Under a Dark Summer Sky

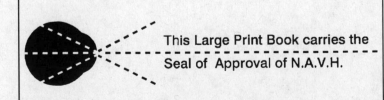

This Large Print Book carries the
Seal of Approval of N.A.V.H.

UNDER A DARK SUMMER SKY

VANESSA LAFAYE

THORNDIKE PRESS

A part of Gale, Cengage Learning

GALE
CENGAGE Learning·

Farmington Hills, Mich • San Francisco • New York • Waterville, Maine
Meriden, Conn • Mason, Ohio • Chicago

GALE
CENGAGE Learning·

LIBRARY OF CONGRESS CATALOGING-IN-PUBLICATION DATA

Lafaye, Vanessa.
    Under a dark summer sky / Vanessa Lafaye. — Large print edition.
        pages cm. — (Thorndike Press large print historical fiction)
    ISBN 978-1-4104-8209-9 (hardback) — ISBN 1-4104-8209-X (hardcover)
    1. Secrets—Fiction. 2. Hurricanes—Fiction. 3. Large type books. I. Title.
PR6112.A335U53 2015b
823'.92—dc23   2015016782

Published in 2015 by arrangement with Sourcebooks, Inc.

Printed in Mexico
1 2 3 4 5 6 7 19 18 17 16 15

HISTORICAL NOTE

Life in the Florida Keys of the 1930s was easy compared to many other places during the Great Depression. Although residents lacked most of the modern conveniences we consider necessary today, food was plentiful and winters were mild. Sun-seeking tourists were attracted to the glorious beaches, riding Henry Flagler's fantastic East Coast Railway all the way down to Key West. But it was also a time of high racial tension across the South, with every aspect of life segregated by Jim Crow laws, and Florida was not exempt from this.

Even so, it is not hard to understand why a group of homeless, jobless World War I veterans would jump at the chance to join a public works project there. It was by far the best opportunity they had come across in years. There were three such work camps spread throughout the Keys.

The local people who had lived there for

generations, known as Conchs, had to adjust to having these hard-drinking, disturbed, and even dangerous men living in their midst. Imagine the effect today if someone dumped 250 Veterans Affairs hospital patients in a tiny, isolated, backward town with a brutal climate and no adequate facilities. You would expect there to be serious problems. The veterans did nothing to endear themselves. The Conchs were unprepared to deal with them. Nor did anyone receive any help from official sources. Against this backdrop came the most powerful hurricane ever to strike North America, on Labor Day 1935.

This book is a fictionalized account of those events.

CHAPTER 1

The humid air felt like water in the lungs, like drowning. A feeble breeze stirred the washing on the line briefly but then the clothes fell back, exhausted by their exertion. Despite the heat, they refused to dry. The daily thunderstorms did nothing to reduce the temperature, just made the place steam. *Like being cooked alive,* Missy thought, *like those big crabs in their tub of seawater, waiting for the pot tonight.*

She bathed the baby outside in the basin under the banyan tree's canopy of shade, both to cool and clean him. His happy splashes covered them both in soapy water. Earlier that morning, asleep in his new basket, his rounded cheeks had turned an alarming shade of red, like the overripe strawberries outside the kitchen door. You could have too much of a good thing, Missy knew, even strawberries. This summer's crop had defeated even her formidable preserving skills, and the fruit had been left to rot where it lay.

The peacocks called in the branches overhead. Little Nathan's cheeks had returned to a healthy rose-tinted cream color, so she could relax. With a grunt, Missy levered herself off the ground and onto the wooden kitchen chair beside the basin and brushed the dead grass from her knees. There was no one else around, only Sam the spaniel, panting on the porch. Mrs. Kincaid had gone to see Nettie, the dressmaker, a rare foray from the house, and Mr. Kincaid was at the country club, as usual. He had not slept at home more than a handful of nights in the past few months, always working late. The mangroves smelled musky, like an animal, the dark brown water pitted with the footprints of flies.

Nathan started to whimper like he did when he was tired. Missy lifted him out of the water and patted him dry with the towel. He was already drowsy again, so she laid him naked in the basket in the shade. With a sigh, she spread her legs wide to allow the air to flow up her skirt and closed her eyes, waving a paper fan printed with "I'm a fan of Washington, DC." Mrs. Kincaid had given it to her when they came back from their trip. Mrs. Kincaid had insisted on going with her husband, to shop. Their argument had been heard clear across the street, according to Selma, who didn't even have good ears.

Even so, Selma knew everyone's business. Before anyone else, Selma knew when Mrs. Anderson's boy, Cyril, lost a hand at the fish-processing plant, even before Doc Williams had been called. She knew that Mrs. Campbell's baby would come out that exact shade of milky coffee, even though Deputy Sheriff Dwayne Campbell had the freckles and red hair of his Scottish immigrant ancestors. She just knew things, and Missy had no idea how.

Selma had helped when Missy first went to work for the Kincaids ten years ago. She showed Missy where the best produce was to be found, the freshest fish. People told things to Selma, private things. She looked so unassuming, with her wide smile and soft, down-turned gaze. But Missy knew those eyes were turned down to shield a fierce intelligence, and she had witnessed Selma's machinations. Missy was slightly afraid of Selma, which gave their friendship an edge. Selma was that bit older and had more experience of things generally. She seemed able to manipulate anyone in town and leave no trace, had done so when it suited her. After Cynthia LeJeune had criticized Selma's peach cobbler, somehow the new sewage treatment plant got sited right upwind of the LeJeune house. It took a full-blooded fool to cross Selma.

Missy sighed and stroked Nathan's cheek. His lips formed a perfect pink O, his long lashes quivered, and his round tummy rose and fell. Sweat soaked Missy's collar. When she leaned forward, the white uniform remained stuck to her back. She longed to strip off the clinging dress and run naked into the water, only a few yards away. And then she recalled: there was still some ice in the box in the kitchen — no, the "refrigerator," as Mrs. Kincaid said they were called now. She imagined pressing the ice to her neck, feeling the chilled blood race around her body until even her fingertips were cool. They would not mind, she thought, wouldn't even notice if she took a small chunk. There was no movement at all in the air. The afternoon's thunderclouds were piled like cotton on the horizon, grayish white on top and crushed violet at the bottom.

I'll only be a minute.

Inside the kitchen, it was even stuffier than outside, although the windows were wide open and the ceiling fan turned on. Missy

10

opened the refrigerator, took the pick to the block. A fist-size chunk dropped onto the worn wooden counter. She scooped it up, rubbed it on her throat, around the back of her neck, and felt instant relief. She rubbed it down her arms, up her legs. She opened the front of her uniform and rubbed the dwindling ice over her chest. Cool water trickled down to her stomach. Eyes closed, she returned it to her throat, determined to enjoy it down to the last drop, when she became aware of a sound outside.

Sam barked, once, twice, three times. This was not his greeting bark. It was the same sound he made that time when the wild-eyed man had turned up in the backyard, looking for food. Armed with a kitchen knife, Missy had yelled at him to get away, but it was Sam's frenzied barking that had driven him off.

"Nathan," she groaned, racing to the porch. At first she could not comprehend what her eyes saw. The Moses basket was moving slowly down the lawn toward the mangroves, with Sam bouncing hysterically from one side of it to the other. She could hear faint cries from the basket as Nathan woke. She stumbled down the porch steps in her hurry and raced toward the retreating basket.

Then she saw him.

He was camouflaged by the mangroves' shade at the water's edge, almost the same green as the grass. He was big, bigger than any she had seen before. From his snout, clamped onto a corner of the basket, to the end of his dinosaur tail, the gator was probably fourteen feet long. Slowly he planted each of his giant clawed feet and determinedly dragged the basket toward the water.

"Nathan! Oh God! Someone please help!" Missy screamed and ran to within a few feet of the gator. But the large houses of the neighbors were empty, everyone at the beach preparing for the Fourth of July barbecue. "Sam, get him! Get him!"

The dog launched himself with a snarl at the gator, but the reptile swung his body around with incredible speed. His enormous spiked tail, easily twice as long as the dog, surged through the air and slammed into Sam with such force that he was flung against the banyan tree. The dog slid down the trunk and lay unmoving on the ground.

"Sam! No! Oh, Sam!"

The gator continued his steady progress toward the water. Missy swallowed great gulping breaths to hold down the panicky vomit rising in her gut. Everything seemed to happen very fast and very slow at the same time. She scanned the yard for anything that would serve as a weapon, but there was not even a fallen branch, thanks to the diligence of Lionel, the gardener. The gator had almost reached the water. Missy knew very well what would happen next: he would take Nathan to the bottom of the swamp and wedge him between the arching mangrove roots until he drowned. Then the gator would wait for a few days or a week before consuming his nicely tenderized meat.

And then she imagined the Kincaids' faces when they learned the fate of their baby son, what they would do when they found out that a child in her care had been so horribly neglected. The gator's yellow eyes regarded her with ancient, total indifference, as if she were a dragonfly hovering above the water. And then suddenly the panic drained from her like pus from a boil and she felt light and calm. She was not afraid. She knew what she had to do. *That precious baby boy will not be a snack for no giant lizard.*

Missy's thoughts cleared. Despite the ferocious mouthful of teeth, she knew that most of the danger came from the alligator's back end. She began to circle nearer the head. She need only spend a moment within the

13

reach of that tail, which was as long as she was tall, to snatch Nathan from the basket. If she succeeded, then all would be well. If she failed, then she deserved to go to the bottom with him. The gator had reached the waterline. There was no more time.

Movement on the porch. Suddenly Selma was running down the lawn toward her, loading the shotgun as she ran.

"Outta the way, Missy!" she cried, stomach and bosoms bouncing, stubby legs pounding. Missy had never seen Selma run, did not know that she could. "Outta the way!"

Missy threw herself to the ground, hands over her head. Selma stumbled to a halt and regained her balance, feet spread wide apart, stock of the gun buried between her arm and her bountiful chest.

"Shoot it, Selma!" yelled Missy. "For the love of Jesus, shoot it, NOW!"

There was an explosion. The peacocks shrieked and dropped clumsily to the ground and fled for the undergrowth. The air smelled burnt. And there was another smell, like cooked chicken. Missy looked up. Selma was on her back, legs spread, the gun beside her. The baby was screaming.

"Nathan," Missy whispered and scrambled to her feet. "Nathan, I'm coming!"

The gator was where she had last seen it. Well, most of it was there, minus the head. The rest of the body was poised to enter the water.

"Oh, Nathan!" He was covered in gore. It was in his hair, his eyes, his ears. She scooped the flailing baby from the basket and inspected his limbs, his torso, his head, searching for injuries. But he was unhurt, it seemed, utterly whole. She clutched his writhing form to her, made him scream louder, but she did not care. "It all right, honey, hush now, everything gonna be all right."

"The baby?" asked Selma, propped on her elbows. "Is he — ?"

"He fine! He absolutely fine!"

"Thank the Lord," said Selma, wincing as she got to her feet, "and Mr. Remington." She rubbed her shoulder. "Helluva kick on him though."

Missy said nothing, just cooed and rocked Nathan with her eyes closed. He still cried, but fretful, just-woken crying, and it was a joyous sound to hear. Her uniform was sticky with blood transferred from his little body. She looked up suddenly. The Kincaids would be home in a few hours to get ready for the barbecue, and when they learned what nearly happened, she would be fired.

And that might not be the worst of it.

"Missy," said Selma firmly, "come on. We got a lot to do."

She felt cold under the hot sun. "Oh, Selma, I'm done for."

"Listen to me, girl. This ain't the biggest mess I've seen, by far." She shook Missy by the shoulder. "Come on now, pay attention. First we get him cleaned up, and that basket too." She scrutinized it with a professional eye. "Yeah, this ain't too bad."

The bundle at the base of the tree stirred, emitted a soft cry. "Sam! He alive! Oh, Selma, how bad is he?" He had been an awful trial as a puppy, eating the legs right off the living room furniture and weeing in Mr. Kincaid's suitcase, but Sam had been Missy's only companion most days.

"Give me a minute," said Selma. She bent over the dog, stroked his ribs, felt his legs, his head. "Nothing broken," she pronounced. "Just knocked out. Be some bad bruises. I'll give you something for that." She straightened. "Call him."

"Sam, here, boy! Come here, Sammy!" The dog's eyes opened slowly. He raised his head, whimpered as he struggled onto his front legs, then straightened his back legs. "Good boy, Sammy, good boy!" Missy could not look at the carcass by the water's edge. "What about . . . what do we do with . . . that?"

"What do you think?" Selma was already striding toward it with great purpose. "We eat it. By the time my people is done here, won't be nothin' to see but a few peacock feathers."

CHAPTER 2

As she hurried home, Missy's heart thumped crazily, like a moth trapped in a glass. Her feet sped along the familiar road, shoes whitened by the dust of crushed clamshells. To have come so close to losing Nathan . . . Were it not for Selma's quick action, the boy would now be tucked under the water somewhere, awaiting the gator's pleasure. The very thought of his blond curls stirred by the current, his blue eyes empty and sightless, the gator's jaws open for the first bite . . . *Oh, dear Lord.* Sweating hard, she forced her steps to slow. One deep breath, then another, then another. "Breathing and praying," Mama always said. "The only two things you got to do every day."

The pounding in her chest began to ease. Nathan was safe. There was no need for the Kincaids ever to know about the incident. All thanks to Selma . . . and someone else. She stopped for a moment to say a thank-you to the sky.

Hard to believe that the huge pile of bloody meat would soon be cleaned up and gone, but Missy had no reason to doubt Selma's word. It seemed all of her extended family had answered the call to help with the carcass.

Missy had prepared to help too, but Selma had said, "You go home, make yourself pretty for the barbecue. I take care of Nathan till Mrs. Kincaid get home." The baby bounced happily on her hip, all cleaned up, his favorite wooden elephant in his mouth.

Missy had picked a speck of gore from his hair, on his miraculously unharmed head. "Well, okay, then. Thank you. See y'all at the beach."

The Fourth of July barbecue and fireworks display was the high point in Heron Key's social calendar, the only one at which coloreds were allowed — on their own side of the beach, of course, but no one could partition the sky when those fireworks went up. Most years, she had missed it because of work. This year would be different because Mama was going to watch Nathan for her.

Just as she turned to leave, Missy had heard something that froze her feet to the

19

bloody grass. It was Selma, calling, "Henry Roberts, you think just 'cause you been to Paree that you too good for this work? Get your scrawny ass down here and help." Henry had given his sister a wry salute, stubbed out his cigarette, and joined the others to swing his machete over the carcass.

So he really was back. Selma had gotten the news only a week ago, since which time Missy had lived in a state of feverish anticipation. He did not seem to recognize her, for which she was grateful, looking as she did like someone who had been through a wringer. Heart thudding, she studied him with sideways glances, at once desperate to be somewhere else but unable to turn her eyes away. He looked so different, no longer the young man she had seen off to war all those years ago. He was thin, ribs clearly visible through the open front of his sweat-stained shirt. Gray stubble marked cheeks no longer smooth. He took a dirty rag from his pocket and wiped his neck. There was a long, curved scar there, like a great big question mark. He looked, she thought, just like the millions of hopeless souls lined up at the soup kitchens in the North, seen in the newspapers that Mr. Kincaid threw out.

So, she thought, the war's been over for seventeen years and he never saw fit to come home until Uncle Sam sent him and a load of other dirty, hungry soldiers to build that bridge to replace the ferry crossing to Fremont. If this was supposed to make the veterans feel better about having to wait for the bonus they had been promised by the government, she figured the plan was less than a complete success. It sounded like there was a lot more drinking and fighting than bridge building going on at the camp.

Since hearing he was back, she had both dreaded and hoped for a chance meeting. In her daydreams, they met at church or maybe in town. She would be wearing the yellow dress with the daisies, and a white hat and gloves. She would be poised, head high, and would walk past without noticing him. He would be in his uniform, like he was when he left, shoes polished to a high shine, sharp creases in his pants. He would tip his hat to her, then do a double take and say, "This beautiful woman cain't be Missy Douglas. She was just a child when I left. Ma'am, may I escort you home?"

"Is that little Missy Douglas?" His voice had startled her out of the memory, that voice she had longed to hear for eighteen years but had thought never to hear again. He wiped the blood from his machete and

21

hooked it to his belt. Sweat darkened his collar. He passed a dirty rag over his forehead. For a moment, she had wished the gator had taken her down. Blood caked her face, her hair. Even her shoes squelched with it. "I should've known," he had said with a slow smile, "you'd be mixed up in this somehow. You bite that gator's head off all by yourself?"

Her mouth had opened and closed uselessly. She could not think of one single thing to say, still caught up in the daydream she had nurtured for eighteen years. All that time, while he was away, she had prayed and wished and cajoled God and the angels and the apostles and the universe to bring him back to her, and now here he was.

She narrowed her eyes against the glare off the road. Her steps quickened again. It was going to take some time to get clean of all traces of the gator. Henry was back, yes, but what else? Changed? Most certainly. Broken? Very possibly. She had heard the stories, of how the veterans needed to be drunk to sleep, how their hands shook so badly sometimes that they could not hold their tools, how any loud noise could provoke either tears or vicious violence. *Just how badly damaged is he?* Her need to know was perfectly balanced by her fear of knowing.

But then, she realized, everyone had changed, including her. Nothing stayed the same, not after so many years. What would he think of her? Of what she had become — or, more importantly, not become? Still living with Mama, doing for the Kincaids, never been anywhere or done anything of note. Taking an encyclopedia to bed every night.

He had stood there, waiting for her reply. That same smile, in a much older man's face. And then, to her everlasting shame, she had fled.

Missy's feet scattered the chickens in a bad-tempered flurry as she raced up the porch steps and flung open the door. Mama shrieked and rushed toward her. "My God, chile, what they done to you? Where you hurt?" She patted Missy all over. "I knew this day would come, didn't I tell you? But you too smart to listen to your old Mama anymore. When I catch the devil who did this to you, I'm —"

"I'm fine, Mama." Missy stripped to her slip and pulled off the stinking shoes. "There was a gator. He went for the baby, but Selma blew his head right off. Her people chopping it up now. You shoulda seen her; she saved Nathan, and me, and my job. She was" — she paused, choosing the right word for what Selma had been that day — "magnificent."

"Lord, the words you use . . . Give me those things." She held out her arms. "They got to be boiled right now."

Mama set the washtub on the fire and filled it with seawater. Fresh water was reserved for the rinse. She had warned Missy umpteen times not to use those big words outside the house. One day, for sure, the wrong person would hear, and it would be her undoing. She piled the bloody clothes into the water with a scoop of carbolic and stirred with a big stick. Growing up, she recalled as she stirred, Missy had few friends. Her preference for books over swamp games made the local kids think she was stuck-up. And now Missy was a grown woman, she showed every sign of ending her days alone. Too smart for local fellas, too proud to play dumb. At Missy's age, Mama had already had two babies and been married to Billy, a shiftless fisherman. He drank his pay every week before doing them all a favor and going to sea one night in a storm, drunk as a skunk. The boat washed up a few days later down the coast, with only an empty bottle on board and Billy's

24

gaff. He probably just fell in and drowned, but she liked to think of him as Jonah, living out his days in the gullet of some giant fish. He'd have plenty of time to think on what he'd done to them and, most of all, to little Leon. She caught her breath, pressed a hand to her side. Even thinking of the child's name shot a jolt of pain right through her.

She continued to stir. The red had begun to lift from the white of Missy's uniform. She skimmed the pinkish foam from the water. Had it not been for Henry Roberts stepping in to help when Billy died, things would have been a whole lot more desperate. Although he was little more than a child himself, he watched Missy so Mama could go out to work. It gave her time to get back on her feet. He was so sweet with Missy, even when she followed him around everywhere like a duckling, no doubt embarrassing him with his friends. But he was never unkind, always patient with her. Every night, he read her those stories that turned her into such a bookworm, stories of places she had never heard of, with names like Zanzibar, Ceylon, Treasure Island. She'd come in to find their heads together over a book in a circle of lamplight. And when he went away to war, it just tore Missy apart, much more so than losing her daddy.

She had heard he was back, with that group of dirty old vagrants at the veterans' camp. *Well, Henry Roberts,* she thought as she tipped away the filthy water, *you got some explainin' to do.*

Missy filled the bathtub with brownish water from the cistern. It had its own aroma, which she was accustomed to, and would at least rid her of the slaughterhouse reek of blood. She could hear Mama's humming from the other side of the partition. As she stepped into the bath, the water went dark. She scrubbed and scrubbed, held her nose, and submerged her head. Although she came up feeling cleaner, she knew it would be days before she lost the stench.

Water dripped from the end of her nose. Selma had saved every one of Henry's letters from France, had never given up hope, had always believed he would come back, one day, to be with his people. She kept a room in her house for him, prepared for the day of his return. But when that day finally came, it was not as she expected. He was back, but not really back, Selma said. He would not use the nice room she had, would not stay with his people, but instead would live out at the collection of dirty, smelly shacks they called a camp. Worse still, it turned out he had been there for months already — almost a year! — before he made contact, avoiding the town the whole time. He explained none of it to Selma. Missy had never seen Selma cry, but when she learned that he had come home with no word to his people, her face had just crumpled into folds of disappointment. Even so, she still started to take meals to him, walking the five miles each way to deliver her casseroles, her fried chicken, and of course her famous peach cobbler. She pronounced that her hogs ate better than the veterans. The whole town could smell the camp latrines when the wind blew the right way. Missy had heard Mr. Kincaid say many times that the camp was a disgrace, to the men and the country.

Missy scraped dried blood from under her nails as she went over the events of the afternoon. It had been such a close call. The Kincaids would be home by now. They were a strange couple; everyone said so. When Selma first told her about Mr. Kincaid's drinking, Missy had been indignantly defensive of him. Then she began to notice the signs: the mouthwash on his breath when he came home at night, the overly precise way he spoke, the scratches around the lock on the Cadillac driver's side door. It had started when Nathan was born. Selma knew why. "Some men," she had said, "cain't look at a woman the same after a baby come out of there. I've known men to walk right out of the hospital and keep on walkin'." And Mrs. Kincaid kept growing fatter every day, although Missy was careful with her portions. It was as if the woman thought she could get his attention just by taking up more space in the room. Her secret eating and his secret drinking . . . None of it made sense to Missy.

And yet the Kincaids must have loved each other once, or else why did they get married? They seemed to have everything needed for a happy life. Such a nice big house, with its wide sitting porch and high ceilings, one of the first in town to get electricity. It was meant to be filled with many more babies, but it seemed certain now that Nathan would be the only one. *The baby is safe, thanks be to the Lord, and Mr. Remington.*

Missy's stomach cramped with hunger. She had eaten nothing since daybreak. There would be plenty to eat at the barbecue, as always. A hog had been roasting on embers, buried deep in the sand, for two days already. It would take center stage,

28

the meat smoky and succulent, dripping with Mama's famous sauce and surrounded by the platters of salad and corn bread. There would be fresh, sweet coquinas, dug from the beach that morning and cured in Key lime juice, and fried conch. There would be turtle steaks, harvested from the kraal that morning. There would be Key lime pie and Selma's fresh peach cobbler. And there would be bottles of beer, lots of them, glistening like jewels in their barrels of ice. She had heard about the starving folks up north, lined up for hours just for a cup of thin soup, and others in the Midwest, trying to farm land that had turned to dust. *Is that why Henry came back after all this time? Because he tired of being hungry?*

She scrubbed her hair, her ears, her face, with the precious sliver of Ivory soap she had been saving. There were so many questions she itched to ask him. That long, raised scar on his neck, shaped like a question mark. *What tale do you have to tell?* She traced a finger down her own neck in the same shape. She hoped he would come to the barbecue and hoped just as strongly he would not. The veterans had been invited, she had heard, against the better judgment of many.

She called from the bath, "He was there,

Mama. He came to help." The sounds of sloshing from the kitchen ceased.

"How he look?"

"Like Doc Williams." Henry did not just look older, as Missy expected. More than that, he had the same look that Doc Williams had when he came back from the war. There were the deep, puffy bruises under the eyes that never went away, not even after years of home cooking and Florida sunshine. It was as if the soldiers had been tattooed, from the inside, by whatever they had seen. *It had to come out somewhere,* Missy thought. It came out through their eyes.

The sloshing resumed in the kitchen. Mama called, "He gonna be there tonight?"

"I 'spect so," she said, hoping Mama might not hear.

Mama's head appeared around the partition. "You didn't ask him?"

Missy could not admit she had run away without a word, like a silly little girl. She sank lower in the water. Red bits floated on top. She wanted to get out, but Mama stood there, hands on hips. "Not as such, no."

Mama pulled her to her feet and began to rub her dry with a rough towel, each stroke emphasizing her words. "Have. I. Not. Taught. You. Any. Manners. Girl." She

30

turned Missy around to face her.

Missy saw herself in Mama's eyes, not as a grown woman, but as a child again. All the years of worry and hope were there, all they had endured together. Nothing had turned out good in a long, long time.

"Come here, chile." Mama wrapped her in the towel. They stood like that for a few minutes, Missy's head on her shoulder. Mama rubbed her back. "Gonna be all right, everything gonna be all right, you see. Now," Mama said, pulling back to look hard at her face, "big question: What you gonna wear?"

Missy stepped out of the water. "The yellow dress, with the daisies."

CHAPTER 3

Doc Williams put a roll of bandages into his old black leather medical bag, topped up the Mercurochrome antiseptic bottle, and put that in too. He snapped the latch shut, thought for a moment, then opened it again and added another roll of bandages. As he was forever telling the boys in his Scout troop, "It's always better to be prepared." He shut the bag again and rested his weight on its familiar bulk. It had accompanied him to war and back, probably still had French mud in the hinges. And blood in the leather. "Almost time, old friend." He patted it fondly.

Through his front window, he could see men carrying plywood and sawhorses, setting up for the barbecue that evening. Zeke went by on his old bicycle, Poncho the macaw in his usual place, clinging to Zeke's shoulder. The bird's flamboyant, cobalt tail brushed Zeke's scrawny haunches. Doc had been to Zeke's shack on the beach not long ago to treat his chronic leg ulcers, but as the man spent most of every day standing in seawater, yelling at the waves, there was little he could do to help. Zeke had not always been like that, he remembered. He used to work on his uncle's pineapple farm, spent all his free time in a little skiff, sat for hours on the still brown waters of the mangrove swamp, patiently waiting for a tug on his fishing line. He knew all the best spots, even took a few tourists out. And everywhere he went, Poncho went too. People said it was the storm of 1906 that did it. Zeke was the sole survivor of his family of sixteen. His little sister was torn right from his arms and crushed by flying timber. Ever since, he had raged at the sea, with only Poncho for company at his lonely shack.

As Zeke pedaled past, Doc noted that the leg ulcers had worsened. He worried that he had ceased to relate to patients as people. They had just become collections of ailments to him: Zeke was ulcers, Missy's Mama was uncontrolled diabetes, Dolores Mason was the clap (again). It had started during the war, of course. It was just wound after bloody wound. They could have been cadavers, except for the screaming. And

33

then, when the war was all but won, the Spanish flu arrived to finish off many of the men who had survived the battles. Any faith that remained had left him as he watched them drown in their own fluids, helpless to ease their suffering.

Peacetime medicine, of course, was supposed to be about listening to the patients, but sometimes, even after all these years, they appeared from him simply as talking lumps of meat — no different from the hog that was even now being disinterred from its sandy grave.

He sighed, rubbed his glasses with his shirttail, tried to muster some enthusiasm. The heat made his head hurt. There was beer in the icebox, but he needed to stay sharp for the evening. He had been dreading the barbecue for a long time, and not just because of the inevitable stomach upsets from Mabel Hickson's potato salad or the minor burns from the reckless handling of fireworks. Someone would wander into the surf after too much beer and need rescuing, or maybe even resuscitation. The soft shush of the waves came to him through the open window. The ocean, which looked so innocent now in the afternoon sun, waited patiently to embrace the unwary.

He was prepared for all of that. He was also prepared for the violence that would well up after whites and coloreds had been marinating in liquor and old grievances for hours, each in their separate areas on the beach. You could set your watch by the fight that would break out between Ike Freeman and Ronald LeJeune. No one remembered where the hatred stemmed from, including Ike and Ronald. Some folks thought a milk cow was involved. And it didn't help that Ike's grandfather had been owned by Ronald's grandfather, and not very well treated at that. So once a year, they pounded the tar out of each other. It was a kind of ritual. And Doc would be there to patch them up.

He poured a glass of lemonade and allowed himself to remember the little migrant girl, as he did once a year. He had only been back from the war for six months, still waking Leann every night in the grip of his terrors, still haunted by visions of horror during the day. They were always with him. Even when he played with baby Cora, he saw the piles of amputated limbs like a grotesque doll factory, felt the sinuous coils of intestines twined around his ankles, heard the screams from a hundred shattered faces. The Fourth of July barbecue that year had promised to be a much-needed dose of wholesome good fun, to help ease him back into normal society. He almost looked forward to dealing with the everyday sorts of injuries that would occur, so unlike the industrial destruction of bodies during the war.

The girl was only six years old, with an innocuous-looking puncture wound on the sole of her foot. She had stepped on a rusty nail while running around with the other children during the fireworks display. Her mother, one of the many who came to harvest the Key lime crop, simply washed the wound and applied honey to it. By the time Doc was called, the child's jaw was locked tight. There was nothing he could do but hold her while the paralysis raced up her little body and finally stopped her lungs. He had heard rumors from an old army buddy that someone was working on a tetanus vaccine, but it would be far too late to help this girl. After that, his nightmares took on a new dimension, much closer to home. And he would never again look forward to the Fourth of July barbecue.

This year promised to be the most difficult yet, thanks to the arrival of the veterans. Against his advice, the town had invited them to the celebrations. It had been hard for him to take such a stance, given his service record, but his frequent visits to the camp had convinced him that it was unwise to include them. His eyes fell on the *Heron Key Bugle*, with yet another outraged headline: VETERANS ARRESTED AFTER PAYDAY BRAWL. Such headlines had become depressingly regular, although the damage had been limited to property. So far.

He pressed the cool glass against his throat, remembered his shock on the first visit to the veterans' camp, the utter squalor of it. He had been called to aid a poor old sergeant from Minnesota who had been poisoned by the deadly smoke of the oleander wood used for his cooking fire. Doc could not imagine why no one had warned him against the innocent-looking shrub with the pretty pink flowers that grew wild all along the coast. The men were housed in stifling, overcrowded "cabins," which sounded quaint but were actually just flimsy wooden partitions held together with a canvas roof. Whites and coloreds still had separate quarters, equal for once in their misery; the latrines would have disgraced the trenches of France — the stench alone was a real health hazard. Doc had shared his concerns with the superintendent, Trent Watts, but it was like talking to a block of granite. The men had nothing to do but drink when they weren't working on the bridge to Fremont in the awful heat and humidity. And it was clear they felt they were being punished by Washington for marching on the Capitol to demand the bonus promised to them. And now this, the final insult: condemned to a close approximation of hell, in a place no one knew existed, where the country could forget what it owed them.

Doc's contemplation was interrupted by a face at the screened door. "You decent?" It was the voice of Deputy Sheriff Dwayne Campbell. Amiable, shambling Dwayne, his uniform always unkempt, buttons straining at the belly. Doc had seen little of Dwayne since he attended the birth of Dwayne's mulatto baby, Roy. He had heard that Dwayne seemed to accept the child, which many men would not have done. Noreen Campbell, by all accounts, had not fared so well. There was talk of savage beatings that left no visible marks — Dwayne was careful — but since she did not seek medical help, Doc could do nothing. He had always liked Dwayne, whose open, freckled face carried a permanent look of mild surprise. The deputy was not blessed with great mental agility, but he usually took a sensible approach to conflict, and his physical bulk on its own seemed to calm most situations.

"In here, Dwayne. Just getting ready."

"Not sure there is such a thing, Doc, not this year." Dwayne had also advised against including the veterans in the barbecue. He removed his hat and wiped his forehead with a handkerchief. The skin at his hairline showed white where the hat's brim protected it from the sun.

Doc had hoped to be reassured that Dwayne would draw on his years of experience to face the evening with the same ease and calm he brought to most problems. The tension in the big man's jaw and shoulders said otherwise. Doc wondered if something had happened at home but decided it was the wrong moment to delve into Dwayne's domestic situation. The priority was to get through the next twelve hours.

Dwayne took a seat at the kitchen table. "Got any more of that lemonade?"

Doc poured him a tall glass and thought he noticed a slight tremor in Dwayne's hand as he took it. Dwayne drank the liquid down without pause or breath and set the empty glass on the table.

"We warned 'em," he said as he wiped his mouth with the back of his hand. "And they went ahead anyway. Leaving you and me to pick up the pieces."

Doc could see both sides of the argument. How could the veterans be excluded, on this of all nights, when the nation celebrated the people who gave it its freedom? They had given their limbs and, in many cases, their sanity in the service of their country. Yet he was convinced they were a danger to others — and themselves. "Maybe it will be all right," he said and heard the note of foolish optimism in his voice. "Maybe everyone will just get along. Is that really so impossible?"

Dwayne regarded him in silence, eyebrows raised. The man was wound tighter than Doc had ever seen him.

"Okay, then," Doc continued. "What's the worst that can happen?"

Dwayne tipped his chair back, hands folded on his paunch. "Oh, I don't know, how about this: maybe they drink the place dry and then go looking for more in folks' houses. Maybe they decide to take what they want from the women. My guess is it's been a mighty long time since those boys got any. They're psychos. You know that better than anyone. Drunks and psychos." He leaned forward, arms on the table. "Would you want them in your house, if you had a wife and child?"

Doc made no reply, just cleaned his

already spotless glasses again.

"Sorry, Doc," Dwayne mumbled. "I know it ain't easy for you."

"Never mind, Dwayne. That was a long time ago now." *Five years, four months, thirteen days, to be precise.* He could probably even give an accurate account of the number of minutes since Leann had left, taking Cora with her. He had changed, she'd said. He'd seemed numb to the world and everyone in it, even her and Cora, except at night, when he screamed and screamed. They had tried separate bedrooms. He woke once to find his hands around Leann's throat, her eyes wide with terror, her fingers trying to pry his away, Cora wailing in her crib, and no idea at all how he had gotten there. She left soon after. They lived with her parents now in Georgia. He got regular notes from Cora, in her achingly precise child's hand. She did well in school, Leann said, in her infrequent letters.

Doc blinked hard, tried to focus. Dwayne said something about getting some extra police in for the barbecue. Doc regarded him over the top of his glasses. "You say you got help coming?"

"Yep, some fellas from over Fremont way."

"But they'll hang back, right? Just come

41

in if there's trouble?" He could imagine the effect of a group of unfamiliar cops, bored and milling around with nothing to do. Incendiary didn't begin to cover it.

Dwayne suddenly scraped his chair back and stood up. "I'll do my job," he said and jabbed a finger in Doc's chest. "You do yours." He grabbed his hat and left by the back door, allowing it to smack loudly into the frame.

Doc watched Dwayne stomp across the hot asphalt toward the beach and rubbed his chest. Only a few nights ago, that same kitchen chair had been occupied by another angry man. Henry Roberts had been drinking stronger stuff than lemonade. Their service in France together had created a bond of shared memories that even Jim Crow couldn't break. Henry had sat there, making slow work of a glass of bourbon while the mosquitoes droned and the crickets sang and moths pirouetted around the bare bulb overhead. Henry had the loping shuffle of the hobo on the rail. His clothes had been washed to a noncolor between brown and gray. They smelled musty. The skin of his face, stretched tight over his bones, spoke of a long habit of hunger . . . so different from the cocky young man who had boarded the train to war with him all those years ago.

Doc had recognized the look in Henry's eyes. It was the same look he saw in the mirror each morning. It did not invite questions. The past was the stuff of nightmares; the present was something to be endured; the future was . . . Well, Doc had learned hard lessons about the foolishness of having a plan. His plan had been simple: raise his family, treat his patients, and grow old peacefully alongside Leann. But it seemed the universe had other ideas.

Doc had thought Henry was different. He always had a plan, always some scheme or other. Doc had no doubt he would succeed at something. But then he had disappeared after the war, and no one, not even Selma, knew where he was. He was just one of the tens of thousands adrift on the backwash of the war. As Henry sat at the kitchen table and turned the glass slowly between his hands, Doc noticed the shadows in his eyes, of defeat, of hopes destroyed, of shame . . . the bitter ashes that remained when anger burned up a person's heart.

"So what's the plan these days, Henry?" Doc had asked.

"No plan, Doc," he said with a swirl of his glass. "I used to think I'd make some money, enough to see Grace and Selma right, and then go back to France."

"You got a sweetheart there?"

"Yeah." Henry's smile split the somber planes of his face. "Thérèse. Met her when we were camped outside her village, told her I'd come back. One day." Then the shadows returned. "Although I guess she's long married by now."

Doc remembered how the soldiers had been welcomed by the French locals — all ranks, all colors, it didn't matter. "It must have been hard, coming back here, coming back . . . to this." His eyes took in the separate door for colored patients to use. Just like everything else in town, from the separate serving hatch at Mitchell's store to the separate diner on the highway. Doc had even seen a driving map of the South that showed which restrooms colored people were allowed to use.

"You could say that," Henry said softly, his eyes on the brown liquid in his glass. "I just . . . We thought, you know, when we came back, that things would change. That they'd be different. And instead . . ."

"It was worse than before," Doc said. He thought back to those heady days when they had first come back, so flushed with victory and pride and faith in the future. That initial euphoria had curdled so quickly, once it became clear the men had brought newfangled ideas home with them. The rest of America, it seemed, shared none of the veterans' sense of a new era. They liked the old era, the old order, just fine, thank you very much. Doc recalled the headlines. It was almost like some kind of mass insanity had taken hold. There were riots in the cities, lynchings in the country, as far south as Fort Lauderdale. Even down in sleepy little Heron Key, they felt the cold wind of change. And then came the stock market crash of '29, which only made people cling tighter to the comfort of old, familiar things. "I understand why you feel like that," he began and tried to imagine what it must have been like for someone like Henry, an officer who by rights should have been on course for prosperity. "Why you want to go back to France, to the way of life there. But we need people like you, if things are ever going to change here."

Henry's gaze had flickered into life. "And end up with a noose around my neck? Or worse? I heard about a guy upstate, accused of raping a white girl, forced to eat his own dick before they shot him full of holes. Little kids cut off parts of him, Doc." He had slammed his glass onto the table. The liquid sloshed onto the Formica. "For keepsakes,

Doc. Keepsakes," he said more quietly. "And what are people like you doing about it?"

Still some anger left in him after all. It had given Doc hope. You had to care about something to be angry. Far better that than the flat hopelessness that bent Henry's shoulders into the posture of defeat. And Henry was right, he conceded. Where did Doc get off, talking about change, when he had lost any stomach for a fight? It lay buried somewhere in the French mud.

He checked his bag one final time. *Maybe it will be all right tonight. Maybe people will just get along.* With a last look around, he hefted the bag and went out into the late afternoon sunshine. *And maybe that hog will fly out of its hole in the ground.*

Dwayne walked quickly for several hundred yards before he felt the tension begin to seep out of his pores with the sweat. He had been unfair to Doc, who only ever meant well, but the man's interference, his habit of looking over the top of his glasses like a schoolteacher, had gotten on Dwayne's last nerve. He slowed and went to rest in the shade of a palm at his favorite picnic table on the beach.

Ever since that little brown baby had come

out of his wife, he had felt like he was living in a fever dream. He was well acquainted with them, having suffered with the Spanish flu in 1918. He had almost died during a week in which he lost all sense of reality and time and had been left with permanently impaired hearing. No one knew the extent of it, not even Noreen, thanks to his lip-reading skills.

A hermit crab crawled up to his boot. Dwayne picked it up gently in his palm and marveled at the delicate engineering of the claws, the phenomenal strength needed to haul that shell around everywhere. At that moment, his own responsibilities felt just as heavy. The whole town depended on him to make the evening run smooth and safe. He had taken every precaution possible, installed every backup available, yet he could not shake the sensation of shadows brushing against him, even in the bright, slanting sunlight.

The crab pinched the flesh of his palm, not hard, more like an experiment. *Roy would like this,* he thought. At only a few months old, he already took a keen interest in the world — the pelicans, the herons fishing in the mangroves, the peacocks. Even the march of ants across the wooden floor would transfix him. The little lizards that sped along the porch, miniature dinosaurs with bright eyes, were a source of special delight. Roy clapped and giggled each time he saw one, which was about forty times a day.

How was it possible, he wondered, to love the child while hating its mother? How had he become this person? He, who had always used his strength to help the weak and vulnerable? It was Noreen's fault. Each time his hand went out to strike her, he felt physically sick yet compelled, as if some invisible force took control of his limbs, made him shout unforgivable things at her. She still refused to name the father — in fact, refused to say anything at all — which only enraged him further.

Dwayne had insisted that Noreen stay home tonight. After all, Roy didn't belong on either side of the beach. He couldn't be with the whites, and the coloreds wouldn't want him either. He feared this would be the case for the boy's entire life. And Dwayne could do without the curious looks and well-meaning comments while he tried to do his job. The anger toward Noreen, always smoldering, reignited inside him.

But even so, he could remember that things had not always been like this. Noreen, when they first met, had called him her

48

"gentle giant." The first few years were good. No babies, but not for lack of trying. Then he began to notice she seemed distracted. She no longer waited up for him to finish his shift. She no longer listened avidly to all the details of his day. Instead, she cleaned and tidied around him while he talked, her mind clearly elsewhere, and this while he struggled to cope with the extra workload caused by the veterans' arrival twelve months previously. He was working harder than he ever had in his life, all thanks to them, and when he came home, he just wanted some appreciation. But when he reached for her in the night, she pretended to be asleep, so it felt like he had to force himself on her. The pregnancy was such a welcome surprise that he buried his doubts in happy plans for the baby, while she became more pale and withdrawn as time went on.

The whole town was laughing at him now, he knew that. He felt it each time he attended a disturbance or took someone down to the county jail. He knew what they were thinking: How was he supposed to keep the criminals of the district in check when he couldn't even control his own wife? It was the lack of respect he minded the most, as if his badge meant nothing just because his wife was a whore. She had ruined him, and Roy was a daily reminder of that — would be for the rest of his life. The flame of anger burned higher. He felt it rise up through his feet, as if it came from the very earth, through his legs, his groin, his torso, to his neck and finally to his head where it burned coldly. Dwayne set the crab onto the sand and raised his boot to crush it. He felt the approach of trouble, like the whiff of the camp latrines that sometimes carried all the way down the beach. Everyone would look to him when it came.

He lowered his foot harmlessly. On dainty claws, the crab tiptoed away across the sand.

CHAPTER 4

Selma sluiced seawater over the bloody tools, then scraped them clean with handfuls of sand until they shone. The gator steaks were laid out on her kitchen counter, ready for the grill, covered by a fishing net to keep off the flies. The iron smell of raw meat filled the small space.

Her back ached from the butchery, and her shoulder throbbed from the rifle's recoil. Blisters shone on her hands, in just about the only places not already calloused. She tore a chunk from the aloe plant beside the kitchen door and rubbed its soothing juice over her skin.

Her husband, Jerome, had gone fishing with some of his boys, said he would meet her at the beach. He had struggled for years to find an occupation worthy of his talents: bartender, pineapple farmer, bus driver. He had a turtle kraal for a while, but Selma had to do all the killing for him because he couldn't stand how they screamed. After she witnessed the way he hacked away at the poor creatures' throats, she could well understand why they did. But meat was life, any meat that didn't already have maggots in it. Her mother, Grace, had taught her that, during the hungry years.

None of Jerome's schemes had lasted for more than a few weeks. He had even tried selling encyclopedias door-to-door for a while. This was one of the strangest things ever to happen in Heron Key, as most of his customers couldn't read, and neither could he. The only good thing to come out of it was when he gave his entire sample set of the *Encyclopedia Britannica* to Missy when he quit. He was all for putting it on the fire, figured it would burn real well, but Selma had persuaded him otherwise.

Now, it seemed, he was a fisherman. *Good thing that fish don't scream.*

She stripped off her blood-spattered apron and dunked it in a bucket of seawater to soak. Leaning against the sink, she kneaded the sore muscles in her neck and wished Jerome had stayed to help. They had been married fifteen years, and every day of it had been a battle of one kind or another — to get Jerome's lazy ass to work, to raise enough food from their tiny plot . . . to swallow the sad knowledge that it would only be the two of them, forever. That last was like the taste of bile in her throat.

And yet, at the beginning, she recalled, it hadn't been so bad. He could make her laugh, one of the few people with that ability, and she had figured the babies would come fast. When they did not, and he began to drift from one job to another like a leaf on the tide, she realized he would never change and made her peace with that. She didn't complain. She didn't run away. (Where to?) She just put one foot in front of the other and kept moving forward.

The sun had reached the low point of the day when it shone straight into her kitchen window, marked with spatters of grease and dead flies. She scrubbed at the glass. The sounds of bickering chickens drifted in on the breeze that lifted the palm fronds. She and Jerome had built the house together, expanded it out from Grace's little shack over the years into a modest home. The sitting porch was the best in the neighborhood, her chickens the tastiest around. The secret was plenty of oyster shells for their gizzards to work on and lots of wild herbs in their feed. The hens in the yard were, as always, competing for rooster Elmer's attention. He preened his russet feathers in the slanting sun, oblivious. Baskets of tomatoes, onions, and cucumbers waited in the shade of a palmetto. The walls of the shed were lined with gleaming rows of jars, relishes, jams, and preserves, all neatly labeled.

Missy often teased her, as Selma's idea of a shortage was having only one strawberry shortcake in the house instead of two. But after a childhood so poor that she was sometimes forced to exist on fish bones and grass, Selma treated hunger like an enemy, always waiting to strike. She remained vigilant at all times. Her weapons were grits and corn pone, her defenses made of swamp cabbage and fried fish. Their little house was a fortress of food.

She stepped over the bucket where her apron soaked to reach the shelf in the corner. In a neat row were laid a rattlesnake's skull, two dried raccoon paws, a crunchy brown bunch of shallots, and a crab's shell. A muslin bag held a lock of Missy's hair and a shred of Henry's shirt.

It had not taken long for the magic to work, just a few weeks. The hardest part was bringing Henry back to Heron Key in the first place. Now *that* had been hard. She had tried every spell handed down to her by Grace, who had brought the knowledge with her from Haiti. Selma had written it all out in her unschooled hand before Grace died, in the bulging, tattered book beneath the shelf.

Selma stroked the book's rough cover, made from an old burlap feed bag. Those last weeks with her mother had been a whirl of activity. Grace had chosen her own time, sure as if she had walked into the sea to drown. It had happened when Henry had been gone for fifteen years. Selma had felt Grace's haste, her need to finish things off; her mother was preparing for her most important trip, but she would not need the battered old wicker suitcase for it.

"Selma," Grace would say, "I got somethin' to learn you."

And Selma would scoop up the ragged collection of pages in their shabby binding and begin to write. They would sit for hours together in the dappled shade of the pines around Grace's tiny shack. The fallen needles made a soft and fragrant blanket on the sand. Dragonflies settled on them, so still were they. Eyes closed, her back propped against the tree trunk, Grace would recite the spells without stumbling or hesitation. The words poured from her mouth faster than Selma's pencil could write. It was, Selma realized as her hand traced the book's contours, her fondest memory of Grace. There were far more of the other kind of memories.

That Grace had the power was beyond question. People in the neighborhood came to her for help with all manner of woes in their lives: to bring or banish love, to heal a sick child, to make a good harvest, to bring misfortune on their enemies. The definitive demonstration of Grace's power had come one Thanksgiving when Selma was thirteen. Dinner was just a scrawny chicken and some stunted sweet potatoes. The air was thick with the smell of other people's turkey and gravy and stuffing. Selma went for a walk in the Key lime grove to distract her hungry stomach and came across Shonuff Thompson, named on account of his stock answer for pretty much everything. He was smoking by himself, on the ground under the thorny branches, skinny ankles crossed. With a nearly toothless smile and the promise of a piece of chocolate, he had beckoned her down beside him. Her mind had shut the memory away but her body remembered — the rough stubble on his chin, the way he had forced her legs apart with a thrust of his knee, his sour, smoky breath hot on her neck, the coral hard under her back.

When she had stumbled home, Grace demanded an explanation for her torn and dirty dress. Selma had whispered the tale through bruised lips, shamed by the blood on her legs. Grace had said nothing for a long time, so long that Selma had thought she had been forgotten. And then Grace had looked at her, a dark flame in her eyes, and said, "Wait, child, and see the Lord at work." A few weeks later, Shonuff was killed by a lightning strike while asleep in the grove under a tree that took a direct hit. To Grace, it was all the same Lord, much to the despair of the local pastor. She prayed equally hard to the old spirits and to Jesus, confident that one or the other would come through.

But they did not. Years passed. The war ended. Still Henry did not come back. At first, there were a few postcards, from California, from New Mexico, from Oregon. Then they stopped. Neither prayers nor spells could bring him back. And when Selma had transcribed the last one in the book, Grace had taken to her bed and turned her face to the wall. Nothing could coax her to eat or drink. She just stopped, like a car out of gas. Doc Williams could find nothing wrong with her. He offered to take her to Miami to see a specialist, but

Selma had declined. She knew why Grace had sickened, and no specialist would be of any help: she had lost her faith, in the old ways and in Jesus. Selma knew Henry was still alive, could feel it, and knew Grace felt it too. On the day when Grace closed her eyes for the last time, a hard, bitter seed took root in Selma's heart. If he would not come back of his own will, she decided, then she would damn well bring him back, using the only method available. Grace had willed her the means; it was time to find out if she had the power. And so she began to work her way through the spells, more in desperation than in hope.

Opening the book, she could still remember the feeling of excitement tinged with dread the first time she had summoned a spirit to bring Henry home — and the crushing disappointment that followed. But she had persevered, through almost the whole book, each time with the same conviction. And each time with the same result. She had saved the most powerful spell for last, the one that summoned the fearsome Agaou. After nearly eighteen years, her hope of seeing Henry again had dimmed to a tiny glow in the farthest, darkest corner of her mind. In desperation, she had gone to the beach at midnight and drawn the *veve* in the sand with cornmeal and ash. She had shaken her snake-bone rattle, scattered a little grilled meat, and spilled her blood on the sand, to send the call of blood to Henry, wherever he was.

And now he was back but, as was often the case with spells, not completely back. It had shocked her at first — he looked so different from the bright, smooth-cheeked young man who had set off all those years ago. Now he looked like an old man, a desperate old man. But she reckoned there wasn't anything wrong with him that couldn't be fixed with enough good food and rest. Of course, it should be her food, and a bed in her house. The camp rations were not fit for a dog, especially when the men worked hard all day under the punishing sun. Yet he would not leave the veterans' camp, behaved like it was his home, rather than staying with his people, where he belonged. And when he confessed that he had spent months in the camp before she knew he was there at all . . . Well, the pain of it, and the shame, burned her up inside, but she figured he had his reasons, reasons she could not begin to understand. Someday she would hear them. Or not. It was Agaou's price. The spirits never granted anything without a price.

She wrung out the brine from her apron and went to get some fresh water from the cistern to rinse it. But first she climbed the steps to look inside. Two bright eyes blinked up at her through the gloom. A soggy raccoon stood on the little platform she had built for this purpose, after one fell in and drowned, ruining gallons of precious water. She lowered a stick and the animal scampered nimbly up it and dropped to the ground with a wet shake.

She rinsed the apron and hung it on the line to dry. Henry and Missy belonged together, anyone could see that . . . except possibly the two of them. *No matter, soon fix that.*

The raccoon eyed her from the shade of a scrub pine, wiped his face with his clever paws. He would certainly be back in the cistern in a few days. *Just like with men,* she thought: once an animal found something it liked, it kept coming back, even at the risk of death. With a tired sigh, she went inside to change for the barbecue.

Hilda Kincaid strained to fasten the buttons of her thin cotton dress, elbows out in a futile attempt to reduce the sweat marks. She was certain that Missy had shrunk the garment, just as she had the other pretty dresses that no longer fit. The shameful trip to Nettie's shop that afternoon had almost undone her. Surely, she thought, there must be some mistake. Those measurements must belong to someone else. She pushed a damp curl from her forehead and yanked on the material where it spanned her hips, creating unflattering horizontal folds. It was the only thing she owned suitable for the Fourth of July barbecue.

Honestly, she'd rather just stay home in a shapeless shift and sit on the porch until the mosquitoes became unbearable. Just rock and watch night fall on the sea and wait for Nelson to come home from the country club, as she did most evenings. He seldom chose to be seen in public with her anymore, which she could well understand, but the whole town would be out tonight. She forced her dimpled feet into a pair of delicate gold sandals. *Maybe we can come home early.*

When she had returned that afternoon, she had been surprised to find Selma in charge. There had been a strange, mysterious vibration in the air, but Selma had explained, with her strong, level gaze, that Missy had spilled juice on her uniform and gone home to clean up. It was entirely plausible, and yet . . . But Hilda knew better than to probe. Selma's eyes invited no discussion. Hilda never felt entirely comfortable in her presence; she moved so quietly for a big girl. Missy had brought her in to help one night with a big dinner party, back when the Kincaids still entertained, and ever since, Selma would just appear at odd times.

Missy's Mama had put Nathan down for the night. There was no reason to tarry, yet Hilda cast around for something to detain her, to put off a little longer that awful moment when she would arrive at the beach and face the stares and barely disguised snickers. She consulted the cheval mirror in the corner. The only way she could view the reflection without tears was to pretend it belonged to someone else. Some fat, frumpy old thing, with disappointed eyes.

She missed so many things. She missed her prebaby body. She missed Daddy, the comfort of his arms, the peppery smell of his pipe tobacco. He always made everything all right. Her one small consolation was that he was not around to see what his princess had become. She missed the seasons, the early years in New Hampshire, before Daddy's emphysema forced the family south in search of a kinder climate. Those years remained in her mind, perfectly preserved, like the leaf she had once found encased in ice. There she had felt safe and oh, so treasured.

Everyone had told her she would get used to the monotonous, wet heat of Florida. She had not. Even after all these years, she longed for the crisp catch of the fall bonfire smoke in her throat, the crystal stillness of snow-covered pines, the raucous choruses of migrating geese.

She stared in despair at the figure in the mirror, the gaping buttons, the bulges at her hips. She pulled harder on the fabric. All her pretty dresses had gone. She could not bear to look at them once the baby weight had set like concrete on her stomach, her thighs. Soon, Nettie would have some new dresses for her, shapeless tents in which she could hide her ravaged figure away. They represented defeat. She only wanted to stay home, away from the scornful glances of the other women who met for coffee and tennis at the country club. Their baby weight seemed to melt away within weeks, like the snow she missed so much. At one time, not so long ago, those same women had wanted to be her friend, when she was the slim, stunning beauty queen, with a future as bright and sparkling as the sea. After all, she had been crowned Miss

Palmetto, two years running. Hilda Humbert as she was then, saddled with an ugly stump of a name but blessed with a fragile beauty that could make grown men weep.

All through her early teens, Daddy had seen off any boy brave or stupid enough to attempt to get near her. She was special, a sacred treasure, a fruit of perfect ripeness to be presented to the best of society at the cotillion ball on her nineteenth birthday. It seemed as if the very stars had aligned to shine for her. Her life, Daddy always said, was charmed. Only the best for her, always the best.

And then, not long after she turned eighteen, Nelson Kincaid had arrived, at the wheel of a cream-colored Cadillac roadster with burgundy interior. She knew very well not to talk to men alone, but when he pulled alongside the curb and asked directions to Delaney Street, her good manners obliged her to respond.

As she leaned down to explain that there was no Delaney Street in town, the occupant of the passenger seat became visible. On a pink velvet cushion sat a caramel lop-eared rabbit. "Oh!" was all she could think to say.

The rabbit rejoiced in the name of Earl, she learned. Men she had been trained to resist, even men as shiny and handsome as Nelson Kincaid, with his wavy black hair and slow, sassy smile. But Earl had captivated her with one look of his deep brown eyes. He began to groom his ears with flicks of a tiny pink tongue. She said, "Oh," again, but this time quietly. And when Nelson asked if he could drive her home, with Earl and his cushion on her lap, she had simply nodded and gotten into the car. All training forgotten. Much, much later, she realized that all was lost in that moment.

Hilda sat on the edge of the four-poster bed and allowed her mind to drift back to those first few weeks after she got into the car. She had known instinctively to keep their meetings secret. He would park in the cool shade of the sea grapes at the end of a quiet track that led to the beach. They would sit in the Cadillac, Earl asleep on his cushion, and listen to the waves and talk. She had never talked to a man like a real person. Whenever Daddy's friends came to call, she was presented as a doll to be admired. And Nelson had done such interesting things, traveled to places in Europe and Asia as a merchant sailor — places that only existed for her in the geography books she rarely opened at school. He promised to take her to those places. They would leave the stagnant, suffocating heat of small-town Heron Key and see the world together.

They had met three times before he even took her hand. She just let hers rest on the seat between them, until slowly he picked it up and held it. His felt smooth and dry. She had been kissed once before, by Tommy Higgins, on a dare at a school dance. His lizard tongue had pushed against her teeth. He smelled of sweat and teenage boy. The whole disappointing episode had left her wondering what exactly all the fuss was about. But by the time Nelson finally kissed her, she wanted him to do it so badly that the first touch of his lips was like ice cream on a hot day — cool, sweet, and delicious. His hands had cupped her face, and he had smelled of hair oil and cedar. She wanted more; her body clamored for it.

She didn't care about anything else, not her friends, not school, not the cotillion ball coming up in a few months. She didn't even care about Daddy. She would walk home after their meetings, every nerve aflame, sure that the signs must be visible to all, and try to compose herself. Rejoining normal life was like surfacing from deep under the ocean. She had seen fish pulled up too quickly from the depths, their eyes

66

popped right out of their heads. So she walked home slowly, to give herself time to weave the lies about reading at the library or a homework session with her girlfriends. The lies came easily, so easily, and this made her feel it must be all right. She lied right to Daddy's face and felt nothing, nothing at all. Her dreams were filled with images of falling, endlessly falling.

Hilda touched her lips, leaned against the bedpost, and remembered the feel of his kisses. It had been a long time since he had kissed her like that, since before Nathan was born. Sometimes she thought of Nelson like a sickness, a disease that had turned her mind against itself. Back then she needed to be with him, to feel his hands on her, like she needed to breathe.

The ceiling fan traced slow circles above her. She recalled the time when the kissing and touching were no longer enough. Nearly wild with frustration, she couldn't concentrate on anything and acted so irritable at home that she risked discovery. In rare quiet moments when the fever lifted from her brain, she observed herself as from a distance and wondered how she had become this animal in just a few short weeks.

When it finally happened — in the back

of the Cadillac, of course — he had had to cover her mouth to stifle her howls of pleasure.

They were careful, or rather he was careful, with his supply of rubbers, which nearly reduced both of them to hysterical laughter. As time passed, her body became attuned to his. They fitted together perfectly, moved together just right. Every day, she woke aching for his touch.

But then came the day when she was alone in the house. Momma and Daddy had gone to the hospital in Miami to see the specialist. Daddy toted an oxygen cylinder on wheels with him everywhere, but even that seemed to be failing. The house was quiet, with only the *tick tick* of the ceiling fan. It was one of those rare Florida spring days, when the sun was just nicely warm, before the arrival of the sweltering summer humidity.

Hilda decided it was the perfect opportunity and called Nelson at his rooming house, holding the phone close to her mouth. He sounded a little strange, taken aback by her urgency, but he arrived within a few minutes.

"Hilda," he said, as soon as she kissed him, "I got something to tell you."

"Later," she said, not really listening as

she led him up the stairs. A bed! They were going to do it in a real bed, for the first time! Just like it would be when they were married. "Tell me later."

"No," he said, and something in his tone cut through the haze of lust in her head. People never said no to Hilda. "I need to tell you now." He took both her hands and stopped halfway up the stairs. "It's important. Let's sit down." He settled on the step above hers. She looked up at him, trying to detect some sign of their usual warmth, but his head was turned to the side. "You know I love you, honey . . ." He stopped, cleared his throat.

Her stomach felt like it was full of angry wasps.

"The thing is," he said, "I never thought I'd meet someone like you . . . You're so beautiful, and young, and oh, so" — he shrugged helplessly, like he had no choice — "and I'm . . ."

"Whatever it is, Nelson," she had said, leaning forward, now full-blown scared, "just tell me. Whatever it is, we'll figure it out."

"Leaving."

"You . . . what?" Of all the things he could have said, this was the last thing she had expected. They were going to be together;

he said so all the time. She had put a hand to her face, so sure was she that he had slapped her.

"Hilda, I never meant to stay so long. I was just passing through that day. Then you appeared on the sidewalk like a vision . . . What's a man to do?" Again the helpless look. "But I've got business up in Miami, long overdue now, thanks to you." He stroked the side of her face. She jerked away from his hand. "Oh, don't be like that, sugar. We had a good time —"

"What about our . . . our plans?" The tears came, big sobs that fractured her words. "You said . . . you said you loved me."

"I do, honey, I do, but we cain't be together, not like that. Your daddy has big things in store for you. You could do anything, get outta Heron Key, go to New York. You don't need me. And I've . . . There's stuff I gotta do."

"Take me with you." She clutched his leg. Miss Palmetto, two years in a row, was begging, and she did not care one bit. Her life would end when he walked out that door. "Oh, please, Nelson, take me with you. I'll do anything —"

"I cain't, baby girl. I'm sorry, but I cain't." He looked away again, and she realized that some part of him had already left.

"You mean you won't!" After all the weeks of feeling so grown-up, she suddenly felt like a helpless child.

"All right," he said and looked at her, but his eyes saw somewhere else, someone else. "You gonna make me say it." That look made her feel so cold and alone. "Someone's waitin' for me in Miami. I've dawdled here too long."

That's all I've been to him, a dawdle. "Oh, no," she sobbed. "No, no." She hugged her knees, wished her parents were there. Daddy would make it right. Nelson's promises had all been lies, all the whispered endearments, just so much malarkey.

Then she looked up at him again and the tears stopped. His black hair had fallen forward over one eye. His lips were moist. She could see right down the open neck of his shirt to his bare chest, which moved with each breath. She felt the heat from his skin, imagined the taste of his mouth. Tobacco and the cinnamon chewing gum he liked so much.

"I'm sorry, darlin'. I'm —" he began.

"Can she do *this*?" She pushed him back on the stairs, tore open the front of her dress. His expression changed. His eyes danced with excitement, pupils blacker than black. She unzipped his pants. His breath

71

quickened. He groaned at her touch. She rubbed against him, used her hands, her mouth, used everything he had taught her over the past weeks. She felt powerful, womanly, to have him on his back. Under her control. He would not forget her so easily.

But then with a roar he was on top of her, the edge of the stair hard in her back. His mouth was hot on hers, her hands pulled him closer, ever closer, and with every thrust, she knew they would be together always.

When finally he rolled off her, his face was closed. "Oh, Hilda," he breathed, "what have you done?"

Her pregnancy had become apparent almost immediately. There was just time, before Daddy died, for him to meet Nelson. It was not a success. Daddy just sat in a corner with his oxygen, too weak even to rage, the room filled with the gasps of his ruined lungs. He was gone by the time of the hastily arranged wedding. Momma had given her away, and she was gone too by the time Nathan arrived. Without Missy, whose services she had inherited with the house, Hilda would have had a nervous collapse.

■ ■ ■ ■

She looked again at the enemy in the mirror, cheeks flushed, eyes bright in some cruel parody of her old self. Her once-fine figure, now buried under mounds of fat. It was no wonder Nelson preferred to sleep alone.

She was hungry, always hungry. There would be such a feast tonight. And she would take a tiny plate and pick at it all evening, while others piled theirs high and went back for seconds. The food called to her like a lover, promising pleasure and comfort and an end to sorrow.

With a last flick of her still-shiny blond hair, she prepared to face the stares, the ridicule, the barely concealed contempt for the oddest couple in town. She planned to get very, very drunk indeed.

CHAPTER 5

By the time Henry finished helping with the gator cleanup, it was late afternoon. They had left no trace of the butchery on the lawn and dispersed just as the big Cadillac carrying Hilda Kincaid crunched down the drive. Missy's secret was safe. Selma had taken the meat home to prepare for the barbecue, trying as usual to persuade Henry back to her house. "Why you want to go all the way back to camp?" she had asked. "You can get washed better in my bathtub. Just look at you; you need a good soak. And I got some of Jerome's clothes to fit you."

"You make good sense, as always, Sister," he had said as he wiped his machete on the grass. "But I got to go back. It's important I be there, for the men." He slipped the machete into his belt.

Her mouth was set in a disapproving line. She seemed to have aged fast while he had been away, but then, he reckoned, eighteen years was half her life so far. At the same age, his mother had seemed like an old woman. There was gray in Selma's hair and tiredness in her walk. He leaned in to kiss her cheek, which she accepted with a glare. He whispered, "See you later . . . Sunny." The choice of this relic from their childhood was deliberate, what he used to call her whenever he was in her bad graces, which was often. It almost never failed to deflect the worst of her ire, like throwing sand over flames. But he always knew they were not extinguished, just smoldering, and could rise up again at any moment.

The muscles in her face fought against the smile. "Git." She slapped his shoulder. "You got a lotta walkin' to do."

Henry headed for the coast road, where there would be a breeze to dry the sweat on his face. The sun was still fierce and seemed to get stronger as it sank toward the horizon, on its way to the sudden, spectacular tropical sunset. He had forgotten the way the sun seemed to laze all afternoon in a slow arc toward the ocean and then, around supper time, drop the world into night like a rock into a barrel.

He was tempted to jump straight into the ocean, clothes and all, it looked so cool and inviting, but this stretch of beach was for whites only. Families had already begun to set up their picnic stations. Fathers fought with beach umbrellas, mothers flicked sand off the blankets, children ran screeching into the waves. A few of the parents eyed him with a mixture of curiosity and suspicion, as if he were an exotic but dangerous animal at the zoo. A little girl sped over to him, a brown ring of melted chocolate around her mouth, stubby legs making hard work of the sand. She offered him her bright red bucket and a shy smile. Right behind was her mother, out of breath and windblown. She grabbed up her daughter roughly and marshaled her back down the beach. He heard the little girl cry, "Why, Mommy?" "Because he's a bad man," hissed the mother, with a backward glance at Henry. "That's why." Her glance took in his blood-soaked T-shirt and filthy pants. He tipped his hat, but she had already rejoined the husband who stood on their blanket, alert, hands on hips.

Henry stepped up his pace, eyes narrowed against the glare off the water.

He fell into the familiar rhythm that had taken him on foot across the country and back. The soft crunch of his boots freed his mind like nothing else. A pelican skimmed the water in an effortless, silent glide alongside him. He realized there was a debt to be paid, to Selma, to Missy. A debt of explanation, for why he had stayed away so long, why he had chosen to ramble aimlessly around the country after the war rather than return home to his people. And why, even after he came to the camp, it was months before he made contact, and after that, only venturing into town rarely. He was grateful Selma had not demanded payment of this debt, but everything in her voice and body said to him, "We have unfinished business, you and me."

How could he explain when he did not really understand it himself? Where to begin? How could he make her feel what it was like, when men you've trained with, lived with more intimately than any woman, get mashed to gristle, their blood in your eyes, your nose, your mouth? What it was like to harvest body parts, instead of cotton, from the fields? What happens to your feet when they're immersed for weeks in a trench filled with mud and shit?

Equally, he lacked the words to tell her about the thrill of fighting alongside white soldiers as valued comrades — French soldiers, because his own countrymen would not have them, but still. The French locals had treated them like heroes, like their own brothers. His boys had played "le jazz" to ecstatic, gyrating crowds in packed clubs. And the women . . . the women. He thought of Thérèse, the last morning before he was shipped home. Her red hair shining in the sunlight on the pillow, the smell of fresh bread from the *boulangerie* below. How to explain that he could step out with her in any bar in town and be greeted with cheers and free drinks, rather than the lynching rope?

He pulled his hat down to shade his eyes and loped on. At first, the homecoming had seemed to meet all his expectations. It looked like everything was really, finally going to be different, just as they had hoped. Even now, he had to smile at the memory of that parade, right up Fifth Avenue. His men had marched proudly in step, exchanged slightly disbelieving glances, nervous grins saying, "Is this for real?" Happy, flag-waving crowds lined their route, the cheers ricocheted like bullets off the tall buildings. There was Li'l Joe, and Franklin, and Sammy, Tyrone, Lemuel, and Jeb. Jeb's little legs had to make two strides for every one of the bigger men's. Together they had marched in hopeful formation toward their future. Henry's plan afterward had been to visit the folks in Florida, but then come back north — to do what, he was not exactly sure, but opportunities for someone like him seemed to ooze from the sidewalks. He would make enough money to give Grace and Selma a comfortable life. Then he would go back to Thérèse, to the room above the *boulangerie* that always smelled of warm bread.

A fine plan. When did it first go wrong? he wondered. When the killings started in Washington and Chicago, the very places where he had thought to try his luck? They heard that Li'l Joe got strung up in Mississippi. Sammy was dragged to death behind a car in Illinois. Tyrone was burned alive for taking part in a labor rally. So he and Jeb had started to walk, away from the riots, away from the burning smell of hate and the rank terror of change. They had worked in fields, slept in barns, sometimes hopped a boxcar, but mostly walked.

During those lost years, he often thought of his mother, his sister, and Missy and the others in Heron Key. If he tried to imagine going back, it was Missy's face he saw, the day she waved him off at the station. The shock and disappointment in her eyes if she could see what he had become — gaunt, weathered, in shabby clothes stiff with dried

79

sweat. He had let them down, all of them. The proud officer, in his shiny shoes, who they had seen off at the station all those years ago, was dead. He sank into the clammy embrace of failure. It was best for everyone if he stayed away. He no longer had a plan. He and Jeb simply existed. They slept in vacant buildings, scavenged in garbage cans for food, did odd jobs. And then one day, while they were in Georgia on a fruit-picking crew, came the call to march on Washington. The government had decided that it would not, after all, pay them the long-promised bonus now, when they really needed it, but rather in 1945, which seemed a century away. This final insult had provoked a reaction, even from the weary veterans. A protest had been organized to explain why this was not acceptable. And so they trekked north to join in.

He could still feel the anger, after all these years, like the smell of smoke that just won't go away. When he and Jeb had arrived at the marchers' shantytown in Washington, it was thick in the air. Thousands of veterans, with their families, had pitched tents in front of the White House. When the army troops arrived to disperse them, at first the veterans milled about in confusion at the sight of their old comrades. Then the soldiers began to fire gas grenades at them, and mounted troops moved in to slash with bayonets, led by a major who someone said went by the name of Patton. The Washington skyline turned orange with the fires of burning tents. Henry saw women and children trampled beneath the horses' hooves. And finally, when it was clear they had lost, he and Jeb joined a slow-moving river of dejected, defeated humanity heading back across the Potomac. Hope gone, faith gone. Only anger remained.

And then, when it had seemed they could sink no lower, a lifeline had found its way to them in the form of a letter from Lemuel. He wrote that a government construction project in the Florida Keys was hiring, for real pay. Not as good as the bonus, it seemed, but better than picking fruit. More than that, Henry decided the location of the project was a sign that the universe wanted him to go home. If it was going to work that hard, he figured, then the least he could do was see what purpose it had for him.

But when he arrived back in Heron Key, he was unprepared for the shock of so many familiar sights and smells, having long ago given up on ever seeing the place again. It looked exactly like it had all those years ago, as if he had only stepped away for a few

81

minutes. He half expected to see his younger self stroll by. It was eerily disconcerting, like an endless attack of déjà vu. He felt like a ghost, haunting a former life where he didn't belong anymore. His men went to town, especially on payday, but he made up excuses to stay behind. The months went by, and still he made no contact. Although his cowardice shamed him, he could face no one from the past, no one who had known him as he was. The extra shame barely registered, just got added to the great big well of it inside him. He was unwilling to face the questions and curious stares of the people he had left behind, even the ones he cared about. The only place he had felt at home was in Doc's kitchen, drinking bourbon after dark. Only Doc, who had served and understood. So once in a while, he snuck into town like a thief.

And then it happened. One night, on his way back from Doc's, he saw her. At first he thought it was a drunken hallucination. Missy passed by in the direction of her Mama's house, head down, weary feet shuffling on the dusty road. Although she hummed under her breath, it was not a happy sound. And then she was gone around the corner. Suddenly he felt completely sober . . . and very, very foolish.

The next day, he had presented himself at Selma's house, as protocol demanded. Reporting for duty.

He thought back to the scene at the Kincaids' house. So now Missy was all grown up. His little Missy, no longer little. She used to leap into his arms each time he arrived to help with her homework, fairly vibrating with the excitement of learning. Even smeared head to foot with gator gore, she was still pretty. And the embarrassment made her prettier still. She was a girl no more, not even a young woman. He had missed all of that. Still working for the Kincaids and living with Mama, Selma had said with a sad shake of her head. He ran his dirty cloth around his neck. Missy could have been something. There had even been talk of her getting a scholarship to college at Howard. And then her useless daddy got himself drowned. Still, where was her husband, her babies? He had wanted to ask Selma, but that would have alerted her extremely keen senses to an interest he was not sure he felt . . . or even deserved to feel.

The coast road bent around the curve of the point that brought him within sight and smell of the camp. The sulfurous stink of the latrines caught in his throat. On the colored side, he could see Jeb sluicing his skinny torso at the pump. The last of his men were here. *His* men. There was Jeb and Franklin, Lemuel and Sonny. That was all.

Henry noticed that his shadow had lengthened on the walk from town. He marched faster, boots kicking up puffs of coral dust. There was just enough time to get clean before they would need to turn around and go back for the barbecue. He did not mind the walk. It was something he knew well how to do. It seemed he had done little else than walk for years and years — always away, never toward anything.

Jeb looked up as he approached.

"Hey, man." He straightened with a grin. "You look like shit." Jeb, whose survival was down to one part blind luck and three parts Henry's protection, was the smallest of them. He joked that he had lied about his height to enlist. By all rights, he should never have even passed basic training, much less been deployed to France, yet he turned out to be fearless in combat and a great comfort to the dying. When Henry caught the shrapnel in his neck, it was Jeb's small hand that stopped him bleeding to death, under fire so intense that it kept even the medics away.

Henry peeled off his shirt. "Guess who's having gator steaks tonight? I had to help

Selma get him ready for the grill. Outta the way, Shortstop."

Jeb nudged the discarded shirt with a disdainful flick of his boot. "Might as well burn that thing. It ain't never comin' clean."

"No chance — that's my best one. My sister can work miracles." Henry stuffed the shirt under the side of their cabin. "She'll be there tonight."

"A woman who looks like you? I scared already."

Henry splashed water in Jeb's face. "That how you talk to your superiors? Where the others at?"

"Where you think?" Jeb indicated the mess hall with a jerk of his head.

Henry rubbed himself dry with Jeb's towel. The little girl on the beach had stayed with him, her green eyes so open and friendly despite his appearance. And her mother's expression, so familiar to him from his years on the road. He imagined what she would make of the veterans when they arrived at the barbecue after hours of drinking beer in the mess. It would fulfill her every fear and expectation. He was surprised to find it bothered him, as he had long become used to reactions like hers. Maybe it was seeing Missy again, or being in the familiar place of his past, but something felt

85

different. He wanted it to be different, and not just for one silly white woman, but for the men themselves. For Selma. For Missy. And yes, for himself. "We'll see about that."

Henry entered the mess hall and said, "Evenin', gentlemen," in his best parade ground voice. The faces at the tables glanced up briefly, then returned to their drinks. Inside the hall was a miasma of sweat and beer fumes. The men looked and smelled like vagrants.

"Oh, hey, Henry," said Sonny, a big placid fellow from Alabama with a lazy eye. "Want a beer?" Sonny had spent the war humping loads from supply ships on the docks of Bordeaux.

"Time to get ready," Henry said. "Anyone goin' to town needs to be cleaned up and standing in formation at 1700 hours. We gonna show these folks we ain't the animals they think we are."

"What do we care what a bunch of Conchs think of us?" This from Two-Step, a heavyset troublemaker from South Carolina with pale eyes and a permanent sunburn, famed for his uncanny ability to evade both bullets and blame. He had spent more time in prison than out since the end of the war. "It's the Fourth of July, motherfucker! They

86

should be kissing my sorry white ass."

Murmurs of assent from the others. Henry's eyes traveled around the room. No one would meet his gaze until it rested on a big, square gunner from Missouri called Max Hoffman. Although he was wide as he was tall, Max had not had an easy time in the camp. Known as "Kraut," he was the target of practical jokes and worse, but he was no pushover. Henry had witnessed him stand up to Two-Step, despite the beating that inevitably followed, which was a rare sight indeed in the camp. Max's eyes registered disgust at Two-Step's performance. He opened his mouth to speak but then, with a small shake of his head, closed it again. Clearly this was not a battle he wanted to fight.

Henry's boys, Franklin and Lemuel, looked uncomfortable but said nothing. Henry understood. They had to live and work alongside these men, who had shown themselves capable of extreme violence over the pettiest excuse.

"You can go fuck yourself, Henry Roberts," Two-Step said with lazy insolence. "You ain't in charge of us." When he was bayoneted in the Argonne Forest, Two-Step had pulled the blade from his body and stabbed it straight into the German's mouth. He and his crew would sooner shoot themselves in the head than take orders from a black officer.

This was too much for Lemuel. "Now, Two-Step, that ain't the way to talk to a officer." Lemuel flicked through the Bible that accompanied him everywhere, including into combat, where it had proved its worth. The stained leather cover was scored with the indentation from a bullet. Lemuel's quotations, however, usually confused rather than illuminated. "Ecclesiastes tell us, *Whatsoever thy hand findeth to do, do it with thy might.*"

"Shut up, you fat baboon," said Milos Dubcek. One of Two-Step's crew, he was a large man with a surprisingly delicate constitution, which had earned him the nickname Sick Bay. He slammed the book shut. "All I know is we gonna have us a *good* time tonight, ain't we, boys?" And he rubbed his crotch with meaningful slowness.

Henry caught a sideways glance from Franklin's one eye. Franklin had been a carpenter in Pennsylvania before he enlisted; now he spent his free time carving delicate sculptures of birds and animals from driftwood. Henry had carried him from the battlefield when Franklin lost an eye in a grenade attack. The scarred socket itched when he was nervous. Franklin scratched at it now.

Two-Step leaned back in his chair, hands linked behind his head. This was not the first time he had gotten in the way. Henry had met many like him in the army, both white and colored, men just out for what they could get. Even among the hard cases in the camp, Two-Step had a reputation for calculated, cunning brutality. His frequent stays in the federal pen had made him an artist of manipulation and subterfuge. Henry avoided him as much as possible, but there had been inevitable clashes, some petty and others not. *I should walk away, just walk away.* As he had done so many times in the past.

But an unfamiliar feeling crept up on him: the feeling that something mattered. He thought again of the little white girl on the beach. He could easily imagine the kind of evening that Two-Step and his crew had in mind. Resolve solidified inside him. Even if it was only for one night, he was determined they would behave like men. He held Two-Step's cold gaze while making fast calculations of weight, angle, and speed. The silence in the tent rang with anticipation.

Henry saw his chance and pushed hard on Two-Step's chair. The man went over on his back, limbs flailing. Before he could react, Henry's boot was on his neck with almost enough pressure to crush his windpipe, but not quite. Franklin grappled with his thrashing legs.

Pale eyes bulged up at Henry, lips bared across a mouthful of ocher teeth. "Help me, boys!" gasped the prone Two-Step. "Help me!"

No one moved.

"Now listen to me!" Henry said. "Those of you not from Florida won't be familiar with our giant cockroaches. They get BIG down here." Two-Step squirmed under his boot just like an insect. "The only way to deal with them is to stomp on 'em. Hard."

Quiet chuckles flickered around the room. Henry did not turn his head to look. He knew he would pay for this at some point. Two-Step could not let this insult go unpunished. But he didn't care. "So I say again: all the human beings should be ready at 1700 hours to march into town, and I do mean *march.* Then we're gonna have ourselves a civilized evening with the other humans. And you know why?" He scanned the faces, one at a time. They had come here from every part of the country, joined together by a desperate hope for something better. Some of them were too far gone to reach, sunk in their swamp of despair, but a few seemed to pay attention. "Not even because of what the town thinks of us, but because we owe it to ourselves. The bugs" — he pushed off of Two-Step's neck — "should stay here in this shit hole where they belong."

Two-Step coughed and gasped on the dirt floor, a deep tread pattern on his throat. Henry saw in his almost-colorless blue eyes a promise: *this ain't over.*

Trent Watts, camp superintendent, observed all of this from the doorway of his office, an unlit stump of cigar clamped between his teeth. Two-Step he knew to be a vicious thug who would as soon cut your throat as look at you, and sly with it. Despite his best efforts, Trent had never managed to tie him to any of the many crimes he had almost certainly committed since joining the project. His enemies suffered terrible accidents, like being crushed by falling timbers that mysteriously loosed their bonds. Property went missing; nothing valuable, of course, as the veterans owned nothing of value. Just little things, like packs of cigarettes or a picture in a tarnished frame. Yes, Two-Step was a slippery son of a bitch who usually got other people to do his fighting for him, patsies like Stan Mulligan and Tecumseh "Tec" Brown, who at that moment were helping Two-Step regain his feet. No, Trent was not at all displeased to see Two-Step on his back under Henry's boot.

But much as Trent would have liked to get Two-Step taken away in handcuffs, Henry was a worse problem for him. For it was Henry who constantly complained to him about everything, from the food to the latrines to the arrangement of the cabins to the goddamn way they folded the flag when they took it down at night. Henry always had a better plan, with that polite smile, that way of talking that managed to sound both respectful and patronizing at the same time. Trent had always known that nothing good would come of having niggers in the army, especially not nigger officers. Henry Roberts was walking proof. He threw down the cigar and moved silently away.

At 1700 hours sharp, Henry emerged from his cabin, ready to lead his men on the march to town. In one respect, Two-Step was right: Henry was not in charge of them, not anymore. The trouble was that nothing had filled the vacuum left by army discipline — and army order — in this desolate camp. In the service, the badges on a man's uniform told you how to behave toward him. Now they were all equals in misery. The supervisor, Trent Watts, had no interest in anything except getting the bridge finished on time and on budget, by any means possible. He did not seem to grasp, despite Henry's repeated pleas, that the revolting food, the ever-present stench of shit, and the cabins that flooded every time it rained were not the best things for getting men to work long and hard in the hot sun. With better food and living conditions, Henry reasoned, the work would get done better and faster, but Watts gave this argument no credence at all. "These men are animals," he had said. "Put them in a palace and they'll still shit in the bed."

It was intolerable, all of it. And yet they did tolerate it, because the alternative was worse: a place in a freezing soup kitchen line in some gray northern town. It was no surprise to Henry that there were men like Two-Step in the camp; the surprise was that all of them were not like him.

He emerged from his cabin to find a group of men standing to attention by the flagpole, all with their serious military faces on. While they could not be described as smartly dressed, they had each made an effort. They were clean, hair combed, beards trimmed.

In a special nod to decorum, Franklin wore a patch over his eye socket. Max Hoffman stood in the mess hall doorway, smoking. Next to him was Two-Step, arms crossed. He spat on the ground as the group passed by, eyes fixed in a hateful stare at Henry.

Henry took his place at the head of the formation. "Gentlemen, now we ready."

They had traveled maybe a hundred yards from the camp gate when there came a scuffle at the rear. Max Hoffman puffed to a stop next to Henry. "I ain't a big fan of cockroaches," said Hoffman.

They fell into step. The sun slanted across the formation, lying in orange bars on the dusty road. Sweat stained their backs and under their arms.

"Henry," said Max, "I hear you from Heron Key? That so?"

"Yep."

They trudged on a bit farther. Henry was very much aware that Max expected him to say more. Sure enough, after a few more silent paces, Max said, "That why you came back here?"

Henry glanced at Max. The man had broken ranks to walk with them. Now he was asking personal questions. Although Henry despised all that Two-Step stood for, he didn't need to go out of his way to find trouble. *What's his game?* But Max's broad face, pink with exertion, showed only open curiosity.

"I woulda gone anywhere there was work," said Henry. He hitched up his pants, which were too big for his skinny frame, despite Selma's cooking. "And since the work was here, it seemed like the Lord intended me to see my family."

Max stared at the sea, hand shading his face, and said nothing for a few minutes. There was only the crunch of boots on oyster shells, the low rumble of conversation from the other men. A pelican buzzed them on its way to the water. Cigarette smoke drifted on the hot breeze. "I had a family too, long time ago. Here." He pulled from his pocket a yellowed, creased photo of a little boy of about six with a big gap between his front teeth. Same square face, pink cheeks, cowboy hat askew on his head.

Henry studied the photo. "That a fine boy you got there. Where he at now?"

Max returned the picture to his pocket with a shrug. Henry knew that kind of shrug. He had used it many times when asked unanswerable questions. "Dunno," said Max. "His mother took him away . . . when my drinkin' . . . well, you know."

"Yeah." A look of understanding passed

95

between them. "Yeah, I do." Henry hesitated one more moment, conscious that he was crossing some invisible line. "That why you here?"

Max shrugged. "I guess so. When it all went wrong, I just started walkin'. I figured I'd walk till there was no more road." He squinted into the sun. "Seems to me like that place is here."

He's right, Henry thought. *This is it, the place where the road ends.* It was where you ended up when you had tried everything else. It was a place of last resort. Every man marching with him left a trail of wrecked hopes and shattered lives, like the shells that crumbled under their boots.

They marched on into the deepening twilight.

CHAPTER 6

When Missy arrived at the beach, Selma already had the gator steaks on the grill, shooing the flies away with one hand while she flipped the meat with the other. A pot of swamp cabbage boiled on the fire with plenty of bacon and sugar. A line of people had formed by the makeshift tables, which were trimmed with red, white, and blue bunting, filling their plates with slaw and fried conch and scoops of sweet coquinas on their way to the grill. A few yards away, a series of posts stuck in the sand ran down the beach to the surf, strung with twine to mark the boundary of the whites' area. Atop each post fluttered a small American flag.

The horizon was awash with apricot light beneath a band of china-blue sky. Ridges of insubstantial clouds mirrored the sand in the shallows. Very unusually, the afternoon thunderstorms had passed over them, driven inland by a strong onshore wind. Missy fanned herself with a paper plate, grateful that at least the air moved.

"Can I help?" she asked. Selma took the plate of Mama's corn bread and set it on the table. Mama had delivered a bucket of her famous barbecue sauce earlier that day to grace the roasted pig to come from Ronald LeJeune. Every year, he made a big show of his generosity toward the colored folks; he so loved playing the beneficent white man. Some coloreds took against his preening and posturing, but to Selma, it was simple: food was food. "You cain't eat principles," she always said.

"In that dress?" Selma eyed her up and down. "I don't think so." Selma's apron was spattered with grease, her wrists marked with welts from the grill, her face shiny with sweat. She slapped at a mosquito on her neck. The air shimmered with them, and their wings filled the air with a constant hum, despite the pots of pyrethrum burning everywhere.

Missy felt suddenly conscious of the pristine yellow of the dress, the scent of oil in her hair. All her careful preparations seemed silly and kind of stuck-up. After all, she was not a girl anymore, someone to primp and giggle at the boys, ribbons in her hair. She was stepping out with no one. She

98

should have come prepared to work.

"You look very pretty," said Selma with a squeeze of her arm and a warm, soft smile that Missy had only ever seen maybe once before. "And you can help by makin' sure there's enough food to go around." She waved her turning fork at Ike Freeman, who had piled his plate with about twice as much food as it was designed to hold. He gripped a slab of corn bread between his teeth as he shuffled slowly through the sand toward a folding chair in the shade of some sea grapes.

"Where's Jerome?" asked Missy. He could usually be relied upon to turn up at a party, if not much else.

"Fishing," said Selma.

A look passed between them. Selma never complained about Jerome. Missy was not sure if this was out of love or pride . . . or maybe both. Her eyes scanned the crowd.

"Henry ain't here yet," said Selma, her tone returned to its normal tartness. "Might not come at all. Get a move on."

Missy took her place behind a big table covered in bowls and platters. Despite Ike's gluttony, there seemed to be no risk of any shortages. She wrapped a spare apron around her waist and let the chatter of the other women flow around her as she served.

She did not know what to expect from the evening, only that a voice in her head said something was going to happen. It did not say whether it would turn out good or bad. Over time, she had learned to listen to that voice.

Lionel, the Kincaids' gardener, stepped up to have his plate filled. That afternoon, he had looked like he might collapse with shock when he learned of the gator's nearly successful raid, then seemed to take special satisfaction in cutting up the carcass. Missy knew he saw the Kincaid family as his personal responsibility. "That a mighty pretty dress, Missy," he said. She spooned some coleslaw onto his plate. "You look like a princess." His weathered features folded into a nearly toothless smile, eyes narrowed to moist slits.

"Thanks, Lionel. Here, have some more." The man was so thin, he looked held together by the ragged clothes he wore every day and washed every night.

He moved away and Missy let her mind wander. She recalled Henry's wry smile, his haunted eyes, that scar on his neck. Who was she to judge anyone, anyway? A woman, no longer young, but still living with her mama. No husband, no babies, no schooling. And why? Because two men had let her down? That was no reason for anything. Men let people down every day, and folks still made something of their lives. She had done nothing, been nowhere. And if she wanted someone to blame, she only had to look in the mirror every morning.

Eighteen years Henry had stayed away, clearly not in any hurry to get home again, not for Grace, not for Selma . . . and not for her. All this time, she had waited and hoped . . . for what, she did not even know. She felt safe when he was there, in ways she could not explain, even to herself. She had not felt safe for a long time.

The line of plates kept coming. Someone put a record on the gramophone, but she didn't recognize the tune. How could Henry not find her ridiculous? She, who might as well still be eight years old, clinging to his neck as he boarded his train. She began to wish she was home with Mama in the yellow lamplight on the porch, with the soft sounds of chickens settling for the night. *This was a mistake. Maybe I can sneak home early.*

And here she was, in this ridiculous, girlish dress, thinking to live out some childish dream. For what? The Henry she had known was gone, that was for sure. If any of him was left, it was buried deep inside him. He had been to the world, to New York, to France. No doubt he had been with fancy, knowing women in all these places, women who wore store-bought dresses and smoked cigarettes in speakeasies. Maybe even, as it was rumored, white women, who wore makeup and curled their eyelashes . . . women who could talk about things, could do . . . things . . . to a man.

Two fishing boats pulled up on the sand. Their crews splashed ashore with garlands of snapper and black drum, dolphin and wahoo, held aloft and heading for Selma's grill. The crowd cheered them on their way up the beach, bare black skin whitened by dried salt.

And then Missy caught sight of something that made her drop her spoon right into the sand.

"What you doing, girl?" asked Violet Hudson on her left. She collected the spoon and went to rinse it in the surf.

Missy just stared, transfixed, as Selma's husband Jerome struggled through the waves with a large grouper on the end of a gaff. The fish must have weighed forty pounds. An even louder cheer accompanied his progress toward the grill. With a grunt, he stripped the fish from the gaff's barbed hook, where it landed with a wet thump on

Selma's table.

Instantly, Missy was a little girl again, waiting for her father, Billy, to come home with his catch. More often, the boat would return empty but for Billy and his collection of bottles, and she would have to help him stagger back to the house to face Mama. Until one afternoon, when Leon had woken late from his nap, cranky and fretful, demanding to see his daddy. Mama had been too tired to argue, so they all went down to the beach to wait for Billy.

Leon was Billy's treasure, the only good thing to come from his miserable life, as he liked to say — often. Missy accepted this. Leon was their gift from the Almighty. Everyone doted on him. Mama got special treatment, from white and black folks alike, when she took him to the store. The other fishermen, with sons of their own, saved the shiniest seashells for Leon. He kept them in a driftwood box next to his cot.

It had been a dull, windy day, and the other boats had come in early with little or no fish. There was talk of a storm, but the wind could not make up its mind and kept changing direction. One minute the clouds seemed about to burst, and then they would pass over. Even before the boat landed, Missy could see her father was drunk from the way he swayed in his seat.

"I gonna surprise him!" announced Leon and raced ahead of them to hide behind a coconut palm. He sneaked peeks at his mother and sister, giggling audibly.

"Shh, he gonna hear you, silly," said Missy.

"Hey, y'all!" cried Billy. He stepped clumsily out of the boat and instantly lost his balance. On his knees in the water, laughing, he waved his arms. "Hey, baby, let's have a party tonight!" His smile was broad and crooked, his eyes unfocused.

The only other contents of the boat were an empty rum bottle and his gaff. Mama was clearly not in the mood. "Yeah, Billy," she had said, hands on hips, "and what we gonna eat at this party?"

"Dammit, woman," Billy said and turned his back to retrieve the gaff from the bottom of the boat. "Why you always —"

At that moment, Leon had raced down the beach, his little feet making silent indentations in the sand. Missy felt a puff of breeze as he sped past her toward his father. Leon made no sound until he reached the water, grinning at the surprised faces of his mother and sister. Then he shrieked, "Daddy!"

Missy had no time even to cry out. Billy moved very fast for someone so full of rum.

Some primitive part of him just reacted to the noise. He had straightened and spun toward it, gaff held in both hands like a spear. And as he turned, Leon's momentum carried him right onto the gaff's barbed hook. It entered just below his rib cage. The vicious point had emerged with a red bloom on his back. He said "Daddy" again, but quietly, just once.

Not long after that, Billy went to sea for the last time. Even at such a young age, Missy recognized that sadness had taken up residence in their home and made himself good and comfortable there. Sure enough, he had been a resident ever since, a permanent presence who followed her everywhere, like an ugly, smelly dog.

She became aware of Violet's eyes on her. Slowly, the sounds of the barbecue returned.

"Missy," said Violet. "You okay, honey?" She replaced the rinsed spoon in Missy's hand.

Missy took a deep, shaky breath and wiped her face with the apron. "Fine, Violet. I fine." But she thanked the Lord that Mama had stayed home.

On the other side of the boundary, Ronald LeJeune settled a large chunk of fragrant, steaming pork on the platter held by his wife, Cynthia. Every year, he used the same family method for roasting the hog: dig a pit, line it with hot charcoal, add some hickory wood and cornstalks for flavor, and then bury the animal for two days. It had come out perfectly once again. All that was left to do was douse it in a bath of Mama's special barbecue sauce.

Dwayne approached. "Looking good, Ronald, Cynthia," he said with an appreciative glance at the platter. "That going to the other side?"

"It is indeed," said Ronald, flushed with heat and pride.

"Do me a favor this year, Ronald," Dwayne said, "and keep away from Ike."

"You know me, Dwayne. There's no one more peaceable in all of Heron Key. It's his fault that things get out of hand. Pure and simple."

Dwayne knew it was neither but had to admit Ronald was mostly correct. That Ike had a short fuse was beyond dispute, and except for this one night, Dwayne could rely on Ronald to be levelheaded, generous, and sober. But something happened at the barbecue every year. Maybe Ronald just saved up all his bad behavior for a whole twelve months to use in a single night. Dwayne knew from long experience that it was pointless to argue. He grimaced, resigned to the brawl to come.

"Cindy," said Ronald, "give Dwayne a plate. Can't have our protector of life and liberty go hungry."

Dwayne made his way to the long tables where people were lined up to fill their plates. Mabel Hickson proudly removed the cover on the bowl of her infamous potato salad and pushed it to the front of the table. "Deputy, can I help you?" she asked with a coquettish flick of her spoon.

"Uh, thanks, Mabel," he said. "It looks delicious, but Noreen wants me to lose some weight." He patted his substantial paunch, then noted the pointed glance she gave the heaped pile of pork glistening with fat on his plate. But there was no way he was going to risk food poisoning just to spare her feelings.

He walked away, intent on finding somewhere comfortable to enjoy his feast. Whatever else the evening held for him, at least he would not have to face it on an empty stomach.

When he was out of earshot, Mabel said, sounding very annoyed, "So sad for poor Dwayne."

Cynthia LeJeune, standing next to her on coleslaw duty, watched his retreating back,

107

all beefy shoulders and solid legs. He settled down to eat a few feet away, on his face the look of a man who likes his food. Cynthia said, "Yes, he's got a hard row to hoe, that's for sure. More slaw, Cyril?"

Cyril Anderson gripped a bottle of beer in the makeshift claw that Doc had fashioned for him after he lost his hand at the fish plant. "Yes, thank you, ma'am."

Mabel said to Cynthia, "I heard that baby Roy's daddy is one of them, out there at the camp, one of them vet'rans."

"Wouldn't surprise me one bit," Cynthia said quietly, licking cucumber relish off her finger. "I hear they live like animals. Stands to reason, in time they start to act like them. And that Noreen has always been a flirt. Black or white, didn't matter." She leaned closer. "Do you know who it is?"

Mabel basked in Cynthia's interested gaze. Nobody usually paid her much attention, not even her husband, Warren. "Um," said Mabel, who wished she had thought this through. Then she remembered what Warren said about one of the veterans, the guy who grew up in Heron Key. Always was a troublemaker, Warren said. "Yes, I do. It's Henry. Henry Roberts. That's what I heard."

At this, Dwayne's fork paused in its trajectory toward his mouth. Even with his poor hearing, Mabel was easily audible. A whisper from her carried as far as a shout from most people. He noted several others glance in her direction, eyebrows raised. The news would be all over town by the morning.

Mabel turned a satisfied smile on the next customer. "Potato salad?"

CHAPTER 7

"There you go," said Doc Williams. "All fixed up." He smoothed more ointment over the rope burn on Jennifer Mason's little hand. She had insisted on taking part in a tug-of-war with some much older children. To her credit, she had stayed on her feet but paid the price with a nasty abrasion.

"Say 'thank you,' Jenny," said Dolores Mason.

"Sank you, Doctor Williams," she said through her missing front teeth.

He tousled her hair, and she ran off to rejoin the big kids.

Dolores sighed. "At that age, all you want is to be older, don't you? Funny how that changes." She flashed an appraising smile at Doc, her eyes half closed against the smoke from her cigarette. Dolores was one of the country club wives who kept trim on a regime of tennis, caffeine, and nicotine. They migrated like a flock of exotic birds between the beauty parlor, the clubhouse, and the tennis court, all brittle chatter and bright plumage. Doc knew her circle well, the ladies for whom the new antibiotics were such a godsend when their indiscretions led to nasty infections.

Doc followed her eyes to the road where the Kincaid Cadillac had just pulled up. Nelson slammed the driver's side door and set off down the beach, dragging hard on his cigarette, leaving Hilda to struggle out of the car. She emerged shakily from the passenger door, tried to smooth her dress, patted her hair into place, and teetered across the sand after her husband. Her sandals would have made walking difficult even on smooth ground, but in the sand, she staggered and fell to her knees. It was obvious that she had already been drinking. It was also obvious that she would not rise unaided.

"Pathetic, isn't she?" said Dolores with a flick of ash in Hilda's direction.

"Excuse me, Dolores," said Doc and went to help Hilda. Although it shamed him to admit it, he had had a crush on her for years — something he shared with all the other males from sixteen to sixty. She had been their very own matinee idol, perfect and untouchable. Everyone had been shocked by her sudden marriage to Nelson, but her decline since then had been marked by a distinct lack of sympathy. There were some folks, Doc felt, who actively enjoyed Hilda's swift, complete disgrace, especially Dolores and her crowd. Doc still found her entrancing.

He raised Hilda to her feet. Her brows were furrowed in distress. He sensed that tears were not far away. "Upsy daisy. Here we go," he said and brushed the sand from her hands.

"Oh, Doc," she whispered. "I'm so embarrassed. Everyone is looking at me."

But it was worse than that. A few people glanced her way, but most had spared her only a moment's attention. They had already returned to their conversations.

"Horseflies," he said. "If I had a dollar for every person who fell in the sand tonight . . ."

She held his arm for support and smiled uncertainly. Her smile could still melt ice cream straight from the freezer. It took him back to the before time — before the war, before Leann and Cora. Before Nelson Kincaid. Back then, everything had seemed possible.

"I need a drink," she said.

He handed over his beer. "There are far

stranger things on this beach tonight than a lady losing her footing. Just look around."

Indeed, there was Zeke, knee-deep in the surf with Poncho on his shoulder, ranting at the sea with fists raised. "Stay back, you monster!" he shrieked. "Stay back!"

And there was one-handed Cyril, setting up the fireworks. Everyone figured he was best qualified, since he couldn't lose the same hand twice.

Up near the road, at a picnic table beneath a stand of palms, were five uniformed officers — Dwayne's insurance policy — failing spectacularly to blend in. Doc had hoped they would be in plain clothes, but maybe Dwayne had reasoned that deterrence was better than interference.

"You're a kind, kind man, Doc," Hilda said with an obvious effort at composure. "Thank you. And now, I should go find Nelson."

Doc had treated Hilda several times over the years and attended the birth of baby Nathan. He could tell when she was on the verge of breaking down. A small tremor in her left eyelid, the slightly vacant gaze, the pitch of her voice a little too high. He wanted to protect her, to say, "Let's leave all these phonies and find a quiet spot to watch the sunset." He wanted to stop that tremor with a touch of his hand, to reassure her that she was still beautiful, that she would always be beautiful to him. That she deserved to be happy. But instead he said, "Best you take off those pretty sandals. Not very practical."

"You're right," she said and slipped them into her hand. "Thank you, for everything. Now, where is that husband of mine?"

He watched her pick her way across the sand to where Nelson stood with his back to her. Dolores had one hand on his shoulder. The rest of the flock was close by, all sharp smiles and trim-waisted dresses. Their husbands were oblivious, engrossed in golf talk. Doc marveled at the human capacity for self-deception, but then decided the men probably knew exactly what their wives were up to. They just chose to ignore it because it suited them. Sometimes he longed for the certainties of the battlefield. At least the enemy identified himself clearly.

Zeke could feel it coming. The signs were there, all around, in the slow, rolling swells. He counted the waves in, felt the immense power of the monster's wake. He knew the ocean as intimately as he knew Poncho's different calls. The bird flapped his cobalt wings once and settled more comfortably on Zeke's bony shoulder. Poncho did not like the yelling, but Zeke knew his duty. He would not rest or falter. He was Heron Key's only defense.

Selma reclined in a folding chair, legs spread wide, a beer bottle half sunk in the sand beside her. Ronald LeJeune approached, platter of pork held proudly aloft as he crossed to the colored side of the barrier. His chest was out, cheeks flushed. A few people had been dancing to quiet music on the gramophone but stopped when he arrived. Every year, it was the same ritual. Food, then a fight. Everyone knew what would happen, yet they seemed hell-bent on repeating the same old tired routine, like a mule in harness. Round and round.

She heaved herself upright.

"Miss Selma," Ronald boomed. "Where would you like me to put this?"

"Thank you, Mr. LeJeune. Follow me." She led the way to the table.

Right on cue, Ike Freeman muttered darkly, "I'll tell him where he can put it."

Selma flashed her hardest look, the one that could usually be relied on to bring Jerome to heel, but Ike was too far gone. There was something in his bloodshot glare that she did not like one bit, some secret that pleased him no end. His grin oozed malice.

"Call me Ronald, please," Mr. LeJeune said to Selma. This was another part of the ritual.

"Come on, y'all," she called. "Mr. Le-Jeune has brought us some of the hog roast."

There were appreciative murmurs. People retrieved their plates and made their way to the table. "May I?" asked Ronald.

"Go right ahead, sir," said Selma. Ronald ladled Mama's thick barbecue sauce over the pork. It smelled smoky sweet, flowed over the meat, and pooled around the edges of the platter.

"Yessuh, nosuh, three bags full, suh," said Ike, this time not trying to lower his voice. "That how it is, Selma?" There were food stains down the front of his shirt. He leered at Ronald and raised his beer bottle with a loud belch. "Happy Independence Day, Roooooonald," he said and took a large swig.

Lionel went to take Ike's arm. "Come on now, Ike —"

Ike shoved him hard, and the old gardener went down in the sand. Someone helped him to his feet. The others stood by warily. They all knew what to expect.

"Leave him be," said Selma with a sharp

glance at Ike. There was something different this year — she could feel it. "Mr. LeJeune, may be best you go on back to the other side."

"It's all right, Selma," said Ronald in a rather bored tone. "It's a shame that some people have to spoil things for everyone else." He turned toward Ike as if to deliver a lecture. "And as for you —"

He did not get to finish his sentence because Ike lunged at him, a flash of metal in his fist.

"Ike, no!" Selma screamed.

Ronald roared in pain and surprise, one hand clamped to his cheek. Blood flowed between his fingers. Violet crumpled in a faint, and no one was quick enough to catch her. Two of the men somehow managed to bring Ike down. He thrashed like a rabid dog under their weight, eyes rolling back in his head.

While he was thus restrained, Ronald took the opportunity to land a vicious punch on Ike's belly. "You worthless piece of shit!" He kicked Ike in the face. "I wish my granddaddy had finished the job when he had a chance!"

The men exchanged a glance and released Ike's arms. He flew at Ronald, swinging. They fell to the sand, Ike on top with his hands around Ronald's throat. Blood from Ronald's face stained the sand all around.

The crack of a pistol shot startled everyone, including Ike and Ronald. Dwayne holstered his weapon and stepped over the barrier in one long stride, the visiting policemen close behind.

"Ike," he said, "you gone too far this time. I'm taking you in. Get him to the station. I'll be along directly."

One of the cops pulled Ike's hands behind his back and snapped on the handcuffs.

"Oh, Ronnie!" cried Cynthia, dropping to her knees beside him. She tried to mop the blood with the hem of her dress. "Someone help my husband!"

Sand caked a long gash in Ronald's cheek. Doc Williams came running with his medical bag.

"That lunatic belongs in jail!" yelled Ronald, blood spraying with every word. "I want him put away for good!"

"Keep quiet, Ronald," said Doc. "This is a bad cut." He stood up and wiped his hands. "I need to get him back to my office, going to require stitches." He helped Ronald to stand. The man's skin had gone gray, and he shivered in the heat. "Help me get him to the car." The men who had restrained Ike half carried, half dragged Ronald back toward the road, with Doc and Cynthia behind.

"Excitement's over, folks," said Dwayne. "Go back to your party. Cyril, get those fireworks going."

Someone started the gramophone. The music wafted over to Selma on the breeze, a jaunty tune she could not place. "You heard the man," she said. "Y'all go have fun." Flies settled on the mound of pork, undisturbed in its lake of sauce.

On the other side of the barrier, the sound of Selma's scream almost came as a relief to Hilda. She had been standing next to Nelson with a smile so fixed it might have been stapled to her face, slowly sinking into the sand and despair. A mosquito stung her neck, but she did not bother to swat it. Her body was already covered in red bites, which would bloom into big welts by the morning. She could not understand why Florida had ever been settled, as everything in the cursed state seemed designed to make her uncomfortable. Everywhere she turned, peril lay in wait, creatures determined to bite, sting, or poison. The very land itself was infested with grasses that cut her tender flesh, innocuous vines that caused painful rashes. The sun was evil, its scorching rays constantly attacking her smooth complexion. The insects nearly drove her insane.

Hilda had downed three mint juleps in quick succession, thinking they would dull the pain of the evening, but they had somehow intensified it. No one spoke to her, so she cast herself adrift from the flow of conversation around her. Everything was magnified and slowed down, so her senses registered each excruciating detail: Dolores's secret smile, the way her hand brushed Nelson's arm oh so casually. The others hung off him like wasps on a peach and he loved it. She could tell, from his half-closed eyes, his lazy grin. Each glance, each touch revealed more of the truth. It cut like a shard of glass being slowly pushed into her flesh. These women, they had once been her friends. Now she understood. It was suddenly clear to her: they were all in on it. Every one of them. *Where did they do it?* Clearly not in her house, since she had barely left it since Nathan was born. And then she realized. *Of course: the Caddy. It had worked for him before.*

Selma's scream brought everyone rushing over to the barrier to get a good view of the fight. Hilda had the chance to observe them all, as if from an airplane high above. The women, with their cute, tennis-honed figures, their manicured nails, their lacquered lips . . . How could she blame him? She had done nothing but stay home and get fat. Was it any wonder he sought satisfaction elsewhere? She went to fill a plate with Key lime pie while they were otherwise occupied. On the way, she picked up another mint julep.

The excitement of the fight over, the crowd dispersed toward the water for fireworks of another kind. Cyril sank the final rocket into the sand at the surf line, pointing out to sea. Zeke stood by, offering encouragement — or at least what sounded like encouragement. "Good!" he cried, bouncing with excitement, Poncho struggling to retain his grip on Zeke's shoulder. "Throw everything you got at him! That'll show the cocksucker!" There were giggles from the small spectators. "Get going," he implored Cyril. "Blast it out of the sky!"

The sunset had been stunningly beautiful that evening, as if the cosmos was determined to outdo any display of spectacle planned by the humans. The horizon still glowed with embers of gold, orange, and crimson, but the sky had darkened enough for a few stars to show through. Torches had been lit, their flames buffeted by the breeze, casting jerky shadows across the beach. Spectators, white and black, gathered at the ocean.

"Stand back, everyone!" called Cyril, the long match clamped in his claw. The crowd went quiet in anticipation, faces turned toward the sky. He touched the match to the fuse of the first rocket. It charred the end of the fuse and went out with a quiet *phut.*

There was a collective groan of disappointment. This happened every year, as Cyril bought the fireworks cheap to make the budget go farther. This year had been especially hard, with the budget cut almost to nothing.

"Ain't you got a flamethrower, Cyril?" came a voice from the crowd.

"Maybe Doc Williams can install one for you!" cackled another.

Cyril struck another match on his claw, hurrying to get the flame to the fuse in the stiff breeze. The fuse fizzled with a disappointing *sssss.* And again. Same result. In frustration, he tried every fuse, to no avail. "Sorry, folks, must have got damp." He rose off his knees. "Or those crooks up in Brooksville sold me a load of duds. Sorry." He put the matches away but left the rockets where they were.

People shuffled back up the beach. Zeke growled his unhappiness. Poncho let out a quiet, disappointed, *"Caw."*

Deprived of the promised spectacle, the crowd seemed caught in a state of suspended anticipation. It was too early to go home, but the engine of the party had stalled. People freshened their drinks, scolded their children, and cast dismayed glances at the line of impotent rockets by the sea's edge.

Then came, from the road, a noise that at first sounded like loud rushing water. It resolved itself as it came closer into the sound of booted feet, marching in formation, crunching over the oyster-shell path to the beach. The veterans appeared from around the bend in the road, Henry at the lead. They came smartly to a halt with a stamp of feet where the path met the sand.

Henry surveyed the scene with a soldier's eye. On the colored side, people seemed to be spooked by something, and there were tearful women being comforted. There was also a great mound of fly-covered meat. Selma looked both tired and angry. Missy, barefoot in a pretty yellow dress, waited alone at the water. On the white side of the beach, there were long drag marks in the

123

sand, coming from the colored side, spotted with what looked like blood. And at the water, a line of unattended, unfired rockets. "Good evening, everyone," he said in his best officer voice. "Looks like we missed quite a party."

CHAPTER 8

Hilda observed the veterans' arrival with little interest. Her feet hurt. Nelson was clearly in no hurry to go home. There was sand in her hair and in her teeth. God only knew how it got there. Nelson whispered in Dolores's ear, his mouth up close to her glossy black hair. They looked like two thoroughbred horses together. Dolores flung her head back to laugh, exposing the strong lines of her throat. Hilda pictured them in the back of the Caddy, Dolores's toned legs wrapped around him, his hands at her narrow waist, his mouth on hers. The pain was overwhelming, like she was drowning in it.

Her eyes rested on the veterans' leader, the one with the big scar on his neck. He was clearly in command, carried himself straight and tall and the others followed. Hilda recognized him. She struggled to focus. Harold? Horace? No . . . Henry.

Selma's brother, been away a long time, back now with the veterans to build that bridge. He had done some work at the house to make extra money, repairing one of the hurricane shutters. *A good-looking man, or he would be,* she thought, *if he got some decent food in him.* An idea began to crystallize.

Henry stooped to kiss his sister's cheek. The atmosphere hummed with electric tension, like there was a great big generator buried in the sand beneath their feet. "Jesus, Selma, what's been going on here?" he asked as he looked around.

"A black jackass attacked a white jackass. Same as every year, but then you wouldn't know about that, would you?" Before he could reply, she said, "Henry, your boys better not make no trouble. We had our fill for one night, I can tell you."

"Don't you worry about my boys," he said with a sideways glance at the men. Sonny twirled a petite, giggly woman to the music on the gramophone. Franklin was in conversation with a pretty girl too, showing her some of his driftwood carvings. Everyone was behaving like civilized people. So far. "They just here to have a good time. Any food left?" He patted his flat stomach.

"I'm starvin'."

She regarded him through narrowed, tired eyes. "Henry Roberts, what the hell's wrong with you?"

"What you mean, Sister?"

Selma gestured toward the figure of Missy, down by the surf. Her dress glowed against the dark blue of the water, which was streaked with the orange and red fragments of the sunset.

She looked so pretty. Had he been anywhere else, had she been anyone else, he most certainly would have been intending some private time with her. He could feel her waiting but did not want to disturb the picture she made.

"I don't know, Selma," he said, suddenly at a loss. Unused to polite company, after so long on the road, he had forgotten how to be with people. Everything felt temporary, like it could all be washed away by the next wave. His former friends and neighbors studied him with guarded smiles. Their curious stares tingled on his back. "I don't think it's a good —"

Selma planted her feet, folded her arms, and leaned very close. Her breath, scented slightly with beer, was hot in his face. "You listen to me now. I put up with you comin' back here after so long, with barely a word for me or your mama, the good Lord rest her soul. I put up with you livin' out at the camp, showin' you care more for those . . . *men*" — she fairly spat the word — "than for your own people. But I will not" — she leaned even closer, her finger pushed into his chest — "I repeat, *not* put up with you breakin' that girl's heart for a second time." Her voice went quiet. "You read me, Henry?"

"Now, Sunny, you just —"

"Don't call me that. I ain't in the mood."

"All right, Selma." He looked again at the figure in the yellow dress. "The whole truth is I ain't the person she remembers." He recalled that little girl, who believed him capable of anything, who trusted him completely. The way she used to look at him, like he was some kind of hero because he knew stuff and could read stories . . . it made him believe too. All that was gone, everything she knew of him, burned away at a shantytown in Washington. He had nothing to offer someone like her. "You don't realize how I've changed —"

"We all changed, Henry!" Selma's nostrils flared, her hands spread wide, taking in the whole beach, Missy included. "S'what eighteen years will do to a body. She been waitin', all that time. For you. Now go on,

128

say whatever you got to say. But be a man. It time you take responsibility for what you done."

When Dwayne returned to the beach, having settled Ike in his cell for the night, he was greeted by an unexpected scene. A group of veterans chatted amiably with the townspeople. Everyone had a beer in hand, but no one was obviously drunk. A big guy with a goofy grin was doing a shambling shuffle. Even the rather scary one with the eye patch seemed to be getting on well with Violet. Some of the white folks had drifted over to get a better look at them. *Maybe Doc was right, and it will be okay after all.*

Something akin to disappointment settled over him. A good fight would be a welcome distraction from the words overheard earlier, which had twined around his brain like a strangler fig: *baby Roy's daddy . . . Henry, Henry Roberts.* They slithered through his consciousness to the point where he could barely wrest his thoughts away. *Could that be the answer?* After so long, wondering, torturing himself and Noreen, was the answer as simple as that?

He forced himself to focus on what he could be sure of: Mabel was the worst kind of fool and an inveterate gossip. She slavered over a hot rumor the way he did a sirloin steak. Yet he also knew that, in small towns, this was exactly how news got around. It was often just a kernel of truth, wrapped in layers of speculation and even pure fantasy.

He jabbed the toe of his boot into the sand, hands sunk deep into his pockets. The timing of Roberts's arrival at the camp fit. Everyone knew the colored soldiers got a taste for white women overseas. And he was well aware of Roberts's reputation for causing trouble with his ideas. In every way, Roberts was the kind of man who could do such a thing.

The sand spilled over his boot. Millions of grains of it, in only a few inches of space. Was there even the tiniest grain of truth in what Mabel said? He had to find out.

His eyes were drawn to the other side of the beach, where Roberts was deep in conversation with his sister. The man clearly thought a lot of himself, just from the way he was standing, back straight, shoulders square. Like he was in charge of something. Dwayne could not help himself, despite all the rational arguments against it. He studied Henry's face, looking for the resemblance. The longer he looked, the more uncertain he felt. There were things that reminded him of Roy in the shape of Henry's face, the tilt of his head. But nothing definitive, nothing that would serve as conclusive proof.

More confused than ever, he was about to turn away, determined to master the turmoil in his head, when he saw something that fixed him to the spot. Henry and Selma were arguing. From their posture, Dwayne could tell it was about something important. Then Selma's lips formed the words that made up his mind. She said to Henry, "Now go on, say whatever you got to say. But be a man. It time you take responsibility for what you done."

Hilda watched and waited for Henry to finish talking with his sister. When he set off down the beach, she saw her chance and rushed around to meet him. She hugged him with a cheery, "Welcome home, Henry!"

With deliberate care, he removed her hands and stepped away. "Evenin', Missus Kincaid."

"Call me Hilda, silly!" She gave him a playful slap.

"Now, Hilda, I mean Missus Kincaid —"

"Dance with me, Henry, c'mon." And she began to shuffle around him in a stumbling approximation of the beat coming from the

131

gramophone. She tried to put his arms around her but he held her away stiffly, his smile taut. She was acutely aware that everyone had stopped to watch the display.

The shocked stares on both sides of the barrier fueled her determination. Now she had their attention. Now they would see. She was not someone to be mocked and ignored. After all, she had been Miss Palmetto. Two years running. "No one else will dance with me," she said, loud enough for Nelson to hear. "Not even my own husband." She switched to a stage whisper. " 'Cause he likes those other girls better."

Nelson flung his cigarette aside, separated himself from the group, and strode toward her. He took Hilda by the arm and began to drag her back across the barrier. His fingers dug painfully into the soft flesh of her arm. She caught Henry's eye.

Henry said mildly, "Hey, you don't need to hurt the lady."

"You," growled Nelson, "keep your hands off her. And keep off our property." To the crowd, he said, "Pay no mind. My wife's not used to being in public." Quietly to her, he said, "You're embarrassing yourself. Quit it."

"Oh, pardon me," she said as she jerked free. "I meant to embarrass *you.*"

They stood there, glaring at each other, breathing hard. Nelson broke away. "Fine," he said and turned to go. "Do what you want."

"I want," she said with a tremor of the lips, "to go home."

"Feel free," he said over his shoulder.

"When . . . when will you be back?"

"When I damn well choose to, woman," he said and returned to the group on the other side. One of the men patted his back. Dolores just shrugged at Hilda and sent her a look that said "game, set, match."

Hilda looked around at the faces, black and white. She saw sadness and disgust there, compassion and disapproval. Her pretty sandals were stained and stretched. Her dress was awry, caught in the sweaty folds of her stomach. Damp hair stuck to her forehead. There was only one thing left to do. With a last look at Nelson, she began walking toward the road and home.

Down at the water, Missy affected an air of cool at Henry's approach, just like in her daydreams. She thought of the last time she had seen him before he left, in his uniform with his duffel bag, waiting for the train that would take him somewhere she could not imagine. He had shown her the place on the map: Iowa. It was a funny shape, surrounded by other funny shapes, several shapes away from the fingerlike projection she knew to be Florida. She had hopscotched her fingers across the map. It didn't look very far away. She and Mama could go visit him. They could bring him some of Mama's corn bread, which he loved so much. He had said there was no ocean in Iowa. She had frowned at this. "That crazy talk," she had said. "Crazy" had been her favorite word at the time. "How the people go fishing?"

"No fishing," he had said. "They eat other stuff, Missy. Cows, mostly."

To which she had responded with a disbelieving huff. *No one ate cows,* she thought, *else where would the milk come from?*

"I'm gonna be an officer," he had said. "You know what that is?"

From the weight of the word in his voice, she had known it was important. "Means you the boss?"

He had laughed at that, head thrown back. "The day a black man is the boss won't come in my lifetime, but yes, I will be in charge of some stuff."

"Like story reading?" There could be no job more important than that, she had thought.

"Like story reading. Officer in charge of story reading, reporting for duty, ma'am." He had saluted and placed his cap on her head, where it dropped over her eyes.

She looked out from under it. "Who gonna be in charge of story reading here till you come back?"

"That you, Missy," he had said and retrieved his cap. "That you."

He had looked so strange that day, so grown-up, his uniform beautifully pressed by his mother, Grace. She stood close by, her hands shaking with the effort not to cry, flanked by Selma and Mama. Mama whispered something in Grace's ear. Henry sweated in the heat, unwilling to loosen his tie or roll up his sleeves as some of the others had done.

The train had lumbered to a stop in a blast of steam and a shriek of brakes. Day-trippers and returning shoppers filed off with curious glances at the black man in uniform.

Henry bent down until their eyes were level. "You be good, Missy, and mind your mama." She flung her arms around his neck.

"Come away now, Missy," Mama had said with a hand on her shoulder. "Time for Henry to go."

Grace had gripped him to her, bunching the uniform in her fists. Gently he separated himself, flung the duffel over his shoulder, and boarded the train. Just as it pulled away, Missy had run after it and yelled, "When you comin' back?"

The wind had whisked his words away, but it sounded like he said "summertime." *Well,* she had thought, left alone at the platform, waving until the train shrank to a black speck that got swallowed by the sky, *that's not long. Already been my birthday, which comes in April. Already plenty hot. Summertime not far away. Won't be long.*

Eighteen years. Eighteen summertimes later, and here he was, at last.

She had waited. Grace and Selma had waited. Mama had waited. When the war had ended in 1918 and Doc Williams and the others came back, Grace had fainted right there on the same platform when Henry was not among them. There was no explanation, no dreaded official telegram from the army. They knew he had left France at the end of the war. Sporadic postcards had come from Texas, California, Washington State, enough to confirm he was alive but little else. The years passed. Grace died, like she had been holding on to something and one day just decided to let go. Selma blamed him for that, Missy knew, and a reckoning would take place, at a time of Selma's choosing. But for now, she was just so glad to have him back . . .

In the meantime, there had been suitors for Missy, the few not put off by her reputation for being headstrong. After all, she was a hard worker, had learned her cooking from Mama, whose food was famed over the whole county, and she had a good, steady job. Her rounded, sturdy build, inherited from Billy, was suited to heavy lifting, and her ample hips, swaying beneath her white uniform, had prompted more than one hopeful local fella to ask her for a stroll on the moonlit beach. But after a few such outings, which always ended in sandy wrestling matches, she had declined the propositions of Heron Key's young men.

And then, finally, the moment arrived, the one she had waited for all that time. He stood there, just a few feet away, hands in his pockets. "Hello, Henry," she said. "Nice to see you."

He had a rather sheepish, tentative look, and she wondered what Selma had said to him. Probably told him what would happen if his boys acted up tonight.

"Hello, Missy. You look very pretty."

She felt his eyes on her. For so long, she

had dreamed of him being there, right where he stood, looking at her like that, on a beautiful night like this. Only now did she realize she had absolutely no idea what to do or what to say to him. "Oh, this old thing . . ." She laughed self-consciously, thought of all the high-toned fancy women he must have known, and felt very, very foolish. Was it true that even the white women in France went with the soldiers? An image of Henry in a creamy-limbed embrace sidled into her thoughts.

"Let's walk," he said and took off his boots. He kept his eyes on the surf curling white around their toes.

They strolled to the end of the beach where the fishing boats were pulled up on the sand, washed by the waves and the warm light from the torches.

"Is Missus Kincaid always like that?" he asked.

"No, she used to be gorgeous, like a movie star. Then Mr. Kincaid came along and knocked her up. She started to eat and ain't really stopped. She pretty much stays in the house since Nathan was born, and in the meantime, Mr. Kincaid . . . Well, you seen it. She been good to me, though, and Nathan is a little cutie."

They sat on the end of an upturned boat,

let their feet dangle in the water. The breeze brought the sound of laughter, children whining, the clink of beer bottles. The soft voice of Larry Adler's "St. Louis Blues" came from the gramophone. It all felt so normal and yet so strange, like waking from a dream to find it was real.

All the lines she had prepared to say just melted away like her footprints in the sand. Heat radiated from his skin and a musty smell he never used to have. Like something washed but not clean. His eyes, with those same curled-up lashes she always envied, were fixed on the horizon. His arms were corded with thick veins. He rubbed the scar on his neck. There was tension in his shoulders, and she realized he was nervous too. The scene suddenly struck her as too funny.

She laughed out loud. "Look at us, Henry Roberts, acting like we two strangers!" She squeezed his hand.

He exhaled. "You right! How you been, girl?" He squeezed back, friendly like.

She had held his hand so many times in the past, but this was different. "Oh, you know, nothin' ever changes in Heron Key. You could come back in another twenty years and the place still look the same."

There was an awkward silence, occupied

by the ugly, lumpy truth of his long absence. All those summertimes he had missed. She felt the empty years collapse inside her. His hand was rough, crisscrossed with shiny scars.

"Yeah, but not the people," he said. "The people ain't the same, none of us." His expression darkened again.

"Oh, I don't know." She jostled his shoulder. "Maybe on the outside we different, but not on the inside. That don't change, not really. We still the same people."

"You is, Missy," he said. "You still the same sweet girl that I left, but I's different. Don't you see?" He turned to face her, his features twisted in shame. "I messed it all up. Got nothin' but the clothes on my back, nothin' to show for all those years. Nothin' to offer . . . anyone. I let everyone down: Selma, my mother . . . you." He turned his face to the sea again.

"Henry Roberts," she said, "look at me. I said, look at me." He turned back, and in his eyes she saw lost years and infinite loneliness. "I ain't the same," she said. "I ain't a girl no more. You think you the only one who messed up? I done nothin', been nowhere. I wasted my whole life so far, and ain't nobody's fault but mine. I still take a damn encyclopedia to bed with me every night." Missy never cussed. The word felt good in her mouth. It unlocked other words, long held back. She sat up straighter, tried to make him see what she saw. "You been to war, you been to France. The way those boys looked at you tonight . . . they'd walk right into the mouth of hell if you were leadin' them. You got them home, Henry. The rest, that don't matter. I proud to know you." She suddenly felt embarrassed. It was more words than she had spoken together for quite a while — perhaps ever. "I talk too much. You didn't come all this way to hear me flappin' my gums."

There was a long pause. The waves whispered to the sand, tickled her toes. Only at this moment did the realization strike her, with the force of a hammer. All these years, she had thought of herself as powerless, no more than a leaf on the wind, but the truth was a lot worse than that. She was scared, pure and simple. Scared to take a chance, scared to leave behind the familiar contours of Mama's house and Heron Key. Just plain scared. The things she might have done, places she might have seen . . . they flickered before her now like an old-fashioned lantern show.

He stared at the surf where it nudged the boat. The tide was coming in fast. When he looked at her again, something was different. It was like he saw her, really saw her, as she was now, for the first time.

"You think . . . ?" he began, then stopped himself and started over. "You think it might not be too late? For an old soldier to make a new start?"

"I know it ain't too late." She looked at the water, where the moon made silver ripples on the waves. "Only too late when you dead." Another thought came to her: *Maybe it ain't too late for me neither.*

Another silence while he thought about this. "Why there ain't no Mr. Missy?"

Don't you see? It only ever been you. Only you. "Oh, I just ain't found the right fella, I guess," she said breezily, "and I is really, really fussy."

"Well, I'll have a think about that for you. I might know someone."

"Much obliged." She had to look away.

"In the meantime" — he seemed to choose his words carefully — "what you say we get reacquainted, away from all . . . this?" He cast his eyes up the beach, where Selma had them under surveillance. "You can show me what hasn't changed around here? We could go for a walk one evening?"

She knew by rights it was a mistake to make it too easy but didn't care one bit.

142

Her mouth opened to accept, but the sound of breaking glass and a woman's cry of fright startled them both. They ran back up the beach to find a scene of destruction in progress.

Dwayne stood at the edge of the mayhem, thumbs hooked in his belt, assessing the situation. A big, sunburned guy with malice in his pale eyes was engaged with six pals in a spree of demolition. They smashed a bunch of bottles, turned over picnic tables. They helped themselves to the booze with the clear intention of draining every last drop. One of them pushed Mabel's bowl of potato salad into the sand. Women pulled their children close, and men shuffled around impotently. It was exactly, down to the last detail, what he had expected to happen.

He had left the extra manpower back at the jail with a case of beer as a thank-you, figuring the night's main event was over after the fight. Although he was armed, he did not like the odds against him. The wild look in the veterans' eyes told him that he might have to shoot every one of them. He was perfectly prepared to do this, but it would mean endless paperwork.

"Ladies and gentlemen," the big one with

the pale eyes announced, as he kicked over a table covered in glasses. "On behalf of all of us who fought for you in the filth of France, we have this to say." And he belched long and loud. Another doubled over with laughter. His pal drained a bottle of rum and smashed it against a palm tree. The others dispersed to find their own amusement amid more sounds of destruction.

Henry raced up to him. "Enough, Two-Step. You got no cause to act like this."

"You in charge of these men?" asked Dwayne. "You best get them under control or it's on you."

"Him? He ain't in charge of jack shit," sneered Two-Step. "Nobody owns us, not anymore. Right, fellas?"

One of Two-Step's crew tried to pull a struggling woman into an embrace while the others slurped down more liquor. Dwayne figured he had maybe sixty seconds before the whole situation got completely out of hand. He had no intention of letting that happen.

An odd assortment of men approached Henry: a big man with a lazy eye, another guy with only one eye, a shambling fellow with a Bible clutched in his hand, and a little guy who looked about twelve years old. "Trouble, sir?" asked the little one.

144

"Nothin' we cain't handle, Jeb," said Henry. "These," he said to Dwayne, "is my men. Sonny, Franklin, Lemuel, Jeb."

"We'll swap business cards later," Dwayne said. He stared hard at Henry, tried to focus on the job and only the job. He considered what the sheriff would want him to do, he in his fancy office two islands over. Dwayne had had one hell of a day and really, really wanted to hit someone.

"Looks like you need one more, Henry." A well-muscled veteran with a blond crew cut approached.

"You sure, Max?" asked Henry with a glance at Two-Step. The outcome of the next few minutes was only half of it. What mattered was later, once they were all back at the camp. Things would go very badly for Hoffman.

Max shrugged it off. "I reckon so."

"You siding with the niggers, Kraut?" growled Two-Step. "Why ain't I surprised? Well," he said and rolled up his sleeves. "I'm gonna enjoy this even more."

And with that, fists began to swing.

They were fairly evenly matched, and neither side seemed to make much headway. Although Two-Step's gang had the weight advantage, Jeb was surprisingly effective for a small person. And for a guy with only one eye, Franklin had a vicious right hook. Lemuel was yelling random Bible verses, timed with haymaker punches. Sonny sat calmly but firmly on top of someone, like the man was a park bench. Max and Henry each had their hands full.

Dwayne was just about to resort to his pistol to bring things to a close when a strange sound came toward them from the water. It was a loud hissing, like a dozen bad-tempered snakes.

The explosion was enormous, deafening, brilliant. All the rockets fired at once. The sky was filled with a cacophony of colored light. Huge blooms of red, orange, blue, green, and white covered the treetops and rained down little sparks everywhere. Along with the big bangs were pops that sounded exactly like rapid gunfire. Children broke out of their parents' grip to race with delight down to the water, squealing with excitement.

The explosions had a different effect on the mass of fighting veterans. A big pile of Two-Step's men were suddenly undone. Stan threw himself to the ground, hands over his head. Tec could be heard to whimper softly.

"Gentlemen," said Dwayne as he slipped the handcuffs onto Two-Step, "y'all are under arrest on account of ruining our party."

"That ain't illegal," gasped Two-Step.

"It is now."

"Thank you," panted Henry, wiping blood off his nose.

Dwayne hauled Two-Step to his feet and shot a hard glare at Henry. "Don't mistake me for your friend," he said and marched away.

CHAPTER 9

Three hundred miles to the south, a tropical storm passes over the Bahamas. On the verge of dissipating, it receives a sudden, mammoth infusion of energy from the superheated waters below. It gorges on this energy, gaining momentum from the very earth's rotation, spinning harder and harder, sucking air into its empty heart. It howls toward the still, summer-hot waters of the Straits of Florida, in search of more food.

Doc Williams was dreaming of Cora, as she was that day when Leann took her away. She wore her sundress with the frogs on it, her face shadowed by a white hat. She reached out her arms to him, crying, "Daddy, help me." He was running after her, on all fours like an animal, but faster than any animal, through the palmetto scrub. Branches flayed his face, his hands propelled him over the sandy soil, and still she flew ahead of him, just out of reach, her face a dark emptiness beneath the hat.

Something shook him awake. He was sweating, and his breath came in ragged gulps.

Dwayne's voice: "Doc, wake up." Another shake of his shoulder, harder this time. "Come on, wake up."

"Wha— time?" It was still dark. *I must have dozed off for a few minutes.* After he stitched up Ronald's cheek, Doc had had no desire to return to the party. The evening was soured for him. He figured someone would fetch him if he was needed. Instead he had finished the night on his porch, with only a bourbon bottle for company. The last thing he remembered was the fireworks, which seemed to happen later and more colorfully than usual. Cyril normally only managed a few disappointing fizzles, whereas this was a full-blown spectacular. He had raised his bottle to the lights in the sky but could not think of a single thing to wish and passed out in his chair. Probably Dwayne was there to tell him someone had cut themselves on a beer bottle. If Mabel had poisoned them all again with her potato salad, he was going to read her the riot act.

"A little after three thirty," Dwayne said. "Get up."

149

"Okay, okay, I'm coming." He struggled to his feet with Dwayne's help. "Need some coffee. You want some?"

"No time for that. It's Hilda." The big man's face looked matte white in the porch light, his eyes sunk into shadows. "She's been attacked. Lionel found her on the road. She's in my truck. Doc, it's bad."

His tone cut through the alcoholic fog. Doc's brain cleared, eyes focused on Dwayne. He had never seen him look so worried, not even that time when the Klan announced a rally nearby. "What happened?"

"We don't know yet. Lionel was walking home, thought it was a deer in the road. She's been beaten, mostly on her head and face." A pause. "I haven't checked for other . . . injuries. Leave that to you. She's been unconscious since Lionel found her."

Doc felt around for his medical bag. "What was she doing walking alone at that time of night?" he asked, his sleepy brain two steps behind. "Why didn't she go home with Nelson?"

"I'll fill you in later. I called Nelson. He's on his way."

"Where was he?" Something was very wrong about this. It made no sense.

"Where do you think?" Dwayne asked on

150

his way back to the truck. "Help me get her inside."

They laid Hilda on her back on the examination table under a bare bulb haloed with moths. A fan in the corner moved the air in feeble bursts. It took all of Doc's training to resist the impulse to gasp. She could have been anyone, a stranger, such was the damage to her face. Both eyes were swollen shut, nose obviously broken, one lip torn, and what looked like teeth marks coming through the other. There was a strange pattern across the bridge of her nose. Blood had turned her blond hair dirty brown.

She moaned softly, and her breath came in uneven gurgles. Doc leaned in close to catch the words but only got, "Make . . . stop . . ."

"It's over, Hilda," he said into her ear. "You're safe."

His professional eye cataloged other details. The soles of her feet were cut. A slim, expensive-looking gold watch was still on her wrist, diamond engagement ring still on her plump finger. Her nails were torn and bloody and there were bruises on her arms. *She fought back.*

"Excuse me, Dwayne, while I examine her. Hilda," he said gently, "I'm going to undress you now."

Her eyes were tiny slivers between swollen lids. "Doc," she said. Her damaged mouth formed the words clumsily, her teeth stained red. There was a gap in front where one had been knocked out. "I —"

"Quiet now, Hilda," said Doc. "You're okay. We're gonna get you fixed right up. Nothing but a few scrapes and bruises. You're gonna be fine."

Headlights swept through the room. Outside, the scrape of tires on gravel, the slam of a car door. Nelson entered, dragging with great intensity on his cigarette. From his overprecise movements, Doc could tell he was still drunk.

He was nearly overwhelmed by the urge to punch Nelson right in his pretty mouth. To have been blessed with a treasure such as Hilda and leave her to walk home alone late at night . . . He forced himself to focus on the examination. Gently, he unbuttoned her dress and noticed that her silk drawers were in place and undamaged. He carefully palpated her limbs, listened to her lungs, tested her abdomen for soreness. The damage seemed to be confined to her head and face. *Who hates you enough to do this? Someone who wanted you never to be beautiful again.*

Nelson cleared his throat. "Is she . . . Will she be okay?"

"I don't know," said Doc. *Where were you when she needed you?* He studied the body on the table. His skills with the needle were adequate for patching people up on the battlefield but not for fine plastic surgery. She might have brain damage. The nearest hospital with the right facilities was ninety miles away, over small, rough roads. His best would have to be good enough. "If she pulls through, she will be . . . different."

Dwayne entered with a curt nod in Nelson's direction. "How is she?"

"There's a nasty bruise on her temple. Need to keep an eye on that." Doc wiped his hands, pushed his glasses higher up his nose. "Broken cheekbone, broken nose, and a bunch of cuts that need stitches." He glanced at Nelson, who seemed extremely calm for someone in his situation. "She wasn't . . . violated. I've sedated her. Got to keep her here for treatment and observation."

"For how long?" asked Nelson.

"I don't know," Doc said again. He could not fathom Nelson, not at all. Most husbands would be focused on what could be done to help. They might pray, or cry, or beg Doc to save her. They might be filled with murderous rage. *He looks like he has somewhere else to be.* "She should really go to the hospital, but I don't want to move her just yet. She's still in shock." And yes, he admitted to himself, there was another reason: she needed someone who cared about her. "Nelson, send Mama to me. I need her help." Everyone called Missy's Mama by that name, Doc included.

Nelson nodded. "Did she say . . . anything?" His eyes were bloodshot. Stubble darkened his normally smooth jaw.

"No, she said nothing."

"When can I talk to her?" asked Dwayne.

"In another twenty-four hours, I'll know more."

"So if you don't need me for nothin', I guess I'll go —" said Nelson.

"Where were you?" shouted Doc, hands clenched together. "Why was she walking alone? At night? What's wrong with you?" Anger suffused his muscles with electric tension. He had never been a fighter, always looked for a way to go over, under, around a conflict. Even as a boy, he would run away, much to the disgust of his father. But at that moment, he could have cheerfully dismembered Nelson without the need for any tools.

"Doc," said Dwayne, with a hand on his

arm, "there was an argument, after you left, between the Kincaids. They —"

"My . . . wife," said Nelson quietly, picking tobacco out of his teeth, "was drunk, and when she's drunk, she'll go with anybody." He said to Dwayne, "You saw her, dancing with that . . . that —"

"Henry Roberts," said Dwayne evenly. "She tried to dance with him, Nelson, but he refused."

"Yeah, but you could see it in his face, he wanted to," said Nelson. "That's what they all want, all of them who've been away. They come back thinkin' they're better than they are. That's what they all really want."

"It's a fair question, Nelson. Where were you while your wife was being beaten?" asked Dwayne.

"At the club," he said. "We went there after you carted off those idiots from the camp."

Dwayne crossed his arms, said nothing. Doc had seen this before. The big man used silence as an interrogation tool. Few people could withstand the power of it or resist the urge to fill the vacuum with words. And so it proved this time.

"What?" Nelson asked as he lit another cigarette from the butt of his last one. "Why you looking at me like that? You think I

155

. . . ?" He looked from Dwayne to Doc. "My own wife?"

"Plenty worse things been done by a man to his wife," said Doc, deliberately avoiding Dwayne's eyes.

"There's at least five people who'll tell you where I was," said Nelson, " 'cause they were with me."

"I'll need those names," said Dwayne.

"Sure, sure," said Nelson with a bitter laugh and a shake of his head. "And then once you've wasted enough time talking to the good, upstanding people of this town, you'll maybe go and look for the nigger bastard who did this. Ain't got far to go, Deputy. Just follow the smell." And he went out into the night, leaving a cloud of smoke that hung in the air long after he had left.

Hilda was floating, floating, not on water but on clouds. The clouds were soft but supported her weight easily. She felt light, free. Pain was there too, but like a bell ringing far, far away. She could ignore the ringing if she chose and just float. Before, the pain had been close, oh so close. It had filled her up in a blaring, pounding symphony of pain. And then Doc's face had appeared and it moved away. Someone had held her hand. She let the soft clouds take her.

Dwayne arrived back at the station just as the darkness of night was giving way to a pinkish gray dawn. A burst of noise greeted him when he opened the door.

Two-Step yelled, "We got rights! I want my lawyer!"

His pals, crammed with him into one of the holding cells, shouted their agreement, along with slurs about Dwayne's parentage. Stan banged the water ladle on the bars. "And you got to clean this up!"

Ike snored in the other corner of the cell, despite the racket around him, a pool of congealed vomit at his feet.

The visiting cops were sitting around a card table between the cells. They were several hands into a poker game, judging by the pile of pennies on the table. One of them said, "I'll see your five cents and raise you a SHUT THE HELL UP!" toward the cells. He tossed a handful of pennies on the table.

"Everything under control?" Dwayne asked.

"Yep," said the cop. "Goddammit, Floyd! You keep cheatin' and you ain't gonna play with us no more." To Dwayne, he said, "Guy in charge of the camp, Superintendent Watts, is on his way over to take charge of those animals." He indicated Two-Step's cell with a sharp jerk of his head.

"Who you callin' animals, pig?" asked Two-Step. "Oh, you mean the animals that bashed in that lady's head tonight?" He leaned forward through the bars, hands folded casually. "Those animals?"

"How do you know about that?" asked Dwayne. "Maybe you managed to fit some assault and battery onto your dance card tonight too? From what I hear, it's your specialty. And there was plenty of time" — he consulted his notepad — "between when she wandered off and you turned up to ruin the party. Maybe you made a little detour."

"I know all about it," said Two-Step, "thanks to the Four Stooges here." He nodded toward the cops at the card table. "They must think locking us up makes us deaf too. But I tell you something." He lowered his voice, beckoned Dwayne closer to the bars. "If my boys did get hold of her, she'd be a whole lot more messed up than she is . . . if you get my meanin'." The pale eyes in the plump, sunburned face gave him the appearance of a malevolent cherub.

Dwayne was forced to acknowledge the truth of what he said. There was no way that Two-Step's gang would have confined an attack to just her face. "If you know something, Two-Step," he said with quiet intensity, "you'd better give it up."

"All I's sayin' is look and ye shall find." His slow, sly grin chilled the air in the room.

"I'll deal with you later." Dwayne went into his office to begin the paperwork.

Dwayne was interrupted an hour later by the thick-necked, mean-eyed camp superintendent. He entered the office, an unlit cigar between his teeth. Trent Watts had a well-deserved reputation for strict discipline bordering on cruelty. *I would not want to be in Two-Step's shoes when they get back to camp.* The poker game had broken up, the visiting cops gone home.

"On behalf of the U.S. government," said Trent, cigar clenched in his jaws, "I assume responsibility for these . . . men." He spared barely a glance at Two-Step and his gang. "I assure you, they will not venture into town again without supervision."

"In that case, Trent," said Dwayne, unlocking the cell door, "they're all yours."

The men filed out into the grubby early-morning light. Over his shoulder, Two-Step called, "Missin' you already, Deputy."

Missy was feeding Nathan his breakfast of

159

mashed banana. She and Mama had stayed all night with him, waiting and talking, getting more worried with every hour that the Kincaids stayed away. To pass the time, Mama made her recount every word that passed between her and Henry, especially the part about going for a walk together the following night.

"And what you say?" Mama had asked.

"I told him I might be able to fit it into my busy social calendar, between the cotillion dance and the mayor's ball."

Mama was snoring now, head propped on her hand. Mr. Kincaid came in and let the screen door bang shut. He looked like someone run over by a steamroller. "Good Lord," said Missy. "What happened? Where is Missus Kincaid? We been so worried."

Mama woke with a start and a "Whuh?"

He said nothing for a moment, and she thought he had not heard. Then he said, so low she had to lean in to hear, "Missus Kincaid has . . . There has been . . . She was attacked, on the road. She's hurt bad. Last night, after the party." He sat down at the kitchen table. "Doc is taking care of her. He don't know how long, or if . . . It may be . . . a while."

"Attacked!" exclaimed Missy. "Who did it? Oh, Mr. Kincaid, who would want to

160

hurt her?"

Nathan began to whine, sensing the distress in her voice, so she gave him more banana while she fitted the pieces together in her mind. Hilda had no friends, no social circle at all, since she had shut herself away. The only people she saw were her family and the folks who did for her: Missy and Mama, Selma and Lionel, and a few other workers. Workers like Henry, who had fixed the hurricane shutter that banged in the wind. It felt like someone had filled her stomach with ice and started to twist, although the morning was already hot.

"I think you know very well who did it," he said, but calmly, like it was purely incidental.

Mama poured him a cup of coffee. Her eyes flashed a warning to Missy.

"Can I go see her?" Missy asked, wiped her hands on her apron. "She'll need her things. I'll make up her bag."

Mr. Kincaid sat with his head in his hands. Then he said quietly, "Wilma, you need to go help Doc."

Missy exchanged a look with her mother. No one ever used her real name.

In Hilda's bedroom, Missy hurriedly pulled a bag from the top of the closet. Her hands were clumsy. She put in fresh underwear, just ironed from the day before. *The day before, when everything was different.* She paused and stroked the fine silk. She imagined Hilda in Doc's office, without all her pretty things around her. Hurt, alone, confused. Her husband had lost interest and didn't care who knew. *She a silly, selfish, vain woman most days, but she don't deserve this.*

"Missy," said Mama sharply, "get a move on. Get me her toothbrush, her slippers —"

"She need her makeup," said Missy. "She cain't be seen in public without her rouge, her lipstick, her face powder." Missy felt the tears come and blinked hard. As Hilda got fatter and fatter, she had put more and more effort into her complexion, her hair, her jewelry, curling her lashes just so. As if everything below the neck was someone else's department.

"Missy," said Mama more gently, "she ain't at a hotel. Just the necessaries."

"Mama, could she die? Could that happen?"

"Doc won't let it," she said and shoved a hairbrush into the bag. "Why Mr. Kincaid think we know who did this? What went on last night at the barbecue?"

"All kinds of foolishness. Those country

162

club ladies were hanging on Mr. Kincaid like ticks on a dog. And Missus Kincaid, she got so drunk, she even tried to dance with Henry, can you believe that?"

"She what?" Mama froze midzip.

"Yeah, she sashayed up to him, but he was just polite and respectful to her. No harm done."

"No harm done," repeated Mama to herself and pulled the zipper closed. "We see about that."

Across town, Selma lay awake next to Jerome and watched the stars fade into the blueness of morning. It was not his rumbling snores that deprived her of sleep. She was well used to them. All through the night, she had replayed the events of the barbecue in her mind. Images flashed like the glint of Ike's knife, the glee on his face when Ronald's blood flowed, almost the same color as the lake of sauce around the big, fly-covered mound of pork. That ridiculous barrier down the middle of the beach, utterly flimsy yet imbued with such power. *Might as well divide up the sea or the sky. Will there be one gate for coloreds and one for whites when we get to Saint Peter?* And then the veterans had to come and smash the place up. She could not understand Henry's attachment to that bunch of crazy winos in their stinking huts. As time went on, she reckoned, things got no better. Only worse, always worse. Folks never tired of coming up with ever more inventive ways to hurt each other. Seems they had endless energy for that. It sickened her, all of it. At times like these, she felt the best thing for Heron Key would be to sweep it all away — the stupid grievances, going back nearly a hundred years, and the more recent ones. The coral beneath their feet was soaked in these old hatreds. It needed to be scraped clean, and then maybe they could make a fresh start. *Yes, that's what we need. A fresh start.*

It was time to act.

She pulled on a robe, shuffled around the partition to the kitchen, and lit an oil lamp. No need to worry about waking Jerome; he had put away enough beer to keep him out until noon. She set the coffeepot on the stove to heat. Morning sounds came to her through the open door. Chickens squabbled, the palms rustled in the stiff breeze, and the ever-present surf shushed in the distance. Sure enough, the raccoon was at the cistern again. She just caught sight of his backside disappearing under the lid. She would retrieve him later. Her grievance was not

164

with the animals. They would be spared, as far as she could manage. But the people . . . they would learn a hard lesson. She opened the Bible to a random verse, as she often did when needing inspiration, and was rewarded: *We rejoice in our sufferings, knowing that suffering produces endurance, and endurance produces character, and character produces hope, and hope does not put us to shame.* It was a sign she was on the right path. *That's what we need around here,* she thought. *More hope. And less shame.*

It would be her biggest, most complicated spell ever, and she wondered if her powers were up to the job. It would be better if Grace were there. She would call on her spirit to help. Together, they would do what needed to be done.

As the first warm rays of daylight fell in through the open door, she retrieved the battered book of spells and went to work.

CHAPTER 10

Jenson Mitchell, proprietor of Heron Key's general store, closed his Bible and poured himself another cup of coffee. His morning routine never varied: Bible, breakfast, barometer. It was his favorite time of day, before the store was open, when he could be alone with his thoughts, before customers and deliveries started to arrive. The neatly stocked shelves pleased him with their order and purpose. His mother, Trudy, had cleaned the window at the back where he served the coloreds so it sparkled in the early light.

He turned toward the front window, blew on his coffee, and surveyed the little town with pride. It gave him satisfaction to think that he knew every inch of it. The store occupied the geographical center of the town, which seemed right, well back from the beach but in earshot of it — like everything else in Heron Key. His eyes roamed toward the south end, where Zeke's shack was camouflaged by the mangroves, past the marina in front of him, toward the country club and public beaches to the north. The Kincaids and their wealthy neighbors had their fine houses close to the water, to get the best of the sea breezes. Poorer whites and all the coloreds had more modest dwellings farther from the water, separated from each other by the Key lime grove. The town had been nothing but a speck until the railway joined it up to the rest of civilization in 1906. And now that the veterans were building that bridge, folks rich enough to have cars would be able to drive right across the cut instead of waiting for a ferry. His family had seen it all, having lived in Heron Key for generations, and were proud to be of original Conch stock. Mitchell's store had stood in the same place all that time. The heavy wood construction was tied together with massive steel bolts that fixed the structure down into the coral of Heron Key itself. In a way, he liked to think he was the same, embedded solidly in the town. He was comforted by solid things, things he could see and touch. All was in order on this fine morning.

He dusted some flour off the floor, straightened the measuring scoop inside the sack, and stepped out into the morning with the last of his coffee. The sky was deep sea blue, crossed with great swooping plumes of mare's tail clouds. The sight of their distinctive, feathered arcs stirred a distant memory from his childhood. His daddy used to say, "Mackerel scales and mare's tails make lofty ships carry low sails."

He stood very still, closed his eyes, and focused on the feel of the wind. He had been following the barometer's descent for a few days. There was news of a storm off the Bahamas. He took his coffee around to the back wall of the store where the barometer was fixed . . . and promptly scurried inside to call the weather center eighty miles south in Key West.

His old friend, Fred Simpson, was now chief meteorologist at the weather center. Hard to believe, since they had grown up together and Fred had never shown the least interest in, or aptitude for, science.

"Fred? Jenson Mitchell here. The storm that passed through Andros last night. How bad was it?"

"Good to hear your voice, Jenson. Not a picnic, but not a hurricane. They had eighty-five."

Jenson could picture Fred, in his Key West office, feet up on the deck. Eighty-five-mile-

168

per-hour winds . . . it wasn't trivial for the little Bahamian island of Andros, but they had seen much worse. "Did a fair amount of damage," said Fred, "but not catastrophic. We're watching it."

"Where's it heading?"

"Can't tell yet. It's playing games with us. Ships are reporting that it moves, then stops, then moves again in a different direction. Like it can't make up its mind . . . Reminds me of my first wife." A dry chuckle. "We expect it to hit the Straits next, unless, of course, it blows itself out."

Jenson had seen many a big storm do exactly that. They were highly temperamental creatures. Even small changes in pressure could eviscerate them. Often in the past, the town had been put on high alert only for the roaring lion to come ashore as a fussy kitten.

Even so, Jenson hung up the phone only mildly reassured. The warm waters of the Straits of Florida were a breeding ground for hurricanes. And he trusted his barometer more than anything that Fred's science could tell him.

His mother, Trudy, pushed open the screen door with her generous backside and turned to reveal a fresh orange cake, made with fruit from their grove.

"Brought you a little something to brighten your day. It's getting ugly outside," she said. The early promise of a fine day had quickly faded. Fat thunderheads squatted on the horizon, blown on by a fractious wind. "What's wrong, Jenson?"

He thought for a moment, considered whether to share what he had learned from Fred. After all, there was still every chance that the storm would be little more than a squall by the time it reached Heron Key. And his mother was fragile, underneath her confident, competent exterior, although it had been years since his father's death from Spanish flu. One day, he'd complained of a sore throat, and Trudy had teased him while mixing up some hot lemon and honey. The next day, he was dead. It seemed that his father's childhood polio had weakened his lungs.

Trudy used to be so active in the community, played the old upright piano in church, led the PTA since forever. Now her only solace seemed to be cooking. She still made enough at every meal to feed several people; she didn't seem capable of reducing the quantity. He must have gained ten pounds since his father's death.

"I'm fine, Momma. Just got a lot on my mind."

"Jenson Mitchell," she said firmly and placed the cake down on his desk. "You've never been able to lie to me. Remember that time you broke my anniversary vase?"

"You're right." He smiled. "I told you a seagull flew in and smashed it."

She perched on the edge of his desk. "You even claimed to be able to identify the bird, as if we were gonna put together a lineup for you. Now, what is it, Son?"

He stood and studied the map of the Florida Keys, which covered most of one wall of the office. "There's a storm coming. Pass me the pins from the drawer, please." He fixed a pin over Andros in the Bahamas. "It's just passed through here."

"How bad was it on Andros?" Trudy had lived through many hurricanes, including the one in 1906 that destroyed her house and carried off her mother, whose body was never found.

"Not too bad. I've been on the phone with Fred. They're watching it carefully, can't say yet whether it will hit here."

"Are you going to tell Dwayne?" she asked.

Dwayne had come by at first light with news of Hilda and asked Jenson if he could remember seeing her leave the barbecue. The man looked done in. He didn't need

171

any more problems just now. "Dwayne's got enough to worry about."

"True. And even without that awful business, he won't thank you for getting everyone all flustered for nothing. Besides, everyone in town knows what to do. Won't take us long to get ready if it does head our way."

Jenson knew she was right. Most people kept a shelter stocked for such events, with ready access to supplies for securing windows and heavy objects. Within a matter of hours, the town could be boarded up, streets emptied, shelters full. Even so, he had a feeling, deep inside, that would not go away. It niggled at him, like a stone in his shoe.

"Okay, here's what we do," he said. "Keep an eye on the barometer and stay in touch with Fred. Any big changes from either, and we put out the emergency warning." He paused. A terrible thought presented itself: *What about the veterans?*

Out at the camp, Trent Watts opened his newspaper, brought down specially from Miami. The *Heron Key Bugle* might suffice for the Conchs, but he needed a real paper. *A man had to have some elements of civilization in this godforsaken swamp.* He had been

172

a professional soldier before taking on the veterans' camp and thought he had seen everything a human being could do to hurt another. But the combination of squalid living conditions and backbreaking work in brutal conditions topped even his extensive experience of misery. He settled down to read the paper in his cabin. It was going to be hot as hell again. No point in trying to get clean. Before he came to Heron Key, he would not have believed it possible to sweat while under the shower.

At least there was more of a breeze than normal, although it smelled of rain. He heard laughter and cussing from the cabins. The men were starting to stir. Two-Step and his pals would pay for their excitement last night, but that smug Henry Roberts also needed taking down a peg or two. It was the only way to maintain order. With a yawn, he noted a small box on the front page of the paper with news of a tropical disturbance in the Bahamas. The pathetic Conchs didn't know what a real storm was like. He had grown up in Kansas: twister country. *Good. We need a storm to freshen up the place.* He scratched the bites on his neck. *And get rid of these damned mosquitoes.*

■ ■ ■ ■

Henry lay on his bunk, arms crossed behind his head. The smells of breakfast wafted over from the mess hall but got no answer from his stomach. He felt different, somehow changed, like a vital organ had shifted to a new position. For the first time in oh, too long to remember, he felt awake, really awake, not sunk in a numb half stupor. His senses registered the scuttle of cockroaches, the reek of the latrine, the creaks of the cabin's canvas roof. Everything was sharper, crisper, like he had been living behind a pane of dirty glass. Something had happened to him last night, something important. He had glimpsed the person he used to be when Missy looked at him. She still believed. It made him want to believe. He could not do it, not yet, but the first step was wanting to. Was it true, as she had said, that it was not too late for him?

Missy Douglas. Little Missy. Well, I'll be damned. Little no more. Grown into a fine woman. She had always promised to be something special. And special she was. He pictured her face. Those eyes, slightly turned up at the corners, which gave her a permanent look of mild amusement; the gap between her front teeth; the smile, which spread across her face like sunshine. Even Two-Step's arrival at the party had not spoiled the night for him. Punishment would follow, for all of them, he knew that. But he did not care. He grinned stupidly.

Franklin asked, "So that was her, in the flowery dress? The little girl you always telling us about?" He stuffed the cuffs of his pants inside his boots to stop sand flies getting at his ankles and tied the laces tight.

"Yep," confirmed Henry.

"Didn't look so little to me," said Jeb with a leer.

"She changed while I was away," said Henry. He sat up on the bunk, took a shirt from the pile, sniffed, and wrinkled his nose. Every one of them smelled rank, even when they were just washed. It was so humid, nothing dried completely.

"I'll say," said Franklin. "Y'all looked real cozy down there."

Henry levered himself off the sweaty bunk. "We good friends, that's all. Why that so hard to believe?"

"Then you wouldn't mind fixing me up with her, would you?" asked Jeb. "I could do with some of that, yessir. I mean, seeing as you're just good friends and all." Jeb had been with maybe two women ever, in

France, and both of them were paid for. Women just wanted to mother him.

"If any of you touch her —" Henry began, then stopped when he saw Jeb's triumphant grin.

"Just good friends," chuckled Franklin. "If you say so, Boss. When you gonna see her?"

"Tomorrow night, we're going for a walk."

"Oh, Henry," cooed Jeb, in a high girlish voice. "You so big and strong." He looped his arms around Franklin's neck in a lady-like swoon.

"Now, my little punkin' pie," said Franklin, in an eerily accurate impression of Henry. "Open them bomb bay doors. I'm —"

"Enough," said Henry, smiling despite himself. "Time to go to work."

That's all we are — just two old friends, out for a walk.

The men arrived for breakfast to find Trent standing on one of the chairs. "Attention, everyone. Shut your traps and listen."

The burble of conversation dried up. Trent addressed the crew rarely, and it was never good news.

He lit a cigar. The assembled workers waited while the pungent fumes filled the hall.

"Ladies, you all know about the despicable behavior last night from some of our ranks." He let his gaze rest on Two-Step, who did not even blink. "You embarrassed yourselves and your government, and worst of all, you embarrassed me." He jerked a thumb at his chest.

He dropped down from the chair and strolled to the center of the room. "If I could still court-martial you, there wouldn't be enough of you left to form a firing squad." He gestured at them with the cigar. "You're pathetic, you're a disgrace to the uniform, and it's beyond me how you were ever privileged enough to wear it."

Henry began, "Mr. Watts, with respect, sir, there were only a few —"

"Shut up, Roberts. I'm talking here. In my day, every man in the unit was responsible for his fellow soldiers. That's what it means to be a comrade." His gaze traveled around the assemblage. Feet shuffled but no one spoke. "You numb nuts clearly don't understand this word. Since a few of you chose to behave like uncivilized morons, the rest will suffer. For two weeks" — he fixed his stare on each sweaty, disgruntled face — "you are under a 1700 hours curfew."

There were low grumbles of discontent

and a few mutterings about unfairness.

"You got something to say?" Trent swung his head left, right. "You think I can't make this worse? I surely can. Want to make it three weeks? Just try me."

Henry imagined Missy waiting for him on the beach where they had arranged to meet the next night at sunset. "But, Mr. Watts, that means —"

"I know very well what it means but don't recall asking for your opinion, *Mister* Roberts. You will work at the bridge site each day and return to camp, where you will stay until work begins the next morning. No exceptions. No excuses. No whining." He spat on the ground. "You brought this on yourselves. Anyone caught breaking the curfew is out of a job. Now git. Go make yourselves useful."

Dwayne entered Doc's office and closed the screened door quietly. Hilda was unconscious again. Doc and Mama had repaired the wounds, but the swelling had worsened. Her entire head was a patchwork of purple bruises and black stitches.

"I don't like the look of this," said Doc. "Don't like it one bit. Pressure is building up in her skull. Look at her eyes." They bulged slightly under the swollen, discolored lids.

"What can you do?"

"The drugs I've given should bring down the swelling, but they haven't started to work yet. If it gets much worse, there will be permanent brain damage, even . . ." He shook his head. "We'll give it another twenty-four hours and then get her transported to Miami if there's no improvement."

Dwayne moved closer to the bed. "What's this?" He indicated the odd pattern of marks on the bridge of her nose.

"Not sure," said Doc, washing his hands at the sink. "I think it's from a boot, the sole of a boot."

Someone stomped on her face. The bastard. The marks were of a distinctive crosshatch pattern. "In that case, Doc, we need to find the owner of those boots." For the first time since they had carried Hilda, bleeding and broken, into Doc's office, Dwayne began to feel some hope of catching who did it. Her breath came in shallow gasps. "Doc, will she live?"

Doc steered him into the other room. "She may be able to hear us. I don't know if she will live."

Despite his extreme fatigue, Dwayne

179

heard the pain in Doc's voice. It was clear he had not slept either. His glasses were greasy and slightly askew, and his eyes were dull with exhaustion. Grayish stubble shadowed his cheeks.

"Doc, you need to get some rest."

"You're one to talk. I will . . . when I know she's going to pull through." He removed his glasses and rubbed his eyes. "Have you got any leads?"

"Not yet," said Dwayne, his jaw tight with frustration. He had driven around town all morning, talking to people who were still at the party when Hilda left. No one saw anything, which he could not believe. Someone must have seen something. It stood to reason, with all those people around. "After Hilda's little performance, everyone lost interest in her. It was like she disappeared. I can't find anyone who actually remembers seeing her leave." He had ruled out Ike on account of him actually being in jail at the time of the attack. And Two-Step's crew were excluded because Hilda was still alive and unviolated when he took them in. He was running out of obvious suspects, which meant only one thing: lots more hard work.

Doc studied her face again, then turned to Dwayne. "The veterans all wear boots."

Dwayne met Doc's tired eyes with his own. "I am well aware of that, Doc."

As he pulled up to the police station, Dwayne spotted Ronald waiting for him. His morale slid onto the floor of the truck. *Oh Jesus, what is this?* A large bandage covered Ronald's wounded cheek. Dwayne climbed the steps to the door. The weather now well and truly matched his mood. Angry curtains of rain arrived, blown sideways by the sudden wind.

"Come in, Ronald, and tell me what I can do for you."

Ronald took the seat opposite Dwayne's desk. Papers covered every bit of the scarred wooden surface and flowed onto the floor in gentle drifts. Dwayne skewered a handful on the metal spike on the corner of the desk. "I've come to ask about the progress of your investigation."

"What is it to you, Ronald? Shouldn't Nelson be here instead? Jimmy!" he called out.

A freckled face beneath a green John Deere cap appeared around the door frame. "Yes, Uncle Dwayne?"

"Get me some coffee!" Jimmy was Noreen's nephew. Dwayne had hired him to do menial tasks, to please Noreen's family, and already regretted it.

"Yes, Boss!" said Jimmy. The face disappeared.

"I'm representing the concerned citizens of Heron Key," said Ronald. "We are sick of the menace of the veterans. Poor Hilda is the last straw."

Ronald had always been pretty sensible, if a little pompous, but there was a new edge to his voice, his words distorted by the bandage on his cheek.

"I understand your feelings." Dwayne spread his hands in what he hoped was a conciliatory gesture. "Last night's display by the veterans was inexcusable, but the superintendent assures me that they are all under curfew for two weeks, and after that will only be allowed in town with a chaperone." Dwayne felt the need to steer the conversation back in the general direction of reality. "But we don't know," he said carefully, "that any of the veterans were responsible for the attack on Hilda."

"Oh, yes, we do," said Ronald darkly. He was sweating, his eyes rimmed with red.

"What do you mean? Jimmy," he shouted out the door, "where is that COFFEE?"

Jimmy hurried in and sloshed coffee all over Dwayne's papers. As he mopped up the spillage, Dwayne made a silent vow never to employ one of Noreen's relatives again.

"Who else would it be?" exclaimed Ronald. "We never had this kind of trouble before they came. They're either criminals, or sick in the head, or both. It's obvious: the man who did this horrible thing to one of our ladies is at that camp." He smacked his fist onto the nearest pile of papers. "We demand justice for Hilda."

Dwayne's tired brain struggled to cope with the wild inconsistencies in Ronald's argument. Ike's attack on him seemed to have tipped him over some kind of edge, followed as it was so quickly by the attack on Hilda. They seemed to have merged in Ronald's mind, into an irrational, unfocused, but very real desire for vengeance.

But he had to admit one thing: Heron Key had never seen an attack like the one on Hilda before the arrival of the veterans. There had been plenty of minor crimes against property, and of course there were some amateurish attempts at larceny, the same as you would find in any small town, nothing exotic. The veterans' camp was the first influx of outsiders the town had seen since the original Bahamian pioneers in the 1890s. That they were a deeply troubled

183

bunch of souls was not in dispute, but were any of them really capable of such viciousness? *Of course they are. They're all trained killers.*

Dwayne knew he must retain control of the investigation, could not be seen as anyone's patsy. "I am following several leads at the moment, which include the veterans but is not limited to them."

"You're wasting time!" Ronald leaped to his feet. "He'll get away! He could already be gone. You've got to surprise him, tonight!"

There was spittle around Ronald's mouth. His face had gone very red, which made even more of a contrast with the white bandage. Dwayne thought he looked like a man about to have a heart attack. "They're Americans, Ronald, just like you or me. They have rights."

"They're not like you or me," said Ronald. "Not at all. And if you don't do what's necessary" — he sat back, folded his arms — "then the citizens of this town will."

Dwayne did not like the fervent light in his eyes. He had seen it before, many times, in the light of burning crosses.

CHAPTER 11

By midmorning, Trent Watts was already in a foul mood. It was partly the weather, which would play hell with their schedule. Rain pattered steadily on the roof. He looked outside. The other cabins sagged into the muddy ground. He doubted they'd be able to put in a full day. They were already behind, because everything took longer here than elsewhere. If it wasn't the heat sapping the men's strength, it was the unreliable local labor, which supplemented the veterans' efforts but disappeared during fruit-picking season. Or the damned climate. You couldn't keep supplies dry. Cement set to blocks inside the sacks, wood warped, rope went moldy. Water was the construction worker's worst enemy. He'd rather build in the desert.

Then came the phone call. Even before he answered, Trent had a sense that it would not be good news. It was that busybody,

Jenson Mitchell. The man was not unhelpful, just so careful and methodical about everything that even the smallest request turned into a federal case. "Mr. Watts," he said, "I'm calling to let you know that a big storm may be on the way. I assume you have an evacuation plan?"

Trent sighed. Here it was again, Mitchell's nose butting in where it didn't belong. The Conchs were panicking over a little wind and rain. He'd seen cows and tractors flung fifty feet into the air by a twister before. "Mr. Mitchell, I thank you for the concern, but we'll be fine here."

"With respect, Mr. Watts, if it does come, you're going to need more protection than you've got. There isn't room for your men in the shelters in town, so —"

"You mean, you're not sure?" Trent gripped the phone between cheek and shoulder while he fished around his desk for a fresh cigar. It would take at least two days to organize a train to evacuate the men, not to mention all the lost work time and resulting delays to the schedule. His superiors in Jacksonville were already on his ass most days, asking how he was going to make up the lost time. He could well imagine their reaction to a request for evacuation ahead of a "possible" storm.

186

"We're watching it," said Mitchell, somewhat guardedly, "and talking to the weather center in Key West. These things can blow up fast, and when they do —"

"I think you mean if, Mr. Mitchell. If." He snipped the end off the cigar and stifled a yawn. These people made him so tired. They hadn't been to war, didn't know what real danger was. "I'll put in a call to Jacksonville. That's all I can do." A shape filled his doorway. The deputy sheriff. He had been expecting his visit, but even so, he wondered just how much worse his day could get. "Now you'll have to excuse me. I have a visitor. Good day to you."

The deputy shook the water from his hat. "Morning," he said. "Nice weather for ducks." He grimaced at the lame remark. Tiredness seemed to weigh him down like a sodden overcoat.

"Yep," said Trent. "Take a seat." Dwayne sat in the folding chair opposite Trent's desk. "Just had your Mr. Mitchell on the phone, telling me it's time to build an ark. That your opinion too?"

Dwayne did not answer for a moment, just stared at the silver waterfall spilling across the doorway. "Jenson is a better storm tracker than any of those fancy scientists down in Key West. He can feel a big one coming, just by the wind and the waves and his barometer. If he's worried, you should be too. For that matter, all of us should."

"Well, I'll take that under advisement." He lit the soggy cigar. "I assume you've come about the attack on that woman last night?"

"Yes. We have reason to believe that one of your men might have been involved." He had to raise his voice over the noise of the rain on canvas.

"Oh, really? And why is that? Aside from the fact that it's always easier to accuse outsiders? That's just lazy, Deputy." Although he had no love as such for the veterans, who he thought were mainly deranged, work-shy drunks, Trent did not need a scandalous crime attached to his project.

"I'm also pursuing other leads, I can assure you. However, a boot print was left on her nose," Dwayne said. "Here, I've made a sketch." He pushed a limp piece of paper across the desk. "I need to see your men's boots."

Trent took a moment to study the drawing. "You sure this is from a boot? Don't look like nothing we wear here."

Dwayne shrugged and pocketed the piece of paper. "Well, even so, we've got to check.

188

Your cooperation would be much appreciated."

Trent could tell that Dwayne was beyond exhaustion, most likely not thinking that straight, although there was no mistaking his determination. He also realized that if Dwayne had any clear leads, he wouldn't need to look at everyone's boots. In Dwayne's position, Trent would take the camp apart, from top to bottom.

He thought it entirely plausible that the attacker was among his men. There had been no witnesses, and it sounded like the lady herself wasn't talking and might never do so again. These men were desperate to keep their jobs, which was the first decent paid work that many had received in years. It would not surprise him at all if whoever had bashed her head in thought he was free and clear. *That Henry Roberts thinks he's so smart. He could have done it, no question. And he was dancing with her.* He blew a smoke ring. It wobbled upward, then dissolved into the sagging roof. An idea began to form as he studied the deputy's weary face. It might be very much in his interests to help Dwayne's investigation. The image of Henry's boot on Two-Step's neck flashed into his mind. "You'll have it, Deputy. Come back at dawn on Sunday. They won't be expecting anything then. That's the best time to catch them unaware."

After Dwayne left, Trent stared at the phone, deciding what to say to Norbert Grimes in Jacksonville. The storm, he felt certain, would prove to be a figment of the Conchs' rum-soaked imaginations. There was nothing to link any of his men to the attack on that woman — yet. But that could well change. He could feel his career prospects flowing away like the river of mud that had formed outside his cabin. If he wanted another of these government contracts, he needed to demonstrate his capabilities to handle just such difficult times.

He made some quick calculations. In terms of the press, a story about a veteran attacking a woman in a place most people had never heard of would be unlikely to get much coverage outside of the local area. He could deal with that in his own time. But it would be just his luck for the storm to cause one of his men to get a splinter in his pinkie. Then Trent would carry the can, not the bosses up in Jacksonville. He took a deep drag on his cigar and picked up the phone.

As the afternoon wore into evening, the rain eased and the sky began to clear, so that by sunset things looked very different.

At the country club, Missy mopped rainwater from the porch. The country club was a handsome, rambling building with white-painted walls and dark green shutters and trim. It had been built by Ronald Le-Jeune's grandfather and attracted sport fishermen from all over the country, especially moneyed Yankees looking to escape the northern winters. She sometimes helped out at the club when extra hands were needed.

The air had begun to steam once the sun came out. It hummed already with mosquitoes, despite the pot of pyrethrum smoldering beneath the porch steps. Do-lores Mason and Cynthia LeJeune rocked slowly in their chairs, glasses sweating in their hands. Missy listened with one ear to the conversation, lulled by the rhythmic, wet slap of the mop and the creak of the chairs. Dinner was under control, unless Missus Mason decided she wanted the okra after all. The men were indoors, absorbed by a new fishing rod that Mr. Mason had purchased in Miami.

The clouds had gone, leaving a blaze of color on the horizon. Lazy, pink-tinged waves brushed the shore. From the beach came the faint scratch-scratch of the staff raking up the storm's debris.

"Looks like it should be a nice day tomorrow," ventured Cynthia with a swirl of her glass. The ice clinked softly. "Although I hear that Jenson is watching a storm. I sure hope it blows itself out; my nerves can't take much more." She had acquired a permanently tearful look since the barbecue and constantly twisted a moist handkerchief in her heavily ringed hands. "My poor Ronnie." She sniffed.

"Yes, terrible," agreed Dolores, although to Missy's ears, she sounded less than interested. Dolores's face suddenly lit up. She leaned forward. "Have you heard the latest? Turns out one of those . . . men at the veterans' camp is baby Roy's daddy." She arranged her toned legs to display the fine bones of her ankles. Missy was suddenly alert.

"Which one?" asked Cynthia. Her heavy-lidded eyes blinked slowly. She always reminded Missy of a sleepy old turtle.

"The one who comes from here, that big buck with the scar on his neck." Dolores sipped her drink, nibbled some mint between her small, white teeth, and tossed it on the floor. Missy's mop whisked it away. "Henry something."

"Henry Roberts?" asked Cynthia.

Missy banged the mop into the chair. "Careful, girl," snapped Dolores. "Yes, indeed," she continued as she leaned back in her seat. "Henry Roberts."

"Poor Dwayne," mused Cynthia with a small shake of her head. "Right under his nose. That's got to hurt, a proud man like that." She settled herself more comfortably in her chair and swatted a mosquito on her neck. "And Noreen always seemed like such a mouse. Never thought she'd do such a thing." She drained her glass. "Just goes to show, everyone's got a secret."

Dolores twined her string of pearls around a lacquered fingernail, eyes out to sea. "So they do, Cynthia," she said, almost to herself. "So they do."

Missy averted her gaze from the two women lest they see the shock there. She kept her jaws clamped shut to prevent the words from escaping her mouth. *It ain't true! You wrong!*

She pushed the mop around the chairs in quick, tight circles. There was no way he would do such a thing. Not Henry, not the man she knew. He was a good person, maybe the best she had ever met. But then a droplet of doubt trickled into her mind and turned black and white to muddy gray. The mop's progress slowed. He had been gone a long time, done things she could never imagine. How well did she know him, really? She would have placed any bet on what the old Henry would do, but now . . . he had changed. A voice in her head said: *It ain't likely, but it ain't impossible neither.*

No, said the other voice in her head. *Some things don't change about a person, no matter what happens to them. Who they are, in their heart, stays the same.*

She did not know what to believe. The mop smacked again into the chair and Dolores shouted, "Missy! What's wrong with you?"

"Sorry, Missus Mason."

"Quit that mopping now and get Mrs. LeJeune a drink."

"Yes, Missus Mason. Right away."

She went into the clubhouse, struggling to corral her thoughts, which were leaping around her head like a herd of wild ponies. The glassy eye of the giant stuffed sailfish glowered at her from the wall above the drinks cabinet. It always looked as if it was about to swoop down and skewer her with its long, needle-sharp nose.

And then it was like that pointy nose skewered the bubble of panic in her head. It came to her, with calm certainty, what she must do. She would talk to Henry, and they

194

would clear the whole mess up. Yes, that was the answer. She would talk to him, and he would make it all right. Her limbs relaxed as she realized that it was just a rumor, the kind that happened when folks couldn't find the truth. They reached for the next best thing. This was the juiciest scandal that Heron Key had seen for some time, far better than the time when the pastor spent the money from the poor box on bootleg hooch that he kept hidden beneath the altar.

It would be all right. She exhaled. It was going to be all right. *I just got to believe.*

When she returned to the porch, Missus LeJeune was dabbing at her eyes with a hankie. She reached a trembling hand toward the glass on Missy's tray. "How can something so terrible happen here? Of all places? Poor, poor Hilda. Have you been to see her?"

"No," Dolores said and lit a cigarette. She leaned back and picked a shred of tobacco from her teeth. Smoke veiled her face for a moment, but in that instant, Missy thought she saw a look of pure contempt cross her pretty features. Then it was gone.

Missy took up the mop again and made slow, careful work of the porch steps.

"It's awful," said Cynthia. "Just awful. It's a miracle she's still breathing. But I tell you one thing: she may come through this, God willing. But she won't be pretty anymore, that's for darn sure." She sighed and re-arranged her bosom. "I took Doc some mullet from the smokehouse. The man looks like he hasn't eaten in a week."

"What a good idea," said Dolores, suddenly a lot more cheerful. "Missy," she called. "Fix one of your pineapple upside-down cakes for me. I'm going to take it to Doc Williams. And I've changed my mind — we will have the okra tonight."

"Yes, Missus Mason." Missy ceased her mopping. The rest of the dinner, of fried chicken and mashed potatoes with giblet gravy, was almost ready. She would make the cake after she cleaned up from dinner, which would be sometime after midnight, if the men got drinking.

As she hurried to pick the okra, her thoughts once again began to spin. She turned it over and over in her mind. *It could not be true . . . could it?*

She went to pull more onions. The okra needed lots and lots of onions.

At the end of the day, Henry and his men loaded their gear into the back of the truck for the return trip to camp. The engine came to life in a burst of shrieks and splutters. The driver attempted to avoid the worst of the potholes, but it was still an extremely bumpy ride. A plume of choking coral dust rose from the road, blown by a stiff wind.

"That asshole, Two-Step," said Franklin. "He's ruined it for all of us. Violet Hudson seemed to like me." His one eye registered angry disappointment.

Henry studied his scarred face. It had been a long time since anyone treated Franklin as a civilized man instead of a dangerous vagrant. Henry had seen him give Violet the little sandpiper carved from driftwood. It was Franklin's favorite.

"The Bible tells us *it is hard for thee to kick against the pricks,*" Lemuel said.

Henry laughed. "For once, Lemuel, you got it just right."

"When you gonna see your 'old friend' again?" asked Jeb, just audible over the grinding of the truck's gears. His slight frame was nearly jostled out of his seat.

Henry and Lemuel each laid a hand on him to hold him steady. "She busy tonight, serving at a dinner party up at the country club. We supposed to meet tomorrow night, but I need a plan for how to get out of camp and back." There was no way he could fail to turn up for Missy — worse still, without being able to communicate with her. She

197

still believed in him after everything he had done.

"You wait till it gets dark," said Jeb. "Then you sneak out. We cover for you."

Henry thought about this. It would mean arriving late, but he was sure Missy would understand, once he explained.

"Uh-huh." Lemuel nodded. "We sure will."

"That right, on one condition," said Franklin. He scratched at his empty eye socket. "You be back before dawn and you bring us some of Selma's peach cobbler."

"That two conditions," Sonny pointed out.

"Hey, fellas," said Jeb. "At least the weather's on our side. I hear there's a storm coming."

"You wouldn't know it to look at that sky," said Franklin.

"It's coming, all right," said Henry. There was a brisk wind, laden with moisture. It was a welcome change from the baking heat of the past few months, but he knew to be wary.

"Good news for us!" exclaimed Jeb. "Means we get a day off!"

"And we lose a day's pay," said Sonny gloomily.

The truck hit a particularly deep pothole, which threw everyone onto the floor of the bed at the back, even Lemuel. A muted "Sorry, boys!" came from the driver's cab.

"I always wanted to see one of them big storms," said Franklin as he raised himself painfully back onto his seat.

Henry eyed the racing clouds. They looked to be in an awful hurry. "I believe," he said, "there's a good chance you may get your wish."

Later that evening, Ronald wiped his mouth and sat back with a satisfied if lopsided smile. "Missy, please tell the kitchen they have done themselves proud. I do love that okra."

Missy circulated with the coffeepot. "Yes, Mr. LeJeune."

"It was all delicious," said Cynthia.

George Mason was drunk, slumped in his chair, although Missy noticed everyone pretending not to notice. Dolores said with a tight smile, "Honey, have some coffee."

Missy poured some into his cup on its dainty bone china saucer.

"Dwayne seems to be making progress," said George. "I assumed you're pleased he went to the camp today?" His accent sounded funny to Missy. Mr. Mason was originally from New York.

Ronald forked the last bite of lemon

meringue pie into his mouth. The bandage on his cheek constrained the movement of his jaw. It clearly pained him to move. "It's the obvious place to look. But he's running out of time. If he doesn't come up with something by tomorrow, then . . ." He passed his fork around the plate one more time.

"Then what?" asked George.

"Then the good people of this town will decide," said Ronald, "what . . . additional measures may be needed."

"Measures? What do you mean?" George sat straighter in his chair. "This is America, Ronald, not the jungle."

"That's right, George, and we aim to keep it that way."

"And the law? Where does that fit with your plans?"

"The law works differently down here," said Ronald, with a sip of his coffee. "Missy, this needs a drop of brandy."

"Yes, Mr. LeJeune."

There was a small pause. George regarded Ronald through half-closed eyes. "I hear from Jenson Mitchell that a storm could be headed our way. They'll have to evacuate the veterans. They've got no chance out in the open if it does get bad."

"As my daddy used to say, God's will be

done," Ronald said.

George opened his mouth to respond, but Dolores interrupted. "How is he . . . How is Nelson holding up?"

"As you'd expect," said Ronald. "He's mad as hell. He and Hilda have their problems, but she's still his wife, after all."

Missy thought this made Hilda sound like an expensive possession, like a car or a prized golf club. She watched Dolores's eyes brighten at Mr. Kincaid's name. Some months before, Missy had taken the beach path for a change on her way home and come across the Cadillac parked in the shade of some sea oats. It rocked steadily on its wheels. She had hurried past, but not before glimpsing Mr. Kincaid's familiar face pressed against Dolores's neck. Her mouth was open, her eyes closed, arms locked around his shoulders. When Missy had reported the sighting to Selma, she had just shrugged and said, "The whole town knows. Now you know too."

Missy saw a look of pure, distilled sadness on Mr. Mason's face. *So does he.*

He lowered his eyes. "Missy, my dear, I find that my coffee requires some brandy as well."

CHAPTER 12

The next afternoon, Mama's face told a tale when she returned from Doc's. Missy met her with a glass of lemonade as she heaved herself up the steps to the Kincaid porch.

Mama took off her favorite hat, the blue one with red flowers. She sank into a rocking chair and narrowly missed Sam's tail. He had arranged himself on his back to catch the breeze on his pale, rounded stomach. After a long drink, Mama asked, "Got anything stronger?"

Mama didn't drink. Not ever. It wasn't like some people, who say they don't drink but really mean *except* at Christmas or *except* on their birthday. Being married to Billy, she liked to say, would drive anyone sober.

"No, Mama. Mr. Kincaid, he drank it all. He got some put away secret, but I ain't found it yet."

Mama drained the lemonade glass.

"Where he be?"

"Gone to the country club, I think. How is Missus Kincaid today?"

Mama shook her head uncomprehendingly. "Wife at death's door, and he out cattin' around." It was the first time Missy had heard her say a slur against the Kincaids. Mama stared for a long moment into the mangroves. "I ain't never seen anyone hurt that bad and still breathin'."

"But Doc will fix her up, won't he? He can do that?"

"Doc is tryin', chile, and if tryin' is savin', then she'll surely walk out of there alive, with God's grace. But she hurt real bad."

"Who would do such a thing?" Missy asked. The person who had enough hate in them to do this to Missus Kincaid was still out there, somewhere. He could be close by, maybe crouched behind the hibiscus or listening beneath the honeysuckle. She pulled Nathan's basket closer to her chair. He stirred slightly, then settled, fists bunched.

"I don't know." Mama rubbed her eyes. "Someone strong, Doc said. And fast."

"Last night, when I was servin' at the club, I heard Deputy Campbell been out to the camp to look for him."

Mama shrugged and placed her glass on

the wrought iron table by the potted geranium. "He got to, baby."

"Why he ain't lookin' at the men in town? Coulda been any one of them. What about Ike? He mean and crazy enough to do it."

"Ike a magician, far as you know?"

"No, but —"

"Because Ike was locked up in jail when it happened. Deputy Campbell not lookin' only at the veterans, but it sure makes sense it was one of them. You seen how they carry on."

Missy sprang to her feet, which startled Nathan into crying. She lifted him from the basket onto her shoulder and stalked up and down the porch. "Why people here have to be so lazy? Always jumpin' at the first thing they think of?" Her voice rose above Nathan's cries. Mama eyed her curiously. "All's I'm sayin' is just because somethin' looks like a rock and holds still don't mean it be a rock." When she was eight years old, showing off to Henry, she had leaped onto a great, greasy turtle carcass, thinking it was a big rock. Up to her ankles in rotten turtle guts, it was the shock of that slimy flesh between her toes . . . That was the worst, she decided, when you think you know what something is and then find out it's something completely different. "Just because," she said more quietly, "something seem like it should be true don't make it true." She sat down and hugged Nathan to her. He squirmed, clearly unsettled by her voice. Usually the warm baby smell of his neck made her feel calm and safe, but now it put her in mind of little Roy, and she returned him to his basket.

"You hear somethin' else over at the country club last night?" asked Mama, and from her expression, Missy could tell she had heard it too.

Missy nodded. Nathan's cries subsided into whimpering, but he stared up at her in confusion.

"That crazy talk," said Mama. "Just sewage from dirty minds." A pause. "What? You think Henry be Roy's daddy?"

"I don't know, Mama. I just don't know. He changed so much, since he been away." She was due to meet him shortly at the beach, only now she wasn't sure if she wanted to. One thing she did not doubt was that he would give her the truth, whatever it was. That much she could count on. *What if I don't want the truth?* "You really think . . . you think he didn't do . . . this?" Mama knew Henry better than she did.

But instead of answering, Mama picked a crimson hibiscus from the bush next to her chair. "One thing for certain, chile, you won't find out nothin' by sittin' on this porch." She stuck the flower behind Missy's ear. "Now go on, he be waitin'."

After Missy left, Mama lifted Nathan from his basket and rocked him back to sleep in her chair. Missy wanted the comfort of her certainty, but Mama had lived long enough to know that there was no such thing, not where people were concerned. Missy's life had been clearly bounded so far, with a rhythm as predictable as the tides. Mama bore the responsibility for that. After Leon and Billy had died, her only thought had been to keep Missy safe. Henry was not safe. He oozed anger from his skin. Something deep inside him had broken while he was away. Missy would have to decide for herself about Henry, damaged as he was. And there was nothing in the world, she thought, harder than that.

Henry was not at the beach when Missy arrived, although she was fifteen minutes late because she had dawdled on the way. She paced the sand, trying to come up with a way to ask the question. Now the time was upon her, it was more difficult than she had expected. It had seemed a lot easier that afternoon, when she decided that all she needed to do was ask him, straight up. Now she realized there was more at stake. His answer could change things between them, forever. Just as she had gotten used to the idea of him being back . . . it felt like her heart had been pulled up and down and around again since she first saw him on the Kincaids' lawn, only a few days before.

A dead crab washed up to her shoe, the pale pink shell almost translucent. When she was little, storms were a source of special excitement because the waves brought so many treasures onto the beach. The whole town went out the next day to scour the shoreline. They found chunks of mahogany, brass deck fittings, glass flagons, and once a fine leather satchel. She knew, as did everyone who combed the beaches, that every piece of booty had been fashioned by tragedy. Somewhere far out to sea, a ship had been broken by the wind and water. People had died, fast by drowning or slow, clinging to wreckage. Their belongings had made it to dry land, but they had not.

This evening, the beach was a sorry sight in the weak, watery light. Nothing interesting or valuable had washed up. The sand was littered with tattered palm fronds, assorted fishing floats, ragged coconuts.

Parcels of dead fish, bound up in broken nets, jostled bits of splintered timber.

There was only one way to find out what she needed to know. "Just ask him," she said aloud.

Outwardly, he had changed so much. The gaunt, scarred person beside her at the party looked like the older, sadder father of the man who she had seen off at the station, all those years ago. The things he had seen and done were beyond her imagination. How could a person not be changed by that? When she looked real close, into his eyes, there was still a flicker of the old Henry there. Weak it was, just a fragment of light, but still there. Just enough to give her hope. *Only too late when you dead.* She had said that, and at the time, she really believed it. But now . . .

The waves brought more trash onto the beach in an ugly, oily rolling motion. They seemed to hang back, like they didn't want to get caught up in the twisted mess on the sand. It put her in mind of the conversation at the country club dinner. Marriage, it seemed to Missy, was just a lot of empty words, forgotten as soon as they were said. Married folks reserved the worst treatment for the one they had promised to cherish for life. Mr. Mason seemed to love his wife, but she only had eyes for Mr. Kincaid. Mr. Kincaid had a beautiful wife and child but seemed to care for neither. Doc Williams's wife had run off with their baby when he had only been back from the war a little while. And then there was Deputy Campbell and his wife, and their little brown baby. She prodded the crab with her foot. It rolled over to reveal its underside, eaten away by other creatures. Only the shell was intact. *That all bein' married is about, makin' things look good on the outside, while inside is just . . . empty. I'd rather be alone all my days.* She figured this was, on current evidence, exactly where she was headed.

Mr. LeJeune's words came back to her. She wasn't sure what he had meant by "additional measures," but it could not be good for whoever got scooped up in Deputy Campbell's trawl through the camp. *That could be Henry.* At the time, she had been too distracted by other thoughts to pay much attention, but now the importance of this registered like a slap, and worry joined the mass of feelings that swirled inside her. Mr. LeJeune's tone of voice and the glitter in his eye put her in mind of a rattlesnake. She had disturbed one once, in a pile of dead leaves beside the Kincaids' porch, and had only been saved by the swift strike of

209

Lionel's shovel. The snake had the same look of malevolent purpose that she had seen on Mr. LeJeune's bandaged face last night.

She straightened the hibiscus behind her ear. Darkness cast its net over the sky. Lights twinkled along the shore. She scanned the beach in the direction of the camp, squinted to make out Henry's familiar shape against the dingy sand and cloud-colored sea. It was the hour when day turned to night, when the light played tricks on the eyes. A bluish-gray haze settled over the outlines of the palms. Early stars began to appear.

He was not there. He was not coming.

Part of her was not surprised. *What did I expect?* Some things never changed. She felt foolish and tired and old. Her knees ached from scrubbing the Kincaids' floor. Her back ached from fetching Nathan every time he cried, which was often, as if he could sense something bad had happened. That Mrs. Henderson had arrived, all full of concern for Nathan and his father. Missy didn't trust her, any more than the other country club ladies, but Mr. Kincaid accepted her help with a shrug.

Part of her was relieved. For a little while longer, she did not have to face whatever truth Henry had to tell.

Another part of her was desperately, child-ishly disappointed, which was ridiculous. After all, they were just old friends, out for a stroll together. Nothing more.

She pulled the flower from her hair and tossed it into the restless water.

Out at the camp, Henry waited impatiently for darkness. He could easily imagine the names Missy was calling him about now and grinned to himself at the look she would have on her face, all surprised when he turned up.

It was too late for their planned walk on the beach. He would go straight to Mama's to find her. They could sit on the porch, do anything, he didn't care. At least the rain had stopped. Wisps of cloud crossed a shin-ing sliver of new moon, which he took to be a sign. *I'm a lucky man. Not many people get a second chance.*

When they had returned from the bridge site that afternoon, Trent had counted them all back, reminded them of the dire consequences of breaking curfew, and retired to his cabin for the evening. He had seemed even more bad-tempered than usual.

Henry and his boys were playing gin

rummy by candlelight. The night sounds of the camp came to them through the open flap. Crickets sang to each other. Men cussed as they sloshed through puddles on the way to the latrine. From the drinkers in the mess hall, there was laughter. At least Trent hadn't decided to punish them by cutting off the beer. That, Henry knew, was likely to lead to mutiny. But for the time being, it seemed that everyone had heeded the curfew.

When it was finally dark enough, Lemuel dug out some sand from under the edge of the back side of the cabin. Henry wiggled out. He wore a black shirt borrowed from Franklin that had the advantages of being clean and rendering him almost invisible.

"Have fun, Son," whispered Jeb, "and don't be late. You know how your mama worries."

"Henry," said Lemuel seriously. "*Walk while you have the light, lest darkness come upon ye.* That's Job."

"Um, okay. Thanks, Lemuel," said Henry.

He slipped quietly up to the perimeter fence using the same stealth that had brought him so close to German lines that he could smell them before they knew he was there. Cutters taken from the bridge site made a hole in the fence. Once on the other side, he made for the road. All the tiredness left his body. His legs felt light and springy, the night air moist in his lungs. Coral crunched under his boots. The friendly moon smiled down at him.

He was home. He said the word aloud, quietly: "Home." It felt good. His long dormant habit of planning had returned in full. The first order of business was to persuade Trent to fix up the camp so it was fit for humans. The latrines should be moved away from the swampy low ground that was forever drawing filth into the open. The cabins all leaked in the rain, the canvas rotted to the point where it was almost transparent in places. The cabins were never meant to stand up to conditions in the tropics. No amount of patching would fix the roofs. They had to get new ones. Better yet, some solid structures that would give real protection from the weather. They needed a hurricane shelter. They needed to hire Selma to oversee the cooking. He had made these points to Trent before, but with no result. Now he felt as if the power of his logic would just demolish any resistance.

Everyone would win. Once the men had better housing and food, they would be more productive. His veins felt full of light, his head a kaleidoscope of possibilities.

There was something about Missy. Being around her made him feel he could achieve anything, the way he used to feel. Before the war, before the horrors that followed homecoming, before the lost years on the road. When he was with her, he believed.

He quickened his steps.

Mama had a squawking chicken by the neck when Missy shuffled dejectedly into the yard.

"Back already?" Mama asked as she broke the bird's neck with one quick twist of her wrist.

Missy just nodded and flopped onto a chair on the porch, staring at her worn, dusty old shoes.

"He not there?" asked Mama as she plucked with great dexterity. Soon her ankles were mounded with feathers, which she would use to restuff their thin mattresses. "That a shame, baby. Never mind, dinner be ready soon. Come on inside and help me with the peas."

Missy did not raise her eyes. For the first time in maybe her whole life, she had no appetite. "Not hungry, Mama. Think I'll just set here awhile."

"Missy Douglas" — Mama's tone was sharp — "you get in this house and help me with them peas. You ain't too big for me to take a switch to, you hear?"

Missy hauled herself out of the chair. The disappointment at Henry's nonappearance settled into her limbs and made her feel heavy and sluggish, like moving through deep water. The future stretched before her, dull and flat as a swamp. The pattern of all her days was fixed: get up, do chores, go to work, do chores, have dinner with Mama, go to bed with the encyclopedia. One day, Mama would be gone. She could not imagine that time, could not fathom the depths of loneliness it would bring. Like a winter that never ended. Although she had no experience of cold weather, she had seen pictures of snow in books. It made everything so white and still, took away all the colors from the trees and flowers, the sun just a weak ember in the sky. Nothing but empty stillness, forever and ever. *That what loneliness look like.*

Whatever Mama said, Missy was too old to be treated like a child. At that moment, she felt every one of her twenty-six years. As she opened the door, she began to say, "Mama, I ain't no —" when she saw him. Leaning against the sink, looking oh so pleased with himself, in a tight black shirt that accentuated the muscles he had earned on the construction site. And Mama beside him, grinning like a crazy person.

Before she could stop herself, she blurted, "Where was you? I waited. I was there. You said you be there!" She didn't care that it sounded pitiful, just like the child she was no more. She was ferociously, ridiculously, glad to see him. Waiting for him that evening had only served to remind her how much she hated doing that very thing. It seemed like she had been waiting all her life for Henry Roberts, in one way or another.

"I sorry, Missy," he said, but he was trying not to grin as well. "They put us under curfew, on account of the fight at the barbecue. But I sneaked out anyway, because we was supposed to go for a walk. And that was important to me."

Missy turned her face away in embarrassment. He had risked his job to come see her. The question burned inside her, but for now, it could wait.

"Do you forgive me?" he asked.

"I suppose so." Up close, she could see the curls of gray in his hair, his eyebrows.

"All right then," he said. "And I make you a promise. I will never disappoint you again. You hear me?" He took her hands. His palms were warm against hers. They stayed like that for a few moments while Mama busied herself with the peas, humming noisily on the porch.

"Now," asked Henry, "what's a man got to do to get fed around here?"

CHAPTER 13

Some hours later, plates washed and chickens fed, Mama and Missy talked quietly over an unconscious Henry. Mama had her sewing basket between her feet, darning on her lap. Missy just sat and watched him sleep. His eyelashes curled up where they rested on his cheek. His chest rose and fell. A small snore escaped his mouth.

He had begun to drift off even before they had finished dinner, head propped on one hand, eyelids drooping.

"You put knockout drops in this chicken, Mama?" he had asked as he yawned and rubbed his eyes. "Guess I better get back to camp." The lamplight smoothed the corners of the little room. The curtains hung motionless in the muggy air.

"Naw, Henry," Mama had said, bustling to the sink. "You best stay here. The road too dark and you too beat. Like as not you'll get lost, end up in old Zeke's mangrove swamp. Gator'll have you, and that'll be that." She wiped her soapy hands on her apron. "Here." She got out a patchwork quilt that was more darning than cloth. "In case you get cold."

"Mama, it's ninety degrees," he had said sleepily.

Missy had met Mama's eyes. It was a sign of how long he had been away. People in Heron Key had a different temperature gauge. Seventy degrees was sweater weather. When the thermometer hit sixty, it was time to get out the winter coats. The quilt was light and soft from endless washings. He settled into a saggy, heavily patched armchair with his feet on Mama's sampler stool. His head began to loll right away, like it was filled with lead weights. "Guess I could catch just a few winks," he said, "long as I'm back at first light for roll call . . ." And with that, he was asleep.

Missy whispered, "Do you think . . . ?"

"Think what?" Mama took a thread between her teeth and bit it off cleanly.

"Just wondered . . . He goes all over, to France, and California, and New York . . . and then, just by chance, he ends up back here, of all places. Seems kinda strange, don't you think?"

"Ain't nothing to do with chance," Mama said. "The Lord has a plan for that boy. And for you too." She tied off a stitch and stretched her arms above her head to the sound of popping joints. "Time for bed. Tomorrow I'll be over at Doc's to help change Missus Kincaid's dressings."

That the woman still did not wake was a worry, but Mama hoped it meant all her energy was being used for healing. As she and Doc had worked to clean and dress the wounds, each one had revealed itself. Hilda's body was a testament to pain. They found her missing tooth, embedded in her tongue. They straightened her broken nose as best they could. Doc said she had opened her eyes briefly. That she could still see was surely a miracle.

Mama looked over at Henry, whose face in repose regained some of its boyish softness. *What happened to you?* The rumors in town had grown from whispers to open talk about him . . . about how being in France had given him all kinds of ideas that had no place in Heron Key, how he had danced shamelessly with Hilda at the barbecue, even laying hands on her. How he and Missus Campbell . . . A black man who could bed one white man's wife could easily beat the tar out of another, no problem. Once the line was crossed, it made it easy to cross another and another, went the thinking.

She looked at Missy watching Henry, her eyes studying him like he was a ghost that could just evaporate any minute into thin air. *Plenty of people willing to believe a lie, if it filled a need.* And the town definitely had a need, and a burning one at that: it needed a name and a face to fit a crime, and any of those crazy veterans would do. And Mr. Kincaid spending almost all his time at the club, just coming home for clean clothes and more cigarettes, didn't bother to check on his wife . . . It wasn't right, none of it.

Mama could sense the anger bubbling like lava through the town, could almost smell it in the air, with each day that passed without an arrest. And if Hilda died, which could well happen . . . *Dear Lord, please make her well, or there will be hell to pay. And still may be, whatever happens.*

It was barely dawn when Missy felt it, a change in the air around her bed. She had not really slept, her head too full of questions and the sound of Henry's snores from one side and Mama's from the other. The floor creaked slightly. A dark shape stood over her. She started to scream, but then the shape said, "Missy, it's me." His face

221

came into focus in the gray morning light from the bare window.

Henry sat down on the edge of the bed. She should have felt embarrassed by his eyes as they traveled over her white nightgown, but she did not. He said, "I got to go back now, but I can sneak out again, I reckon." Half of his face was in darkness, the other half lit by the pale glow from the window. Somewhere a rooster crowed.

"Wait, don't go yet." She scooted over to the wall to make room. "Set a minute."

He sat down, grimaced, and removed a large object from underneath him: volume M to Z of the *Encyclopedia Britannica*. "I see now that you weren't kidding about this," he said.

She took the book from him, smoothed the worn ocher cover with her hand. "It helps me get to sleep. I pick a page at random, any page, and it always seems to be the right thing for that day." Shadows from the past crowded around her, old memories of the people they used to be.

"What you read last night?"

Almost overcome by the nearness of him, conscious of her thin cotton nightgown, she blurted, "Voyeurism."

"From the French, *to see*. But it means more than that, don't it?"

"Yes, it's when you watch someone, and they don't know you doing it. Like last night —" She caught herself just in time, but his bemused expression said he knew exactly what had happened.

"You was watching me, when I was asleep."

Desperate to get out of the hole she had dug for herself, she pulled her knees up and wrapped her arms around them. "So you speak French then?"

He smiled in a sad way. "A little. I picked it up from . . . people I met there." His eyes went to the square of watery sky.

"What was her name?"

He turned to look at her. "You a surprising young woman, Missy."

She shrugged. "Don't take a genius to work it out. We heard stories of how the . . . ladies there, even white ladies . . ." She did not know how to finish the sentence. Her insides churned at the thought of his hands on Missus Campbell's pale, skinny body.

"It true, what you heard. That did happen." Now he stared at her hard, like she had an answer to some important question.

"You a grown man," she said, trying to manage an air of worldly disinterest with a shrug. "Ain't got nothin' to explain."

"Oh, but I do, Missy; I do." And he leaned

223

right in, to where she could feel his breath on her face. "You see, I figured I'd go back to France one day. They got a better way of livin' there. Whites and coloreds, they's just all people. Not like here." His eyes got that clouded look again. "When I come back after the war, I got . . . You could say I got stuck. Me and the others who fought. I lost my way, Missy, and it seemed like I had nowhere to go. Not France, not Heron Key, just . . . nowhere."

She could not imagine how that felt, she who had always been surrounded by familiar people and things, as much a part of Heron Key as the palms and the coral. What did it feel like to lose your place in the world? It must be like purgatory, she decided, a place that often got talked about in church. It scared her more than hell, where there was at least something going on all the time. But if a person was just to drift, unattached to anything or anyone, in endless emptiness . . . She could conceive of nothing worse.

He turned to find her eyes on him. "What is it, Missy?"

Just ask him. "I don't know —"

"Ever since last night, there's been somethin' on your mind. I can always tell with you. Like that time you let all the turtles loose from old Simpkins's kraal? Or when you thought you'd caught chicken pox from one of the hens?" A dry chuckle escaped him.

And he looked, just then, in the weak light of dawn, like the old Henry again. The lines and the scars and the gray stubble were all smoothed away by the gentle glow. It took her back to a time when she could say anything to him, anything at all, and it would be all right. He had always been part of her life, and always would be. The warm cloak of the past wrapped itself around her.

"They say you baby Roy's daddy." There. It was out. The words hung in the air like ash.

And then his face was old again and she wished she could claw the words out of the air and swallow them down, if it would erase the lines from his face. He said nothing for a long moment, and then, "Do they now? And you, Missy, what you think to that? You believe I did that?"

His eyes seemed to fill her whole field of vision. She saw her reflection there, and all the memories of their time together. The questions, the doubts, the fears . . . they all melted away under his gaze. "I do not." And it was true — the certainty she had sought was there as she looked at him. Without a conscious decision, she put her arms around him, leaned her head on his shoulder. "You somewhere now."

"I know. I with you, Missy."

They sat like that for several minutes. She felt the thump of his heartbeat against her cheek and the warmth of his skin beneath her hand. Then he loosened her arms, got up, looked down at her like he had a lot more to say. The hens clucked beneath her window, impatient for their breakfast.

She watched him move quietly to the door. He paused there and whispered, like an afterthought: "Thérèse. Her name was Thérèse."

Henry strode toward the coast road. He dared not risk missing the roll call, and yet he could have easily stayed with Missy on that hard, narrow bed for a lot longer. Maybe forever. He thought of the soft weight of her pressed against him. It had taken a tremendous effort of will to keep his eyes off the fullness of her body under the thin nightgown. Had she been anyone else, he would have taken her right there, with no care for Mama in the next room or the curfew or anything. As he had done with others on so many occasions in the past.

But this was Missy, and that made it all different.

His head, which had been fogged for so long, suddenly felt newly scrubbed clean. When he had said Thérèse's name, it was like a spell had been broken. For so many years, he had kept her image in his mind, her red-gold hair on the pillow in the room above the *boulangerie.* It summed up everything he wanted to move toward — and everything he wanted to leave behind. And it summed up all he had lost. But when he said her name, just now, to Missy, instead of the usual pang of longing and regret, he felt . . . nothing.

Instead, his eyes were filled with the sight of Missy. She had said, "You somewhere now." And he had felt it, at that moment, a feeling of settled contentment, of belonging, the first time in . . . he could not remember how long. Maybe it was the first time ever.

A band of flamingo-pink light had begun to spread along the horizon, which reflected on the waves rolling alongside him. There was just enough time for him to slip back into the cabin before roll call, if he hurried. Nearly running now, the speed of his steps matched his racing thoughts. A new kind of plan appeared in his mind, one that he had never considered during all the years that he had been away. It came to him fully formed, so clear it was like watching a newsreel, but in color.

He saw a pretty little house by the water, where cool breezes lifted the curtains that Missy had made. There was a vegetable patch and chickens around her feet. He would work doing maintenance on the big wooden houses like the Kincaids' and the old country club, which he happened to be walking past. Those places always needed repairs to the damage from the relentless sun and salt.

They would have babies, he decided. There was still time. They would have a little boy who he would teach how to fish and make things with tools, and a little girl with Missy's shy smile, who he would read stories to. Selma would love that too — she always wanted to be an aunt. Missy could stop doing for the Kincaids and take up . . . what?

Of course!

The answer came to him so suddenly that he halted in his tracks. She could start the first school for coloreds in Heron Key. God knows they needed one, and she was more than capable, having a whole entire encyclopedia stored in her head.

He ran faster. He had run a lot over the years, but this was different. It felt like, for the first time, his tired old feet were taking him *toward* something.

Their kids would go to college one day and come back talking about strange things they had seen, completely beyond their parents' comprehension. He and Missy would grow old and care for each other. He could see it all, every detail, them sitting side by side on the porch he would build. They would rock in their chairs and talk at day's end, in the golden light of the setting sun, surrounded by good smells from the kitchen.

He halted again, shook his head. It was so real, he could almost taste it.

But then he recalled the thing she had struggled to voice. He had known, from the moment she arrived last evening, that something was wrong. He could always tell when she was troubled. But he had been completely taken aback to learn what it was: "They say you baby Roy's daddy." *Where on earth did that come from?* He had a hard time even picturing Noreen Campbell, had maybe seen her a handful of times. He recalled a slight, pinched blond with downcast eyes. There was talk of regular beatings.

He knew how it worked, had seen it before, how a rumor could burn through a town like wildfire. It didn't matter how it started. All that mattered was whether the important people believed it. Missy did not. He could count on Mama and Selma to see through it. Doc likewise. The only other person who mattered was Deputy Campbell himself. According to Doc, he was a decent man with a good heart . . . and a tendency to violence where his wife was concerned.

The pinkish clouds were giving way to blue. The storm had cleared and it looked like they should get a full day on the bridge site. He picked up his feet and marched quickly on. But still the thought bothered him, like a burr in his shoe. After the fight at the barbecue, the deputy had said, "Don't mistake me for your friend." Henry had taken that as the normal hostility the veterans were accustomed to from the townspeople and thought no more of it. But now . . .

Deputy Campbell's a decent man. Doc knows him well. No decent man with an ounce of sense would give it any credit. No one in such a position of authority would believe it . . . would they?

Dwayne steered his pickup onto the coast

road in the direction of the camp. Jimmy was in the passenger seat, as excited as a red-haired terrier on his first hunt. The boy had slept on a cot in the station, having been upgraded from clerk duties to help with inspection of the veterans' camp.

"What we gonna do when we catch him?" asked Jimmy. Such enthusiasm at this early hour was almost too much for Dwayne to bear.

"We take him in for questioning," said Dwayne with a yawn, "and do a lot of paperwork." Dwayne had told no one, not even Noreen, of how desperate he would be if the morning's search did not turn up a match for the boot print taken from Hilda's nose. He had very little time left.

He and Noreen had argued last night, as they had almost every night since Roy had been born. Dwayne was sure they had been happy once. There were vague memories of Noreen smiling at him. Then he wondered if he had just imagined it. Maybe they had always been at each other's throats like this and would be for the rest of their lives. *No, it was different once. Before the baby.*

The argument was, of course, always the same. The only difference was Mabel's whiny voice in his head saying, "There he is; there's Roy's daddy."

Henry Roberts. Now he had a name. Mabel was hardly a reliable source of information, but she had a knack for digging up dirt on people. Dwayne needed confirmation although, if he was honest, he was unclear how it would help. Would it make him feel better to know whose mouth had been on Noreen's, whose black hands had stroked her nakedness, whose name she called out instead of his? Would it change the fact of Roy? It would do none of those things, and yet he felt compelled to know. The need gnawed away like a tapeworm in his gut.

He had waited until they were having dinner. Roy was in his cot, a milky smile on his plump cheeks. "What if I were to tell you," Dwayne had asked, eyes intent on her face, "that I know who it is?"

Noreen pushed the greens around her plate without much interest. She had become so thin, like she was trying to disappear. *When did that happen?* There never had been much to her, but her shape was almost gone. Her pale blond hair was lank and dull. She shrugged. "I'd say good for you."

"Henry Roberts," he said, alert to any display of emotion on her face. He thought he saw her shoulders stiffen, but she gave nothing away. Frustration steamed like a geyser inside him, threatening to bring dinner up with it. "It's him, isn't it? Henry Roberts. Why don't you just admit it?"

"Why?" she had spat. "Why do you want to know so bad? What difference would it make? It won't change anything, will it?"

"I need to know. Why cain't you understand that?" He threw his plate against the wall, where it shattered. Food slowly smeared a brownish track down the wall. "I need to know!"

Wailing had erupted from Roy's cot. Noreen went to pick him up. Dwayne had caught her by the wrist. "I can make you tell me," he had said in a low voice. "You know I can." His other hand had drawn back to strike. She had flinched and covered her face, but not before he recognized the shameful truth: months of beatings had not produced the result he wanted. Rage burned right to his fingertips. His hand had shaken with frustration, with the desire to connect with flesh, and then suddenly it was not Noreen in front of him but Hilda. He had seen her right there, her bloodied mouth and nose, her bruised and swollen eyes, the torn lobes where her earrings had been. Her battered lips had spoken the words that chilled his heart: *For shame, for shame.*

He had dropped his hand, released Noreen's wrist. She had scooped Roy into her arms, wiped his nose with her apron. "There, there, hush, baby boy, hush now. That just your . . . daddy. He cain't help it." Her gaze had flickered to Dwayne, and in that look, he had seen weary resignation and something else, which shamed him in all his physical strength: defiance.

"You okay, Uncle Dwayne?"

Jimmy's voice broke into his thoughts. He throttled the pickup toward the camp. Jimmy's spare frame bounced with every bump in the road, one hand clamped on his cap. "Yeah, I'm fine."

The search just has to produce a match, Dwayne thought. It stood to reason. He was determined to remain in control of the situation and not give Ronald and his friends an excuse for the kind of lawless violence that had taken place elsewhere in the state. In Daytona Beach, in Tampa, in Plant City, and Fort Lauderdale, even in the capital, Tallahassee, he had heard stories of how the mobs wrought their vengeance. The authorities seemed powerless to stop them. Or more likely, he thought, they just lacked the will to stop them. *I'll be damned if I'm gonna let that happen here.*

So far, the lynchings had not traveled farther south than Miami, and he wanted to believe it could not happen in Heron Key. He had lived there all his life and knew the people to be basically decent, if prone to normal human weaknesses. Sure, they had their share of problems, but since the end of Prohibition, the town had enjoyed a peaceful time. Everyone left their doors unlocked at night, looked out for each other's children. Rare incidents like the fight between Ike and Ronald at the barbecue could be put down to an excess of alcohol and bad blood. Few people in town owned anything valuable enough to attract real thieves.

He thought again of the look on Noreen's face when he had said Henry's name. It made a lot of sense that an outsider had attacked Hilda.

The camp came into sight around the bend. He gunned the engine.

I'll find you, if I have to take this entire camp to pieces.

CHAPTER 14

As Henry crept closer to the camp, he could see that something strange was going on. Although his time with Missy had made him later than he intended, it was far too early for the place to be so busy. A few stars still shone faintly over the ocean, ahead of the rapidly rising sun. Normally only the cook was up at this time, preparing the miserable slop he had the nerve to call breakfast. An unfamiliar pickup truck was parked inside the gate. The veterans stood in groggy groups outside their cabins, scratching and yawning like they had been pulled from their beds. Barefoot. Trent shouted orders in their faces, clipboard under his arm.

Henry circled around to the swampy latrine side to consider how to rejoin his men. He had planned to slip back into the cabin the same way he left, but that would not be possible now. He managed to catch Jeb's eye as he craned his skinny neck. He mimed an attack of stomach cramps. Jed blinked; he understood. Then Henry waited on the boards over the filthy mud for his opportunity.

The deputy sheriff made his way from cabin to cabin, trailed by a young, red-haired man. At each stop, Red lifted the men's boots, one pair at a time, so the deputy could examine them, each time referring to a small piece of paper. This made no sense to Henry, but he guessed it was something to do with the attack on Missus Kincaid.

He was unsurprised that suspicion had fallen on the veterans. It was entirely predictable for a small place like Heron Key to close ranks against the outsiders. He had seen it many times in his travels across the country. Doors were slammed, curtains pulled shut, children tucked protectively behind their parents' legs. Still, it saddened him. While the veterans did little to endear themselves to the townspeople and included some characters even he was wary of, it was not beyond the realms of possibility that someone from the town was responsible for the attack. The veterans, he felt, deserved the same treatment as the townspeople: no better and no worse.

The deputy arrived at Henry's cabin, the

last to be inspected. Trent consulted his clipboard. His voice carried over to where Henry waited by the latrines.

"Where's Roberts?" he barked, eyes swiveling to take in the parade ground.

"In the john, Boss," said Jeb. "He a sick man, on account of the crap we had for dinner last night." He shrugged. "Crap in, crap out."

Lemuel snickered, silenced by a look from Trent.

"That right, Boss," said Franklin loudly. "He could shit through the eye of a needle right about now."

The resulting hilarity continued while Henry strolled over to join them, very obviously doing up his pants and trying to look drained. Trent regarded him closely. "How long you been in there?"

"Hours, Boss, I reckon," said Henry with a weary sigh. "Was woken in the night by a terrible rumbling. Thought it was an earthquake in my stomach."

Murmurs of sympathy rippled through the assembled men.

"Boots, Roberts," said the deputy. "Off."

Henry handed the smelly footwear to Red, who wrinkled his nose and held it at arm's length for the deputy to inspect. He studied them for a long moment, compared them to his piece of paper, before he finally said with a note of disappointment in his voice, "Clear."

Hands on hips, the deputy surveyed the scene like it had done him some kind of personal injury. His eyes wandered across every sleepy, unshaven face and every building while the men waited and the temperature rose. Full morning sun broke over the camp. It filled out the shadows and reflected off a shaving mirror left by the water pump, which sent a shard of light right across the side of Henry's cabin.

"Mr. Deputy, sir," said Two-Step. "I think if you were to look over there —"

Trent barked, "Did anyone ask for your opinion?"

"No, let him speak," said the deputy.

"Well," said Two-Step, "I saw Mr. Roberts hide something over there." He pointed to the side of the cabin. He had the expression of a satisfied spider, enjoying the fly's struggles too much to bite just yet.

Henry caught his eye and thought, *People see what they want to see. Payback.*

Instantly the deputy straightened, alert as a gun dog with a scent. He strode over to the cabin and tugged at a lump that stuck out from under the wall. Then he stood to reveal a T-shirt covered in brown stains. It

239

was the shirt Henry had worn to butcher the gator before the barbecue. That gator never existed, as far as anyone knew in town, and he was determined it should stay that way, for Missy's sake.

"Whose is this?" asked the Deputy.

Jeb sent Henry a warning glance, which he ignored. "Mine, Deputy," he said. "It mine."

"These stains look like blood to me."

"That's because they are," said Henry, his tone level.

Two-Step offered, "Just like I said, Deputy: seek and ye shall find."

"You can shut up now," said the deputy.

Jeb's narrowed eyes flashed with alarm.

The deputy stepped closer. "You mind telling me, Mister Roberts, what activity you were engaged in when you got covered in blood?"

There was something in the man's eyes, in his voice, that cut right through Henry. It was the hint of triumph, like he had proved some kind of point. He had found what he was looking for; everyone could sleep safe in their beds now. In the country of the damned, a stained T-shirt was the flag. But he could not bring himself to cooperate, especially if it implicated Missy. "I do, as it happens."

"You do what?" Trent glowered.

Franklin's one eye registered apprehension. Lemuel bit his lip. Jeb whispered, "You gone crazy?"

"Mind, Boss," said Henry calmly. "I mind. It ain't the deputy's concern. It ain't her — Missus Kincaid's blood on the shirt."

"Then tell us," demanded Trent, so close to Henry's face that he could see every pore, smell the odors of stale tobacco and beer. "Whose blood is it?"

"No, Mr. Watts. I . . . respectfully decline."

"I've had enough of this vaudeville routine," the deputy said and cuffed Henry's hands together. "I'm arresting you on suspicion of grievous bodily harm on the person of Hilda Kincaid."

"But, Uncle Dwayne," said Red, anxiously shifting from foot to foot. "We didn't find no match to the boot print. Don't that mean —"

"Shut up, Jimmy, and get in the truck," said the deputy.

Mama arrived at Doc's later that morning. He had begun the process of changing Hilda's dressings. The roses from Lionel had started to look sorry for themselves, so she gave them fresh water and replaced the jar on the bedside table.

"There you go, Missus Kincaid," she said. To Doc, "Can she hear us?"

"I don't know," he said. "Maybe, some of the time. She's been mumbling but I can't make it out." He tossed the bloodied bandages aside and took the clean ones from Mama. She washed a bad cut on Hilda's forehead.

"How she doing?" Mama asked. She could detect no change, no flicker of waking.

"Well, there's no infection," he said with a tired creak in his voice.

Mama had helped out at Doc's since he came back from the war. They understood each other after long years together. They had plastered broken bones, sat up with sick children, and eased the passing of the dying together. She knew that the bruises that flowered into extravagant yellows, reds, and purples were part of normal healing. Of more concern was this unbroken sleep. The wounds were clean, already trying to close, but the brain lagged behind.

"I'm not happy about her blood pressure," he said.

Indeed Mama thought the eyes looked more swollen than the day before. "You sending her to the hospital?"

He removed his glasses, polished the

lenses on his shirt. "Not yet. She's still too weak. In this condition, the trip could . . . do more damage. We'll give the drugs another day to work and then see how things look."

Mama spied the cot in the back room. So Doc had taken to sleeping in the office. This was not a good sign, nor was the slightly fevered redness around his eyes. "Doc, you been eatin'?"

"People have been very kind," he said distractedly, "as you can see."

His desk was piled with plates and dishes, mostly full of food. Flies were making a meal of what looked like smoked mullet. With no icebox, the food was not fit to eat.

"Doc, you got to take better care of yourself, or else how you gonna take care of her?" she asked sternly.

He blinked behind the smeared lenses of his glasses, as if he did not understand her words.

She took the bandages out of his hands. "Now, look here," she said. "This is what we gonna do. I'm gonna finish this up while you lie down and rest." He started to protest, but she held up a hand. "Then I'm gonna get rid of this rotten food and bring you some fresh. And then," she said in her no-nonsense voice, "I'm gonna sit here and watch you eat it, every bit." He was the only white person she would ever talk to like this.

He did not resist as she led him to the back room. Just then, there was a knock, and a cheery "Hello? Anybody home?" came from the screened door.

Dolores Mason glowed in her white tennis dress. She entered with a glass-domed plate on which sat a magnificent pineapple upside-down cake. Mama recognized it as Missy's specialty. "Just brought you something to keep body and soul together," trilled Dolores. "Morning, Mama."

"Mornin', Missus Mason." Mama never had much to do with the country club set, but she heard often from Missy that Dolores Mason seemed to get younger every year. Her skin was clear, just touched with a honeyed brown from the sun. Her arms were lean and sinewy. Missy said she ate very little, mostly vegetables and some fish, but smoked like a chimney. Meanwhile, George Mason seemed to be aging faster than normal. He was a nice enough man when sober, Mama heard, which wasn't often.

Dolores handed the plate to Mama and stood next to the bed. "Oh, Hilda," she said as she leaned over her face. "You poor thing. What did they do to you?" Hilda stirred.

Her eyes trembled behind their lids, and her hands twitched slightly. "How is she, Doc? Has she said anything?"

"Nothing I can make out," he answered. "We have to be patient."

Mama observed Dolores closely. The woman was no friend of Hilda's. Everyone knew that and the reason behind it. So why was she there? To make herself feel better about the whole thing with Mr. Kincaid? Mama smiled to herself. In some ways, poor old Hilda had gotten one over on the svelte young woman who had so publicly stolen her husband. Hilda was now the center of everyone's attention, which was the spot that Dolores usually had all to herself.

"You poor man," Dolores said, laying a manicured hand on Doc's arm. "You look done in. You must get some rest. Take him home, Mama. I'll sit here with Hilda while you're gone."

"I —" he began.

"Honestly," Dolores said, "it's no trouble. At a time like this, we must all put aside our personal . . . feelings and pull together." She smiled, showing her neat, small white teeth.

"I'm not leaving, but thanks all the same," said Doc.

"Me neither," said Mama.

Dolores looked from one to the other, smile fixed firmly in place. Then, with a shrug, she picked up her pocketbook and said, "Well, all right then, suit yourselves. I'm always here for you," she said and gave Doc's hand a squeeze.

The screen door smacked closed behind her. Doc slumped into a chair. "What just happened?"

Mama shook her head. "You been run over by the Dolores Express."

Back at the police station, Dwayne had begun to fill in the forms for Henry's arrest. They had come in through the back door, but even so, several people had seen Henry in his truck and would draw their own conclusions. It would not be long before the news spread. He needed to take advantage of this period of calm to extract the information from Henry. *I've got you, Roberts, and you're going to pay, for everything you've done. And I mean* everything.

Henry sat in a corner of the cell, apparently unconcerned, as if he were waiting for a bus. He had said nothing on the way back in the truck, which put Dwayne on his guard. Innocent people — and many guilty ones — were always quick to tell you all about it, in his experience. Henry's silence was disturbing. It was not normal. Jimmy, by contrast, had chattered nervously for the whole way back, until Dwayne had threatened to make him walk to town.

Jimmy led Henry to sit across from Dwayne at his desk.

"Mister Roberts, you understand the nature of the charge against you?" Dwayne asked formally.

"I do."

That flat, confident stare again. It unnerved Dwayne. "And what do you have to say in your defense?"

"It wasn't me. I wasn't there." Henry paused. "And I trust in American justice."

Dwayne studied Henry for a moment. He was cool and collected where he should be stammering with fear — a black man, accused of battering a white woman, on the edge of Florida's lynch belt. Dwayne could not fathom it, any of it. This annoyed him. "Where were you after the barbecue at two in the morning?"

"Asleep in my bunk, in a cabin surrounded by my men, who will all vouch for me." Henry sat back and folded his arms, like he was the one in charge.

"Of course they will," said Dwayne, making some notes on the form. *Suspect was cooperative but full of himself.* "Now it's time to tell me about the shirt. Where did the blood come from?"

"It's nothing to do with Missus Kincaid," he said, "and for that reason, I respectfully decline to say."

"Whoever attacked Hilda would have been soaked in blood," Dwayne said, leaning forward. He held the T-shirt close to Henry's face. "They would look, in fact, just like this."

"That may be, but it's not what happened." He leaned toward Dwayne so their noses were almost touching. "And anyway, I hear that you came to the camp this morning to look for a boot to match a print?" He raised his eyebrow. "Mine don't match, and neither did anyone else's in the camp, did they? So now you're trying this" — he cast a disdainful glance at the T-shirt — "to make it stick to me."

Dwayne felt his temper start to rise. *I'm in control here. I ask the questions.* He had been so intent on finding the owner of the boot, and when that didn't happen, the shirt had been like a gift. But there was no way to prove that the blood on the shirt was Hilda's, and with Henry refusing to explain, it was completely circumstantial. His alibi might be false, but it would be hard to break, with the men on his side. Any judge in the county would throw it out of court. Yet Henry was hiding something, he was sure of it. Maybe protecting someone. But who?

"Here's what I think happened." Dwayne leaned back and laid down his pen, arms crossed over his paunch. "After the way Missus Kincaid flung herself at you at the barbecue, you figured you'd have some of that. So you followed her when she left. But she didn't want you, and she fought back. This made you mad, because men like you are used to having any white woman you want, aren't you, Henry? You had them in France and . . . other places." An image of Henry on top of Noreen, her laughing, urging him on, doing all the things she'd never do with her own husband. Dwayne stumbled, tried to recapture his train of thought. "She was drunk. You're a big, strong guy, easy for you to pull her off the road and beat her to a pulp."

Henry said nothing for a moment, just regarded Dwayne levelly. "This lady been . . . interfered with?"

"No, but —"

"So tell me why," he asked, "if I'm crazed with lust for this woman, why don't I rape her? Ain't that what men like me" — he let the phrase hang in the air — "always do?

249

And why don't I kill her? Why do I let her live, when she can finger me? Why, Deputy Campbell? It don't make no sense. None of it does."

"Everyone in town saw how you danced with her, laid hands on her," said Dwayne. He felt blood rush to his face. *Where did those words come from?* He had started to sound like Ronald. The stained T-shirt had seemed to confirm that his gut instinct about Roberts was right, but now his certainty started to unravel. He needed something solid to stand on, something that would not just turn to sand beneath his feet.

"They saw what they wanted to see," said Henry with a dismissive shrug. He paused, eyes narrowed. "Why you lookin' at me like that?"

While Roberts was talking, Dwayne's mind was searching for evidence of a different kind. He regressed the man's features to those of a baby. He took his face apart in his mind and tried to reassemble it into Roy's. The nose was different, and so was the chin. There was maybe something in the shape of the eyes, possibly a similar tilt to the cheekbones . . . He could not be sure, of any of it. Who could say how Henry's and Noreen's looks would combine? It felt like the entire foundation of his life had crumbled away, eroded by doubt. He wanted it to be true. He needed it to be true.

And still Roberts sat there, calm, unafraid, even relaxed. He should have pissed his pants by now, but instead he looked arrogant beyond belief.

Anger and frustration boiled together inside Dwayne like acid, threatened to burn a hole right through him. He could be sure of nothing. His muscles trembled with the effort of control. His fists itched to pound that cool smugness from Roberts's face. Dwayne said nothing, just continued to stare. The answers were there, he knew it, but he could not bring them to the surface.

"Sorry, Deputy," said Henry, "but you taken a wrong turn somewhere. Missus Kincaid a nice lady. She been good to me. I got no reason to harm her." He stood up. "And you got nothin' to hold me, so —" He turned to leave.

Dwayne was out of his seat so fast his chair went over with a crash. One of his hands grabbed Henry's collar, and the other pulled back to strike with all his considerable strength. The truth was inside Roberts. *I will thrash it out of you, so help me God.*

"Uncle Dwayne!"

He felt Jimmy tugging on his arm. For a

251

split second, he almost tossed him aside, but the boy's expression of open-mouthed shock stopped his hand.

Dwayne still gripped Henry's collar tight, breathing hard. In Henry's eyes, he saw alarm but also sadness, like Dwayne had failed some test he didn't know he was taking.

Dwayne swallowed hard, released his hold. *How did this get so out of control?* Just a few minutes before, he had been conducting a normal interrogation, as he had hundreds of times before. He tried to regain his composure. Roberts had tricked him somehow; that was the only explanation. He struggled to focus. Pictures of Henry and Noreen together filled his head. The urge to punch Henry in the mouth — the mouth he had kissed her with — was undiminished. If anything, it was stronger. He could take no more. He had to escape from Henry's steady, direct gaze.

"Jimmy!" he barked. "Put him back in the cell."

He pushed past the startled Jimmy, desperate for air.

Jenson Mitchell had woken from a troubled sleep with a profound feeling of wrongness. There was a metallic taste in his mouth and gooseflesh on his arms although the night had been oppressively hot.

He got up from his narrow bed at the back of Trudy's house, his old bedroom. No sense in keeping the house he had built once his wife was gone. He didn't want to spend every day avoiding reminders of her. The same flu that took his father had taken her too, strong and young as she was. And Trudy's house, big and empty without Eldridge, was closer to the store. He pulled on some clothes and sat on the edge of the bed. The barometer was still dancing around. While it had ceased to plummet, which was cause for some relief, the behavior was not normal. He decided it was time to check with Fred again.

Once at the store, he felt no better. The air glued the shirt to his skin. His nerves felt jangly and itchy, as if a mild electric current were passing through him. His ears tingled, and his eyes were sore, yet the sky was clear. The only sound was the faint sigh of the waves slowly breaking and the cries of a few sea birds. And then came another sound, of the telephone in his office. He got there on the last ring.

"Jenson," said Fred, and just from the way he said his name, Jenson knew something had happened. "Seems that our friend is on

253

the move. Heading northeast. I've ordered the lanterns to be put out tonight."

The warning lanterns, placed along the coastal lighthouses and weather stations, signaled the approach of a damaging storm. There would be two red lights, one above the other, to indicate a northeasterly heading. Although this would bring it in the direction of Heron Key, Jenson knew that storms often lost their power once they made this turn. "What's your best bet for landfall?"

"Now, Jenson, you know I'm not a gambling man," said Fred, which was belied by Fred's many weekends spent in Nassau's casinos. "But if I had any money, I'd put it on Coquina Bay."

This was a wealthy enclave between Miami and Fort Pierce, a favorite of golfers from up north. It was close enough that Heron Key would feel the sting of the beast's tail as it passed by — if it made it that far.

"That is," added Fred, "if it doesn't blow itself out, of course, which is more than likely."

"Every chance of that," agreed Jenson. There were still too many uncertainties for his liking. "What's your advice?"

"It's moving real slow from what we can tell. We'll get plenty of warning if it does head for land. Stay by the phone."

Jenson hung up, his mind already calculating what needed to be done. Fred had never lived through a big storm. Jenson was just a child when the one came that took his grandmother, but he had a very clear memory of that day. A giant hand had picked up their house and pushed it a hundred yards down the street. He heard the terrible grinding of the house against the road, even over the noise of the wind. Glimpses of the town flashed past through the empty holes where the windows used to be. Then it tore the roof off and sucked his grandmother into the sky. The last he saw of her was the soles of her shoes.

He knew the next twenty-four hours would be critical. It was time to make a list of people to call.

CHAPTER 15

Dwayne sat in the cab of his truck, head in his hands, and waited for his heart to stop pounding. He kept seeing a grotesquely deformed creature made from Henry's face stuck onto Roy's little body. The inspection at the camp had been an embarrassing waste of time. He could not claim to be any closer to identifying Hilda's attacker. Ronald and the others would not wait much longer. He heard there was a meeting planned at the clubhouse for the next evening. At a total loss for what to do next, he cast around the cab for a cigarette. His scrabbling dislodged the piece of paper with the boot print. It fluttered onto his lap.

He crumpled it into a ball to throw out the window, but some memory stopped his hand. He smoothed the paper out again. Earlier that morning, while inspecting the boots at the camp, something had bothered him. It was not simply that the drawing found no match among the men's boots; it was that, as the inspection had continued, he had begun to doubt whether the pattern belonged to any boot at all. Although the men wore different makes and sizes, there should have been some basic similarity, just variations on a template. Yet the drawing he held in his hand, he now realized, was of a completely different character.

There was still the option of checking the footwear of all the men in town, but he was coming to realize that this would just compound the time wasted so far. In the excitement of finding Roberts's bloody shirt, he had let emotions cloud his judgment.

I have been looking in completely the wrong place.

He started the engine and headed for Doc's office.

Henry leaned back against the rough concrete of the cell. Water dripped slowly from the ceiling, making a muted *plink* in the bucket on the floor. Ike snored extravagantly in the next cell. The man had only woken twice, to piss on the floor and demand a lawyer. He still stank of the vomit encrusting his shirt.

Henry caught Jimmy's eye. The boy had

been observing him from behind the pages of yesterday's paper for some time.

A cold draft of suspicion made him shiver in the sweltering jail. The deputy had stared at him like he wanted to see through to Henry's very bones. The rage in him went beyond Hilda's attack. There was something personal in that stare, more than just a professional lawman's desire to obtain a confession. Henry had seen plenty of them in his travels, been threatened many times, even beaten by a fair few. And yet some part of him still wanted to believe that Dwayne Campbell was different, that justice was still possible, even here, even now. Despite all the evidence of his senses, he wanted to believe. *He a decent man. Doc said so.* He tried to focus on that thought, but the image of Dwayne's staring eyes would not leave his mind.

He got up and began to pace the dimensions of his cell. Eight steps, turn.

Missy would have heard of his arrest by now. He remembered her face, as it had looked the previous night in the yellow lamplight. He felt calm. That's what thinking of her did to him. He should have been frantic, given his situation, but he was not.

Eight steps, turn.

I trust in American justice. Now why had

he said that? Just to show Dwayne that he wasn't dealing with an ignorant hick?

Eight steps, turn.

Did he even believe it? Since returning from France, he'd seen every kind of abuse of power, from the small-town cops like Dwayne to the federal government. He had seen his fellow soldiers trampled by their former comrades on orders from Washington. He had seen the smoldering bodies of sharecroppers whose only crime was wanting a fair price for their goods. He had seen the newspaper reports that a mob held a man to be lynched. The reporters had time to get the story, but still all the authorities did was cut down the corpse when it was over.

Eight steps, turn.

Despite all the evidence of men's brutality, it was Missy, and her basic goodness, that made him believe again. It was hope, he realized, so long absent from his life. She restored that in him, made him want to believe the best in everyone. It felt like a dead, gangrenous limb had been healed, with fresh blood in the veins, new skin on the bones. *Deputy Campbell a decent man. Doc said so.*

Eight steps, turn.

But then he thought back to the night of

the barbecue, the way Dwayne had stared, even before Missus Kincaid was attacked. Something was very, very wrong.

Eight steps, turn.

Doc woke to the sound of voices raised in argument. There was a high-pitched woman's voice, which sounded stubbornly irate and clearly belonged to Mama. The other voice was lower, with a note of urgency that cut through his grogginess. Dwayne.

"You got to leave the man be," said Mama, blocking the doorway with her substantial bulk. "He needs rest, or he won't be no good to no one."

"Let me by, woman," said Dwayne. "This cain't wait."

"It's okay, Mama," said Doc, slowly getting off the cot. He felt like he had slept for days, but the sun's angle told him it was maybe a couple of hours. A plate of Mama's fried chicken had restored him somewhat. He wiped the lenses of his glasses and squinted at Dwayne's silhouette in the doorway.

Mama withdrew, with a scowl at Dwayne. She gathered up her hat, her pocketbook, and the plate and left. The slam of the screen door signaled her disapproval.

"Doc," said Dwayne, "I got to take a look at Hilda."

A frown creased Doc's forehead. "What's going on, Dwayne?" The man was clearly agitated. In his hand, he clutched a dirty, creased scrap of paper. "What happened at the camp this morning? Did you find a match?"

Dwayne shook his head. "No, not to any of the boots. I did find a bloody shirt belonging to Henry Roberts, so I arrested him on suspicion."

"You arrested Henry?" Doc was now extremely glad that Mama had gone home.

"Had to, Doc." Dwayne spread his hands. "The man refuses to explain it. Arrogant son of a bitch." He paced the small space. "Cool as a cucumber, he was, and his shirt absolutely covered in blood. Says it's not hers, like that's enough. What possible, innocent explanation could there be for that much blood?"

"An animal, maybe?" But Dwayne was not listening. "Then why are you here, if you think he did it?"

"He knows more than he's saying. I can feel it, Doc." Dwayne flopped onto a wooden stool. "But something ain't right." He held up the scrap of paper. "None of the boots matched, and I think I know why.

I'm starting to think . . . to think it ain't a boot print at all."

"That does change things," agreed Doc. "What else could it be?"

"Dunno," said Dwayne. "That's why I got to take another look."

"Is there another reason, Dwayne, why you arrested him?" Doc had heard the rumors, just like everyone else, that Henry might be Roy's father. He didn't believe them, but Dwayne was desperate for an answer. Doc hoped he would resist the urge to abuse his position of authority but imagined that the temptation would be overwhelming. He wondered how long his principles would stand up to such strain.

Dwayne's eyes slipped to the floor. His shoulders slumped. He said nothing for a long moment, then looked up. "I cain't deny that I wanted to get him alone. Not to hurt him, you understand, just to ask him. But when it came to it, I couldn't. I just couldn't." He searched Doc's face for an answer to his pain. "I'm a pathetic excuse for a man."

Doc laid his hand on Dwayne's shoulder. "No, you're not. Maybe it's just . . . it's different when the man is sitting there with you. Maybe you just realized that knowing won't help after all."

"Maybe . . . I thought it would make it easier to bear somehow, if I knew, but now . . ." He shook his head. "One thing I do know is that we got to think again about what made this mark." He held up the crumpled piece of paper. "It's the only thing we got to go on."

The way to deal with any of life's traumas, Doc knew from experience, was to focus on the work, just the work. As for the rest . . . well, that could wait. "We'd better hurry," he said. "The wounds are healing fast."

They stood on either side of Hilda's bed, the only sounds her slow breathing and the soft whoosh of the fan in the corner. Although Dwayne had a clear memory of how she looked on the night of the attack, he was shocked anew at the extent of damage to her face. He realized the healing would make it look worse, but even so. Between the swelling, the stitches, and the bruises, she resembled something found on a slaughterhouse floor. She had been a very pretty woman; some even thought her beautiful. No more.

Doc gently pushed a lock of hair from Hilda's forehead. Dwayne noted the way his face softened when he looked at her. Doc had been alone a long time now. It was clear that Leann and Cora were never coming back. It was common knowledge that Nelson had neglected Hilda before, and this pattern had continued. He seemed to spend all his time holed up with Ronald LeJeune. *Maybe something good will come out of this after all. If she lives.*

"I've been thinking," said Doc, "about the force of the blows needed to do this kind of damage. If someone used their fists, their hands would be lacerated. They might even have broken fingers. I'm pretty sure they'd need treatment, and I'd hear about it. So it must have been —"

"An object," interrupted Dwayne. "They hit her with something . . . something that made that mark." He pointed to the fading crosshatch pattern of red lines on her nose. "The object, whatever it was, could have got smashed from the force of that blow."

They both leaned in close. Their eyes met over Hilda's unresponsive form.

"You thinking what I'm thinking?" asked Doc.

"I believe I am, Doc. I believe I am."

Hilda drifted on dreams, dreams of falling at the feet of a familiar figure standing over her. The figure held something in its hand. The figure swung it at her head, again and again, like it was a game, until the object broke with

264

the sound of splintering wood. Words filtered through the haze but she could make no sense of them. She knew the meaning of each word but not how they went together. She tried to recall the figure's face, but it hurt too much. The only way to avoid the pain was to sink back down again, below the surface, and sleep. Just sleep.

Back at the jail, Henry watched while Jimmy read the farming report for the third time in between fascinated glances in his direction. It was clear from his swagger that Jimmy thought himself better than a floor sweeper, a bucket emptier. It was also clear that he idolized his uncle Dwayne, while he chafed under his discipline.

"Jimmy," Henry called, "can I have some fresh water, please?"

Jimmy filled a cup and passed it through the bars, careful to avoid contact.

"Thanks, Jimmy." He drained the cup and handed it back. "I'm Henry."

"I know who you are." The boy took a step back. "Where'd you get that scar? In a knife fight?"

Henry's hand went to his neck. "You could say that." An easy smile. He kept his voice low and even. "Don't worry, I ain't gonna try nothin'. Your boss must trust you a lot, to leave you alone, in charge of everything."

Jimmy shrugged, thumbs hooked in his belt loops, just like Uncle Dwayne.

"Your boss, he a good man, I can tell," said Henry.

Jimmy cleared his throat and spat. "S'pose so. Most of the time, anyway. My momma says —" He stopped himself and blushed right up to his hairline.

Henry leaned casually on the bars, hands loose in front of him, like they were chatting together over a backyard fence. "It's all right, Jimmy. Who I gonna tell, locked up in here? What your momma say?"

"She says . . ." He hesitated, glanced warily at the door, pulled his John Deere cap low over his eyes. "She says that Aunt Noreen gonna leave him, on account of him beatin' on her all the time."

Henry thought for a moment. "That a bad business, for sure. Why he do that?"

"Because," said Jimmy, and his eyes swept over Henry in a slow, calculating arc, "she won't tell him who is the daddy of her little nigra baby. But there's folks think they know who it is."

Henry kept his tone light although his heart had begun to beat faster. "Folks sure do like to talk."

"Don't you want to know what they say?" asked Jimmy. His cheeks were pink underneath the freckles. He leaned forward, feet nearly dancing with excitement.

"Up to you, Jimmy. You in charge here."

"So I am." He stood a little taller. "They say" — and he stepped closer to the bars, staring intently at Henry — "they say that baby's daddy is . . . *you.*" He whispered the last word. "What you got to say to that, then?"

"That what your uncle thinks?"

"Uh-huh," said Jimmy, with a gratified grin. "Indeed he do. So is you or ain't you?"

Henry turned his face away to collect his thoughts. The fears he had pushed to the back of his mind now crowded around like a flock of vultures. After a few moments, he heard Jimmy sit down again with a disappointed huff and a shake of the newspaper.

Henry had always been good at thinking on his feet, but now his brain felt filled with molasses. To hear Jimmy say it out loud gave shape to the dread he had tried to deny. Icy fingers of fear squeezed his bowels. He had not known a feeling like it, not since the battlefield, with the raging storm of shells and gunfire all around. There, among dead and dying comrades, he had accepted death as an occupational hazard. He did not welcome it but accepted it.

This was different.

There was nothing better for keeping a small town happy than a scandal, and they didn't come much juicier. It was one of the reasons why he'd left Heron Key all those years ago, to find someplace where people cared about ideas and world events, rather than just who stole whose milk cow back in 1895. *And who dallied with whose wife.*

He searched his memory for some reason why Dwayne would think he had done it. He couldn't recall ever speaking to Missus Campbell. It made no sense. And then came the realization that winded him like a punch: reason had nothing to do with it. If the deputy sheriff thought Henry was the father of his baby, all bets were off. A white man would have paid a heavy price. For a black man . . . there was no limit to the price he would pay.

Things suddenly fell into place: the smoldering looks from Dwayne, like he could barely control himself; the delight on his face when the bloody T-shirt was discovered at the camp.

Henry sat down heavily on the bench, more dispirited than at any time since his return, and stared at the stained concrete floor. There was a brown patch shaped like an eagle, its beak open, talons extended to skewer its prey. It made horrible, brutal sense.

This isn't about the attack on Missus Kincaid at all.

His boots didn't match the print they found. There was nothing to connect him to the attack. The bloody shirt was just an excuse to bring him in and get him alone. And he had walked right into the trap, high on happiness after his night with Missy. He might as well be the mouse, impaled on the eagle's claws.

Doc was wrong. The deputy is just another hick lawman who uses his badge to settle any old score.

Henry sunk his head in his hands. He had completely misjudged the situation, his normal defenses down. There would be much sympathy for Dwayne among the townspeople, who were already minded to blame the veterans for any trouble. Henry had heard what white mobs in Florida did to men like him. There was no worse crime, in their world. The jail's thick concrete walls would prevent any sounds from escaping into the street. *And that will be just the start of it.*

Nothing Henry said would make a damned bit of difference. There was no way to prove his innocence, nothing definitive that Dwayne would accept. And Henry had known plenty of decent men driven to savagery in extreme circumstances. He had seen them rip flesh from their enemies' bodies with bloody howls of joy. Good men who, when at home, would lift a grasshopper out of harm's way. Decency, he knew, was a veneer, hair-thin in places.

No, the idea had clearly caught light in Dwayne's mind and already burned too bright for Henry to extinguish. The only answer was to escape, to run, as he had so many times before. He would head north and be out of the state in a few days if he traveled by night.

From the next cell came a soft, malign chuckle.

Henry said, "Yeah, Ike, like you ain't up to your ass in it too."

Ike stuck his grizzled chin between the bars and leered. "You gonna burn, baby. You gonna burn."

Henry thought of Missy, of what they could have had together, what they could have built. He pictured the look on her face when she heard he had gone. It would mean the end of all his newly hatched plans. To have come so close to happiness, only to lose it over a damn fool deputy sheriff with a wayward wife was too much. His chest ached with the disappointment of it all. He became aware he was gasping for breath.

But wait . . . His heart lifted as he realized there was a simple answer. *She'll come with me, and we'll start a new life together, somewhere away from all this.* Yes, that was it. It would be hard for her, at first, to adjust to a new place, but he counted on the look he had seen in her eyes last night. And hadn't she said she wanted to do something with her life? Well, here was her chance, with him. He would show her the great cities of the north, maybe even go to France. He didn't care where they went, if they were together. What had seemed desperate and hopeless suddenly became bright with promise. His breath came more easily, and his vision cleared. There was still a chance, if he was smart enough. And lucky enough.

But first he needed to focus on the job at hand. His training came back to him, and he scouted the contours of the jail, looking for weaknesses, assessing his options. Jimmy eyed him curiously from across the room.

And Henry knew what he had to do.

Sometime later, Dwayne returned to the jail. He strode over to Henry's cell, where he stood quietly for a long moment. Henry's demeanor had changed completely while he was out. The relaxed confidence was gone and in its place was extreme wariness. Through narrowed eyes, Henry followed Dwayne's every move. A vein pulsed in his forehead.

Dwayne turned to Jimmy. "What's been going on here?"

"N-nothin', Uncle Dwayne."

Dwayne just raised an eyebrow and waited.

"Well," said Jimmy, "I just wanted to show you I can get people to tell me stuff too. So I told him . . ."

"You told him what?" Dwayne's voice had gone deep and quiet.

Jimmy straightened his cap, swallowed hard. His large Adam's apple bobbed. "I told him . . . I told him that people sayin' . . . they sayin' he's Roy's daddy."

Dwayne said to Jimmy, "I'll deal with you later. Bring him to my office, then go back to your momma." To Henry, he said, "You and me gonna have ourselves a little private talk."

Dwayne sat at his desk and shuffled some papers to calm his temper, collect his thoughts. On the way over from Doc's office, he had tried to make sense of what the evidence was telling him: that no boot had made the mark on Hilda's face and that Henry was not involved. There was still the matter of the bloody shirt, which had to be explained.

And as for the other business he had with Henry . . . He felt tired, just tired to his marrow. He was tired of the way Noreen flinched when he came near, tired of the whispers and knowing looks from people in town, tired of feeling like every step he took led him deeper into the swamp. He had been fighting to get at the truth of what Noreen had done. Now that he was so close to finding it, he wondered why he had bothered. What would he do, once he had the knowledge? How would it make things any better?

He felt much more in control this time. Things were clearer in his mind. Roberts would not get the better of him again.

He heard the heavy cell door creak open on rusty hinges, then slam shut. Henry said, "I don't feel so good."

"Come on," said Jimmy. He led Henry into the office, where he appeared to stumble. In a flash, Henry snatched the paper spike off the corner of the desk and pressed its vicious point hard against Jimmy's throat.

Dwayne was on his feet in an instant, hand

on his holster. "You idiot," he hissed. "What do you think —"

"Put your gun on the desk, Deputy. Slow now." Henry's eyes were wide but in control, his voice level. "I got no interest in hurting this boy, so don't make me." He jabbed the spike harder, his arm around Jimmy's neck. Jimmy yelped.

Dwayne obeyed. "Henry," he tried, "listen, you don't want to do this. I know you weren't involved in the attack on Missus Kincaid." He spread his hands. "We can work this out."

"Yeah, like they worked it out in Tallahassee, and Tampa? Like they did in Greenwood?" He began to shuffle back toward the door, still with Jimmy in his grip. "No offense, Deputy, but I'd rather take my chances in a swamp full of gators. Your key ring, please."

"Henry, you have my word. Just put the spike down and let Jimmy go. No harm will come to you. We'll forget all about this."

Dwayne thought back to their previous meeting, how he had come so close to beating Henry senseless, had wanted to with a desire akin to lust. He saw that Henry read his thoughts. In that moment, the argument was lost.

Henry said quietly, "Now, Deputy

Campbell, you and I both know that ain't so." He stuffed Dwayne's gun into his pocket. "Keys. Now. Give them to Jimmy. Now get into that cell over there."

And with that, he locked Dwayne into his own jail cell. Dwayne sat miserably on the bench.

Henry continued toward the front door. "Now, Jimmy, you gonna lock the door behind us, you understand?"

Jimmy's throat bulged against the spike. "Yes," he gasped, his eyes rolled back in terror.

"If you hurt him," said Dwayne, hands on the bars, "I swear —"

"He won't be hurt," said Henry. "I just need to borrow him for a spell. And your truck. Good-bye, Deputy Campbell."

He heard the cough of his truck's engine, followed by the scrape of tires as they drove away. Then there was silence. Dwayne was left alone with his thoughts, and Ike's gleeful cackle.

CHAPTER 16

It was that funny time of day when late afternoon turned to early evening. But there would be no colorful sunset tonight. Thick, dark clouds had been rolling in all day. An irritable wind had sprung up to worry the laundry on the line. Then came a series of miserable squalls, so Missy had moved Nathan inside. She rocked him and sang:

> Precious Lord, take my hand,
> Lead me on, let me stand,
> I am tired, I am weak, I am worn;
> Through the storm, through the night,
> Lead me on, to the light:
> Take my hand, precious Lord,
> Lead me home.

He seemed fascinated by her voice. His legs kicked and he stared at her mouth with those round blue eyes while she sang. She touched his nose with his favorite wooden elephant. He grabbed it from her hand and gummed the trunk. His teeth had started to come through, so that lately everything went into his mouth — seashells, driftwood, even Sam's bone. The dog had looked on in affronted confusion while Nathan chewed contentedly until Missy had whisked it away.

As a girl, she had always expected to have children one day. It was just what folks did. Then as she got older and more settled on her own, she had let go of that certainty with some sadness. It was just part of the bigger sadness of being alone. Over time, she had come to accept that there would always be other Nathans who needed her, and that would be her place.

"It ain't too late," she said to Nathan and wrestled the elephant from his grip. It was time for a bubble bath and then bed. Hopes she had long abandoned, things she had thought impossible, had come back into focus since Henry came home. It was like she had been looking through a dirty window for a long time. The glass was clean again. "Only too late when —"

Mama burst into the kitchen, hat askew and sweat on her upper lip. "They arrested Henry," she panted. "Dwayne brought him in from the camp, something about a bloody T-shirt they found in his cabin. People say he the one that —"

"Course he ain't, Mama!" Missy leaped from her chair. "We got to go down there and straighten this whole thing out." But she felt a weight land heavy on her heart. The arrest would be proof enough of his guilt for the kind of folks who already believed.

"Take Selma with you," said Mama as she collapsed into Missy's vacant chair. "I stay here with the baby. And, Missy," she said, "watch yourself. There's an ugly mood out there, and I ain't just talkin' about the weather."

Missy shuffled along beside Selma. The sky matched her thoughts: dark gray and heavy with rain. Why would God bring Henry back to her, only to snatch him away like this? Despite her brave words, she was scared for him. Mama was right about the mood in town. Folks on street corners stared at them as they passed, muttering behind their hands.

The weather got worse as they walked. The wind pulled at their skirts, sprayed sand on their bare legs. She studied Selma's profile. Everyone knew she practiced the old ways, with knowledge inherited from Grace. Just talking about such things would give Mama apoplexy. For her, there was the one true church, and all else was blasphemy. The devil's work. Still, she had to ask. "Selma, is there any way . . . is there anything you can do . . . I mean, can you . . . ?"

Selma said nothing, just trudged on. Then, very quietly, she said, "I brought him back once, and look how good that turned out. Got to work with man's law on this one."

A pickup truck appeared ahead, driving fast right toward them. Just before they jumped out of the way, it skidded to a stop in a cloud of dust. At the wheel was a young white man in a John Deere cap with a shocked, frightened expression, and Henry was on the passenger side, looking grimly determined.

"Missy!" he called. He took the keys from the ignition and jumped down. It was then she saw the gun in his hand. "Now just stay calm, Jimmy," he said, "and everything gonna be all right."

The white boy stared straight ahead, hands clenched on the wheel. Missy thought she saw his lip tremble.

"What's happened?" demanded Selma. "Where you get that gun?"

"They let you go?" Missy asked. She

didn't know what to think, filled with equal parts hope and dread.

"Not exactly," said Henry with a look over his shoulder. He was fairly humming with tension. "I ain't got time to explain. I got to leave. Now. Missy, you trust me?" he asked, more seriously than she had ever seen him.

His eyes were focused on hers. They were filled with desperate longing, deep as the sea. She nodded. "Yes, but —"

"Then come with me. We'll go away together, anywhere you want. Start over. You can go to college, or do whatever —"

"Wait, I cain't think!" For years she had dreamed of something like this, but it was not how it should be. His excitement had the metallic shine of desperation, like the gun in his hand. The boy at the wheel of the truck seemed turned to stone. It was wrong, all of it — every part of her body said so. Yet he stood there in front of her, Henry, saying these things. His words came too fast; she needed more time.

"Missy," he said with yet more urgency and another look over his shoulder. "I explain everything once we away from here, but we got to go *now.* You comin' with me?"

Her whole life, the things that felt so solid and kept her tethered to the earth were all in Heron Key. Without them, how would she live? Wouldn't she just float up and away, to be lost forever? *But I be with Henry. He keep me safe.* She squeezed her eyes shut tight but could not picture it. It was not real. This was real, this dusty street lined with familiar stores, and their little house, and the beach, and . . . "What about Mama? And Selma? What about Nathan? I got to say good-bye. I got to get a bag —"

"Don't you see, Missy?" He was trying to smile but only managed an ugly grimace, which turned him into a stranger. "We ain't got time for any of that. You got to come right now, as you are. Missy, *please.*"

She stood still. "Why? Why we need to go like this?"

"You know what they think I done," he said, close to her ear. "All of it. I ain't waitin' around for their so-called justice. I got no choice, Missy. I got to run. You got no idea, no idea what they'll do to me if I stay."

They had attracted the attention of a small knot of people, storekeepers and customers, drawn outside by the commotion. Henry shoved the gun in his pocket. She had never seen him so afraid. The acrid sweat of fear dripped from his face. "But how this gonna help?" She gestured at the truck. "If you run, they just say it's 'cause you guilty. And takin' a white boy with you? That just gonna make it worse. You always sayin' things won't change till we change 'em. Stay — stay and fight."

"I cain't win, Missy," he said with a dejected shake of his head. "Not this fight."

A group of men left the barbershop and strode in their direction, frowns all around. Henry said, "We got to — I got to go, right now. Come with me. Please."

She tried to reach out for him. If she could just touch him, maybe he would see there was another way. But Selma's arm went around her shoulders, as much to hold her back as to support her. "He right, Missy," she said. "He got to go. Let him go."

"No, wait, don't go, please." It was all happening too fast. A minute before, her biggest worry was him being in jail. Now she realized this might be the last time she ever saw him. Tears of frustration and loss scorched her eyes. "If you run, if you go, like this," she said as she strained against Selma's arm, sobs choking her voice, "you won't never be able to show your face here again. Never."

"I know," he said, but he was already turning away from her. "I sorry, Missy. I so sorry."

And then he was gone. The truck headed

off just as the clouds released their burden. She watched the pickup until it disappeared behind the heavy curtain of rain. Fat raindrops splashed down her face, but they were not enough to wash away the tears. Not nearly enough.

Henry held Dwayne's revolver to Jimmy's side as they made their way up the coast road. The truck's engine coughed and slowed. "Keep drivin'," he said.

"Wh-what you gonna do to me?" Sweat darkened Jimmy's collar. His voice was hoarse with fear, and his cap drooped forlornly. The dashboard lit his face with a sickly glow.

"Don't talk."

Rain spattered the windshield and mixed with the dust on the glass. The coast road brought them alongside the camp. He would not be able to stop to say his good-byes, but at least he could see the place one more time, imagine his boys in the mess hall with their first beer of the evening. They thought he was in jail, which was bad enough, but not as bad as being on the run. Yet more people he had let down . . . He thought of their familiar faces, creased with confusion and worry when they heard what he had done. As the truck passed the camp, the wind carried to him the sound of laughter from the mess hall.

What am I doing? Leaving all this behind? He wondered if Missy was right, if he could have stayed and argued it out. She seemed so certain, but she had not seen the homicidal glint in the deputy's eyes. He was a man barely in control of himself — Henry had seen enough of them in his time to recognize that look — and it would only take the tiniest excuse to push him over. Had Jimmy not been there to intervene, Henry might already be just a smear on the jail cell wall.

He wanted to think that he would make it up to them, to Missy, to all of them — one day. But deep inside, he knew it was the last time he would see Heron Key. He had an infinite capacity to accept disappointment and despair, built up over long and bitter experience, but hope — hope fairly ripped the heart out of him. For a brief moment, Missy had given him hope.

Of all the journeys he had been forced to make, this one was the hardest. He had always been in a hurry to leave places, to keep going, always in motion. But now all he wanted to do was stay. It had not been long since he returned to Heron Key, compared to how long he was away, but the place held on to him with a grip of steel. The only way to wrench himself free was to leave the best part of himself behind. And that, he decided, was where it belonged.

"Where to?" asked Jimmy.

"North," said Henry. He had never felt so weary in his life. "Just north."

Trent's day had started so well. Roberts was in custody and the other men were subdued. They had gone off meekly to work that morning, leaving him free to catch up on paperwork. Things were under control again, just as he liked them to be. He had allowed himself a sigh of satisfaction and a fresh cigar.

Then the weather deteriorated. The rain blew in sideways. The storm flags were out, which replaced the lanterns during the day. They crackled in the stiff wind. And then Jenson Mitchell had called again to advise Trent that the storm was now officially classed a hurricane, although still not predicted to hit Heron Key.

"Mr. Watts, you have to get your men out of here," he had said. "They're very exposed. If —"

"But, Mr. Mitchell, you've just said it's not headed here." He stared at the rotting canvas roof of the cabin. A spider had built

285

a nest in the frame. Out of the fluffy white ball would soon pour hundreds of tiny beasts, rushing to infest his gear, trail across his face while he slept. *God, I hate this place. This ain't purgatory. It's hell.* He fried the spider's nest with the end of his cigar. Mitchell's calm, soft-spoken voice nearly drove him crazy.

"Whatever the weather center says, my bet is on the barometer. I've never seen it drop so fast. I urge you to get the men out. Just think of the potential consequences."

Trent had done little else since mid-afternoon. The sky was a washed-out non-color he had never seen before, a kind of yellowish gray. The wind seemed to blow hard from several directions at once. The surf was a disorganized mess of brown and white. "I can't order an evacuation based on your gut, Mr. Mitchell, but I will confer with my superiors. Good day to you."

His first conversation with Norbert Grimes up in Jacksonville had not gone well, and he did not relish a second. Yes, the sky looked strange and angry, but that could just mean the daily downpour was on its way. Trent had become accustomed to them. Towering thunderheads of darkest purple would barrel in, deluge them for a few minutes, and the steamy sunshine would return. It could simply be more of the same.

Before the war, where he spent several weeks in a freezing trench, Trent had always thought of himself as a cold weather man. As a boy, he felt more alive during the winter than any other time of year, like he was energized from the inside out. The crack of falling ice, the swish of his sled, the deep, total silence of falling snow, more quiet than anything in the world . . . these were his favorite sounds.

That all changed during the winter in France. For a time, he had ceased to remember what it was to be warm, that there even was such a thing as warm. He lost three toes to frostbite and would have lost more if his tour of duty had not ended. The Heron Key contract had seemed just the thing for his scarred old body. A tropical sojourn was just what he needed, with palm trees, clear water, white sand, and friendly local women with suntanned faces.

He scratched at the mosquito bites on his arm. It seemed that the local insects found him a lot tastier than the women did. They regarded him as no different from the veterans, whom they considered to be dangerous drunks and criminals. He realized that his bald head and armfuls of tattoos might not help, but he still resented being lumped in together with the crazy sons of bitches under his supervision.

The phone rested on his desk like a genie's lamp. How to make it work for him? How could he communicate to Grimes, up in the civilized world, what life was like on Heron Key? How precarious it was, on this little spit of land, barely above sea level? He doubted that Grimes had ever considered it, from the vantage of his safe, hygienic metropolis. And what if Mitchell was right and the storm did devastate the camp? Whose name would forever be associated with it? Not Norbert Grimes. He picked up the phone. The remains of his lunch curdled in his gut.

It was clear from Grimes's tone of voice that he was less than thrilled to hear from Trent again, probably because he was preparing to head to the golf course. "You can see my position," Grimes said. "It's a helluva lot of egg on my face if it turns out to be a false alarm. Like last time." The sound became muffled as Grimes covered the receiver. "Be right with you, Bill!"

Trent stifled a groan of frustration. Grimes was an administrator, had never been in the field, but he did happen to be married to the governor's daughter.

Trent knew all too well about "last time" and why Grimes had brought up the incident from the past. It was too good an opportunity for him to pass up. It had taken place a few weeks after the veterans' camp was set up. Most of them had no experience of the tropics, Trent included, but all knew enough to fear the deadly yellow fever. It was impossible to avoid the mosquitoes, which swarmed so densely at dusk that they resembled earthbound rain clouds. The men were all alert to the symptoms: flu-like fever and bloody vomit, followed by the classic yellowing of the skin that signaled liver failure. It was so highly contagious that it could take hold of the camp within a day or two.

So when Mo Hendricks, an infantryman from Chicago, collapsed and died a few days later with those very symptoms, Trent had been straight on the phone to Grimes to request an evacuation. Grimes was not convinced and ordered a postmortem, and the conclusion was that Hendricks had died of acute alcoholism. Ever since, Trent had been tainted by Grimes's insinuations that he was liable to panic.

Having survived a year in the trenches of France, panic was the last thing that Trent was liable to do. He could barely prevent the resentment from seeping into his voice. He had withstood the most extreme circumstances ever, and never, not once, had he panicked. Not even when, stranded for three days in a flooded shell hole, he had eaten the rats that came to feast on his dead comrades. *I wonder how long Norbert would have lasted there.*

Grimes's exasperated sigh trickled into Trent's ear. He just imagined the man's longing look at his golf clubs, anticipating his first cocktail of the evening. Grimes asked, "Trent, what does the weather forecast say?"

"It's a hurricane now, for sure. Looks like it will hit north of here but could still —"

"So if it's going to hit elsewhere," asked Grimes, "why the panic?" Trent dug his fingers into the wood of the desk to stop himself shouting. Grimes continued, "Try to look at it from my point of view."

That would be from the fifteenth hole, I guess? Trent took a deep breath and decided to make one more attempt — and document the conversation in his log. It was all he could do. "Mr. Grimes, I'm not panicking. It won't take more than a stiff breeze to flatten the camp, much less a bad storm. Hell, the water comes right up to the perimeter sometimes at high tide. The locals

290

have seen telltale clouds, and the barometer keeps falling. We need you to order the train now —"

"And by the time it arrives," said Grimes, "this whole thing could have blown over, and not only will we have wasted taxpayers' money, but we'll look like idiots who got suckered in by the local folklore. Keep me informed, Trent. I've been advised that we can get those boys out of there in three hours if we need to."

Easy for you to say, 370 miles away. "Yes, Mr. Grimes."

Trent hung up the phone and stared at nothing for a moment. He was not a believer in much of anything, not fate, or destiny, or even God. But he felt himself in the grip of something huge, some force of incredible strength. As a boy, he had once lost control of his sled on an icy hill and tumbled helplessly, over and over, completely at gravity's mercy. He opened his log on the desk and checked his watch. *1730 hours,* he wrote. *I spoke to Mr. Grimes and advised him of the deteriorating weather situation . . .*

Down at his shack in the mangroves, Zeke was frantic. He spun around the little room so jerkily that even Poncho could not maintain his grip. The bird perched on the

291

back of a spindly wooden chair to clean his feathers.

Zeke felt the monster's breath. It blew hot on his neck. He could hear its roar. *Not far away now.* He would remain at his post. He would defend the town to his last heartbeat. But a warrior needed a weapon.

He had found it in the drainage pipe after yesterday's big rain, covered in weeds and mud. Although it was broken and stained, he sensed it still had power inside. He had seen the way the rich folks treasured such weapons.

He took it by the handle now and swished it experimentally through the air a few times, as he had seen the folks in white do it. The air made a satisfying *hum* sound through the sagging strings.

He would need all the power left in his weapon. As darkness spread across the sky, he saw it: two red lights appeared up the coast. The monster had opened its eyes.

CHAPTER 17

Jenson dumped a heavy sack of potatoes in the back room of the store and stretched his tired muscles. The sounds of preparation could be heard all over town: windows being boarded up, shutters secured, loose objects and animals stowed away, supplies gathered into shelters. Water had been decanted from the cisterns, as it would get contaminated even if they did not blow over. His store had sold out of candles and matches and most of the canned goods. If the storm was bad — and he grimaced at the hopefulness of that "if" — it could be days before they got any fresh food in. The Coast Guard's hurricane warning buoys had started to wash up on shore, dropped to alert islanders and boaters. The marina had emptied out overnight. The boat owners with any sense had fled to safer moorings by now.

He and Trudy had almost finished their

work. The store would serve as the main shelter for the town, as it had so many times before. They had moved most of the stock to the back room to create as much space as possible.

As he unpacked their old lanterns, he could not get his last conversation with Trent Watts out of his mind. He had clearly failed to persuade the superintendent of the threat. How could he communicate to someone who had never experienced a hurricane what it was like? How it could tear your home to pieces, snatch your loved ones right out of your arms? How it could throw cars and trees around like they were toys?

The barometer's descent had begun again, faster than he had ever seen it. But they were ready, he felt. The tidy interior of the store reassured him. It had served them well in the past. There was no reason to believe that this time would be any different. Fred was still confident the storm was in no hurry and would come ashore well to the north of Heron Key. Jenson had done everything possible to prepare. So why then could he not shake the feeling, deep in his bones, that it was not enough? And that this time would be very, very different?

Trudy deposited another box of canned pears. She straightened, hands braced against the small of her back. "You think we're ready?"

"Yes, we are . . ." The image of the veteran's camp lurked in his head, the men going about their normal routine with no earthly idea of what was bearing down on them — and soon, according to the barometer.

"Tell me," she said and took a seat on a sack of cornmeal.

"I can't help thinking about them . . . the veterans." His eyes toured the store again, calculating. "Do you think — ?"

"No, we do not have room for them here. There isn't room in the town for that number of men, not with hundreds of locals. And, Son" — her tone softened — "even if we did, you can't have men like that cooped up with women and children for hours on end."

"I guess you're right." He sighed. "It's just that —"

"There are plenty of people, official people, who have responsibility for them. It's their job to see them right, not yours. Now come on," she said as she stood up and stretched. "We got enough to do already without spending time worrying about a bunch of" — she hesitated, searched for the right word — "people, who by rights shouldn't even be here." She studied his face closely. "There's something else?"

"You've been through a lot of these storms," he said. "Anything feel . . . different to you?" He could rationalize the feeling away in any number of ways: that Fred had the most accurate information, from shipping and spotter planes, and that Heron Key's preparations had always seen them through the storms of the past. But his gut did not agree. There was something different this time, and he had no idea why. It was completely indefinable. It pinged around in his head like a bead of mercury each time he tried to get a fix on it. It was telling him, in his most primitive core, below the level of conscious thought, that he should do just one thing, and quickly: *run.* Just *run.*

She shrugged. "Can't say so, not really. The worst ones come when it's hottest, and it's plenty hot now. But I trust your gut, Jenson, more than anything Fred has to say. What's it telling you?"

He thought for a moment about how to answer.

No one's interests were served by a panic. His mother had never been susceptible to that. So he looked at her steadily and said, "This may be worse than we thought."

■ ■ ■ ■

Trent surveyed the camp at dusk. Although the wind blew hard enough to ripple the cabin walls, it did nothing to freshen the air. He had ordered the heavy equipment at the bridge site to be weighed down with concrete rubble. If the storm was anything like the twisters of his childhood, there was no telling what could take to the sky.

He had left yet another message for Norbert Grimes, to say that a relief train was now urgently needed. Grimes had not returned his call. Trent's eye traveled over the flimsy structures of the camp. Waves already dampened the cabins closest to the surf line, which advanced much faster than a normal tide. Trent had done all he could. A delivery of fresh water had arrived at the station and awaited transfer into the storage tanks. He would deal with that later. His priority was to get the men out of Heron Key . . . and he just might not come back. He was tired, tired of the heat, and the rain, and the mosquitoes, and the Conchs. He was tired of the stinking latrines, the lousy food, and the petty annoyances that kept the men in a constant state of agitation. He was tired of being told what to do. Yes, the money was okay — and he had to admit that any money in the current economic situation was a blessing — but he figured there had to be less miserable ways to make a living. The only thing that raised his spirits was the knowledge that Henry Roberts was locked up.

The waves deposited a line of dirty foam at his feet. Sand stung his face. *So much for the tropical paradise.* More than anything, he yearned for the vast, empty plains of Kansas, nothing but open fields stretching to the vast blue horizon. There, a man could see weather coming a long, long way off. He ground his cigar into the damp sand and went back to his cabin to complete his log for the day — and make another phone call.

About ten miles south of Miami, Henry and Jimmy stopped for the night. Their progress had been slow on the little back roads, and Henry had intended to continue while it was dark. But after he fell asleep and woke with a start to find Jimmy had pulled over, he realized the need for rest could not be ignored.

The truck was parked under the spreading branches of a huge old oak tree. Gray clumps of Spanish moss gave it a forlorn, unkempt look but effectively hid them from the road.

"Uncle Dwayne be real mad at you," said Jimmy around a mouthful of sandwich. "You in big, big trouble." Just before dusk, they had found a food store that served coloreds. Henry bought some dried-out sandwiches and bottles of warm Pepsi-Cola for them.

"Yeah." Henry slurped from his bottle. "I had worked that out." The sweet, fizzy liquid soothed his parched throat. They had not stopped since leaving Heron Key, not even to piss. He had made Jimmy hold it until he was sure they hadn't been followed. They sat in darkness to conserve the truck's battery and remain invisible.

"When you gonna let me go?" Jimmy asked for about the fifteenth time. The boy's voice had a whiny, fretful edge that ran along Henry's nerves like a cheese grater.

"Georgia. I'll let you go when we get to Georgia." He glared at Jimmy. "Or, if you ask me again, the answer is Kentucky."

All afternoon, the sky behind them had continued to blacken as they made their way north. When Henry looked back, all he could see was a curtain of dark purple clouds that stretched right down to the ground. The rain had followed them. It tapped with insistent fingers on the roof of the cab. The wind moaned softly through the old tree's branches and made them creak and sway. Henry thought he'd never heard a more mournful sound.

Jimmy gave him a sideways glance. "So I guess you is Roy's daddy after all. Otherwise, you wouldn'ta run."

"No, Jimmy, I ain't." There was no moon. No stars shone through the thick foliage above. The darkness was complete. Henry felt suspended in time and place. He figured the only way to shut Jimmy up was to tell him what he wanted to know. And what did it matter, anyway? Once they got to Georgia, he would never see Jimmy again.

"But you did beat up Missus Kincaid, didn't ya?"

"Nope."

"Then why you run? Why the hell we here?" Jimmy's voice was thick with exasperated confusion. He smacked the dashboard with his fists. "Ow."

"Because, Jimmy, what I did, or didn't do, ain't the point. Only thing folks care about is what they think I did."

"But Uncle Dwayne ain't like that! He a good man, really —"

"All men is animals inside, Jimmy. Best you learn that lesson fast. Some just have thicker hides than others. And when they get angry, well, they capable of anything. And I do mean *anything.*" He could feel Jimmy listening intently. Somewhere close by, a peacock cried. It always sounded to Henry like a woman's scream. "I seen it myself, in the war, so many times. And what was that you told me about your uncle? How he beats on your aunt Noreen?"

"Yeah, but —"

"You saw what happened at the jail, Jimmy. Would you have stuck around, in my shoes? Truth, now."

Jimmy said nothing, just stared into the darkness beyond the windshield. Henry could almost hear the wheels and cogs turn inside the boy's head.

"He ain't been himself since Roy came along. But it cain't be as bad as you say. You trying to trick me. Uncle Dwayne said you was tricky."

Henry stretched his cramped limbs and yawned. He would have to let Jimmy go soon, for his own safety. The temptation to beat some sense into his thick head was very strong, but he had promised Campbell not to hurt the boy. "Go to sleep now. We can probably make it to Jacksonville tomorrow."

"I cain't sleep, not like this."

"Okay, then watch me sleep. And just to make sure there's no funny business . . ."

301

He locked their wrists together with Dwayne's handcuffs.

"Aw, c'mon, you don't have to do that!"

"Good night, Jimmy."

In a few minutes, he heard the boy's deep sleep breathing. Henry thought of Missy, safe in the shelter of Mitchell's store, surrounded by family and friends. They would tell her what she needed to hear: that he had to go, that she was better off without him, that he would always be in trouble of some kind. It was no life for someone as special as Missy. She would find someone who would treat her well, someone she could rely on. And she would forget about her old friend Henry. *She is better off without me.*

He thought of his boys, settling into their bunks for the night. After their experience in the war, nature held no fear for them, but they had never seen what a hurricane could do. Trent Watts might be sadistic and cruel at times, but he could not be accused of stupidity. He must have organized a way to get the men out of the storm's path. There would be no room for them to shelter in town, even if the townspeople had been willing to spend hours at such close quarters with them. Given the state of the weather, he figured the evacuation train must already be on its way. In a few hours, they would be enjoying themselves in Miami. *Good luck to you, boys. We meet again someday.*

As for his own future, the only option was to put as much distance as possible between himself and Heron Key. He would figure out the rest later. Missy's face appeared to him, her eyes bright with tears.

Suddenly overwhelmed by the magnitude of his loss and frustration at the pointless ruination of his hopes, he wanted to smash up the truck until it was nothing but twisted metal. What had he said to Jimmy? *All men are animals.* With that thought, he fell into a deeply troubled sleep . . .

. . .and dreamed he was back at the bridge site, working with the boys to sink the huge pylons into the sandy soil. Everyone was there, even Li'l Joe, Sammy, and Tyrone, dead all these years. They laughed in the sunshine, heads thrown back, and moved the huge chunks of concrete around as if they were cardboard props in a play. Their strength was limitless. They could finish the bridge in a few hours, and then they would stride across the land to the next task, Paul Bunyan–style. Heroes all, just as they had hoped.

But then the earth just collapsed under them, like a sinkhole big as Lake Okeecho-bee. It opened up and sucked them down into a huge, dark emptiness, and their laughter turned to screams. It was like the screams he had heard often in the war, born of a terror so pure that it produced sounds almost unrecognizable as human.

He jerked awake. The sound was inside the cab with him. He had slumped against the truck's window. A layer of sweat adhered his face to the glass. He looked across at Jimmy, whose mouth was open, his eyes stretched wide. Henry followed his stare. The soft, slanting light of early morning shone on a pair of naked legs dangling from one of the branches that arched over the truck. Some of the toes were missing. The body's face was hidden up in the gloom of the tree. It must have been there, gently turning in the breeze, while they slept, oblivious, so dark was the night.

A group of five white men arrived and stood beneath the carcass, gazing with interest at the truck.

"Shut up, Jimmy! Shut up!" Henry ordered. Jimmy ceased screaming, but it looked like he might cry. Henry's sleepy brain struggled to make sense of the situation. Hysterics from Jimmy would not help. "This is what we have to do. Jimmy, listen to me." The boy swallowed. His Adam's apple juddered. His hands shook. "I'm your prisoner, Jimmy. You're taking me to Miami, on instructions from the deputy sheriff. You got to make them believe, Jimmy. If you do this, I will let you go as soon as we're clear of them."

There was no response. Henry unlocked the cuffs. "Jimmy, you're okay. You've had a shock. Nod if you can hear me. And breathe, just breathe."

Jimmy nodded, but his hands continued to shake, his eyes fixed on the body that turned gently in the wind.

"Can you do this, Jimmy? Tell me now." Henry's hand was on Dwayne's gun.

Jimmy exhaled. "Yes, I can do this." He breathed loudly through his mouth. "I can. Do this."

Henry considered briefly whether to trust the boy, then quickly decided it was beside the point. But just in case, he prepared to move into the driver's seat. "Here, put the cuffs in your pocket. Make it look official. And take this." He handed the gun to Jimmy.

The boy looked at the gun for a long moment. His resolve seemed to falter. "Uncle Dwayne never let me touch his gun. I only ever used my daddy's shotgun for hunting deer. I ain't never fired a pistol. Like as not, I'll end up shooting myself."

"You carry a gun so you don't have to fire it. Remember what I told you: it's not what you do but what people think you do. You just gotta look like you could shoot the buttons off their shirts. Wait." He removed Jimmy's John Deere cap. "That's better."

Jimmy took a pinch of chewing tobacco from the glove compartment and shoved it in his gum and jumped down from the cab. He looked so young. *We are dead. This is never going to work.* But then he left the truck and approached the group of men with a swagger that was pure Uncle Dwayne, thumbs hooked in his belt loops, gun stuffed in his pocket. *I should have removed the bullets. He's going to blow his foot off.*

Jimmy strode into the group with a big smile and shook hands all around. A long conversation ensued, none of which Henry could hear properly. The men regarded Jimmy with guarded expressions as they stood casually beneath the hideous form in the tree. They barely glanced at Henry. He might as well have been luggage. Henry cast his eyes to the floor of the cab and hunched his shoulders in a posture of surrender. The image of the mutilated feet stayed in his head. Trails of blood wound around the legs like black worms.

More muffled conversation. Henry sneaked a quick peek. Jimmy's head was up, his shoulders back. He laughed at something and clapped one of the men on the shoulder. *Don't push your luck.* They looked like people at a normal social gathering. Jimmy's hand rested comfortably on the gun. He spat liberally on the ground.

After more shoulder slapping and handshaking, Jimmy made his way back to the truck with a fond wave. His grin looked like it had been carved into his face. He waved some more to his new friends as they drove away. It was several miles before he spoke. All he said was, "I need a drink."

With no hope of finding a liquor store at that hour, he had to make do with strong coffee from a diner. Since they could not be served in the same establishment, Jimmy brought the steaming cups out to the truck. The waitress watched suspiciously from the window, hands on hips.

"You did it, Jimmy," said Henry after a gulp of the bitter liquid. He tried to banish the thought that it tasted of someone else's saliva. "Your uncle woulda been proud of you. Thank you." The homey smell of coffee filled the cab, which only increased his sense of unreality. Here, just a few miles away, it was a normal morning, where people did normal things. They drank coffee, had breakfast, went to work. Meanwhile, not far away, a vision of horror swung from an old tree.

Jimmy said nothing, just gripped his coffee cup as if he needed the warmth, although his freckled cheeks were shiny with sweat. He was most likely still in shock, Henry figured, and not only because of what he had seen, but also because of what it meant. Henry knew how it felt to have his certainties, those treasured things he believed to be true, yanked from under him. The boy would need time to adjust to that loss.

Henry's own pulse was still ragged. When his eyes had first flown open, for a fraction of a second, he had thought the legs of the slowly turning corpse were his own, that he had somehow become a bystander at his own death. It would not have surprised him, as he had felt fate's soft wings brush against him many times. But this time was close, closer than ever before. Had he not run from Heron Key when he did . . . A chill passed through his body, like a cold jolt of electricity, as he took in the full realization of what might have happened. The murderous fire in Dwayne's eyes had stayed with him. The memory remained undimmed with every mile they traveled.

Jimmy cleared his throat. "They said — they said they had come to harvest, that he was just about — ripe. Been there five days." Jimmy's voice was dull and flat with none of the youthful squeakiness. "One of them said — he said he wanted a toe. As a souvenir. For his granddaughter." He slurped his coffee. "When they saw me, with the cuffs and the gun, they thought I was there to . . . interfere. But I told them I was just passing through, not interested in anyone's business but mine. They wanted to know . . . they wanted to know what I planned to do." He eyed Henry askance. "With you. Asked if I needed any . . . assistance."

Henry was acutely aware of the danger they had faced during those few long minutes. The thought struck him that Jimmy was probably safer, at that moment, with an escaped black prisoner than with his own kind. For those locals to carry out a murder so brazen, they must have had no fear of the law. Jimmy had been very, very lucky to pull it off. Henry studied him. Jimmy's face was different, not as soft as before. "Do you really think they bought it?"

Jimmy turned toward him and Henry saw that his eyes had aged overnight. There was a new, sad seriousness in the lines around his mouth. "Yeah, I think so. Yeah."

"What did he . . . What did they think he'd done?"

"Raped a white girl." Jimmy stared through the windshield again, like he could still see it. "Maybe. They weren't real clear about that. Henry," he said as he threw the dregs of his coffee out the window, "you were right. Let's get outta here."

They made the outskirts of Miami at midday, following the railway tracks, by which time hunger demanded another stop. There was a store near the depot with some black men at the window lined up to buy food. Jimmy swung the truck around and Henry joined the line. He had not asked again when Henry would release him but seemed content to just keep driving.

Two men in overalls stood at the front of the line. One of them nodded. "Howdy."

Henry nodded back. A harassed old woman was busy dispensing food for their lunch pails through the open window. "You together?" asked Henry.

"Yeah," said the man, "but don't worry, we'll leave some for you." His eyes took in

Henry's gaunt frame in its dingy clothes. "Plenty left, ya see? Hey, Moses," he said. "What time you make it?"

His companion squinted at the sky. Dark, fast-moving clouds obscured the sun. It felt like early evening rather than afternoon. "Time we be gone, Clarence. Got to make the Keys before the storm."

"Where you fellas headed?" asked Henry.

"Going down to pick up some army boys, ya see?" asked Clarence. He scuffed his boot in the dirt. "Was supposed to see my gal in Lakeland, but they pulled me in for this instead."

Henry had started to understand that "ya see?" wasn't really a question. It was Clarence's way of ending a thought. But he needed to know more. "Did you say army boys? In the Keys? Whereabouts?"

"We got to make a few stops, ya see?" asked Clarence. "The last stop is the bird one, can never remember the name. Raven? Pelican? Moses, you remember — ?"

"Heron?" asked Henry.

"That the one," said Moses. "Some asshole up in J'ville thinks you can get a relief train down there in three hours. Gonna take that long just to get her juiced up. Train shoulda been sent yesterday. We got to get in and out fast, and this shitty weather won't help." He shut his lunch pail. "Thank you, ma'am. Come on, Clarence."

Henry looked over at the truck where Jimmy waited, eyebrow raised quizzically. He pointed to his watch, clearly keen to be off. They had made good time through the morning. It should be possible to get most of the way to Georgia by morning. He would be free. Safe and free. He could start again, somewhere fresh, where no one knew anything about his past, or the veterans, or Heron Key. He could go back to France. He could go anywhere. He was free. He should have been looking forward, toward a new life somewhere. But all he could do was look back, toward the black horizon.

He imagined them — Jeb, Franklin, Lemuel, Sonny — waiting patiently for rescue while the storm bore down on them. He imagined Missy in the shelter. He had abandoned her to face its fury on her own. He thought of the clearing, with the old oak tree and the horrible fruit hanging from its branch. And he thought of Dwayne's face, teeth bared in rage, his fist pulled back to strike.

And then it hit him like a physical blow, the realization that had been growing since they left Heron Key: the farther north they traveled, the less free he felt. It was like he was attached to the place by a long rubber band that was now stretched to its absolute limit. Missy had reminded him that things would only change when folks decided to change them. She was right. Yes, there were risks for him back in Heron Key, from the storm and the law, but finally he understood. He had left his people behind. Without them, he could never be truly free. Risks didn't matter at this point. Choices mattered. And there was really only one.

"Is there any chance," he asked Moses, "you could take a passenger?"

CHAPTER 18

Down in Heron Key, Dwayne went to his favorite thinking spot at the beach. Eventually he had managed to raise the alarm, and someone got the spare keys from Noreen. IIe could not meet her eyes when she opened the cell door, nor Ike's when he released him. Ronald wouldn't like it, but Dwayne would deal with him after the storm had passed. The beach was the only place where he could avoid the smirks and questions, the only place where he could clear his head. He sat at the same old, scarred picnic table he always used. It didn't matter about the weather. He needed to calm his thoughts, which were as jumbled as the flotsam washing onto the sand.

There was little time left. Ronald and his cronies would be at the country club by now, organizing their action against Henry. It almost made him smile to imagine their surprise when they found out he was long gone. Dwayne had done his duty and reported the escape to police upstate, but he was under no obligation to inform the likes of Ronald.

There was another, darker reason why he had told no one in town. It was partly that his damaged pride hurt worse than a jellyfish sting — he should have been prepared for Henry to make a move — but there was some part of him that wanted Henry to get away, wanted to deny Ronald his vengeance. Nothing Dwayne had done would change the outcome anyway. It was only a matter of time. A white boy with a middle-aged black man would not be hard to spot.

His mood darkened to match the dirty-looking clouds. Milky gray waves heaved themselves onto the shore. He had wasted precious time chasing a phantom. He had no other leads, and now a damned hurricane was about to destroy any chance he had of finding them. Hilda's attacker would certainly be gone once the storm was over, if he was even still around. The chaos of the cleanup would be the perfect cover for someone wanting to disappear. And from the look of the sky, they did not have long to wait. The storm had come much quicker than Jenson had predicted.

He had failed, for the first time in his

career. It might cost him his job. It would definitely cost him respect in the community. He could easily imagine the *Heron Key Bugle*'s headline: WORST CRIME IN RECENT MEMORY GOES UNSOLVED. But he did not see what else he could have done. His only choice was to accept it, take the responsibility and the consequences.

But still he sat there as the palm trees started to shake and crackle in the wind and the rain spattered his shoulders. Wind-whipped sand stung his face. Yet still he sat there, pondering. The answer was there in his head, he could feel it, just out of reach. With his pocketknife, he carved the pattern of marks from Hilda's face into the table's weathered surface. The scratch of the knife on the wood was like a chick pecking at the inside of an egg. The answer was there, so close; he just needed to focus and think harder.

But his concentration was disrupted by strange sounds from down the beach. It was only Zeke, yelling at the sky as usual. He was always very agitated when a storm was on the way. Dwayne squinted in the strange, hazy yellow twilight. Usually Zeke just shook his fists, but today there was something in his hand. A big stick . . . no, not a stick. It had a rounded head. Zeke

316

swiped it through the air like he was playing a game against an invisible opponent.

Suddenly Dwayne realized what Zeke held in his hand. He looked again at the marks he had carved into the table, then leaped to his feet and ran toward the figure in the water.

As he approached Zeke's shack, he slowed. Zeke was easily spooked, especially in this state. The wind whisked most of Zeke's words away toward the mangrove swamp, but it was clear from the wild swings of the tennis racket that he was very upset. Waves lapped at his scabby knees. He wore only his usual frayed shorts, almost more hole than fabric. Ribs poked through the thin skin of his chest, which was dotted with tufts of white hair that matched his beard. Poncho was perched on a rotten piling nearby, feathers aflutter, eyes narrowed against the wind.

"Zeke," called Dwayne. "Can I see that?"

"It's my weapon! I got him on the run!" He flailed the racket at the sky. "Be gone, cocksucker, back to the hell you came from!"

The frame of the racket's head was broken. A section of it flopped each time Zeke swished it through the air, but there was no mistaking the distinctive crosshatch pattern of the strings.

"It's broke, Zeke. Give it here. I can fix it, make it work better."

Zeke paused. His breath came in ragged gasps. "You can . . . you can do that?"

"Think so. Give it here."

Zeke handed him the racket with some reluctance. Dwayne fitted the broken edges of the frame together. There were brownish stains in the grain of the wood. And on the base of the grip, the letters *DM*, written in fuchsia nail polish. "Where did you find this, Zeke?"

Zeke tried to snatch the racket. He was surprisingly quick, but Dwayne was quicker. "Give it back," Zeke demanded. "Cain't you see? It's almost . . . here." He rasped this out in a hoarse whisper, which Dwayne could barely hear over the noise of the wind. Zeke's eyes bulged and spittle whitened the corners of his mouth.

"Tell me where you found it." Dwayne raised the racket out of Zeke's reach.

"You said . . ." He made a grab for it and missed. "You said you'd fix it for me!"

"Where, Zeke, tell me where!" He was yelling now, partly to make himself heard over the wind, partly from frustration.

Zeke ceased his leaping and seemed to deflate. His bloodshot eyes darted fearfully toward the horizon, as if he could see something there, something vast and terrible. "In the storm drain," he said. "After the big rain."

It fit. That drain was fed by a ditch that ran alongside the road where Hilda was attacked. It all fit. A woman. Why hadn't he thought of that? Someone who played as much tennis as Dolores Mason could bring considerable strength to bear on such an object. She also had plenty of reason to want Hilda off the scene. He could have kissed Zeke at that moment. "I need to take this to the workshop, but I'll bring it back soon."

"No!" screamed Zeke with such vehemence that Dwayne turned back. "Give it to me," Zeke begged. "Please. I need it."

These were the most coherent words he had ever heard from Zeke. For a brief moment, the man's eyes were lucid and clear. It made Dwayne wonder about the person he used to be.

But the racket's insistent weight in his hand demanded his full attention. He sloshed back toward the shore. Behind him, he could hear Zeke resume yelling, empty-handed, at the sea.

On the road to the country club, Dwayne

leaned on the accelerator of Doc's truck and fought for control against the wind. The wipers could not keep up with the sheets of water blown sideways across the windshield. He really should have been home by now, where Noreen waited for him to take her and Roy to the shelter at Jenson's store. But he was so close, he could not stop now. The detour would not take long. He needed to see Dolores's face when he confronted her with the evidence. He would have to be satisfied with house arrest until the storm had passed. It would have to be enough. It *was* enough.

He arrived at the clubhouse, tennis racket stuffed in an old bag he found on the floor of the truck. In the main dining room, he found Ronald with about ten other men. It was dark inside, with shutters fixed over the windows and only lanterns to illuminate the room. The white bandage on Ronald's cheek glowed in their flickering light. A thick pall of cigarette smoke hung in the air.

Dolores stood next to Cynthia with a drink in her hand. Dolores had an air of annoyed distraction, like her thoughts were somewhere else entirely. Rain clattered incessantly at the windows, as if someone were throwing handfuls of marbles at the glass. The building was solidly constructed and had survived many storms in the past, but there were audible creaks from the timbers. Tentacles of sand crept under the door to be swept away by Violet's broom.

"Good of you to come, Deputy," said Ronald, "but we were just on our way to see you. It's time for Mr. Roberts to face the consequences of his actions."

There were nods and vague noises of agreement, but Ronald was clearly in charge. Dwayne regarded each of them in turn. All respectable landowners, farmers, businessmen. Churchgoers, every one. He marveled at how easy it was to turn supposedly good people. All it took was a suspicion, steeped in old grievances, ignited by hatred. He sensed they did not all share Ronald's fervor — especially George Mason, who looked distinctly uncomfortable — but were prepared to go along.

"Get on with it," said Ed Henderson. "I got to check on *Princess*." Everyone knew Ed loved his boat more than pretty much anything, including his wife, Marilee.

"Yeah," said Warren Hickson. "We ain't got time for this. Storm's come in a lot faster than the weather report said."

"I won't keep you, gentlemen," Dwayne said, "and ladies. Henry Roberts is no longer in custody, the main reason being that he did not attack Hilda." He felt no need to enlighten them about Henry's escape.

"Is that so?" Ronald folded his arms over his belly. "You must have thought different when you arrested him this morning. What changed your mind?"

Dwayne set the grubby bag on the banquet table. It made a solid *thump* on the surface, which shone with the soft, mellow luster of decades of beeswax polish. "This is what changed my mind." He removed the racket from the bag. "Dolores, I believe this is yours?"

Her eyes widened, and her hand reached out. "My racket, you found it!"

George stepped toward her. "Is that the one I got for you in Boca Raton? With the special grip you wanted?"

"Yes, it is." Her hand dropped to her side. "I left it — I mean, I lost it, a few weeks back." It was impossible to read her expression in the low light. "Where did you find it?"

Ronald advanced, clearly ready for a fight. "I've had enough of this. What does an old racket matter to you?"

Dwayne picked it up. "This is the object used to beat Hilda nearly to death. The pattern of the strings matches marks found on her face." He studied Dolores. Her eyes were shadowed, but her back was straight. Cynthia, on the other hand, looked in consternation from Dwayne to Dolores and back again, one beringed hand over her mouth. The men crowded around for a better look at the racket. "You say you left it somewhere a few weeks ago?" Dwayne asked.

"Yes, I did . . ." She stopped, lost in thought. Her whole concentration turned inward, like her mind had traveled somewhere else entirely and left just her body there.

George moved to her side. "Where did you leave it, honey? Just tell him, so we can clear this up and get out of here."

Wind pounded at the glass. Somewhere at the back of the building, there was a heavy whump and a crash. The lanterns shuddered.

"I don't remember," she said. Her eyes remained focused on the mangled, stained lump of wood and catgut on the table.

"Of course you do, honey. This is your favorite," said George. "Just tell —"

"Dolores Mason," said Dwayne, "I'm arresting you —"

"Now wait a minute," said George, with

an arm around his wife's shoulders. "You don't really think —"

"Get off me!" Her shriek shattered the muggy atmosphere of the clubhouse. She pushed George away and backed toward the windows. "I can't bear for you to touch me!"

Her voice echoed off the polished wooden floor. No one spoke. The windows rattled in their frames. Cynthia sniffed quietly.

All attention was focused on George. He just let his arms drop. Then he slowly went to the drinks table and refilled his glass, right to the rim.

Dwayne thought he had never seen a more hopeless gesture. "Dolores," he asked, "do you want to go to jail? Because if not, you got to tell me." He looked hard into her eyes. "Now, for the last time, where did you leave the racket?"

Her reply was drowned out by the wail of the wind, but Dwayne read the words from her lips. *This,* he thought, *changes everything.* "Say it again," he said.

"In his car," she spat. "I left it in Nelson's car."

The men shuffled their feet. In the sheepish, sideways glances that passed between them, Dwayne saw their collective relief. *There but for the grace of God . . .*

George said nothing, just stared into his

glass with his back to the room. The others seemed stuck in some kind of trance, mesmerized by the drama unfolding in front of them. Even Ronald was lost for words.

The ferocious wind pounded the clubhouse. Dwayne's mind was already on how to find Nelson before the storm forced him to give up and find shelter. "We're done here," he said, collecting the racket, "but, Dolores, don't —"

Something smashed into the big window overlooking the beach. The whole building trembled, followed by the *crack* of splintering wood. A corner of the roof lifted and allowed rain to pour in. Cynthia screeched and clutched at Dolores, who was covered in broken glass. She pushed Cynthia away with a cry and sped out the door, fine trickles of blood running down her arms. Everyone rushed for the exit, except for one person.

"George," called Dwayne. "Aren't you coming?"

But George did not answer. He just swirled his glass and stared at the big sailfish on the wall.

Dwayne ran for the truck. Noreen would be frantic by now, but he had one more stop to make.

I must find Nelson.

■ ■ ■ ■

At the Kincaid house, Nelson was glad he had thought to raise the convertible roof on the roadster before the storm started because it would be a battle in this wind. The only possessions he cared about were packed in two leather cases in the backseat. He looked up at the big white house, which he had always hated. The windows seemed to glower at him with disapproval, just like Hilda's daddy. There was nothing here he would miss. Even Nathan had not been hard to give up. He was just another reminder of how Hilda had trapped him.

When Missy had arrived earlier that day, she had obviously been surprised to find him packing. "Mister Kincaid, sir," she had said. "You going on a trip? In this weather?"

"Yes, Missy," he had said. "Yes, I am."

She began to bustle about, opening drawers and cupboards. "Then you'll be wanting Nathan's travel cot and his bottle and his —"

"Take him," Nelson had said.

She had looked at him with a strange, shocked sadness. "Mister Kincaid, I —"

"He's better off with you," he had said. "I got to go away." He handed her a thick wedge of dollars. "Here. This is for you."

"But when you comin' back?" She had hefted Nathan onto her shoulder, a small bundle wrapped in a blanket.

Nelson noticed the boy clung to Missy like he never did to his daddy. He felt nothing, absolutely nothing. "I don't know. It may be . . . a while."

They had stood there for a moment as the wind thrashed the trees. He could tell she knew what he was saying and was grateful she did not make a fuss.

Time to go. The wind suddenly strengthened, and with it came the rain. A roof tile sailed past. Water surged over the lawn, frothy waves blown clear up to the porch steps. Sam raced back and forth on the porch in a frenzy of barking. The dog had always hated water. Nelson wanted no encumbrances in his new life: no wife, no girlfriend, no baby, no house, no dog.

He ducked inside the car and fired the engine with a sense of pure exhilaration. He was free. Free! At last. For the first time since he had become a man, there was no woman hanging on him, begging him for more, always more. Their bodies, so soft and inviting, inevitably proved to be like quicksand for him. It had always been the same. At first, it had seemed like such a gift.

The women could not get enough of Nelson, any of them. Over time, he made a specialty of rich widows. He was their drug, their legal high, and in return for that, they gave him things — money, Cuban cigars, the Cadillac. He didn't even care much what they looked like. Servicing them became like a vocation. It was his job.

But after a few disastrous breakups, which included one successful suicide and other botched attempts, he had learned to read the signs when they became too possessive and hit the road. *Should have done this long ago.*

He steered the car in the direction of the coast road and just managed to avoid a fallen tree branch. Hilda had been a mistake. He had known it from the very beginning, but she was just so sweet, so pretty, so naive and fresh. And so responsive, it had electrified him. It was like meeting a female version of himself. And then she had tricked him and he was caught, the noose tight around his neck. After the baby, when she got so fat, he had found distraction with the country club ladies. He allowed himself a bitter chuckle as he moved the car into the middle of the road, where there was less water. But Dolores had turned out to be just the same. She wanted to keep him all to herself too. She would have trapped him, if it had carried on. *That's what they all want.*

He recalled the night of the barbecue. It was a rare lapse of self-control, which luckily had turned out all right for him. On his way home, he had found her, waddling down the road in the dark. She had refused to get in the car, just continued to pick her way barefoot over the stones, those ridiculous shoes in her hands. The car's headlights had illuminated every lump and bump, every sweaty fold of her body in the unfashionable dress. She had reminded him of some kind of farm animal, and then the thought hit him with bone-shaking force: this was his future, he and Hilda yoked together forever, in an unending series of embarrassments and compromises. Meanwhile, his real future, the one he deserved, sailed off without him. He was disgusted, as much with himself as with her, for allowing it to happen.

He had no memory of grabbing Dolores's racket. It just seemed to appear in his hand. It was his one chance, and he took it. Hilda had fought back, more than he'd expected. He kept hitting her until the racket broke and she lay unmoving on the ground.

It was over. Henry Roberts had been arrested, thanks to that fool deputy sheriff and some well-placed pressure on Ronald. If Hilda ever woke up, which seemed unlikely, she would probably remember little. And even if she did, he would be long gone.

Nelson was made for better things, better places, with civilized, intelligent people. His time in the stinking swamp of Heron Key was almost over. No more of Hilda's reproachful eyes, no more of Dolores's clinging arms. He was still handsome and vigorous enough to attract the older ladies who had always found him irresistible. Canada appealed, very much. Plenty of rich widows there. And cool pine forests.

He whistled as he steered the car around more debris. The Florida weather was another thing he would not miss. He could already smell the fresh scent of Canadian pine.

On the coast road, Dwayne fought for control of Doc's lumbering pickup truck. The wind suddenly increased in intensity. The truck swerved toward the ocean, like it had been punched by a giant fist. Out of control, he could only wait for the vehicle to stop. Water seeped up through the pedals on the floor. The engine coughed once, twice, and then died. He tried to restart it. Nothing. He tried again but could hear no sound over the wind. One of the heavy beach picnic tables flipped over beside the truck. *Come on, come on.* Water covered his shoes. He pumped the pedals and cursed Henry Roberts for perhaps the hundredth time. His own truck would stand up to this treatment a whole lot better. He turned the key again and felt the hulking vehicle come to life. He steered to where he hoped to find asphalt, felt the tires grip. Noreen was going to give him hell when he got home. She hated water, had never learned to swim. He had tried for years to persuade her, with no success. Roy, on the other hand, loved bath time and at the beach would splash happily for hours in the shallows.

He pushed the engine harder. Of all the crimes he had dealt with as deputy sheriff, the attack on Hilda had affected him the worst. He was used to the petty larceny and other offenses against property. There were plenty of drunken brawls and, during Prohibition, some pretty nasty characters.

And of course there were plenty of couples with marital problems. He had been called to a fair few disturbances, mostly when people had a drink. But no one talked about it. The problems stayed in the home, where they belonged. For Nelson to treat his own wife so . . . to beat her nearly to death, and on a public road. Well, it was completely beyond his experience or understanding.

The windshield fogged up. He rubbed it clear and Noreen's face appeared in the glass. He was careful never to hit her where it would show. There was no doubt that he possessed the physical strength to do to her exactly what Nelson had done to Hilda, but the thought of it revolted him. The idea of a grown man using all his strength against someone so defenseless, swinging the racket again and again at her head . . . it made him feel sick. He wanted — no, needed — to believe he was different. *I am not that person . . . or am I?* There had been a few times (not many, but enough) when Noreen's unbreakable silence had pushed him so far, he had needed every ounce of willpower to hold back. He thought of her eyes, so reproachful and frightened yet resigned and determined at the same time. When the wipers cleared the windshield, it was Hilda's broken, bruised face he saw.

It had gone very dark outside. He turned on the headlights. Between swipes of the wipers, he got glimpses of the road ahead. It was almost covered by water, blocked by big tree branches. He was about to turn off to use a different route when he saw the lights. As he got closer, the distinctive lines of the creamy-yellow Cadillac came into view. Its headlights illuminated the horizontal rain. He could see, by the Caddy's dashboard light, Nelson in the driver's seat, staring straight ahead. Dwayne pulled up alongside and signaled Nelson to roll down his window. There was no response.

"Well, if that's the way you want to play it," Dwayne said as he grabbed his handcuffs and flashlight and stepped out into the deluge. House arrest might have worked for Dolores, but he would have to take Nelson in, storm or no. *Noreen is going to love this.*

The rain hit his head like a shower of marbles. He put up a hand to shield his eyes. Nelson did not appear to notice him.

"Nelson!" he hollered. "Get out of the car! I'm arresting you on suspicion of —" He did not need to finish the sentence. Nor, he realized, did he need the handcuffs. In the beam of his flashlight, he could see why Nelson did not answer. A massive banyan branch had penetrated the car's soft roof and gone straight through his torso, pinning him fast to the seat. His hands were still on the steering wheel, mouth open in a last gasp of complete surprise.

CHAPTER 19

At Doc's office, an argument was in progress.

"It's simple," Doc explained to Mama. "We can't move her and I'm not leaving her. I can do this on my own. Go on, get to the shelter. We'll be fine here. This building has stood through seventeen hurricanes. What's one more?"

Mama scowled. "You doin' what I think you doin'?"

They had watched Hilda deteriorate for the past few hours as the pressure inside her skull mounted. She had had a small seizure an hour previously. Without relief, her brain would mash itself to pulp against the walls of its bony container.

"We have to reduce the pressure. It's the only way."

She tied an apron over her dress. "Best make it quick, for all of us."

Doc knew the procedure, had done it

more than once in the field. But he wished there was another way. He went to the back room where his rarely used instruments were stored. He found the trephine in the box of tools inherited from his grandfather, who was a field surgeon in the Confederate army. The saw's circular blade resembled a set of shark's teeth. The instrument looked much older, like something from the Middle Ages.

When he came out, Mama had arranged the other tools he would need on a clean cloth. The wind sounded like it was trying to shake the glass from the window frames, even behind the heavy shutters. The lights failed, then came back on a few seconds later.

"Get the lantern," Doc said. He injected morphine into Hilda's scalp. He positioned himself at the crown of her head, scalpel in hand.

"We got to sterilize that," Mama said, setting the lantern at his elbow.

"This'll have to do." He doused the instrument in bourbon.

Carefully he cut away a small square flap of Hilda's scalp until he saw the white of bone. Hilda whimpered and thrashed despite the morphine. It took all of Mama's prodigious weight to hold her down. Blood trickled onto the floor. It looked like a pool of ink in the glow of the lantern. Mama dabbed the wound with sterile gauze. Doc poured more bourbon into the hole. "Keep her still, Mama. I'm so sorry, my dear," he whispered. "So sorry."

The lights went out and stayed out this time. Mama brought the lantern close. Doc hefted the trephine. Its circular serrated blade had not seen action for many years, but he had kept it clean and sharp.

Doc placed the blade gently against the exposed surface of Hilda's skull and began to turn the handle. It bit into the bone with a gritty, grating sound, like sandpaper on rough wood. The bone seemed to glow with a pure light of its own.

"When you last done this?" Mama asked.

"Oh, not for a while," he said, slowly sending the blade farther into Hilda's skull. He had not used it since the war. The noise of the storm took him back. If he could keep a steady hand with shells exploding all around, he could do it with a little wind.

He set his glasses straight on his nose. He had trepanned quite a few soldiers and never lost one because of it.

Something big slammed into the side of the building. Mama jerked the lantern and began to mutter what sounded like mingled prayers and curses.

"Bring the light here." It was crucial that he go no farther than the bone itself to avoid damaging the delicate underlying brain tissue.

The room shuddered. The blade slipped out of its cut. A fine shower of dust and dirt drifted down from the roof to turn Doc's hair instantly gray. Mama stretched her apron to make an awning over his head. He met her eyes, saw the question there. But there was no choice — not for him or Hilda. The only thing to do was carry on.

He continued to twist the blade until he felt the resistance cease. With a slight *pop,* the disk of bone dropped to the floor, propelled by a gush of blood and fluid that splashed his shoes.

"We need something to cover the hole," he said.

"I got it," said Mama and fished in her pocketbook. She handed the quarter to Doc, who doused it in bourbon and took a swig himself.

He inserted the coin into the space left by the blade and quickly stitched the flap of skin closed. "Bandage," he said, "and then you must go to your family. I insist."

Mama wrapped the bandage around Hilda's head and fastened it expertly. The wind battered the building like an enraged beast. "You comin' with me." It was not a question.

"No," he said. "No, I don't think so. You go to your family, Mama. I'll see you when this is over."

She retrieved her hat and pocketbook. It was clear from her expression that she considered him beyond reason. "You take care of yourself now," she said. "You hear?"

"Will you be okay getting to the shelter? I'd give you a ride, but the deputy took my truck."

"Never mind about that. It ain't far." She fixed her hat firmly. "I be fine. Don't you worry."

"Thank you, Mama," he said. "Thank you." But his eyes were on Hilda.

Once Mama had gone, Doc settled himself next to Hilda with the lantern and took her hand. The swelling in her eyes had already diminished. For the first time since the attack, she opened them fully. They were still glacier blue but very bloodshot and took a few moments to focus. Her tongue emerged from her mouth to lick cracked and broken lips. He brought a cup of water to her mouth.

"What . . . ? Where . . . ?" she asked. "My

338

head hurts."

"You're in my office," he said. "You're safe now. You've been asleep for a few days."

"What's that noise?" Her voice had a new nasal quality from the broken nose. Her speech was distorted by the swelling in her mouth.

"Just a storm," he said, stroking her hand. "Nothing to worry about." It seemed to Doc that the world outside the circle of lantern light had ceased to exist. Despite the crashes and bangs from outside, there was just him and Hilda, together. *Let the wind blow. I don't care.* He was exactly where he wanted to be, where he belonged.

"Where's Nathan? I need to find Nathan." She tried to rise off the table but immediately fell back in a dizzy slump.

"Take it easy. You've had a bump on the head. He'll be with Missy, at the shelter. She'll take good care of him. She's a sensible girl. They'll be fine. You just rest."

"Face feels funny," she said and raised a hand but he stopped it. Her tongue found the space where her tooth had been. Her eyes widened in alarm. "Oh, Doc, am I . . . ? Am I still . . . pretty?"

His eyes took in the network of red-lined black stitches, puffy with the first stage of healing. He was no plastic surgeon. The work was without finesse. Yellow-green bruises covered most of her face. When these had faded and the stitches came out, the true extent of the permanent damage would be revealed. "Beautiful," he said. "Just beautiful."

She tried to smile and winced where the stitches pulled. "Guess I'll need to keep a serious face on for a while. Nelson used to make me laugh, all the time . . ." Her eyes clouded with pain. "Oh, Doc, I never thought — I never thought he could — he would . . ." Fat, slow tears slipped down the sides of her bandaged head.

"There now," he said, mopping the tears with a handkerchief. "Don't upset yourself all over now." He frowned in confusion. Dwayne had passed through earlier, waving the broken tennis racket in triumph, on his way to arrest Dolores. "Nelson is the one who did this to you? Can you . . . Do you remember . . . anything?"

"Yes. Yes, I do." Her tone was flat, without emotion. No tears now. "I fought, at first, but then I just lay there and let him hit me. Part of me was glad it was finally out, how much he hated me. No more pretending. I'm so tired of pretending. The racket made a sound when it broke, like a bone breaking. I think, Doc . . . I'm pretty sure he only stopped because it broke." She said nothing for a few moments. The wind hissed through the building, testing it for weakness, searching for a way in. "Can I have more water, please?" He held the cup to her lips. "I thought I would die, Doc, right there in the road." She turned reddened eyes to him. "And other than Nathan, I couldn't think of anyone who would mind."

Rage boiled up inside him, so fierce that he had to turn away to shield her from the murderous heat in his eyes. Nelson had vowed to protect and cherish Hilda all her days, and instead he destroyed her face and nearly killed her . . . Worse, almost, he had made her want to die. And why? So he could have his fun with Dolores and her friends, once he decided domestic responsibilities didn't suit him? He could imagine Hilda's pain as she lay there in the dirt under his blows . . . Her parents gone, no friends in town, and now her husband wanted her dead. During his worst moments, after Leann left, he too would have welcomed the darkness, had planned it all out, to the last detail. An overdose of barbiturates and bourbon, the coward's death of choice. But now he realized he was happy, for the first time in many years. "Hilda," he said, "I would mind. Very much." He looked hard into her eyes, hoping to make her see what he could not say, hoping to find, if not an answer to his feelings, at least some comprehension. That would be enough. "I will never let any harm come to you again," he said. "I promise." And he planted a light kiss on her hand.

There was surprise in her eyes. And something else. Her voice was soft. "Doc, I . . . I never realized —"

The wind tore away one of the heavy storm shutters like it was a flake of paint. Water seeped under the door. Hilda asked, "Shouldn't we get to the shelter?" But still she held his gaze.

In her weakened state, with a fresh hole in her head, they would never make it to the store. *Whatever happens, we're together.* "Better to stay put," he said with more confidence than he felt. "We're fine, and the shelter will be so crowded and hot. Much more comfortable here."

"Yes, you're right," she said, and the trust in her eyes nearly broke his heart. "We are better off here."

Missy looked out through a crack in the plywood over the window. It had taken her all afternoon to nail it up around the place. A single candle cast a jittery glow around the familiar contours of the room. She tried again to decide whether to stay or go. Mama had said to wait, but it had been hours since she had gone to help Doc, and the weather had suddenly worsened. Only a little while before, everyone had said the hurricane was still a long way off. No one had been in much of a hurry. Selma had gone to get Jerome and some necessaries.

Missy hated storms. Mama said it was because she was born during a big one. It had nearly carried Missy off. One of her favorite stories as a child was how Henry's mother, Grace, had fought a battle with the wind that tried to wrest her away. Mama said the storm didn't like to lose and, having been denied once, would try again. Missy knew some people like Selma who found storms exciting, were exhilarated by the wildness and the danger. Some crazy fools even liked to ride the storms staked out on the beach. She hated everything about them. She hated the way Mama's little house shook like a frightened puppy in the wind. She hated the dirty flood water that came up through the floor and soaked everything in a stench that lasted for months.

She searched her mind for the right word to describe the unsettling tingle of dread

343

that had been with her for days. *Personal.* That was the word. If it didn't sound so purely ridiculous, she would have said this storm felt personal in some way she could neither define nor understand.

She tried to picture Henry. He was probably out of the state by now. There was only one occasion when she had ever left the county, to accompany the Kincaids to a family wedding in St. Augustine. It was a long, long way to drive in the Cadillac, almost as far as Georgia. They had passed by so many fields and towns, more than she could have imagined. She had wondered if other states had the same air as Florida. Would it smell different? Would she feel different? Would her body know if she had crossed the border into Georgia? She had never found out.

Ever since Henry had gone, she had been telling herself that he was safe. Nothing else mattered. Other feelings had no place. She swallowed the lump of bitterness in her throat as she surveyed the tempest outside. He was right to go — she knew that for sure. She had nurtured a tiny kernel of hope that maybe he would come back. One day, far in the future.

But when she had said as much to Mama, her mother was very clear that she should

abandon such ideas, and quick. When Missy
had protested, Mama had just fixed her hat
into place and said, "Folks have long
memories, Missy. It won't never be safe for
him here." And with that, she had left for
Doc's.

Missy looked out the window one final
time. No sign of either Mama or Selma. It
was unnaturally dark outside, more like
evening than late afternoon. And suddenly
she was overwhelmed by the certainty that
they must leave immediately.

"Time to go," she said to Nathan and
wrapped his blanket tighter. "Most likely
we'll meet them on the road."

Once outside, she realized the strength of
the wind was far greater than she'd thought.
It hit her with such force that she staggered
and nearly fell over. Rain stung her face,
her arms. Briefly she wondered if she had
left too late, that maybe she should go back
inside, but Mama's little house had started
to sway. One of the posts that supported
the porch gave way and the roof sagged. The
shelter was not far. They would be fine. It
was just a matter of one step then another.
She gripped Nathan tighter to her chest.
He made no sound at all, just looked up at
her with his trusting blue eyes. "Don't you
worry, Nathan. We be fine."

Small missiles buffeted her all over. With every step, the strength of the gale seemed to increase. She had to lean over, almost parallel to the ground.

She tried to picture Henry's face again, which helped to calm her in most situations, but it only made her sad now. The wind grew stronger. An icy trickle of fear seeped into her heart. It got worse with each step, although they should have been closer to the store by now. So she did what she always did when she was scared: she sang.

" 'Don't you know, God is able, he's able, he's able, he's able, y'all.' "

That helped. She felt stronger. Nathan felt more settled too, as if the vibration coming through her ribs had soothed him. "You like that? Almost there, precious boy, almost there." She knew it would not be long before bigger objects took to the air. The wind grew stronger still. She dodged a milking stool just in time. In a louder voice, she sang, " 'Clouds may gather, all around you, so dark and sable.' You know what sable mean, Nathan? It an animal, like a muskrat but prettier, with oh such soft fur." Or so the *Encyclopedia Britannica* said. "Words is funny, Nathan; they can do two jobs at the same time. Sable a color too, dark brown." She raised her eyes to the furious sky.

"Nothing like these clouds, though. They is plum, or violet, or . . . burgundy." The unfamiliar word felt funny in her mouth. "And burgundy got two jobs too. It a place, a faraway place, called France, where they don't talk like us and eat different stuff and all." She wrapped herself more tightly around his little body. "Henry been to France, he say —" Her throat closed. She refused to cry. Instead, she croaked, " 'Surely, surely, he's able to carry you through.' "

Except that for the last few yards, she had started to realize they weren't going to make it after all. Bigger chunks of wood, coral, glass, and stone flew at her. Her arms and legs were cut and bleeding. Soon would follow objects big enough to knock her from her feet or crush Nathan against her. She had to get out of their path. The wind sucked the air from her lungs. Her shoes felt made of iron. She must not let Nathan feel her fear. Its malevolent voice urged her to drop the baby and run for her life. She could make it to the shelter without him. Breathless from the effort of standing still, she said, "Tell you what, baby boy; we gonna set down and have a little rest."

She climbed into the filthy ditch, already half flooded, and huddled over Nathan, tried to make herself as small as possible. Nathan whimpered. "I got you, honey. I got you." Henry's smile came to her, and she was comforted.

"For the last time," Selma said to Jerome, "we got to go." She waited by the door with her small bag of necessaries, Elmer the rooster tucked under one arm. People took their pets to the shelter; she was taking Elmer.

Jerome had tied one on the night before with a load of other idiot storm watchers down at the beach and carried on drinking when he woke up. It was his favorite hangover cure. He was sprawled in his chair, cuddling a bottle of rum. "You go on," he said. "I be fine here."

She stroked Elmer's russet feathers. It seemed to calm them both. She had brought the rest of the birds inside, where they clucked nervously around her legs. They had made a mess of Grace's rag rug, but it didn't matter. She would clean it up. Her beans and tomatoes would be ruined, but as long as the salt water held back, they could be replanted. She always thought the worst part of any hurricane was the mess it made.

"You crazy?" she yelled at Jerome. "You

348

seen it out there?" She put her eye to a gap in the window boards. The wind had begun to tear the town to pieces. The street looked like a canal.

"Exactly, Selma," he said. "We safer here. Now come away from the window and have a drink." The single bare electric bulb flared and went out.

If that big wind picked him up a hundred feet in the air, he wouldn't feel a thing.

"Jerome," she said in the voice that usually brooked no backchat, "get outta that chair. We going. Now."

He just wrapped himself tighter around the bottle. With a sleepy smile, he said, "I keep an eye on the house, Selma. See ya later."

Something thudded loudly against the front door. She did not relish even the short walk to Jenson's store, not in that wind. Worse still was the idea of staying put. She knew exactly how much the house could take — and what destruction hurricanes could wreak. As a child, she and Grace and Henry had hunkered down many times, with only the kitchen table for protection. Grace believed the old spirits would save them, and it seemed she was right. One time they emerged to find all four walls still standing but the roof removed cleanly, as with a huge can opener. Another time, the whole house was destroyed around them, but the kitchen table was untouched.

It was the same one they still used. She had prepared Jerome's meals on that table for fifteen years. On the underside, it bore her initials and Henry's, which they had carved during a particularly fierce storm in case it blew away, so someone would know they had been there.

Jerome was asleep in his chair, mouth open. The house shivered like a wet dog, and Selma made up her mind. With one last look at him, she said, "God bless," and left.

CHAPTER 20

In the mess hall at the veteran's camp, the men had been waiting a long time for instructions with nothing to do but drink beer. So they had waited and drank. And waited and drank some more.

"My friend Marvin," said Lemuel, "he been in a hurr-a-cane before lots of times, and he seen a shark swimmin' down the street in Havana."

Sonny nodded solemnly, like this was a bulletin straight from *National Geographic.*

"I got a friend too," said Tec Brown, "and he says snakes travel on the ground in the same direction as the hurricane for days before."

"My friend," said Carl Bukowski, a motor mechanic from Wisconsin, "says you got to leave open a window or else your house'll explode inward from the change in pressure." Carl was a slight, nervous young man who suffered so badly from shell shock that any loud noise could unman him, even Tec's farts.

"And my friend," said Stan Mulligan, "said the best thing to do is put your head between your legs and kiss your ass good-bye!" He cackled and clinked his beer bottle against Tec's.

"Mr. Watts said we'd be going to get the train," said Carl. "He said that, you all heard him. What's taking so long?" He shredded the label from his beer bottle.

"And you believe him?" Two-Step asked. "Because he's taken such good care of us so far?" He spat and crossed his arms. "My money says there's no train. No one gives a shit about us; we know that for sure. They left us here to take our chances."

The little color remaining in Carl's face drained away.

"Don't listen to him, Carl," said Jeb. "The train is comin'. And even if it wasn't, Two-Step, there ain't nothin' in nature could be as bad as what we seen in France."

"You got that right, brother," said Franklin. "I'd face a hurricane any old day. Nothin' scares me no more."

Suddenly the roof screamed like an animal in pain. The men gulped their beer. Carl made a sound like a leaky balloon.

Two-Step stood up with a loud belch. "All

you pussies better prepare for the day of judgment," he said with dark glee. " 'Specially you, Bukowski. Yessir, you'd better wipe your snotty nose and get ready, 'cause it's *here,* Bukowski!"

A lantern blew off a table and went out. Carl shouted in alarm and flung himself to the ground, hands over his head. Two-Step laughed long and loud. The wooden sides of the mess hall rippled like they were made of canvas.

Trent Watts entered the mess on a gust of wind that almost knocked him off his feet. He was wet through, bald head shining. He had briefly considered cutting off the beer but decided the last thing he needed was a mutiny. The room hummed with tension, the air heavy with the smell of fear and hops. The relief train should be almost there by now, although by rights, it should have been sent days before. The speed of the storm's arrival was unlike anything in his experience, from squally rain to destructive winds in a matter of hours. Even Jenson Mitchell seemed taken aback in his last phone call before the line went down, urging Trent to evacuate the men. That time, Jenson was preaching to the choir. At last, help was on the way. They would shelter at the station until it arrived. The flimsy mess hall already looked about ready to collapse.

"Ladies," Trent hollered, "we're going to the station to wait for the train. It won't be long, and we'll have more protection than here at the beach." Water surged in under the walls and scooped out lagoons in the sand. "Watch yourselves out there; got lots of debris."

They filed into the storm. Palm trees knelt in deference to the mighty wind, their trunks bowed to the ground. The air was alive with pieces of wood and metal and swirling sand that made it almost impossible to see. As soon as he stepped out of the door, Carl took a blow to the head from a flying plank torn from a cabin. He went down without a sound. A large flap of skin hung over his eye. Blood soaked the front of his shirt.

"Get him to the station!" Trent yelled.

Stan and Franklin half dragged Carl away, but they had not gone far before Stan suddenly spun sideways with a scream that carried even over the wind, hands clutched to his belly. A wooden fence post protruded from his abdomen. Lemuel scooped up the big man as if he were a child and ran in the direction of the station. The others hung back in the lee of the mess hall, which provided a little shelter from the wind.

Water rose around their ankles. A corner of the roof peeled back, as if pulled away by a giant hand.

"Get moving, ladies, NOW!"

They stepped quickly into the ferocious wind, heads down. And then the entire ocean-facing side of the building came off and flew into the sky, light as a leaf.

Still many miles to the north, the relief train sped onward through the rainy darkness, its headlight illuminating wet tracks strewn with debris. The massive cow catcher on the front of the locomotive could blast through most obstacles, but they had already stopped twice to remove a big branch and a section of fence.

The chief engineer, Ken Cramer, had taken some persuading to allow Henry and Jimmy on board. They had waited in the yard while Moses made the case for them. They could hear nothing of the conversation, just watched it through the office window. There was a lot of shouting. Cramer folded his arms at one point and spat. But Moses had kept on.

Clarence had studied the scene through the window. "Ken ain't a bad man. He just hate any ideas but his own. So the trick is to make your idea his idea, ya see? Moses, he good at that."

The engine was ready. All 160 tons of it snorted and hissed like a racehorse at the gate. Its shiny black flanks seemed to puff in and out with great gusts of steam. It had seemed to Henry like the most powerful thing he had ever seen. And it needed to be. His body fairly vibrated with impatience. If the weather was this bad up in Miami, it would be much worse in the Keys. "Come on, come on," he had said under his breath.

"This looks good, ya see?" Clarence had asked. "Ken's arms is unfolded. He leanin' forward." He clapped Henry on the back. "Congratulations. The deal be done."

Indeed, the chief engineer had looked more relaxed although still dubious. Moses was smiling.

"Well," said Henry, "let's hope that Moses lives up to his name. Jimmy, you don't need to make this trip — it ain't your fight. You can stay here or go up to Pensacola to meet your folks." He did not want to be responsible for putting the boy in harm's way again.

Jimmy did not move. "I'm going with you. Uncle Dwayne been good to me. He's gonna need help. I'll come back up here to get the truck when the storm is over."

Henry regarded him for a long moment.

"The thing that swung it," Clarence said later, "was you being a war hero and all. Cramer fought in France. Almost didn't make it out. Man's only got half a stomach, ya see?"

They sat in the first carriage behind the engine. Moses was assisting Ken in the engineer's compartment. With the rain-swept darkness pressing in on the carriage windows, it seemed to Henry they could have been anywhere: another state, even another country. It could be the blasted, cratered French countryside out there instead of a Florida swamp. Only the hot, muggy air gave it away.

The swaying motion of the carriage made him realize how tired he was. How long was it since he had slept a whole night? He could not remember. "I'm no war hero," he said with a yawn.

"You is now," chuckled Clarence. "What was it like? Over there?"

"Didn't you ask Ken?" Henry did not want to have this conversation, not now. He wanted to blink his eyes and find the train pulling in to the Heron Key station. His whole concentration was fixed on what to do when they arrived, how to find Missy

357

and Selma, how to get his men to safety.

Clarence shrugged in the direction of the conductor's cab. "He won't talk about it, ya see? We only knew about his stomach when we saw him with his shirt off one time. Man, you musta seen some wild shit out there."

Henry bit back his caustic reply. Clarence's face was so openly curious, no malice there, and he had the man to thank for getting him on the train at all. "You could say that." Night had been the worst time in the trenches. The mind supplied what the eyes couldn't see, only far, far worse. Sometimes a flare would go up and illuminate the ravaged, unnatural landscape of shell craters, which stank of rotting flesh. But mostly the men just sat and smoked and waited for the cold comfort of daylight.

As the train clattered on, Henry felt some of the same mixture of fear and excitement as before a battle. The weather had worsened considerably as they moved south. The wind punched the carriage again and again, made it shudder on the rails. The rain smashed against the windows. They would have to be quick to get all the boys on board and away. Likely they had been drinking all afternoon, which would not make them any easier to handle. *Maybe Trent will have the sense to stop the beer.* He hoped to persuade Missy and the others to evacuate too but knew it wouldn't sit right with them. The shelters had always served them in the past. They had never run from a storm before and would see no cause to do so this time.

"But what about the women?" Clarence leaned forward. Henry noted that Jimmy was actively listening while pretending to be asleep. "You must have got your share of those fine French ladies?"

"It's different there," said Henry. "Black, white — don't matter." Henry thought of Thérèse for the first time in . . . how long? It used to be her face that he conjured to get him through the bad times. Now it was hard even to remember her clearly. She had taken on the blurred outlines of a dream. Red hair, he recalled that much, fine as copper silk. Skin the color of fresh milk, with a sprinkle of freckles on her arms. The smell of fresh bread that always clung to her, mixed with her rose cologne. But the rest was clouded. Instead, it was Missy who came to him when he closed his eyes; it was her soft skin that his fingers longed to touch. He pictured her, safe and dry in Jenson's shelter with the others.

"C'mon, man," pleaded Clarence, his arm dangling over the back of the seat. "Give us the lowdown. We want —"

Henry never found out what Clarence wanted, because just then there was a loud shout from the engineer's compartment.

"Hold on!" yelled Ken.

But it was too late. Everyone was thrown to the floor when the train hit something big and hard enough to stop several tons of hurtling iron. Henry felt the carriage buck wildly beneath him and grabbed hold of Jimmy as he was flung into the air. Somehow the train stayed on the rails. Henry covered his ears against the awful shriek of metal on metal. And then there was only the sound of the wind and the rain.

They surged into the engineer's cabin to find Ken on the floor, a bloody gash on his forehead. Moses stood over him, a rag pressed to the wound. "Give me a hand, Clarence!"

They got Ken back into his seat. "It's a crane," he gasped. "A fucking crane. I saw it, but there was no way to stop in time."

"Musta blown over," said Moses. He pulled on a yellow raincoat and hat. "Clarence, come with me."

They returned a few moments later, dripping and panting.

Moses shook water from his hat. More puddled at his feet. "It ain't the crane that's caught us. That's lyin' clear. It's the cables. They knotted around the wheels like Christmas ribbon."

"How long will it take to get it off?" asked Ken. Blood trickled into his collar. Moses gave him a fresh rag.

"Hard to say," said Clarence with a shrug that sent a shower of droplets from his coat. "It's stuck there good, ya see? Two hours, at least. Maybe three."

Henry was all too familiar with the kind of cables used on construction cranes. They would be thick ropes of steel, designed to lift massive loads. It was not an option to cut through them, not without special equipment, which could only be found far away in Miami. No, their only option was to go out and untangle it by hand. A gust of wind rocked the carriage. They could not afford to lose two hours, much less three. "I'm coming too," he said. "Will be faster with more hands."

"Yeah, me too," said Jimmy and pulled his cap down tight. "Let's go."

"We ain't got enough raincoats for y'all," said Moses.

"Don't matter," said Henry. "We gonna get wet tonight anyway."

Down in Heron Key, Jenson's store was a

361

blur of activity as he and Trudy scurried to clear more space. There were nearly a hundred people crammed into the building, and still more people arrived. Parents carried wide-eyed, pajama-clad children, thrilled to be up past their bedtime. Old people shuffled in wearily, all too aware of the tedious hours ahead. People brought food, which mostly remained untouched, but the case of beer was quickly dispatched.

A bedraggled bundle of wet fur stumbled in the door and flopped with an exhausted *smack* on the floor.

"Ain't that Nelson's dog?" asked Cyril Anderson. He picked up the animal in his arms. Sam licked his face all over. "You're okay now, pal. You're okay." He stroked his ears but the dog would not be comforted and kept up a pitiful whining.

Jenson heaved another sack of flour on his back and dumped it outside the rear door. The storeroom was needed for people. Much as it pained him, he had no choice but to sacrifice perfectly good food to the elements.

Breathing heavily, he checked the barometer again and for a moment thought it must have broken. It had been falling steadily for hours, like a stone dropped from a height, but never in his life had he seen a reading so low. It was much lower than the one he received from Fred in Key West, which led him to a dreadful conclusion: the hurricane was many times more powerful than anyone, including Fred, had realized. And it was much, much closer, literally on their doorstep. The phone lines were down, power gone. They were on their own.

He looked around at the faces, shiny with sweat in the yellow glow of the lanterns, and decided there was no benefit in telling them what he knew. It would not help and could make the situation much worse, if there was a panic. There was nowhere safer to be.

The Conchs' basic good humor prevailed, despite the increasingly crowded conditions. People played Go Fish with the older children.

The hot, moist air gradually sent the younger ones to sleep, drooped over their parents' shoulders. The Conchs had seen off many a storm in this fashion. It almost felt like a party, a chance to socialize and swap stories of hurricanes past. As he moved around the store, Jenson caught snatches of conversation, all relating to the hunt for Hilda's attacker. He shook his head wryly. Nothing helped pass the time like juicy gossip.

"I've been saying all along, it must have been a crime of passion," said Warren Hickson. "Stands to reason. Got to feel something real strong to mash someone's face in like that."

Mabel Hickson said, "That kind of shameless carrying on never ends well. As ye sow, so shall ye reap. Potato salad, anyone?"

Just then, the building was rocked by an enormous gust of wind that sent water spraying right through the tiny gaps in the walls.

Still more people came. It was dark as midnight outside, although it was barcly 6:00 p.m. The good humor deteriorated. The party atmosphere dissolved into apprehension as the crowding got worse and the wind grew stronger.

Ronald burst in through the door with Cynthia in his arms. The bandage on his cheek was no longer white but grubby gray.

"Tree branch hit her," he said, panting. "Right when we left the country club. The kitchen blew up. The whole back side of the place is gone, just gone."

Cynthia moaned softly as he deposited her on the floor. Feet shuffled to make room. "Where's Dolores?" Ronald asked. "She was right behind us, but I lost her when Cindy got hit."

"Not here yet," said Warren.

Next through the door was Marilee Henderson with her young son, Tim. She was soaked through, dress mostly torn off her body. Mascara made thick black tracks down her face. Tim's face was pale as milk. He stared fixedly at his mother, as if afraid to take his eyes from her.

"Where is Ed?" she called as she searched the mass of faces. "Where is he?"

Trudy yanked down a curtain from the window to wrap around Marilee's shaking shoulders. Someone found a chair for her. "He's not here yet, sweetie." She knelt beside her and wiped rain and tears from her face. "What happened?"

It was several moments before she could speak. "I begged him to leave, but he wouldn't. He had — he had to check on her, one more time. He had to make sure she was okay. I told him, I said we could always get another boat. He looked at me like I was crazy."

Trudy exchanged a glance with Jenson. The *Princess* was not a big craft. Others of similar size had fled up the coast to safer moorings when the hurricane alerts came. *We are all foolish about things we love,* thought Jenson.

Marilee covered her face. Her body heaved

365

with sobs. She said, so low that only Jenson heard, "You know, I always said — I always said she'd kill him one day."

Water pooled beneath the door. Jenson tasted it. "Salt," he said. He saw comprehension in the taut faces of the crowd. The store was nearly half a mile from the beach, raised up three feet off the ground.

The sea was coming for them.

For the first time, his confidence in the shelter was shaken. Heron Key had never seen a storm like this before. Sam's whining rose in pitch and volume.

Cynthia came to and sniffled. "Ronnie, make it stop. My nerves can't take much more."

"You either shut that dog up," Ronald said to Cyril, "or it's going out, I swear."

"You lay a hand on him," said Cyril quietly, "and I'll finish what Ike started." The lantern's light flashed on the metal claw of his prosthesis.

"Keep calm, everyone," said Jenson. "Anyone who wants a fight is welcome to go outside." He looked hard at Ronald and Cyril. "No takers? All right then. Now let's behave like civilized people. We're all friends here."

He watched his mother rock a crying child. It would serve no purpose to alarm her, but as always, she could read his face. "What is it, Son?"

"We've got no more room, but there are still people missing." He scanned the faces. There were other shelters, like the one out at the fruit-packing warehouse, but most of his regular customers would come to the store. There were plenty more still to arrive.

"We'll make room somehow," said Trudy. "We always do." She turned her attention back to the child, whose eyelids had started to flutter.

But Jenson knew the worst danger did not come from the wind, however fearsome. Earlier that day, he had seen big waves clawing at the beach, as if trying to return it to the depths. As the wind grew stronger, so the waves would get bigger still. Even a moderate storm surge could inundate low-lying Heron Key. This storm was anything but moderate. His barometer had bottomed out at the lowest reading on its scale: twenty-six inches. He had inherited it from his grandfather, who had lived through some terrible storms, one with a reading as low as twenty-eight inches; twenty-six was unheard of. The barometer, the instrument by which he had lived every day of his life, was now just a useless hunk of metal and glass.

Surrounded on all sides by a sweaty crush of people, he had never felt so alone.

"Leave it, Noreen," said Dwayne. "We got to go."

She was still filling a bag with Roy's favorite toys and clothes and food, as if they were off to spend a day at the beach. On the drive back from the country club, Dwayne had heard the roar of the incoming waves, seen the angry way they tore at the beach. At the marina, the mooring lines still held, but the boats jostled about like fat ladies at a buffet. Back home, their house creaked on its foundations. It felt like the whole world was shaking apart. Still she would not be hurried. Such was her concentration that she did not ask why he was so late, for which he was grateful. He did not want to tell her about the country club, or about Nelson's death. It was too much at that moment, and they needed to focus. He had seen the damage already wrought by the wind.

"You know what it will be like," she said and pushed Roy's stuffed tiger into the bag. "All those sweaty people, kids getting fractious with nothing to do."

"Noreen," he said, beyond exasperated, "it's a store. It'll be full of food and drink."

368

He took the bag from her hand and hoisted Roy onto his shoulder. "Come on."

"I wish we knew where Jimmy was." She tied a scarf around her hair. It was patterned with honeysuckle, his present to her on their first anniversary. He had spent hours choosing it, on a rare trip to Miami, and far too much money buying it. But it had all been worth it to see the expression on her face when she opened the box. "When they catch that Henry Roberts," she said, "I'm gonna give him a piece of my mind."

"If he has any sense," said Dwayne, "Jimmy'll be in Pensacola with his folks." He did not doubt that Henry by now would have dumped the boy somewhere safe, if inconvenient. "And you can thank Henry Roberts for taking him away from this storm. Wherever he is, he's better off there than here. Now come *on.*"

Finally he had everyone and their belongings loaded into the truck. Noreen scooted along the bench seat, Roy in her lap, bags stuffed around their ankles. The headlights shone through horizontal rain so heavy and thick it looked like shards of glass.

Dwayne held on tight to the steering wheel, which kept trying to twist out of his hands. A couple of times, he thought they were going over, as the two windward wheels left the ground, but the weight of the truck restored its balance. Water sloshed around their feet. Roy, clinging to Noreen's neck, whimpered each time something struck the pickup. Missiles appeared from nowhere, chunks of buildings and trees, fences and tools, suddenly illuminated as they entered the headlights' beams. He had no time to swerve, could only hope they would bounce off. A coconut smacked the windshield hard enough to craze the glass, but it held.

Everything receded from his mind except the two beams of the headlights on the flooded, debris-choked road. It all fell away, everything that had so consumed him recently — finding Hilda's attacker, finding Roy's daddy, bringing Henry to justice. It seemed part of another life, someone else's life. There was only the whine of the engine in low gear, the barrage of missiles, and the headlights piercing the darkness ahead. Something strange happened to his sense of time. It had only been a few minutes since they left home, but such was his concentration that it seemed like they had spent their whole lives in the truck, forever trying to reach the safety of the store but never quite getting there. He could see little through the windshield and instead relied on the tires to tell him they were still on the road.

"Not far now," he said with a forced lightness. "Almost there." The speed with which the storm had overwhelmed the town was staggering. And still the wind blew harder and the waters rose. Dwayne kept his speed low to avoid slamming into something big or flooding the engine. "And when we get there," he said to Roy, "Momma's got a bag full of treats for you." Roy gave him a weak smile. He already had a fondness for sweets, especially orange blossom honey. *Just like his daddy,* Dwayne thought to himself, then grimaced at the absurdity of it — everything, all of it. Ever since Roy's shocking entrance into the world, he had turned Dwayne's life inside out. "That's my brave boy," he said. To Noreen, "After this is over, everything's gonna be different between us, you'll see."

"You mean that?" she asked, one arm around Roy, the other braced against the door. Her voice shook with anxiety. She really, really hated water and they were now surrounded by it.

"I do." He had said things like that in the past, more than once. The whole business of Hilda's attack had changed him in ways he did not understand or have time to examine. But he did mean it, maybe for the first time. That she still had the capacity to believe him warmed his heart.

He silently urged the truck on. *Keep it together, old girl.* The water only had to rise a little higher to drown the engine, and then they would be stuck. Totally at the mercy of the beast. *God help anyone out on foot in this.*

CHAPTER 21

It took all of Selma's strength to put one foot in front of the other. The wind tore at her clothes like Jerome on payday. The scariest thing of all was that, unbelievably, the wind was still getting stronger, the water on the road deeper. In all her years in Heron Key, she'd never known a storm of such power. *I'm damned if I gonna die naked in public.*

Elmer was gone and so was her bag of necessaries. Eyes narrowed, one hand up to protect her face, the other holding her dress together, she plodded on. Missy and Mama would be at the store by now, she figured, and they'd be wondering where she had gotten to. Rain stabbed like needles at her skin. She'd never seen such rain before. She pictured Jerome back in their cozy little house, asleep with his bottle. Quickly she shoved the picture from her mind. In her heart, she knew it was gone, and him with it. She should feel sadness, but her mind had room for only one thing: left foot, right foot. First one, then the other. Sadness was a luxury to be indulged once she was in a dry room with the lights on and a big cup of coffee in her hand. Then would come the time for sadness.

Already she had passed several poor souls who had lost their grip on life. One was buried beneath a collapsed water tank, only the legs visible. Another had a metal beam where her face should be. *I did this. I summoned you, Agaou. A fresh start, that's what I wanted for this place.* As with everything else, there was always a price to pay for wishes granted. And it looked like the price would be terrible this time.

Stones and broken glass tore at her. A chunk of coral flew past, narrowly missing her head. She shuffled forward, bent parallel over the rising water. A stuffed rabbit floated by, still clutched by a neatly severed child's hand. Inside the scream of the wind, she could hear other screams, but there was no way to find their owners in the treacherous blackness.

She should be within sight of the store by now. What little she could see through splayed fingers was unfamiliar. All the landmarks were gone. Had she taken a wrong turn?

She cast an eye at the malevolent sky. Selma had never minded storms in the past. She liked the brilliance of the lightning flashes, the fierce boom of the thunder. As a child, Henry had taught her to count out the lightning's distance by the time it took for the first crack of thunder. Hunkered underneath Grace's kitchen table, they had counted together: "One one hundred, two one hundred, three one hundred . . ." They had squealed with delight when the thunder's boom shook the air.

Are you watching, Grace? Her mother always warned of the dangerous powers to be found in the tattered pages of the old book. But once Selma had tasted them, she had grown bold. There was nothing to do now but face the consequences, however fearsome. She had thought to reshape Heron Key, drain the swamp of bad blood, break the shackles of the past. Well, it was happening all around her. The wind was taking the town apart, reducing it to its basic materials. And she sensed in its destruction a purpose, even a personality, like a gigantic, evil child smashing its toys in a fit of temper. *Of course, it is you, Bade.* The *loa* of the wind shared his duties with Agaou. It meant that Sogbo, the *loa* of lightning, would not be far away.

Sure enough, just at the moment when she thought to set herself down and wait for the gods to deal with her, lightning shattered the sky. Something white caught her attention among all the gray and brown and black. An island of white. No, not an island. Faint sounds came from the white thing, barely audible beneath the incessant yowl of the wind. It sounded almost like singing.

She stumbled closer and stopped. *I know that uniform.* And she gave thanks to Sogbo. "Missy!" she shrieked, loud as her voice would carry, which was usually enough to stop a grown man in his tracks at fifty paces.

Missy raised her head to reveal the small bundle beneath her. Selma sloshed toward her, arms outstretched. "Give him to me. Come on, girl, we almost there!"

Missy handed Nathan to Selma. He started to cry, which gladdened Selma's heart almost as much as if the sun had shown his face right there and then. "Good boy, Nathan," she cooed, baby on one shoulder, hand reaching for Missy.

Missy pushed through the water, uniform caked with mud and weeds, stinking like a swamp. "Oh, Selma," she began, eyes full of tears. "When the ditch flooded, I thought —"

"Ain't got time for that now, Missy. Almost there. C'mon." She put her free arm around Missy's shoulders and propelled her forward in what she prayed was the right direction.

And then it was there, right in front of them, like it was just waiting to be discovered: the familiar outline of Jenson's store. Missy let out a sob of relief. Selma stormed up the steps.

But something was wrong.

A crowd of maybe fifteen people was crammed into the remaining corner of the front porch. They held on to whatever they could find — railings, shutters — anything to keep from being blown into the rising water. Violet was there with her small son, Abe, tucked between her body and the wall of the store. Lionel clung to Ike, whose thickly muscled arms were twined around the only roof post left.

"Where's Mama?" Missy called. "She inside?" No one answered.

Selma tried the door. It was locked. "Let us in!" she hollered. "Let us in!" But the wind tore the sounds from her mouth.

The door opened a crack and Ike put his shoulder to it. They tumbled inside, into the mass of people packed together tighter than bristles in a brush.

"What the hell kind of foolishness is going on here?" asked Selma. "Why the door locked?" The air was thick with the smell of bodies and cigarette smoke and . . . something else. She searched the faces for an explanation. Trudy Mitchell looked like she wanted to murder someone, which was highly unusual. Jenson would not meet her eyes — equally unusual.

Ronald stepped forward. "Because, Selma, as you can see, there's no more room."

"There is *always* more room," growled Trudy.

"Momma —" Jenson began.

"Trudy," said Ronald, "we agreed to abide by the will of the majority."

"The will of the . . ." Selma studied the people in the dimness, taut faces shiny with fear. All white. And she knew every one of them, knew more about them than even their own families did. Secrets, they told them all to Selma. They had to, if they wanted her help. No one else knew Warren Hickson had another wife and child in Fort Lauderdale, who he visited every two weeks. No one else knew Cyril's mother, after her eleventh child, put saltpeter in her husband's coffee. No one else knew Ed Henderson spent all his time on the *Princess* because he was fascinated by one of the deckhands. The secrets twinkled in their eyes, little pinpricks of light. "And what might that be, Mr. LeJeune?"

Nathan began to wail, as if to remind them he was there. Missy soothed him. "Quiet now, my boy. We safe now."

But Marilee Henderson reached for him. "Give him to me, Missy. You're done in."

"He fine," said Missy and shifted him higher on her shoulder. Her limbs shook with exhaustion, but he weighed nothing as far as she was concerned. She would carry him forever if need be. "We got this far together. We fine," she said firmly.

Ronald turned to Selma. "You must see the sense of it. The shelter isn't big enough to hold everyone, so we have to choose." He paused, as if unsure what to say next. "So I'm sorry, but that's the way it is. We decided, all of us." He gestured to include the whole room. No one spoke. He cleared his throat. "The coloreds . . . you folks, will have to go."

"Go? Go where, Mr. LeJeune? You know what it's like outside. You'd send us out into that banshee storm?"

Violet sniffed. Abe wiped his nose on her skirt. Lionel put his twig-like arm around her shoulders.

Cynthia said, "Ronnie, can't we —"

"You know we can't, Cindy," he said quietly.

The wind slammed into the building. The force was like the impact of a solid object. Water sprayed through the walls. The lanterns went out. Children cried out in the dark, and women screamed. Someone turned on a flashlight.

"This isn't our way," said Jenson. "These people are our neighbors. We'll make room. We'll —

"You idiot, you'll kill us all!" said Ronald. "We made a decision, all of us." The bandage on his cheek cast strange shadows on his face, like it was some kind of malignant growth. The crying subsided into quiet sobs. "It's agreed. We all agreed."

Ike stepped forward into the circle of light. "I should have finished you when I had the chance." There was no mistaking the menace in his voice.

A metallic click. "Take one more step, Ike," said Ronald. "Just one more." The flashlight's weak beam glowed dully on the barrel of the revolver. "I don't want it to be this way. It doesn't have to be this way. Not if you go now. Please. Just go."

Selma looked around but no one met her eyes. The store shook like a die in a cup. Her skin prickled with the electric tingle of imminent panic. She stared into each face, willing each to remember this moment. Her gaze settled last on Jenson, who looked like a man torn apart from the inside.

She straightened her shoulders. "We going," she said. "And when we gone, y'all best think on how you gonna explain this to your Maker. Because you be seein' him soon, I promise you that. Real soon." On her way past Jenson, she murmured, "For shame."

"Where's Mama?" cried Missy in desperation. "Anyone seen my Mama?"

Violet said, "I ain't seen her since she went to Doc's."

Missy buried her face in Nathan's neck. Marilee stepped forward. "Missy," she said gently, "you've got to leave the baby here, with us. He belongs here. He'll be safe here."

"No! No, you cain't. I won't let you. I —"

But Selma took him from her arms and handed him to Marilee. Nathan howled in distress, stretched pudgy hands out to Missy, and kicked his feet. Selma said, "She right, Missy. You got to leave him. These his people. And he safer here."

And with that, Selma opened the door to . . . silence.

Traitorous stars shone within a circle of

swirling cloud. Their light touched only water, as far as she could see, punctuated by a few blasted trees and pieces of wood, where there should be dry land. Houses, businesses. Just piles of timber and crushed concrete.

"It over!" shouted little Abe. "We can go home now!"

"It ain't over," said Selma. "We under the eye." She made a quick study of the circle of clear sky above them. It was devilishly small, which meant the back side of the hurricane would be upon them soon. She reckoned they had maybe twenty minutes. Probably less. There was only one place she could think of where there might still be room to shelter. "Run, everyone!" she yelled. "Make for the station! Get in them boxcars quick, and stay there!"

"But what about Mama?" said Missy. "I gotta find Mama." She clutched at her empty, Nathan-less arms. "I got to find her." Her bare feet stumbled around in an aimless circle.

"Missy!" But she did not seem to hear. Selma took her by the shoulders and shook her, hard. Missy's eyes were wild with grief, her mind poisoned by it. She had lost too much, too fast. Doc's office was not far. While things were calm, she had time to get there and back. Just about enough time. To be caught in the open, once the eye passed over, was . . . *Well, no time to think on that now.* Despite the humid heat, Selma shivered. "I'll find her if she at Doc's. You take the others to the station. You hear me? Get in them boxcars and don't come out, not for anything, you understand?" Missy acknowledged her with a nod. "Come on, girl," Selma said. "MOVE!"

As Selma's splashes faded into the distance, Missy looked around at the scared, tired faces of the others refused a place in the store. Old Lionel looked about ready to drop, but he had an arm around a tearful Violet. Something was wrong with Ike. He seemed to be arguing with someone who wasn't there. None of the others were in much better shape. Several had already been hurt on the way to the store.

She didn't want to run anymore. She wanted to be alone, with her memories of Nathan and Henry, and pray for Mama and wait for Selma.

They all stood in a miserable huddle, looking expectantly at her.

A small hand tugged at hers. Abe said, "Selma say you take us."

"Go on," she said. "I be along soon."

But Abe would not release her hand. He

began to pull her in the wrong direction. The rail yard was not too far, maybe two miles away, but it would be easy to get lost in the darkness with all the familiar landmarks gone. For her whole life, she'd had an unerring ability to find her way, wherever she needed to go. So much so that the other kids used to leave her deep in the swamp to see if she made it home, and she always did. Just about the only learning she ever got from Billy was how to steer by the stars, but more than that, she could always tell the right way from the wrong way by how it felt.

She cast a look at the sky. The storm's eye had begun to move away. Nothing but darkness behind.

"Not that way," she said. "This way."

And just like that, they were off.

Dwayne had lost his bearings. Impossible to do, he would have said, a few hours before. They should have reached the store by now, but the absence of landmarks meant they could have been driving in circles. There was no beach to use as a reference point. All was wind-whipped water, in every direction.

The truck's wheels thumped into something hard. He tried to back up but there was only the grind of metal on metal. And then a wave broke over the hood and poured into the cabin. They were submerged up to their waists. With an angry hiss of steam, the engine died.

Noreen's eyes told him she understood what it meant. They would have to make it on foot. He would carry both her and Roy. She was far too slender to stand up to the current that barged against the side of the pickup.

Just as he was considering the logistics of this, all went quiet. There were splashes as airborne objects dropped into the water, like puppets with their strings cut. His ears rang with the absence of sound. No wind. Nothing.

He leaned out of the window and looked up to see the malevolent eye circling slowly above them. With each turn, it brought a new bout of destruction closer. The back side of the storm could only be minutes away. Once it arrived, they would have no chance in the open. They would have to stay in the flooded truck.

But Noreen was struggling to open her door. "Come on," she said. "We cain't stay here. We got to be close to the store by now."

He pulled her hand away. "We have to stay here! There's more coming. The truck is big and heavy enough to hold together. Noreen, it's the only way."

Too tired and scared even to cry, Roy had made no sound for some time. His dark eyes were alternately wide with fear and droopy with fatigue. The supplies so carefully packed for him floated in a sodden mess around them.

"We got to get Roy inside," she said. "He's hungry and thirsty."

"Hang on," said Dwayne and plunged his hand into water around his feet. He felt around until his fingers found the outlines of a milk bottle and raised it from the black water with a smile of triumph. "Here you go, my boy."

Roy sucked on the bottle without stopping until it was half-empty.

"That's better," said Noreen and wiped off his milky mustache. She kissed his cheek. "Hard to believe it ain't over," she said. "It looks so calm out there now."

Indeed, without the wind and with the water smoothing over the damage, what was left of Heron Key looked placid, even serene in the starlight. But Dwayne knew beneath the surface lay the wreckage of buildings, homes, and lives. Probably many lives.

"Noreen . . ." he began. How to start? It felt like there was too much to say and not enough words to say it. "I'm — I'm sorry. I mean, for everything, for —"

"I know, Dwayne," she said and squeezed his hand. It was the first time he had felt her touch for months, maybe since Roy was born. "I'm sorry too."

Something bumped against his door. He looked out of the window and down into the sightless eyes of Dolores Mason, who floated on her back, her red lipstick black against the gray pallor of her face. The current pushed her body into the side of the truck with a solid *thwack.*

"What is it?" Noreen asked.

"Nothing," he said and sent Dolores on her way with a hard shove. "Just a branch."

The veterans arrived at the train station to find it dark and empty. Trent peered up the tracks for sight of the locomotive's headlight, but there was only rain and wind screaming in the blackness. *It should be here by now. Something's gone wrong.* In the pale flashlight beam, he could see waves lapping the embankment, which was the highest point on Heron Key. Carl was unconscious and Stan was on the way there, moaning in pain. The post remained in his stomach, on Trent's instructions. He had seen too many men bleed out when such projectiles were extracted by well-meaning comrades. His only chance of survival was to leave the wooden stake right where it was until they could get medical attention . . . which could be a long time.

A gust caught the roof and tore half of it away. The rest of the structure began to tremble. The realization struck him that even the solidly constructed station would not protect them for much longer. They had to move. He swept the flashlight across the yard. An empty train stood on the siding. The heavy boxcars would be safer while they waited. Assuming, of course, the wait was not long. *Where is that damn train?*

But it was going to be tricky to get the men inside, given the strength of the wind. They would have to form a chain to make it across. He explained the plan to the men nearest to him and hoped the rest would follow.

Big Sonny was the first to attempt the crossing. He stepped off the platform into the full force of the wind and was blown off his feet and left clinging to the rail. The rest of the men hung back, unwilling to follow, especially those without the advantage of Sonny's bulk.

The remainder of the station began to disintegrate around them. This was clearly too much for Two-Step, who hollered, "I'm not staying here! There's no train coming for us."

"We've been left here to die!" said Sick Bay. "We've got to save ourselves!"

"Wait!"

It was the one they called "Kraut." Trent struggled to recall his real name. Mick? Mo? No, Max. Max Hoffman.

"Mr. Watts is right," said Max. He stood between Two-Step and the edge of the platform, hands spread wide. "Everyone just stay calm. We're safer waiting here. We've got to stick together and —" A chunk of masonry flew right into the side of his head, and he was felled like a tree. He landed on his back, eyes unseeing and open to the rain.

Angry voices surged around Trent. Wet, terrified faces jostled, ghostly in the flashlight's beam. He recognized the smell from the trenches: fear had overwhelmed some of their bladders. He could see Two-Step's point entirely. It looked like he had led them into a death trap. "No!" he shouted. "That's not true, I promise you —"

"Another lie!" said Two-Step. "We can make it, fellas! Look, over there. Shannon's filling station!" The concrete building was maybe a hundred yards away. Part of the roof was gone, but the walls were intact. "Who's with me, boys?"

Trent figured there was room for maybe twenty people inside — if they made it across the open ground, which did not look likely. Huddled on the platform were close to two hundred men. And how long before the wind flattened that structure too? No, he had to stop them. He made one last attempt. "Wait, I've got a plan —"

But it was too late. A group of men jumped down with Two-Step, running toward the gas station. When they were almost halfway there, one of the fuel pumps took to the air and slammed into them. Several bodies lay unmoving, face-down in the dirty water. Another grabbed hold of a telephone pole and clung there grimly. The wind simply lifted the pole from the ground and sent it hurtling into the sky. Two-Step let out a high, girlish scream as a piece of window glass cleaved right through his thigh. He fell, then tried to get up, but the wind pushed him down again. He grabbed the severed leg and began to pull himself through the mud.

Trent could see his mouth screaming "Help me!" over and over, but no one moved.

Two-Step flailed on, like some deranged

swimmer, sliding in the mire. And then the wind lifted him up and carried him away into the night. A few men made it to the gas station. The remainder of his group flung themselves behind the bulk of a massive water tanker, still full of ten thousand gallons.

When Trent turned to face the rest of the men still waiting, they appeared ready to follow him almost anywhere.

"What's the plan?" asked Sick Bay.

On the other side of the platform, Sonny had managed to regain his feet and reach the boxcar. He grabbed hold with one hand and stretched the other toward the waiting men. Trent set about getting the biggest ones onto the tracks first. They would have to carry the wounded. The dead would be left where they lay.

"Sick Bay, grab hold of Sonny," Trent yelled. "The next one grab hold of Sick Bay, and so on, until we get a solid line of men. The others use them to cross. Got it?"

Sick Bay set off toward Sonny. He was blown over twice but got up each time. A cheer went up when he clasped Sonny's outstretched hand. Others followed, and soon the line was complete. Men began to cross, holding their comrades for support.

Jeb stared wide-eyed. Each man had to

fight his way across, and they were all easily twice as heavy as him. "Guess this is the last stop for me," he said in Franklin's ear.

"Come here," said Franklin. "Get on my back."

Jeb climbed on, arms tight around Franklin's neck. "All aboard," said Franklin. And he stepped off the platform, to be met by waiting hands.

Franklin stumbled. Jeb clung on, eyes narrowed. The wind clawed at his shoulders, tried to loosen his arms and pull him off. Franklin held on, legs wide apart to maintain his balance. He took another step along the line, which swayed under the might of the gale. It was clear that Jeb's weight was holding him back. Jeb knew what he had to do. He loosened his grip on Franklin's neck. Franklin's eye swiveled around in surprise, his lips formed to say, "No!"

Jeb closed his eyes and let go. A big hand grabbed his collar and wrenched him from the wind's grasp. He just had time to register Lemuel's grin before he was flung bodily into the safety of the boxcar.

CHAPTER 22

On the relief train, still several miles away, Ken Cramer stared through the deluge. He nudged the locomotive forward, as much by touch as by vision. It was impossible to gauge the depth of the water covering the tracks. Moses, Clarence, and Henry leaned out of the windows with no more success. "Can't see a goddamn thing," Moses complained.

"Fellas," said Ken, "this is about to get real interesting."

After they had freed the train from the crane's cables, it had sped south to collect veterans from two other work camps on its way to Heron Key. It had been a slow and dangerous operation just to get them on board, as the wind lifted people right off their feet. Included in the wet huddle of humanity were a few locals who had decided, with uncharacteristic alacrity, to evacuate as well.

Shouting came to the engineer's cabin from the passenger carriage. Ken dispatched Henry. "Go calm them down, Roberts. You're one of them."

On his way through the swaying carriage, a hand grabbed Henry's arm. "What the hell took you so long?" demanded a sunburned blond bull of a man with USMC tattooed on one bicep and a bloody rag wrapped around the other. "We had no chance out there." The man's face was flushed with rage as much as sun. "Sitting ducks, that's all we were. Sitting fucking ducks." He nodded at a sodden woman with a bedraggled dog on her lap. "Beggin' your pardon, ma'am." He passed a hand over his face. The atmosphere in the carriage was a strange mixture of seething resentment and relief.

Jimmy turned around in his seat. Water dripped from the brim of his cap. "It weren't our fault," he said. "The crew couldn't have worked any harder. It's them assholes up in J'ville, left it too late to order the train, ya see?" He also nodded to the woman. "Beg pardon, ma'am."

Henry noticed Clarence's distinctive cadence in Jimmy's voice. The boy was very taken with the train and the men who made it run. He seemed to be having the time of his life. Henry had forgotten what that felt like, the thrill of adventure. And Jimmy had been a tremendous asset in the effort to free the train from the cables. The operation was considerably speeded by his youthful strength and energy. In fact, Henry wondered if they might not still be stuck were it not for Jimmy. He had whooped and hollered as they hauled on the cables under the merciless, pounding rain. After an hour of this, he and Clarence and Moses were all panting and fatigued, while Jimmy looked as fresh as when they started.

Henry said, "Take it easy, Marine. We doin' the best we can." He took in the man's bandage, his eyes wide with barely controlled fear. One of his legs shook but he seemed not to notice. Henry had never seen a marine so scared. He knew them to be the toughest sons of bitches around. "What happened to y'all?"

The marine's massive head hung down. "The camp killed our men when it blew apart. We had nowhere to hide. It just cut us to pieces. We expect that, in a war. We trained for it. You can attack, take the other guy out. But not here. There was no way to fight back, nothin' we could do. Just nothin'. It ain't right." He wiped angrily at his eyes. "It just ain't right."

"No, it ain't," Henry said through clenched teeth. "Someone is gonna pay when this is all over." All he could think of was Lemuel, Sonny, Jeb, Franklin, left out there to face the same thing. Why weren't they evacuated sooner? At least the locals had shelter, but the men had none. *I should never have left.*

He stared into the blackness outside, trying to get some sense of the train's momentum. Rain clattered against the glass. It was impossible to tell, but it felt like they were moving forward with agonizing slowness. No doubt Ken was intent on avoiding another collision. It felt like Henry's blood could boil from the frustration of it. Although he could do nothing to stop the slaughter — neither in war nor in the storm — his men looked to him for leadership, even after all this time. And he was not there. Were it in his power, he would have jumped down onto the tracks and pushed the train all the way to Heron Key.

"You think anyone gives a shit about us?" asked the marine. The woman with the dog just gave a tired wave of her hand at his language. "Hell, I bet those bastards in Washington are having a party —"

Henry was thrown to his knees by the train's sudden deceleration. Jimmy helped him up and they looked out the windows. "I think," said Henry, "we've arrived."

Ken entered the carriage. "This is as far as we go, can't make it to the depot. Water's too deep ahead, already higher than I ever seen, and getting deeper. Roberts, you need to get your people on board right now. We can't hang around."

"Listen," said the marine.

Complete silence pounded Henry's ears. Empty not only of train noise, but of any noise at all.

"Hey, everyone!" the marine called to his comrades. "It's over! Come on, we've got to help get the rest of the men on board." And he moved toward the carriage door.

Henry peered at the sky and quickly moved to bar his way. The marine was easily a head taller and fifty pounds heavier, but Henry held up his hands. "No, wait, y'all got to stay here."

"We'll be fine. You could use our help. The storm's passed." The other veterans scuffed their boots, plainly torn between their duty and wanting to dry off in the train.

"It's not safe!" Henry said. "It's not safe. If you want to save yourself and your men, you will not get off this train."

The locals in the carriage stayed put. The woman with the dog said, "He's right. We're under the eye. Only a fool would go out now."

"There's worse to come," said Henry. "Much worse, in only a few minutes. Please, wait here." He jumped down into the black water.

"Where you going then?" asked the marine.

"To get my people."

The other man appraised Henry for a moment. "Then we're coming too. You're going to need help, if they're anything like mine. As a famous marine once said, 'Who wants to live forever?' Come on, men, we've got work to do."

With a grin, he jumped down beside Henry and was instantly swallowed by the darkness.

Missy peered into the darkness ahead. The stars were almost gone, covered by rolling coils of cloud, and the wind was up again. She reckoned they still had about a mile to go, but it was slow. The ground beneath their bare feet was a treacherous maze of debris, and the water that covered the road hid chunks of wood, glass, and cement. Abe had already fallen into a deep hole and emerged with a gash across his arm. There was a lot of blood that showed shiny black against his dark skin, but he did not cry. Violet bound it with a strip torn from the hem of her dress and they carried on.

It felt to Missy like they had been walking for hours, such was the concentration needed for each step forward, feeling with her toes for the safe place to put her feet. They were badly cut but she ignored the pain.

The road itself had been washed away in several places, leaving fast torrents that they could only cross with their arms linked together. They were right in the middle of one such torrent, up to their waists in it, when Lionel cried out and went under. In an instant, he was gone, swept into the blackness by the white water. The others were nearly knocked off their feet but somehow managed to right themselves.

They stood there for a few moments, clinging together and calling Lionel's name. There was no answer.

"Missy," Violet asked in a trembling voice, "maybe we should turn back?"

The wind blew harder. Only a small circle of stars remained visible in the sky. Ike held a sputtering Abe on his shoulders, clear of the rushing river that had torn the bandage from his arm. The others braced themselves as best they could against the force of the water, but it was clear that they were not able to hold their positions for much longer.

They could not go back; there was no shelter there. They could not stay still. The only way was forward. Missy said a prayer for gentle, harmless old Lionel . . . *He don't deserve this.* It was so utterly unfair. She didn't deserve it either. All her life, she had done the right thing. Every time fate had slapped her in the face, she had just carried on without complaint. Lightning crackled in the clouds above, followed fast by the bass boom of thunder, like the storm was tuning up its instruments, ready to play its big final number.

And that was when it happened. Something inside her just broke apart under the weight of fear and helplessness. She was suddenly and completely overwhelmed by a determination, hard and clear as glass, that they would make it to the station. Her grief and fear turned to anger at her powerlessness against the forces that hurt the people she cared about. She was tired of being blown around like a leaf, with no say in anything that mattered. Anger rose up her spine like a column of molten steel. Her back straightened. She was angry at the storm, for destroying her home and wreaking havoc on her town. She was angry at

400

the small-minded people who accused Henry and forced him to flee, and those who had turned them out into the storm. She had failed to stop any of it. She had failed to stop Henry leaving. She had failed to protect Nathan.

By God, I will not fail at this.

"We cain't go back!" she yelled above the rush of the water and wind. "We got to keep going! Ain't far now!"

"You heard Missy!" said Abe. "Ain't far now!"

With an enormous effort of will, Missy braced her feet and pushed forward against the weight of water, pulling on Violet's arm to bring her along. And so they began to move. Far above them, the stars disappeared.

At the remains of the train station, the veterans were hunkered down miserably inside the boxcars. The air was sour with their breath, from the exertion of getting everyone inside, and the fumes from their filthy, soaking clothes. Rain slanted down so heavily outside that it obscured what was left of the station. They were surrounded by a wall of water reaching up to the sky. Trent felt many pairs of hostile eyes focused on him.

"This is your fault," said Tec. "You've known this storm was coming for days. You coulda got us out before. Two-Step was right. There ain't no train comin'. We're stuck here."

Trent took a moment to choose his words. The atmosphere was a combustible mixture of terror and anger, which could ignite at any moment. Although the accusation stung, he could see Tec's point. It would serve no purpose to defend himself, would probably just inflame them further. And it made no difference to their situation for them to understand who was really responsible. Tec was right — they should have been evacuated sooner, and now they were stuck.

Lemuel said, "Ain't no good pointing fingers, Tec." He removed the Bible from inside his shirt. Water dripped from the pages but the binding still held. "As the good book says —"

"Shut up, Lemuel," said Sick Bay. "Tec's right. Since it looks like we're all gonna die here, I vote that you go first, Trent. You are the leader, as you keep telling us." When sober, Sick Bay's disposition was sunny, even placid, but when drunk, he became bad-tempered and downright aggressive. He had been drinking since early that afternoon.

Trent shifted away from the group into the corner of the boxcar. There was no mistaking Tec's intent. The faces of the others told the same story. He could see it in their eyes: for all those times he had imposed his will on them, driving them to work harder under the awful conditions of the camp. This was probably their one and only chance for payback. And in the chaos of the storm, no one would ever know.

"Fellas, hang on a minute," he said, hands up ready either to placate or punch them. "You have every right to be angry. But I'm angry too. I've been trying —"

Tec's fist sent him to the floor of the boxcar. There, the heavy boots found him. The first kick went to his kidneys, the second to his stomach. He curled into a ball, hands over his face. The next kick would be to his head. What bothered him most was not the pain, as he had felt much worse, nor even the unfairness of it all. No, what bothered him most was that, for all the times he had come close to death, all the times in France when he expected to be taken, it was always in the service of some purpose, with even some dignity. Not curled up on the floor of a stinking boxcar, getting stomped to death like a cockroach by his own men.

He looked up to see Sick Bay's boot raised, ready to smash down on his head. In a flash, Trent realized he had only one chance, while the man's balance was off. He flung himself at Sick Bay's leg and bit down as hard as he could. The skin tasted salty, the blood metallic in his mouth. Sick Bay staggered with a howl to fall on his back with Trent straight on top of him, hands around his throat. It felt good — the pulse of the artery under his fingers, the springy firmness of the windpipe between his palms. Arms pulled at him but he retained his grip. Months and months of frustration congealed in his hands and he squeezed harder. Sick Bay's face turned a satisfying shade of brownish red, like a bruised apple.

"Fellas, listen!" Sonny cried. "Listen!"

While they had been fighting, the rain had stopped, like someone had turned off a faucet. The wind had ceased.

The men who had been shouting encouragement fell silent. Intent on strangling Sick Bay, Trent had not noticed the lack of noise from outside. He had no idea how long it had been since the storm finished. It felt like they had been cooped up in the boxcar for hours already. He released his hold on Sick Bay.

"Hey," said Sick Bay rather hoarsely, hand to his throat, "you can see the stars!"

"Let's go, fellas!" said Tec and jumped down onto the tracks. "It's over!"

The men stumbled out into the still night air, the absence of the train no longer a concern, now the storm was over. They were jubilant, smiling, arms around each other's shoulders. They had survived the worst night of their lives.

Tec even helped Trent up. "No hard feelings, eh?"

Trent just shook his head in wonderment while his heartbeat returned to normal. But then the chattering mass of men shut up and parted to reveal a group of colored people approaching from the direction of the town. A woman was at the front in a torn and filthy uniform that might have once been white.

"Can we help you?" Trent asked.

"My name's Missy Douglas," she said, "and we need some place to stay."

He recognized the name. Roberts's men had teased him about a girl called Missy. "Why aren't you at the store?"

"No room at the store," she said without emotion, "for people . . . people like us."

He was struck by the simplicity of her words. If he had been denied shelter by a bunch of niggers, he would have taken a terrible revenge on the next one he saw. She looked exhausted to the point of collapse, but there was fire in her eyes. There was a little boy holding closed a big gash in his arm. A man with wild eyes dragged his right leg like it was broken. All were soaked through.

"Come, sit down," he said to her and helped her into the boxcar doorway. The others followed. The veterans stood around curiously, unsure what to make of the newcomers. Trent turned away to deal with them but she caught his sleeve.

With great urgency, she said, "Mister, you got to get them back inside. It ain't over. This just the eye."

"What do you mean?" he asked. The men had poured onto the tracks to wait for the train, scattered for maybe five hundred yards.

"There's worse coming — it right behind us. You got to get them inside, and fast."

Trent set off at a run after the men. There was little hope of persuading them to return to the smelly confines of the boxcar while the sky was clear, but he had to try. *Might as well tell ketchup to get back in the bottle.*

Missy turned to find a big man with a lazy

eye smiling at her. "Missy," he said, "my name's Sonny. I one of Henry's boys. He talk about you all the time."

"Yeah, but he didn't say how pretty you was," said a little guy who looked about twelve except for the weary worldliness in his eyes.

"You must be Jeb," she said. "Henry talk about you all the time too." Just saying his name caused a pain in her chest. More than anything in the world at that moment, she wanted to feel his arms around her and hear him say it was going to be all right. But he was somewhere else, far away and safe, somewhere the wind didn't tear your house to pieces, somewhere bodies didn't float down flooded streets.

"I'm Franklin," said a man with a crumpled hole where his eye should be. He saw her glance at the wound and covered it with his hand. "Sorry, ma'am, I lost my patch in the storm."

"Franklin?" called a small voice from the back of the boxcar. "That you?" Violet shuffled forward. Her dress was torn and stained, her hair a wild mess from the wind and water. One eye was swollen shut where a stone had flown into her face.

Franklin hugged her off her feet. "Violet!" She slumped into his arms.

"Look at you," he said. "You got one eye, like me now. Don't matter — we got two good ones between us. That all a person needs." He turned to Abe, who lurked behind his mother's legs. "And who is this young man?"

"My name's Abe," he said. "I hurt my arm." The gash was long and deep and pink as a shark bite.

"Well," said Franklin, "let's see about that. I ain't no doctor, but I seen plenty of soldiers hurt worse than this." He tore his shirt into strips to bind the wound.

"You was a solider?" Abe asked, eyes wide.

"Yup," said Franklin. "We all was. Still are, come to that. There." He pulled the bandage tight. "Now you a soldier too."

A whistle sounded, high and clear in the quiet air.

Missy looked up to see the bald man's head appear in the doorway, eyes lit with excitement. "It's here! The train's here!" he exclaimed. "Just like I said it would be. Come on, fellas, all aboard!"

"We comin', Mr. Watts," said Jeb.

Missy clasped his shoulder. "Please don't go. It ain't safe out there. The storm, it comin' back, and —"

Lemuel patted her with a big paw. "Don't you worry, ma'am. We be halfway to Miami by then."

"Franklin," Violet said, "listen to Missy. Please don't go. It ain't safe. Stay here, with us." She put an arm around Abe's narrow shoulders.

"With you?" Inside the question was another question. He took a tentative step forward. "Do you mean . . . ?"

Violet took something from her pocket. A sandpiper, carved from driftwood. "Look. I keep this with me all the time. It make me feel safe. You . . . make me feel safe."

Jeb cuffed Franklin on the shoulder. "Yeah, best you stay here. Don't want you crampin' my style when we get to Miami." And then, with a wink, he was gone, along with Sonny and Lemuel.

Franklin called after them, "Y'all take care of Jeb now, ya hear? He ain't old enough to drink!"

Jeb, Sonny, and Lemuel sloshed along the tracks in the direction of the train. In the beam of the locomotive's headlamp, the scene ahead of them was one big, heaving mass of men. Although keen to board, they were in no hurry, enjoying the respite while they smoked in the welcome stillness under the stars.

"What you gonna do when we get to

Miami?" Jeb asked Lemuel.

"I gonna get me a big ole steak and a bucket full of beer." Jeb threw him a surprised glance. Lemuel did not drink.

"All's I want," said Sonny, "is to sleep in a real bed, just for one night."

"Shit," said Jeb, "what's wrong with y'all? We survived a hurricane. You got any idea how much the ladies gonna love that story?"

As they approached the train, Jeb heard a familiar voice, which cut through all the noise and confusion. He searched the crowd, eyes darting from face to face until he saw him.

"Thank us later!" Henry shouted in exasperation. "Just get your asses on board. NOW!" The unruly group of veterans surrounded Henry, all wanting to shake his hand. The train's long-delayed arrival and the horrors of the past few hours had released in them a kind of euphoria, making them even more difficult to manage than usual.

"Boss!" cried Jeb. He and the others pushed their way through the crowd to Henry's side. Lemuel lifted him into the air. Sonny asked, "You just cain't stay away from your old pals, huh?"

Henry's face split into a huge grin that disappeared just as quickly. "Hurry now, boys, and get on that train. Storm's not done with us yet." With a wary look at the sky, he said, "I got to find Missy and Selma. Where's Franklin?"

"Franklin gonna wait it out with the locals inside that boxcar over there," said Jeb. "With his sweetheart."

"Speakin' of which . . ." began Sonny.

Henry's eyes passed from one man to the next, forehead creased in confusion. "Why you fellas all grinnin' like fools?"

Jeb clapped him on the back. "There's someone in that boxcar you got to see."

Henry broke into a run. Over his shoulder, he said, "Get yourselves on board the train — that's an order! I'll deal with you later."

CHAPTER 23

It had taken Selma longer than expected to slog through the filthy water to Doc's office, and with every step, she had regretted her decision. She was on a fool's errand, she knew that, had known it when she set off. She could feel Mama was gone. Of course, she couldn't tell Missy that. And yet here she was, in the open, under the eye of a hurricane. And for what? To confirm what she knew already, what the collapsed roof of Doc's office told her when she finally arrived? There might be someone alive under the massive pile of jagged timbers, but she figured the chances weren't good.

She forced herself to move faster through the water, heading back in the direction of the station. The others would be safely inside the boxcars by now, whose enormous weight should stand up to whatever the storm still had to throw at them. Unseen objects brushed her legs. Some were soft.

She closed her mind to what they might be. A dead raccoon floated by, its clever paws curled over its face, finally overcome by the element it craved. Out of nowhere, a very much alive cottonmouth snake sped toward her across the water, its white jaws glowing in the darkness, opened wide to strike. She snatched up a broken fence post and swung it like a baseball bat. It connected with the snake's head and sent it hurtling into the gloom. *Shame about that; cottonmouth's good eatin'.* When the storm finally finished with them, there would be nothing to eat or drink, maybe for days. For Selma, that was her worst nightmare. With deep sadness, she thought of her shelves of carefully stored preserves and canned goods lined up neatly in the shed and the fresh lemon cake she'd made just that morning. All gone.

She thought of the faces of the people at Jenson's store, people she had lived alongside her whole life, people she thought she knew. Their expressions, a mix of shame, mortal fear, and determination, would stay with her always. It was time to accept that nothing would ever change Heron Key, no amount of death or destruction. It would go on as before, as it always had. And if she didn't like it, well then there was only one choice. *If I want a fresh start, I'll need to find it somewhere else.*

Her whole life had been spent within a twenty-mile radius of Heron Key. She had never wanted to be anywhere else. Missy had shown her pictures of other places, in discarded copies of the Miami newspapers and of course in her beloved encyclopedia. Maybe she would go to Georgia. People said it was nice there. But why not somewhere completely different, somewhere far away from all the memories? Jamaica? Aruba? *Hell, why not France? Henry sure liked it there.* He was the traveler in the family. From the time he was little, he had talked about the world. He used to draw pictures of the continents in the sand, then fill them in with different kinds of seashells. Just as she felt Mama's absence, she felt Henry's presence, and not far away. *Where you at, brother mine? What made you come back here?*

No, she realized, she would never leave Heron Key. They were joined together forever. And anyway, she figured people were the same wherever you went, didn't matter how far. The only way to get away from them was to fly to the moon.

The eye started to cloud over. She was still some distance from the station. Wind stirred the water into peaks. She needed to speed up.

The ground suddenly became treacherously uneven. *Must have left the road.* She felt her way along with bare toes, shoes lost in the water. Her ankle twisted as she stepped into a hole. She pulled her foot out and tried to quicken her strides against the weight of water, pushed her legs harder, and leaned forward.

And then she stumbled.

Her right foot plunged into a hole and stuck fast. Sharp edges of something heavy gripped her ankle tight. They bit into her flesh when she tried to twist free. As she felt around beneath the water, her hands told the awful truth: her foot was impaled on a sharp object. It went right through. Pain and anger forced a cry from her mouth. She hauled on the trapped foot, but the jaws only tightened. A quick look at the sky and her inner clock told her there was little time left. Agaou's hot breath blew hard against her now. The water suddenly retreated, and that was when she knew: the surge was coming. She would stand no chance out in the open. She felt the return of the storm's fury, just moments away now.

Only one choice remained: she must lose the foot. Plenty of people got along fine with only one. She pulled and pulled with all her

415

strength. The teeth bit harder, sunk deeper. She was well and truly stuck, just like a bear in a trap.

Her hands cast around for something, anything, sharp enough to cut but met only useless pieces of wood. "No, no, not like this," she growled into the empty darkness. "Help!" she called. "Someone help!" But there was no sound except a faint, distant rumble, coming closer.

She looked up at the sky just in time to see the stars disappear.

"Come on, Dwayne," said Noreen. "We cain't stay in this truck all night. I need to go to the bathroom, and Roy's diaper is dirty. Look, the water's gone right down, we should just —"

"Be quiet a minute," he said. "You hear that?" Dwayne sensed a change in the air. Noreen was right — the water had suddenly receded, as if someone had drained a bathtub. But the wind was up again, worse than before. There came a sound, at first unremarkable. It was a low, scratchy thudding like the footfall of some giant animal. He felt it in his gut more than heard it with his ears. It was the vibration of something incredibly heavy, approaching at great speed.

Noreen had opened her door. "Well, I'm going —"

"No, don't!" he yelled, but it was too late. The surge was upon them.

The enormous wave struck the truck and flung it along as if it were made of balsa wood instead of heavy gauge steel. All the glass gave way and the water rushed in.

He heard Noreen scream and reached out for her but found Roy instead. He fought to keep the baby's head above the torrent. It engulfed Dwayne up to his chin, tried to fill his mouth and nose. It flowed through the cab like a raging river and swept Noreen out of the open door. He caught her hand just in time.

"Dwayne!" she screamed.

The water poured across him with such force that his grip on Roy's body weakened. He needed both hands to secure him.

"Hold on!" he yelled, but Noreen looked from him to Roy and back again. Then, very deliberately, she closed her eyes and let go of his hand. And vanished.

The water closed over Dwayne's head. His hands held Roy above the surface, just under the roof of the pickup. The boy's body had gone limp. And still the truck continued to fly sideways, pushed along at great speed by the wave's watery fist.

Dwayne expected a crushing impact at any moment, which would wrench Roy from his grasp. His lungs burned for air. He managed to raise his mouth into the roof space, took a big gulp of air, and went under again. He would keep Roy safe until he could breathe no more. That was the only thing that mattered. It seemed impossible that there was so much water in the sea, and yet it still kept coming.

Dwayne's world shrank. There was only the airspace, Roy's warm body in his hands, and the fight for breath. The waves developed a rhythm, like the surf, and he began to time his breaths to coincide with the low water. His arms ached. His hands began to go numb. He carried on like this for what felt like hours but was probably only ten minutes. A dead moray eel floated through the cab. Its silky tail caressed his cheek.

There was no more feeling in his hands, but Roy's weight was still there. With each gulp of air, he had just enough time to check that the boy was breathing.

The truck struck something solid that halted its sideways progress. Dwayne struggled to make his hands retain their grip. They felt like two pieces of dead meat. The muscles in his arms were on fire. The water receded slightly, enough for him to keep his face clear. Whatever had stopped their progress had absorbed the impact of the truck without smashing it. He could just make out the lines of graceful arching branches in the space where the door had been. Mangroves. Of course. They could withstand almost any amount of force, even hurricane winds, and they now held the truck in a cushioned embrace. He took several grateful breaths.

"Roy, you okay?"

Roy opened his eyes. Dwayne realized they were not alone. Several naked corpses, anonymous in death, were twined like lovers around the mangrove roots.

Zeke's voice: "Give him to me."

Without a moment's hesitation, Dwayne passed Roy to Zeke. His arms dropped into the water like they had been cut off. The return of blood to his hands was excruciating. He could not move his fingers. The wind once more began to pound the truck with water and anything else it could find. A chunk of cement big as a bowling ball slammed into the door frame beside his head. It seemed that the elements, having failed to drown the truck, were now intent on beating it to death.

"Come on," said Zeke. "In here."

Dwayne could see nothing beyond the edge of the mangroves. Feeling began to return to his hands. He pulled himself along in the direction of Zeke's voice. Once he got inside the trees, the wind and water's power was greatly diminished. He was able to stand and breathe freely. As he pushed toward Zeke's voice, behind him came the awful sounds of the truck's demise, as more and more missiles found their target.

He came across them deep inside the forest. Of Poncho there was no sign. Zeke had Roy afloat on a raft made of old tire inner tubes, which rocked gently with the motion of the trees. The boy stretched out his arms to Dwayne. Dwayne snatched him up, hugged the little body tight to his chest. At that moment, it felt like he could happily remain there for the rest of his life, in that same spot.

Then his eyes were drawn to something pale, caught between two branches. It was a scarf, printed with honeysuckle.

Over at Mitchell's store, the mood had been somber since Selma and the others had been forced to flee.

Jenson Mitchell sat alone in the back doorway. He knew it was extremely reckless and irresponsible. It was not safe to be out under the eye. He looked up. The circle of cloud was almost gone. Dirty water slapped the back steps. They had not yet seen the worst of this hurricane, if the back side winds brought a surge. It would not take much to overwhelm them. He should be inside, helping to calm people, reassure them — his friends, his neighbors, the people he had known all his life. But he could not. He needed to be away from everyone.

A few people had come outside to stretch their legs and relieve themselves, as the toilet had overflowed some hours before, but most had remained inside, despite the awful conditions. It was not clear whether it was out of fear of the storm, or of losing their place, or both.

He studied them as if they were an unknown species. Were it not for Trudy, he would simply have walked away and left them to their fate. He had always considered himself to be a good, honest man — not a great one, never that, but a good one — someone who would try to do his best by others in any situation. He had failed, and the bitterness of it nearly choked him. He could have — should have — done something.

Although no one could deny that Heron

Key had its share of problems, all his life he had been glad, even proud, to say it was his home. He thought about the generations of his family and all they had invested in the town. The store wasn't just a place to buy provisions; it was a place where people came to get and give news, ask for help, or just talk to someone. Despite the terrible destruction of the town, he knew it could be rebuilt, would be rebuilt. But by far the worst damage, he felt, could not be repaired with any amount of money or labor: the storm had destroyed the vision of life he had treasured. It was gone. Forever.

Trudy stepped outside to join him. "Come back in, Son. It's not safe out here." The wind had come up again. She pushed the hair out of her face. The sky was once more a mass of indigo clouds. "There was nothing you could have done."

"I could have stopped him," he said miserably. "I could have grabbed Ronald's gun and —"

"Ronald wasn't the only one who wanted them to go," she pointed out. "Others would have taken his place." A shrug. "It's just the way things are."

"The way things are . . ." He shook his head. "Maybe you're right. But without Ronald in the lead, maybe some common decency could have got the upper hand. These are basically good people; you know they are."

"Yes, they are, but good people in fear for their lives don't always do what's right."

He stared at the worn wooden floor, deeply indented by the footsteps of generations of Conchs. "I should have done something, taken a stand. Even if I failed, that would count . . . for something."

"True, and maybe got yourself shot in the process, and the coloreds would still have to leave. And how would that help anyone?" She glanced in alarm at the sky. "Come on inside now."

Just as they closed the door, the wind slammed into the building. It felt stronger, wilder. The gusts of earlier in the evening had succeeded in weakening the structure. Again and again, it struck the store in a frenzy of force. With a terrible tearing growl, the timbers began to split. There was a loud groan and then a *crack*. To Jenson's complete amazement, the heavy steel anchor bolts sheared away. Three men threw their weight against the door to hold it closed.

The floor lifted and tilted one way and then the other, like a surfboard. The whole building was afloat. The crowd of people fell in a heap, crying and screaming in terror as the walls started to break apart.

And then the rear of the building rose up, as if a hand were trying to spill them out. People began to slide toward the door, scrabbled to retain a hold on anything solid while the world turned itself inside out. Cyril held on to Sam, who was barking hysterically. Warren Hickson clung to Mabel's generous girth. Cynthia's arms were tight around Ronald's neck. "Do something, Ronnie!" she hollered. "I don't want to die!"

The door blew off its hinges and struck Warren. He was swept away before anyone could help him.

"Warren!" shouted Mabel, but then she also lost her footing and went down.

Marilee held on to Tim with one hand, the other wrapped tight around Nathan.

The angle of the floor's incline deepened. Jenson realized in an instant that the whole structure was about to tumble onto its roof. They had to get out or the store would become a mass coffin. Such a wind would bring the sea with it. The wave was coming, would be upon them in a few moments. They had to make for higher ground, and the only place he knew to find it was the railway embankment.

"Listen to me, everyone!" he called over

the noise of the people and the shriek of the gale. "We have to get out of here. Get ready to run, fast as you can! Make for the railway line!"

The room tilted further still, so that people simply fell out of the open door to be snatched by the wind and water.

Cyril cradled Sam in his arms. "Come on, Sam!" He stepped out and they both disappeared. Others followed in a sudden rush. The store was no longer a place of refuge. Even the storm held less terror than being inside while the building was demolished.

Jenson turned to get Trudy but she was not beside him. As the last person spilled out the door, there was a loud crash and a scream from the back of the store. Jenson pulled himself along, hand over hand, until he came to the storage room.

"Momma, where are you?" He could see nothing but dark, swirling water.

"Over here, Jenson!" she called, a ringing tone of pure panic in her voice. "Over here!"

In the far corner, Trudy lay trapped beneath the heavy industrial refrigerator. Her torso was free, her head just above the water, but the rest of her was lost from view, crushed by several hundred pounds of metal.

She cried out, "Jenson, my legs! I can't

feel my legs!"

Tears poured down her cheeks. Her face was white with pain, her eyes frantic. He had never seen his mother panic. It electrified his muscles. He threw himself at the machine, heaved on it with all his strength. It would not move. He went around the other side and did the same thing, with the same result. He cast around desperately for anything to use as a lever, but the building had been emptied of everything and everyone. They were alone in the bucking, disintegrating structure, like on some horrible carnival ride.

"Hang on," he said. "I'm gonna get you out of here! You're gonna be fine!"

The structure tilted farther off its axis. Jenson seized hold of the door frame. Trudy cried out. There was a crunch of splintering wood. A roof beam sailed past his head. The window glass exploded outward as the air pressure plummeted still further. He flung his whole weight against the fridge, again and again, to no discernible effect. There came the *snap* of his collar bone breaking. He could not raise his arm. He turned his body around the other way, prepared to break the other one, but Trudy yelled, "Stop! You can't do it. Not this time, Jenson. The surge is coming; you know it is."

Now her eyes were dry. She spoke quickly, even calmly, although the pain twisted her face into a terrible grimace. "You have to save yourself. You have to get to higher ground. Get out. I'm begging you. Get out. Now."

The building howled and thrashed as if in the jaws of a lion. The roof blew away and rain poured in on them. He looked around at what was left of their livelihood, the place that had served them so well for so long. And then he sat down beside her, steadied himself against the immovable refrigerator. With his good arm, he stroked her hair. Beneath the sound of the wind, he felt the unmistakable throb of the surge's approach. Not far away now. Not long to wait.

He had heard somewhere that the dead retained an image in their eyes of the last thing they saw. He stared hard into her beloved face.

"Now, Momma," he said. "You know me better than that."

CHAPTER 24

Missy lay down on the boxcar floor to wait for whatever else the night would bring. Her heart kept pumping blood around a body that did not belong to her. It felt like the wind had hollowed her out from the inside. Only an empty shell was left, a shell that still breathed but did not feel. She was glad of the numbness and hoped it would last. Being under the eye of a hurricane, she thought, was like lying down in the road, paralyzed, in front of a steamroller. No way to get out of its path. Nothing to do but brace yourself as best you could. And wait for whatever came next.

Around her, the others settled themselves on the hard floor in quiet apprehension. Franklin ripped off part of the door to make a splint for Ike's broken leg. The boxcar was big and heavy enough to protect them, but it was still going to be a rough ride.

All she wanted was to sleep, maybe

forever. Yes, she decided, that was it. End-less sleep. Maybe just let the wind take her. It began to hiss through the boxcar again. The curtain of rain drew itself across the door. It would be so easy to just get up and walk out. There was no reason to stay. Selma and Mama should have been there by now. Mama had never trusted water, not after Billy drowned. The thought of her, out there in it, scared and alone — and Henry was gone. Since he left, she had been tortured by dreams that he had returned, dreams so real that when she woke without him was like a knife in her heart.

And her arms ached for Nathan. She knew rationally that the store was the best, safest place for him, but she still yearned for his warm, sweet-smelling weight against her. She had cared for him every day of his life. The emptiness was almost too much to bear. Their house, their garden, the hens, everything they depended on . . . all gone. Her life . . . she wanted it back, just as it was yesterday, in every mundane detail. She wanted to sit on the porch next to Mama again amid the soft clucking of chickens, shelling peas and talking about the day until the mosquitoes got too bad. She wanted to see that look on Henry's face again, that smile of surprised wonder, like he couldn't believe his luck.

Gone. All gone.

A sharp stone of loss settled in her throat, so big that she found it hard to breathe. She closed her eyes and tried to empty her mind of everything. Really, she had little interest in what was to come. Yes, she had brought her people to the rail yard. But what had seemed like her big achievement was, she saw now, the same as an ant biting a cougar's toe. The cougar would not even notice, and the ant still got stepped on. It made no difference whether she approached the night scared or calm or crazy, like Ike, who sat in a corner, muttering into his hands. Nothing she did made a difference.

A commotion at the door. She turned her back, tried to get comfortable and sink into nothingness, hands over her ears. But then a sound cut through the numbness. She heard it. His voice. *This just another cruel dream.*

"Missy," he said, and she opened her eyes to find Henry standing over her. A shower of silver raindrops fell from his face.

Unable to speak, she just stared. He lifted her off the floor. She clung to him like he was life itself, clenched handfuls of his shirt, unsure whether he was real. She buried her nose in his neck. He smelled awful. *He never smelled bad in the dreams.*

Through her tears, she asked, "You been rollin' in a pigsty?"

He kissed her, hard on her mouth, soft on her cheeks, her forehead, her hands. "Hmm, I cain't say you smell much like roses neither."

"You here," she breathed. "You really here." She squeezed his arms, his shoulders, to convince herself he was really there and not just another figment of her sleeping brain.

"Had to. Couldn't let my best girl have all this fun by herself, could I?" He hugged her to him. "I was a damn fool to leave you," he whispered into her dirty, tangled hair. "You better get used to havin' me around, y'hear?"

She could not help it. Her entire body began to shake with the release of tension, like there was an earthquake inside her. He just held on and waited. When she was quiet, he looked around the boxcar.

"But hang on. Why ain't you at the shelter? Where's Selma? Where's Mama?"

"We don't know," said Missy, her voice choked with emotion. The rush of feeling, held back for the many long hours, swamped her senses. She had to force the words out. "Mama wasn't at the store.

431

Selma went to find her at Doc's, but she ain't come back . . . And, Henry, they took Nathan; they took him from me when they made us leave the store. They —"

"Made you leave the store?" he asked and looked around in disbelief at the tired, battered faces.

"That right," said Franklin. "Missy brought them all here. She got them here safe."

"What the hell —" Henry began.

Shouting came from outside.

A young man with red hair and excited eyes appeared at the doorway. When he took off his John Deere cap to wipe his face, Missy recognized him. He had been Henry's hostage when he ran away upstate. "Henry," the young man said. "You got to come quick. There's loads of men still not on board. Ken's going crazy."

Missy was confused. The young man seemed on good terms with Henry. How was that possible? In fact, it was more than that: the look on his face was the same as she'd seen on the faces of Henry's men when they talked about him.

"What you want me to do?" he asked.

"Keep the men moving, Jimmy," said Henry, "and tell Ken I'm on my way."

"Okay, but don't take too long; you know

how he —" Jimmy broke off and peered through the rain in the direction of town. "What in Sam Hill is — that?"

Missy followed his gaze.

She could make out lots of pale shapes of different sizes in the gloom, moving at speed toward them. Cries of pain and fear reached her ears. As they drew closer, the shapes resolved themselves into bodies. Lots and lots of naked white people were running for their lives, clothes stripped away by the wind. They ran like the devil himself was right behind them. As the air pressure dropped still further, the few remaining structures simply exploded as they ran past.

A water cistern flew through the air and tore into the mass of running bodies. It flattened a man near the edge of the crowd, a man with a square of white on his face. He went down with a loud *crunch* that carried to Missy on the wind. A stout woman dropped to her knees by his side and screamed, "Ronnie, don't leave me!" There was Cyril, recognizable by his metal hand, with a limp bundle in his arms. As they got closer, Missy began to recognize more and more faces. The group that raced toward them, naked and barefoot over the sharp coral and broken glass and cement, had less than an hour before been tucked up in the safety of the shelter. *What on earth made them leave?*

But before she could even open her mouth to ask the question, she saw the reason for their hurry. Behind them reared up a thundering wall of water, easily twenty feet tall, whose crest seemed to brush the clouds.

She heard Henry inhale. "Oh, sweet Jesus." He jumped down and raced toward the crowd. "Jimmy," he shouted over his shoulder. "Get in the boxcar and stay with Missy!"

"Not a chance!" said Jimmy and ran off after him.

The running bodies sped toward the protection of the boxcars, pursued by the massive white-topped wave. Missy herded her people away from the door. "Get ready, y'all," she said. "Make room! C'mon, make room!"

Out in front of the approaching crowd was a woman with a baby in her arms. His familiar cries cut through all the noise and chaos swirling around Missy. She had jumped down and was running toward the woman before she even realized she was moving.

"Nathan!" she cried. "I'm coming!"

He heard her! His head turned, and his eyes searched for her face. Marilee Henderson staggered to a stop and shoved him into Missy's waiting arms. Her body was so badly torn and bruised that there wasn't more than an inch of unbroken skin left.

"Where's Tim?" she asked, frantically looking around her. "He was right beside me! Has anyone seen him? I have to find him!" She turned to run back in the direction of the wave, which was devouring the ground between them in ferocious gulps. The others streamed past, their eyes empty of everything except the determination to keep running.

"No!" said Henry. "There's no time; you —" He grasped her arm.

"Let me go!" she wailed, yanking herself free. "Tim! Tim, where are you? Mommy's coming, Tim!" And she ran straight toward the wave.

"Missy, go!" said Henry. "Get back in the boxcar!" He scooped up a young girl who had sat down on the ground crying, her feet a mass of red. "Everyone!" he shouted. "This way! Follow me!"

Missy ran faster than she ever had in her life. The wind tore the clothes from her body but she did not care. Nathan felt completely weightless on her chest. Her legs pumped, powered by pure adrenaline. She could run all night. Her feet moved so fast that she was surprised she was still on the ground rather than swooping high into the night sky like an airplane. The wave thundered on behind her, close now. But she was faster. Henry was beside her, a limp little girl in his arms. Missy could hear him panting, but it may have been her own breath she heard.

Violet and Franklin were up ahead in the doorway, arms extended to catch her.

"Come on, Missy!" Violet cried.

Only a few more feet to go and they would be safe, all together. *Almost there, almost there.* With one more push, she would make it.

She heard Henry gasp, "Missy!"

And then she was gone.

Up on the embankment, Trent was using every last bit of his strength to get the men on board. His voice was raw from shouting, but still they milled around like they had all the time in the world. The stars were gone, smothered by thick cloud. He thought of what Missy had said, about the back side of the storm. The wind had risen again, which made it even harder to make himself heard. There still seemed to be a huge number of people on the tracks waiting to board, many of them badly injured. They had to move faster.

He approached the carriage and asked the man helping people to board, "Who's in charge here?"

"You want Ken," he said. "Move on down!" he yelled to the men inside. "Keep going to the back!"

Just then, a scowling man in a conductor's cap came through the door from the engineer's compartment.

"I don't like the look of this, Moses," he said to the man in the doorway. "Not one bit. We've been here too long already. Why aren't they on board yet? We shoulda been gone fifteen minutes ago. Faster, Clarence," he said to another man. "You gotta make them move faster."

Clarence was helping a veteran into the carriage whose face was obscured by a flap of scalp. "You look like you been in a war, mister," said Clarence.

"You ain't fuckin' kidding," said the man with a hand up to hold his scalp in place. "Worst carnage I seen in my life. Can't wait to be somewhere else — anywhere will do."

"Where's that bastard Roberts?" Ken yelled. "He's supposed to help clean up this mess."

"Henry had some personal business," said

Moses as he helped another man on board whose forearm was pierced through with white slivers of bone.

"Henry Roberts?" asked Trent. "That who you looking for?"

"Who are you?" asked Ken.

"Trent Watts, superintendent of this camp. Roberts is one of mine." Last Trent had heard, Roberts had skedaddled upstate, but there he was again, like a bad rash. *Why in God's name would he come back, to this?* And then Trent thought of the sweet-faced woman who had brought her people, half drowned and battered, to the boxcar for shelter. She had warned him about the eye. *Well, what do you know?*

Trent shook Ken's hand. "Don't think I've ever been happier to see anyone in my life, Ken. Thank you, I —"

"Thank me when we get to Miami," growled Ken with an exasperated glance at the mass of men still to board. "Which ain't gonna happen unless you speed up this shambles."

"Can you spare a man to help me?" asked Trent.

"I'll go," said Clarence and jumped down into the crowd.

Ken said to Moses, "Let me know the second the last one's on board. I'm going to

438

get her ready to pull out." And he turned to leave the carriage.

Trent hollered with all the power left in his lungs, "Come on, you stubborn sons of bitches. Get your asses on board this train or we're gonna leave you behind! I've moved five hundred head of cattle quicker than this!"

But suddenly he realized no one was listening to him. Their attention had turned away, back toward the rail yard. There was a collective moan, which quickly rose to an awful, haunting cry. It sent a stab of dread right through Trent's heart. He knew that noise, had heard it before: it was the sound men make when they realize they are about to die.

Suddenly the crowd rushed toward the train, in far greater numbers than could fit through the doors.

Trent heard a shout from Clarence. "Holy shit, will you look at —"

The wave cut through the veterans still on the tracks like a blade through a field of barley. Dozens went down and were washed away in an instant.

Trent clamped his hands around the iron rail as the water hit. Eyes shut, head down, he held on and on, waiting for it to end. But it kept coming. It clawed the clothes from his body. It pulled at his arms to dislodge them, but still he held on, even when knocked sideways by chunks of debris and the bodies of men who could hold on no longer. His lungs clamored for air, but he kept his jaws shut. It felt like he was at the bottom of the sea, beneath tons and tons of water. It pummeled him harder. More bodies thumped against him. Hands brushed as they passed, making one final grasp at life. And then they were gone. But the water kept coming.

His grip on the rail weakened. The pressure in his lungs could no longer be denied. The last of his strength left his hands, and he went to join his men.

The weight of water hit the train with such force that all the carriages tumbled off the tracks and down the embankment. The whole train went over like it was made of cardboard. Only the massive locomotive remained upright. Jeb heard shouts of surprise and pain from within the cars as they toppled over and the explosive shattering of all the windows at once.

Inside the train, a river raged through from one side to the other. Carriages swung around in crazy arcs, flipping onto their roofs. Ken clung to an empty window frame, his legs flailing in the current. "Help!" he cried. "Someone help me!"

Moses battled the flow to reach him, but it flung him back each time. With a final surge of effort, he leaped for the window and grabbed Ken's arm. He hung on there, head down against the torrent, and slowly pulled Ken back into the carriage.

Jeb tumbled over and over, slammed against the walls, the seats, curled into the smallest shape possible. *So this is what it feels like to die — in a washing machine.* Still the foamy water poured in, whipped up by the ferocious wind. He struggled to find some air in a world of black water, completely disoriented. There was no way to tell what was up and what was down. Again and again he was thrown against the walls, the roof, the floor.

Just as his will to fight ran out, so did the water. He found himself at the bottom of a panting, spluttering tangle of limbs. Only his face was above the water. "Hey!" he yelled. "Get off me!"

In a sudden rush, he was pulled free. He looked up into Lemuel's familiar face. "Thanks, man," he gasped. The wind boomed around the carriage, making it hard even to hear himself. "Where's Sonny?"

Lemuel put his mouth right next to Jeb's

ear. "Dunno. Last I saw, he was waiting to get on board. Jeb, what do we do now?"

Jeb tried to look out the window but rain sprayed right into his face. A coconut flew past his head. All was in darkness. It was impossible to tell where the wave had deposited them. They might be just a few feet from the embankment, or they might be in the sea. The wind wailed through the carriage like a demon.

"Cain't see a damned thing out there." Jeb looked around. The men began to right themselves, check for injuries. It seemed completely miraculous that they were still alive, just badly bruised and half drowned. "We wait for the light," he said. "Just wait for the light."

"Amen to that," said Lemuel.

CHAPTER 25

Henry retched up a mouthful of seawater. Even before he opened his eyes, he knew something was very wrong. Every limb registered sharp, stabbing pain, yet he instinctively held on to the source of the pain with all his strength. It was the only solid thing in the world of the wind. Its rasping roar filled his ears. It scoured his naked body, tried to wrench him free, but he hung on. Even the rain fell sharp as needles on his flesh.

He opened his eyes slightly. Nothing but cloud above and darkness below. He became aware of a great void beneath him and looked down. Something moved there, a gentle rise and fall, vague outlines all he could make out. It was water, he realized, flowing back to its rightful home, taking with it a solid mat of undulating corpses, trees, cars, and broken timbers.

His hands found the source of the pain.

Big, sharp thorns were embedded in his legs, his torso, his back. And then he realized: his support, which he clutched with the ardor of a lover, was a spiny Key lime tree. The wave had deposited him there, perhaps twenty feet off the ground.

A gust rocked the tree. He gripped it tighter, jaw clenched against the pain. "Is anyone there?" he yelled. No answer. Farther up the tree, he could just discern the unmoving bulk of another body. Impossible to tell if it was a man or woman. It made no sound in answer to his call.

All was blasted and dark. No signs of life. *Maybe I'm dead too.* Maybe the pain was a mirage, an echo of his last moments alive, a memory somehow retained by his flesh. No, the pain was real. He could be certain of nothing else, but the pain was definitely real.

The wind pulled at his limbs, tried to tear him loose. It would be so easy to just let go, let the wind take him to join Missy. He wanted to be with her, wherever she was. She had been so close to the boxcar, just a few feet from safety. He was so sure she would make it. But then the wind had snatched her and Nathan up, her legs still pumping as it carried her away. A chasm of loss opened up inside him and beckoned him in with the voice of the wind. *Just let go,* it hissed. *Everything you care about is gone.*

It would be so easy. *Just let go.*

A movement nearby. From the next tree came a soft moan. He called out, "Who's that? It's Henry here. Henry Roberts!" His voice broke with relief. He had started to wonder if he was the last living soul in the land of the dead.

"Henry?" It was Jimmy, weak but recognizable. "That you?"

He sounded close by, but Henry could see nothing through the thorny cage of branches around him. "You okay, Jimmy?"

"Don't think so . . . Got something in my . . . God, Henry, it's gone right through me! Got to get it out —"

"No, don't pull it out, Jimmy! You got to leave it there!" A gust nearly ripped him from his perch. It took all his strength to hang on.

A scream from Jimmy's direction.

"Jimmy, you there?"

"Still here." His voice was weaker. "Don't think I can hang on much longer, Henry. It hurts real bad."

Henry could just make out the words over the wind. "Jimmy!" he called. "Your uncle Dwayne be mighty proud of you right now." He had to keep him talking, for his own sake as much as Jimmy's.

"You think" — Jimmy coughed — "you think he's still alive . . . down there?"

"Course he is!" said Henry with no basis at all for this. He had seen plenty of bigger corpses already that night. "Take a lot more than a little wind to knock him down."

"I guess so." A pause. "But he just treats me like a kid."

"I tell you somethin'," Henry said with great conviction. "You ain't a kid no more." He tried to ease himself off the thorns, but they just bit harder. "What you done since we been gone . . . well, it's more than many a grown man would do."

Another pause. "Ya think so?"

"Not only that, but I'll tell anyone who cares to listen, including your uncle Dwayne."

"Assuming he don't shoot you on sight, o' course."

"Yeah, good point." Henry thought Jimmy's voice sounded stronger.

"I tried," said Jimmy, coughing again. "I tried to grab her, the girl with the baby. The wind was too strong. It just took 'em both."

"I know, Jimmy," said Henry. "I know." It would stay with him always, his last view of Missy as she flew away. "And, Jimmy? That just what I'm talkin' about."

Another silence. Then Jimmy asked, "You hear that?"

Pitiful cries for help rose up from the blackness below, from people trapped beneath broken buildings and lumber, trees and cars. There was nothing he could do to help them, but the cries continued. He tried to cover his ears to block them out, but the sound seemed to be inside his head.

"Don't listen, Jimmy. You gonna be fine. We'll get down from here and get fixed up, you'll see."

And then, gradually, one by one, the cries stopped.

Henry started. *Must have dozed off for a minute.*

"Jimmy?"

There was no sound except the *shhh* of the wind through the branches.

"Jimmy, you okay?"

And then Henry knew he was alone, really alone. "Oh, Jimmy." He sighed. It felt like all hope left him on that breath.

He was so tired. His body was a collage of pain, some sharp, some dull. There wasn't a part of him that didn't hurt. It felt like he had been clinging to the tree for days, but it could only have been a few hours. Morning must come soon, he reasoned, although it would not have surprised him to find that the world had fallen into perpetual darkness, never to see the sun again.

He had fought so hard, for so long: fought to become an army officer, fought for respect from his comrades, fought the government when they got home, fought to improve the conditions in the camp. Fought to save the people he cared about — and failed. *When was I last at peace?* He had to go far, far back to find it.

He closed his eyes.

He is eight years old, on the beach with Selma and Grace. The midday sun beats down hot on his bare shoulders. Crawfish that he and Selma caught boil in a pot on the fire. Grace uses her machete to hack the tops off some coconuts. He and Selma sip the sweet liquor from the shells.

He draws a map of the world in the sand for Selma and sets about filling in the continents with different types of seashells. He uses his favorite for North America, neat lines of coquinas, like stripy butterfly wings in soft pink, green, and blue. There are spiked cat's paws for Europe, ridged white clamshells for Asia, and speckled limpets for South America. Australia is one big conch, nearly as big as his head, because he likes the smooth, rosy inside. Selma isn't really interested in his map, and that's fine. Grace passes him a plate of crawfish with one of her rare smiles. "Let it cool," she says, "or you burn your fingers." But he grabs the hot shellfish off the plate, cannot wait to taste the sweet meat. Grace laughs as he blows on his hands.

His stomach cramped. He was so hungry, but worse than that was the terrible thirst. The thought of the coconut water made his throat ache.

He finally allowed himself to think of Selma. Until that moment, he was sure she had to be all right. No other outcome was conceivable. She would not permit it, simple as that. It was more likely that the clouds would fall right to the ground or the water would run uphill.

And he always thought he would sense it when she passed, that there would be some sign, some shift in the earth's rotation. But now he was not sure, not of anything. He felt nothing, nothing at all, and he realized: that was the sign. He was empty.

Take me then, if you want to so bad. I'm done fightin'.

He must have slept again, because he thought he heard Jimmy's voice say, "Henry, wake up!" But there was no sound except the wind, weaker than before, weak enough for him to relax his grip on the tree. Rain still pelted down, but on the horizon he saw it. A patch of lightness in the sky. And as he watched, it grew bigger and turned to peach and turquoise. In the quiet left by the wind, he noticed the complete absence of birds. No gulls, no pelicans, no herons, no egrets. Strangest of all, no buzzards, even with the carpet of death below him.

Now he could make out Jimmy, maybe two trees away. He seemed to be sleeping, held in a cradle of branches.

And as Henry looked around in the growing light of dawn, he saw the others. All around him, the trees were draped with bodies. Some had been left in poses that looked almost relaxed, hung gracefully over the branches. Others were twisted into postures of agony.

A child's shoe was snagged on a branch by his head. And on another, a woman's hat. He recognized it. Grayish blue with red flowers, now limp and dirty.

The rest of the branches were festooned with what looked like streamers, which fluttered in the wind. He plucked one, rubbed it between his fingers. It was a piece of cloth, ripped from a shirt. His eyes moved from one tree to the next. All carried the same: every tree left standing in the grove was covered in shreds of clothing.

The sun burned a hole through the clouds, which still poured with rain. It shone like a spotlight on an expanse of destruction so complete that even the soil was gone, stripped away to reveal the bare coral skeleton. Even the palm trees, those sturdy survivors, had been ripped up by the roots. As far as he could see, in every direction, there were only piles and piles of broken wood, like an explosion at a sawmill. There was no town, no veterans' camp, and no sign there ever had been one. Nothing moved except the sea in the distance, where angry gray waves, heavy with bodies and debris, pounded the shore.

The heat began to cook the corpses in the trees. The sour, meaty smell of putrefaction hit the back of his throat. It was a smell he knew well but had hoped never to encounter again. With the heat came the flies. He swatted them away from his face. *Not yet. You cain't have me yet.*

The low morning light revealed the damage done to him by the tree's thorns. He pulled them out, one by one, until he was free.

Figures appeared below and started to pick their way slowly across the wasteland. A few had retained some clothes, but most had not. They clutched at bleeding wounds,

451

stronger ones supporting weaker ones. Cries of pain drifted on the wind, mixed with voices begging for help. He could make out a woman's head on the ground, her mouth open wide but making no sound at all. The rest of her body lay beneath the remains of a house wall. Three men were struggling to get it off her. One had begun to saw at the timbers that pinned her to the ground.

With one last look at the remains of Heron Key, he took the hat with the red flowers from the tree and started the slow, painful climb back down to earth.

EPILOGUE:
TWO YEARS LATER

Dwayne brushed the sand from Roy's pants. He had only just managed to get him dressed and already he was dirty, chasing a lizard around the yard on his powerful little legs.

The boy looked up at him with wide eyes. Noreen's eyes. He seemed to sense the importance of the occasion, even if he did not understand it. Dwayne could see Noreen so clearly in the boy's face, in the arch of his brows and the shape of his mouth. More and more of her came to the surface as he grew.

"Your momma would be so proud of you."

He could not be sure if Roy remembered her. Sometimes he called out for her as he slept, when the nightmares came, but most of the time it seemed Dwayne was the only parent he had ever known. Of course, in a way, he belonged to the survivors of Heron Key too. So many children had been lost that those who made it through had become community property. Whenever they went to get groceries or mail a letter, it took forever because people wanted to fuss at Roy and give him treats. He had become plump and sleek on it, which was fine with Dwayne. He never wanted to see Roy as thin again as he was after the storm. His own paunch had not regained its former glory. For days and days, nothing got through until the Red Cross arrived. Were it not for the turtles that Zeke caught and the water tanker left on the tracks, it could have turned out very differently for them.

"Wanna play with Nathan."

Dwayne smoothed the boy's springy curls. He would forever be amazed at the resilience of children. They had finally found Nathan where the wind had dropped him, nearly forty miles away and still wrapped in Missy's arms. He was almost unrecognizable from the bruising, both legs broken and nearly dead from dehydration. His heart had stopped twice on the Coast Guard rescue plane. You'd never know it now from the way he sped around the place. The only lasting damage seemed to be his somewhat bowlegged gait, a scar that bisected his left eyebrow, and an abiding fear of water. He and Roy had become inseparable.

"Nathan will be there, I told you. You can go play later, but there's something we got to do first." It had taken two frustrating years, but the memorial was finally completed and ready to be unveiled, on the site where Jenson's store used to be.

They were ready. Dwayne swung Roy up onto his shoulders. The boy clutched handfuls of his hair and giggled with delight.

"Are you about ready?" Doc asked. "We're going to be late."

"How do I look?" asked Hilda. She was wearing a dress of sea-blue cotton that matched her eyes. After the months of living in donated Red Cross clothes, it was the first new thing she had bought. She pulled at it where it stretched over the bulge of her stomach. At four months along, she was starting to show. "This doesn't hang right anymore," she said. "I need to get it let out. I wish I could find another dressmaker as good as Nettie."

"You look beautiful," Doc said with a kiss on her forehead. "Just beautiful." She had tried to cover her scars with heavy foundation. The makeup seemed to draw attention to the hard lines and folds left by the sutures. But it made her feel better, and he decided that was more important. She was also self-conscious about the slight droop of her mouth, a reminder of her latest seizure.

"Now come on," he said. "It's time to go."

"I don't know." She fussed at her skirt. "I think I like the pink better . . ."

He winced as Nathan pulled at his hand. "Take it easy, Nathan," she said. "Daddy's back is bad today."

It was time to go to Miami for another operation, to remove yet more wooden fragments from his back. Some were inoperable, too close to the spine to be extracted. They would be with him always, painful souvenirs of that night. When the morning finally came after the storm, he could hear people searching the rubble, calling names of loved ones. He could make no sound, trapped beneath the weight of the collapsed roof. Doc knew that no one expected to find anyone still alive under the massive pile of timber. The only reason he and Hilda did survive was that the debris stopped them from being swept away by the wave, which washed through with merciful speed. But he had been able to do nothing to attract attention, pinned across Hilda's body by the fallen beams. She had been unconscious for hours, but he had felt her slight, shallow breathing beneath him. Had Henry not found them when he did, delirious with pain and thirst . . . well, they would have joined their friends and neighbors on the huge cremation pyres that burned day and night.

He looked around at the home that had begun to take shape. There were still times when none of it seemed real. He sometimes feared they might just be ghosts, floating through other peoples' lives, tied forever to the place where they had died. But no, he thought, ghosts do not use hammers and nails; ghosts do not pour cement. Hilda had wanted the remains of the old Kincaid house demolished. So they had built a new one, of solid construction — with a concrete hurricane shelter. Even after two years, there was still a lot of work to do, but it was a start. He had figured she would want to leave Heron Key behind forever, move up north or out west — anywhere far away. But she would never feel confident among strangers, only among the others who, like her, had survived that night.

"It's okay, Nathan," he said. He thought he would never get tired of being called "Daddy." Nathan seemed to have accepted him, with no memory at all of Nelson. "Put Sam's leash on him."

Nathan clipped the leash to Sam's collar. The dog had been found by one of the rescue boats, afloat in a fruit packing crate, Cyril's claw still attached.

Hilda put some dainty gold sandals on her feet.

"Those are pretty," he said, "but not very practical —"

She placed a hand on his chest. "Yes," she said with a smile, blue eyes shining. "I know."

Henry splashed some water on his face and put on a clean shirt. The morning was already hot and promised a sweltering afternoon. He had been to the memorial site early, to make double sure that everything was in order. It had taken a mighty, concerted effort to get it approved, commissioned, and delivered — all made possible by the American Legion funds, after the state government declined to contribute.

From the other room came, "Can you give me a hand, Henry?"

He went in to find Missy sitting on the bed, struggling with the clasp of her necklace. It was a gold St. Christopher, a present from Hilda and Doc in gratitude for what she had done for Nathan. He fixed the clasp and bent down to kiss her.

She looped her arms around his neck and

he lifted her into the chair, her weight easy in his arms. It had taken him a while to get the hang of it — he had even dropped her once when he forgot to put on the brakes — but they now had a smooth routine. And the plans for the new Heron Key Colored School included all the necessary ramps and fittings to let her get around, even a special bathroom. Henry had made sure of that. He had also harassed the school board into donating a new set of *Encyclopedia Britannica* too. Amazing what could be achieved, he thought, with enough moral blackmail.

The first term would start in a few months. The building would not be ready, of course, and classes would have to be held on the beach to begin with, but that was okay. It was nearly impossible to tear Missy away from her lesson plans, which were strewn across her desk under the window. The desk was one of the first things he had made for her, out of wood taken from Mama's old house.

There were times when his pride in her nearly overwhelmed him. This was one of those times. She looked so fine in her new green dress, another present from Hilda. He just wanted to stand and stare.

"You doing it again," she said fondly.

"I cain't help it." He still sometimes found

it hard to believe she had been returned to him. The Coast Guardsmen who found her and Nathan still sent them Christmas cards. They had just been so delighted to find anyone at all still alive on that spit of sand, especially a woman and a baby. But because Nathan was in such peril on the flight back, no one had realized until they landed just how badly Missy was hurt. For the first few months in the hospital, Henry had just sat by her bed and kept watch, reading her stories, getting fresh food, until finally he brought her home, to the house he had made for them.

Sorrow shadowed her face. "She should be here," Missy said and cast her eyes to the window that overlooked the beach. The waves sparkled in the clear morning light. "It ain't right, without her."

"Yes," he said. There was nothing else to say, no words that they hadn't said over the previous two years.

Another long silence while they both stared at the sea that looked so calm and inviting on this hot day. Then she curled her hand inside his. "Come on, Mr. Roberts, let's go."

He released the brakes on her chair. "Yes, ma'am, Missus Roberts."

■ ■ ■ ■

They gathered in the center of town, where Jenson's store had stood for so many years. The monument was a handsome obelisk of creamy yellow stone, inset with a stylized carving of windswept palm trees. Its contours were covered by a pale drape, the hem stirred by a slight breeze that did nothing to cool the air. The sun was directly overhead, the time of day when shadows disappeared.

Henry wiped the sweat from his face. He was pleased with the final result. He and Doc and Dwayne had wanted to include a list of names on the monument, but it wasn't possible. They would never be sure of all those who died, because so many bodies were taken by the wind and the sea. Many of those found were unidentifiable, once the intense heat and the huge swarms of flies did their work. But not the carrion birds. The flies feasted on their carcasses too.

For days and days, Henry and the other survivors had collected the rotting corpses, whose flesh came away in their hands like soft cheese. He had prayed to find Missy — and also not to find her — as he looked into each face, swollen beyond recognition. The stench was overwhelming, not even dented by the disinfectant they washed in every few minutes. Some of the National Guardsmen wore gas masks, which put the final seal on it for Henry. He had thought there could be nothing worse than his time in the trenches, but this had been many, many times worse. The decomposing bodies had been robbed of their very identities.

At first, they had tried to make coffins for each but quickly realized that the scale of death required faster measures. So they began to burn them all, without pause or ceremony, in huge pyres, blacks and whites, old people and children, townspeople and veterans. Some were mangled, unidentifiable lumps of meat, and others were completely intact. The sky had turned black with the smoke, the sea stained gray with ash.

And as the burning continued, he had searched for her, inside every ruined building, under every tangled heap of wood or metal, inside every crushed car. He had found only carnage or, rarely, folks like Doc and Hilda, still breathing. It was about five days after the storm that he collapsed, from lack of sleep, food, and water and the infection raging in his wounds. Waking up in the hospital, his only thought was to go back to the search, but he could not even get out of bed. When he could finally walk again, he had trudged up and down the corridors to build his strength, and it was on one of these excursions that he heard a nurse mention a familiar name.

It seemed incredible, standing there in the gentle breeze with the glint of sun on calm water and the soft swish of the palms, that this was the same place that had resembled the worst battlefield imaginable, that had reeked of death for weeks as the town staggered back to its feet. He looked around at the few others who, like him, had lived through that night and what followed and saw the experience engraved on their faces.

Violet and Franklin stood together, unconsciously leaving a space for Abe. Even now, Violet still retained the hunched posture of grief, as if winded by a blow. Her boy had died of blood poisoning from the wound in his arm while waiting to be evacuated.

Zeke kept himself apart from the others. He looked tiny, very much diminished by Poncho's absence. It was the first time Henry had seen him wear a shirt.

The American Legion band arrived and began to unpack, their white uniforms and silver instruments flashing in the sun. Henry put a hand up to shade his eyes from the glare and spotted the Legion post commander, Leonard Goodchild. "Good to see you, Leonard," he said and shook his hand. "A mite different to last time."

"You could say that, Henry." Goodchild's men had been among the first relief workers to arrive after the storm. Some of them had never recovered from what they saw during those days.

Cars and buses pulled up, disgorging scores of people Henry had never seen before. There were a lot of Florida license plates but some from out of state too. And they just kept coming.

"Who are these people?" he asked Goodchild.

"Folks who want to pay their respects. This made the national news, Henry." He tilted his head to one side and shaded his eyes with a hand. "You look surprised."

He had only expected a few visitors, figured the unveiling was of little interest beyond the environs of the Keys despite all the press coverage. It was astounding that such a tiny place, unknown to almost the whole country, had become a focus for national outrage over the botched evacuation of the veterans. He heard that the northern papers carried stories for months after the storm, going almost as far as accusing President Roosevelt of manslaughter. At last, it seemed there was to be a public debate about how they had been treated after the war. In death, they had achieved what they never could in life.

For a long time, Henry had followed the investigation into how they came to be abandoned, why so many had died so needlessly. But it was like trying to catch hold of smoke. Each time they seemed close to an answer, those in charge got diverted by more official hand-waving. And as time passed, so the outrage waned and the world moved on.

He straightened his shoulders. In the end, he had realized that having someone to blame helped no one. It didn't bring them back, all those who had been lost. What mattered now was this group of people who stood quietly, fanning themselves in the heat. They still had so much work to do, to rebuild and restore the community. And some things would never be the same, could never be rebuilt.

Ken and Moses arrived. Henry strode to greet them. "Thanks for coming, fellas."

"Wouldn't miss it," said Moses.

"This is Jimmy's uncle," Henry said.

"Dwayne, this is Ken and Moses, from the train."

"He was a good kid," said Ken and shook Dwayne's hand. "I'd have been happy to have him in my crew."

"Thank you for coming," said Dwayne. "And thank you for . . . Jimmy always loved trains. Here," he said. "He'd want you to have this." He handed Ken a faded, stained John Deere cap. "There was this one time when he — hey, come back here, Roy!"

Roy and Nathan had climbed onto the monument steps and were taking turns jumping off. Doc picked up a giggling Nathan. Henry could tell from his expression that his back was bad again.

"Is everyone here yet?" Leonard asked, unfolding his speech.

Jeb strolled up, a fat cigar between his teeth. "The important people are. Hey, Boss." He had yet another new girl on his arm. He had found work in a Miami cigar factory and was on track to become a supervisor. Although Lemuel had survived the storm, according to Jeb, he was lost in the confusion and chaos that followed. Henry and Jeb never saw him again.

It was time.

Dwayne stepped forward to leave a scarf on the steps, patterned with honeysuckle.

Zeke placed a single bright blue feather, gave a stiff salute, and disappeared into the crowd. Doc placed Jenson's barometer, its glass panel fractured, its gauge forever frozen at the impossibly low reading of twenty-six inches.

Henry waited his turn. No trace of Selma had been found. And yet there were times, usually at sunset and sunrise, when he felt her presence so strongly, right by his side, that he had more than once turned to talk to her. Missy did not find this strange one bit, said she had long conversations with Selma all the time. She had told him, "When so many souls get taken all at once like that, bound to happen that one or two fall out the bucket. And Selma, she ain't gonna move on till she good and ready." The old kitchen table from Selma's house had washed up on the beach, legs broken but top intact. Selma's initials were still visible on the underside, right next to his. He and Missy ate dinner on that table every night.

He knelt at the monument steps and placed his hand against the stone. It was warm, almost skin temperature. He said quietly, "See you later, Sunny."

The slow trickle of survivors kept coming. Each person left something of meaning to the dead. Soon the piles of mementos spilled down the steps and onto the ground. And still they came.

Henry looked at Jeb and Franklin and remembered his boys on their homecoming parade up Fifth Avenue. They had been so proud, so bursting with hope and promise. Sonny. Lemuel. Sammy. Tyrone. Li'l Joe. All gone. Gone too were Sick Bay, Two-Step and Carl, Stan and Tec. And Trent Watts, who was never found. Hundreds more. Far from home, in a place they never wanted to be.

He took a crumpled, faded photo of a little boy in a cowboy hat from his pocket and studied it for a long moment. Then he placed it alongside the other tokens on the monument. *Rest in peace, Max Hoffman.*

Missy rolled her chair forward. She leaned over to set Mama's hat on the monument steps, grayish blue with red flowers. Then she sat there for a long moment, head bent, eyes closed. It was strange: ever since she and Nathan were taken by the wind, she'd had the feeling of moving through the air whenever she closed her eyes. Terrifying though it was, while the wind carried them farther and farther out to sea, there was a kind of freedom to it, unlike anything she had ever known.

And when the wind had finally dropped them on that barren sliver of sand and she lay there in a broken heap beside Nathan, who was even too worn out to cry, the fear had drained from her. She used the very last bit of her strength to drag them clear of the water. There was no more. She had done everything possible and found some comfort in that. The pain receded. It was like a blessing to feel the sun again and hear only the quiet lap of the waves. She had laid her cheek on the warm sand and closed her eyes and was at peace . . . so much so that the rumble of the Coast Guard spotter plane engines, faint at first, then loud overhead, had sounded like the hurricane coming back to finish its business with her. Nathan had screamed in terror at the noise. It was only when a seaplane landed later that she had understood.

Since that day, every time she needed to feel that sense of peace again — and there had been many after she first opened her eyes to find Henry by her hospital bed — she took herself back to the tiny atoll in her mind.

Nathan clambered onto her lap. He was growing into a sturdy, bowlegged little boy. The bond between them, already strong, had been forged into iron by that terrible night. Now, when the bad dreams came, he called her name, not his mother's. Hilda was saddened, but she understood that no one except Missy shared those memories with him.

Missy still saw him every day, and each visit always ended the same way. The only story he wanted to hear, over and over, was how he and Missy had flown way up into the sky like birds, very far away. When she got to the end, he would say the final line with her, which never varied: "And then Missy and Nathan went home again together, safe and sound."

He bounced now on her useless legs. "Wanna play cars!" He liked to ride along with her in the chair and pretend he was driving. He still had trouble understanding that she could not get up and chase after him. She caught him staring at the chair sometimes in an angry confusion, like it was personally responsible for spoiling his fun.

Henry went to remove him, but Missy said, "Let him stay." She rested her head against his neck until he grew bored and ran off to find Roy.

Henry leaned down and said, "He be too big for your lap soon."

"I know," she said and stroked his hand where it lay on her shoulder. According to

Doc, the damage to her insides, and the surgery that followed, meant she would never have a child. When it happened, she was too overwhelmed with trying to adjust to everything that had changed in her life. It was just one in a long list of losses. But after she and Henry married, the hard, cold truth of it had landed like a boulder on her heart. Even with all she had to be grateful for and Henry by her side, it had pained her worse than anything, even the loss of her legs.

It was only when Henry outlined the idea for the school that the fog of hurt had started to clear. It would be filled with children, he had said, children who needed what she could give them. At first, the doors of her mind had stayed firmly closed, bolted shut by her misery, but over time, he had painted a picture with his words, of these children learning from books, in a real classroom, even one day going to college. As he had spread the plans on her desk by the window, his face all excited, his voice was like a rope dangling down into the pit where she had fallen. She only had to grasp it in order to climb out. And so she did, hand over hand, one agonizing inch at a time.

It felt like so long ago — and like it had

only been five minutes. Something strange had happened to her sense of time that night. Before the storm, she could always tell the present from the past. It was like there was a solid wall that kept them separate from each other. No longer. That solid wall had become more like a fisherman's net, allowing the past and present to mingle together constantly. One minute, she could be sitting at her desk, working on a lesson, and the next be back there again, up to her armpits in dirty water, dragging Violet and Abe toward the station. Or she could be having dinner with Henry, and then Mama would appear beside her, shelling peas and complaining about the price of flour at Mitchell's store. There were occasions when she felt so adrift on the current of time that she had to clutch the wheelchair to keep from losing her bearings completely. The only constant, the only thing that anchored her, was Henry.

She looked up at him now, squinting into the glare, and knew he read her thoughts. *We somewhere now.*

The sun was hot on her shoulders. Henry shifted position so his body threw a cool shadow across her. A hush fell over the crowd.

"Ready?" Leonard asked, reading glasses

on his nose, ready to remove the drape. The band leader was poised, baton raised, forehead beneath his cap beaded with sweat.

Missy surveyed the assembled locals and visitors, standing patiently in the humid sunshine. The scores of the lost shimmered among them. She heard their whispers in the breeze. They crowded closer, waiting to be remembered.

Doc and Dwayne nodded at Henry.

"Yes," said Henry with a glance at the vast, indifferent blue sky. "Time to begin."

READING GROUP GUIDE

1. Henry has always had a plan for his life, which the whims of history ultimately force him to abandon and just live in the moment. He finds this very difficult, Missy less so, because her expectations are so low. Which way of living leads to greater happiness? And which do you use in your life?

2. Both Missy and Henry feel that they have failed in their lives. Does this do more to draw them together or push them apart?

3. A key theme of the novel is the question "What makes us human?" At several points in the book, characters mention the difference between humans and animals, e.g., the townspeople view the veterans as subhuman, Henry comments on the difference between the human beings and "giant cockroaches" like Two-Step. Then

we see how the storm makes some people abandon their humanity, while others rise to the occasion. What do you think makes us human? And is it just a "thin veneer" as Henry thinks? Or does it go deeper?

4. The storm pushes everyone to the limits of their endurance, where they find out who they truly are. What extreme life event have you experienced, and what did you learn about yourself as a result?

5. Another important idea is that of perception versus reality. Dwayne allows his prejudices to blind him to the evidence of Hilda's attack. Several times, Henry comments that "people see what they want to see" rather than what is really there. Do you agree with this? How much of Henry's view has been affected by his experiences?

6. How much or little has the treatment of traumatized military veterans changed since 1935? Do you think it's possible that such a group could be so treated by today's officials?

7. Hilda worshipped, and was worshipped by, her father. How has this affected her relationships with other men? Do you

know any women whose lives have been similarly influenced?

8. The opening chapters show each character getting ready for the Fourth of July barbecue. Compare this scene to the epilogue, where we see each one preparing for another important event. How has each been changed by the storm? What have they gained and lost?

9. Selma believes that she has summoned the hurricane with her voodoo spell. Other characters place their faith in a higher power who will heed their prayers. Does the universe care about us? Do things happen for a reason?

10. There are clashes between tribes, of townspeople and veterans, between black and white people, between the wealthy and the poor — all groups who mistrust and dislike the other. Jimmy's outlook changes when he is on the run with Henry. Have you ever experienced a radical change of view after getting to know someone very different?

11. There are several parallels between the veterans' experiences of the hurricane and

the battlefield. How are they similar and different?

12. What is your first impression of Dwayne? And how do you feel about him at the end of the book?

13. If you were Missy, would you have gone on the run with Henry?

14. Huge events can be triggered by the smallest incident. One example is when Mabel starts the rumor that Henry is Roy's father, simply because she is piqued. Things then quickly spiral out of control. Has something similar ever happened in your life?

15. Missy believes that people's fundamental natures don't really change, regardless of outward appearances. Do you agree?

16. Missy risks everything to save Nathan; Henry returns to the storm zone rather than save himself; the veterans have lost limbs and sanity in the service of their country. In contrast, Nelson won't even save his dog. Do you know where the boundary of your self-interest lies? What

would you do to help a stranger if it meant personal risk for you?

17. Both Selma and Hilda have very emotional relationships with food. Discuss the very different reasons for this.

18. How much has changed between the races in America since 1935? And how much remains the same?

A CONVERSATION WITH THE AUTHOR

What do you love most about writing?

Those (very) rare moments when you hit on the perfect combination of words, and it resonates through your whole being, almost like poetry. I also love it when the characters surprise me. And I love it when readers talk about the characters like they really exist, because they do for me!

Which book has had the greatest impact on your life and writing?

Birdsong by Sebastian Faulks. I read it when I had been living in England for several years. Being American, I knew nothing of World War I and its effects on a whole generation of Europeans. I saw the veterans parading every year on Armistice Day but had no understanding of what they had been through. *Birdsong* opened my eyes and my mind to an incredibly important historical period that is almost completely overlooked in American education. I then went on to read Pat Barker's Regeneration trilogy, which deepened my interest in the period. So, in a way, it was destiny that I ended up writing about veterans of that war — and having it published during the centenary commemorations. I feel very privileged to be even a small part of it.

What attracts you to historical fiction?

I absolutely love having a framework of real events that I can populate with characters. I love feeding in the little period details carefully, to avoid the kind of heavy-handed exposition that you get with some historical fiction, e.g., "She picked up the Regency faceted crystal goblet and remarked on its typical pattern of grape-vines." It adds an extra layer of complexity to what is already a very complex task, but I much prefer it to writing contemporary fiction. I'm completely in awe of writers who wrote these kinds of books without the help of the Internet for research. I can't imagine how much longer it would have taken to check every fact and answer every historical question, such as "When was the tetanus vaccine invented?" The Internet is the historical writer's best friend.

What is one thing you know now that you wish you knew when you started your writing career?

I used to think that I could only write if I could carve out large chunks of dedicated time. You hear a lot of writers say that it's essential to write every day, even just a little. My life isn't like that. I realized that I would have to snatch any small opportunity, rather than waiting for long stretches to become available, if I wanted to finish writing a book.

Do you write to a plan?

Only in the broadest sense. I have in mind a series of important scenes to include and a spreadsheet where I list each chapter and what it will cover. But when I actually start writing, unexpected things happen. The characters say and do things that I hadn't planned, so I need to stay flexible the whole time. For example, I may have a general idea of where the book ends but no precise idea of how until I reach that point and it reveals itself to me.

What research or preparation did you engage in before writing this book?

Because I didn't set out to write this book, the research took a circuitous route. I intended to write about the lynching of Claude Neal in Greenwood, Florida, in 1935, which I read about in the *St. Petersburg Times,* because I thought it was so outrageous that no one has ever been prosecuted. Then the magic of Google led me to the Keys History website, www.keys history.org, where I found the story of the hurricane and the veterans. I found myself moved so profoundly and ashamed that I knew nothing about it, although I was a Florida native. I felt compelled to write about it, almost like I didn't have a choice.

Which character do you feel most closely connected to?

Henry is my favorite. Although it's traditional for female writers to have more connection with their female characters, I felt Henry's story more intensely than some of the others. I could picture every step of his journey and how it made him feel — the initial euphoria when the war ended and then the terrible, crushing disappointment that destroyed his hopes. Also, I enjoy writing action scenes more than emotions, and male characters lend themselves more to that. Of the female characters, Selma was my favorite. I'm really fascinated by her. She's had a tough life, and I loved introducing a hint of magical realism.

Did you create your cast of characters at the beginning, or did they evolve with the writing?

That's another interesting thing about historical fiction. Some characters are entirely imaginary, but others are needed to play real roles, even if their personalities are entirely fictional. From the outset, I had Missy, Henry, and the Kincaid family in my mind. Dwayne and Doc were also fairly well-formed. The real events required a camp superintendent and the relief train crew. Interestingly, I didn't intend to develop Selma into a main character until I got some really useful feedback from a writers' website where I posted the first two chapters. The reviewers all wanted to know much more about Selma, so I developed her further to include her voodoo skills. It was a very constructive and positive experience, and I highly recommend it to other authors.

Why don't you reveal the father of baby Roy?

Throughout the book, I want the reader to feel the same emotions as the characters, in real time. Dwayne undergoes a huge transformation during the story, and the pivotal realization is that the identity of Roy's father doesn't matter. All that matters is his love for the child. I want the reader to feel, along with Dwayne, the frustration of not knowing the father's identity and then understand that, actually, it isn't the point.

The hurricane seems almost like a character itself. Is this intentional?

Yes. I invested the storm with a personality, partly to tie in with Selma's voodoo beliefs and partly to explore how the characters see themselves in relation in the universe. Are there higher powers, which punish and reward us? Can we influence them with prayers or spells? Or are we alone, with nothing out there but indifferent, empty space? And although the storm was real, I use it to reveal what happens to people when they are pushed to the limits of their endurance and find out what really matters to them. The storm is an agent of change for all the characters, which is often both good and bad.

Where do you get the names of the characters?

This is hard to answer in a way that doesn't sound very affected, because the names come to me on their own. I picture the character, and their name appears. If it doesn't sound quite right, for the period or the setting, then I tweak it, but generally the first name that pops into my head is the one that sticks.

AUTHOR'S NOTE

Although I was born and raised in Florida, I was unaware of the events on which this book is based until I stumbled on them accidentally in 2010 while researching the idea for another book. The story then completely took over my imagination. As my research progressed, I began to realize that it was one of the most scandalous episodes of the period — not just for Florida, but for the United States as a whole.

It was a desperate time for many in 1935.

The nation was still on its knees from the effects of the Great Depression. The economic hardship and competition for jobs did nothing to ease the racial tensions going back as far as the Civil War. These were exacerbated by the return of thousands of black soldiers from the battlefields of World War I, who brought with them new ideas about equality of opportunity that terrified white Americans. Every aspect of daily life was segregated by the Jim Crow laws enacted in the 1880s. It was illegal for blacks and whites to marry or cohabit; all facilities, from hospitals to restaurants to prisons to libraries, were supposed to be "separate but equal" — but of course only managed the former. It was illegal to promote equality of the races in written form. Even in death the doctrine reigned, as whites and blacks could not share the same burial grounds. These laws not only legalized discrimination for whole generations, but also legitimized violence against those who transgressed the laws. I was shocked to learn of Florida's status as "lynching capital of the South" in 1935, having always associated this with the "real" deep Southern states like Alabama and Mississippi. Lynchings were carried out for a variety of supposed crimes, including infringement of labor laws, but there was nothing more heinous than a crime of violence by a black man against a white woman, such as the one for which Henry is accused. At this time, white men ruled supreme, especially those with money. At the other extreme were poor black women like Missy, Selma, and Mama, with virtually no civil rights as we understand them today.

For the veterans, both white and black, life was extremely hard. Many had left jobs to fight for their country but came back to destitution. In 1922, Congress had approved a bonus for their service, due to be paid out in 1945. As the teeth of the Depression bit deeper, these veterans began to pressure Herbert Hoover's government to make an early payment. In 1932, up to 40,000 veterans and their families made camp outside the U.S. Capitol building while Congress debated the question of an early payment of the bonus. (One of the most interesting yet overlooked features of this camp was the complete integration of black and white veterans — for the first time ever. It was not remarked upon by the press at the time and would not be repeated for many years.) The House of Representatives approved the motion, but it was overwhelmingly defeated in the Senate. Many of the

veterans left the scene at this time, even further dejected and dispirited. Those 3,500 or so who stayed behind were perceived as both a threat and an embarrassment to the Hoover administration. Fearing that the police would lack the resources to deal with the veterans, Hoover authorized the army to disperse the crowds. George Patton, charged with commanding the cavalry, said later that it was "the most distasteful form of service." The violence erupted into a national scandal that was a key factor in ensuring Franklin D. Roosevelt's victory in the next presidential election. The penniless, desperate veterans had helped bring down a government — but had to wait until 1936 to get their bonus.

Roosevelt did not have long to enjoy his election victory. With the economy still in critical condition, and the specter of further unrest from the veterans, he was quick to set up public works projects — both to provide employment for the disgruntled soldiers and to rebuild areas devastated by the Depression.

It is not hard to see why this group of hopeless men, scarred by their experiences of war and defeated by their government, would have been attracted to a works project in the Keys. Many had been living rough for years. As I learned more of their story, I began to feel it was important to make more people aware of what happened to these men: that they were housed in appalling conditions and left to die, through a combination of apathy and incompetence, when a major hurricane struck.

Equally, the residents of Islamorada, the town on which the fictional Heron Key is based, were unprepared, either for the veterans' arrival or for the hurricane's powers of destruction. It is easy to imagine the disruption caused by the hundreds of bedraggled, disturbed soldiers on a small, isolated community, which itself was struggling with economic hardship. The tragedy that befell the Conchs was no less shocking in its loss of life. With their long experience of hurricanes, they thought they were ready, but none of their preparations could withstand winds and waves of such magnitude. When the storm finally receded, the area of devastation resembled the photos taken at the epicenter of an atomic bomb: no buildings, no houses, no trees. Nothing

left standing. Even the soil was stripped from the coral bedrock. A large stone angel, a grave marker from the seaside cemetery, was lifted and whisked 150 feet away by the wind. She still resides in the same cemetery, her broken arms never repaired, as a reminder of that night.

Although meteorological science was primitive by our standards, with none of the hurricane tracking systems we rely on today, the risks of storm season were well understood by all. Ernest Hemingway, who lived in Key West at the time, was one of the first on the scene after the storm and helped with the cleanup operation. His conclusion, published in the article "Who Murdered the Vets?" (*New Masses*, September 17, 1935), was clear:

Who sent nearly a thousand war veterans, many of them husky, hard-working, and simply out of luck, but many of them close to the border of pathological cases, to live in frame shacks on the Florida Keys in hurricane months? You could find them face up and face down in the mangroves. They hung on there, in shelter, until the rising water and wind carried them away. They didn't let go all at once, but only when they could hold on no longer . . . You found them high in the trees where the water had swept them . . . and in the sun all of them were beginning to be too big for their blue jeans and jackets that they could never fill when they were on the bum and hungry . . . You're dead now, brother, but who left you there in the hurricane months in the Keys where a thousand men died before you in the hurricane months when they were building the road that's now washed out? Who left you there? And what's the punishment for manslaughter now?

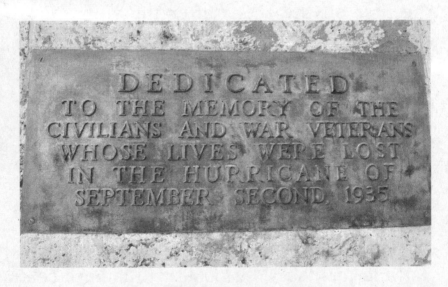

In the investigation that followed, no one was ever prosecuted for what happened to the veterans, despite compelling evidence of official culpability. One of the great ironies is that the same scandal that brought Roosevelt to power almost cost him the presidency, such was the nation's outrage at the veterans' deaths. On September 12, 1935, the *Chicago Daily Tribune* wrote that putting the veterans in the Keys during hurricane season was:

> . . . a piece of criminal folly committed by someone in Washington. The camps on the Florida Keys were established to avert another bonus march on Washington, with all the political embarrassments involved in such a demonstration of discontent . . . Naturally a site was selected as far from Washington as it conveniently could be while still providing free labor for a southern constituency which wanted public improvements at somebody else's expense.

People will say that such a thing could not happen today, but the residents of New Orleans might disagree. We have thousands of damaged soldiers making an uneasy reentry into civilian life, with a shockingly high suicide rate that is an indictment of their treatment by the military establishment and society as a whole.

None of these characters are based on real people. The real hurricane struck Islamorada and the other Keys on Labor Day, not the Fourth of July. There would have been a separate "colored" area of the beach a fair distance away, not right next to the beach reserved for the whites. Such is the license of fiction. Many of the events depicted did not happen, but some of them did, as told by the survivors. General Douglas MacArthur, given the job of breaking up the Bonus Army protest march in Washington, was worshipped as a hero by the very men he drove out with bayonets and gas. Some of the black residents were turned away from a storm shelter in town, which was then destroyed, forcing the white residents to join the blacks in empty boxcars for safety. The tragically late relief train was blown off the tracks by the storm before it could evacuate the veterans. Almost all of the veterans died, and so did many, many of the locals. People were found high up in the lime trees and as far as forty miles away, dropped there by the wind. Unlike Missy and Nathan, they did not survive for long.

Some who did survive have recorded their memories in a fascinating video to be found on the Keys History site at www.keyshistory .org/shelf1935hurrpage15.html, which also has photos of the memorial erected by the American Legion. The decapitated remains

of Flagler's magnificent East Coast Railway, never rebuilt to this day, can still be seen in the turquoise waters off the Keys. They mark the place where, on Labor Day 1935, Nature demonstrated her prodigious power over us.

FURTHER READING

Storm of the Century: The Labor Day Hurricane of 1935 (Washington, DC: National Geographic, 2002) by Willie Drye is a meticulously researched description of the storm and the investigation that followed. The author concludes that the veterans were failed by every level of government with responsibility for their well-being. Even if you do not agree with the author's conclusion, his book is a factual account that reads like a thriller.

For a firsthand narrative of what it was like to live in the isolated, rural Keys of the 1930s, you can read hurricane survivor Charlotte Arpin Niedhauk's *Charlotte's Story: A Florida Keys Diary* (Sugarloaf Key, FL: Laurel & Herbert Inc., 1973), which depicts every aspect of life during an extraordinary year.

And for a study of violence in the period, read Walter Howard's *Lynchings: Extralegal*

Violence in Florida in the 1930s (Authors Choice Press, 2005).

Finally, everyone interested in this period of Southern history must read Zora Neal Hurston's *Their Eyes Were Watching God* (New York: Harper Perennial Classics, 2006), which includes a stunning depiction of what it feels like to experience a hurricane.

ACKNOWLEDGMENTS

My husband, James, for reading endless drafts, commiserating through the bad times, sharing in the joy of the good times, for being steadfast in his support and encouragement, even when I had given up hope; my agents, Tina Betts and Mitchell Waters, for their sage advice on everything from characters to publisher politics; Louisa Pritchard, queen of foreign rights; Kate Mills at Orion and Shana Drehs at Sourcebooks and their lovely teams, for steering me through my first author experience with patience and understanding; the survivors of the Labor Day hurricane, for their courage and resilience; and everyone who pays me the highest compliment there is, of reading the book. I thank you.

ABOUT THE AUTHOR

Vanessa Lafaye was born in Tallahassee, Florida, and raised in Tampa. After obtaining a zoology degree from Duke University, she left the United States in search of adventure and found it. She lived in Paris and Oxford before settling in Marlborough in southwest England with her husband, James, and three furry children. Find her on Twitter @vanessalafaye and online at http://vanessalafaye.wordpress.com.

The employees of Thorndike Press hope you have enjoyed this Large Print book. All our Thorndike, Wheeler, and Kennebec Large Print titles are designed for easy reading, and all our books are made to last. Other Thorndike Press Large Print books are available at your library, through selected bookstores, or directly from us.

For information about titles, please call:
  (800) 223-1244

or visit our Web site at:
  http://gale.cengage.com/thorndike

To share your comments, please write:
  Publisher
  Thorndike Press
  10 Water St., Suite 310
  Waterville, ME 04901